"…not since I picked up *The Hunger Games* by Suzanne Collins, have I been so enraptured by what I was reading! Ms. Nevins' writing is sheer genius, well thought out, extremely well written, and polished to perfection. I have been left ready to beg for the next few chapters…! *Wormwood* is a book I want on my shelf, in my collection, to be able to pick up and return to on a whim…!"

—Christine M. Butler, author of *Birthrights*

"…this is post-apocalyptic fiction at its finest, in part because Nevins is actually showing us the apocalypse as its happening, …and in part because she's taking a nice fantasy-inspired twist on things (with a little bit of religious imagery thrown in there to keep things spicy). On top of the impressive thematic content, Nevins' writing style is crisp and clear, and the narrative chugs along at a crackling pace. …one hell of a solid novel."

—Steven Montano, author of *Blood Skies*

"*Wormwood* is a must read! D. H. Nevins has created something special, a fascinating read by a fantastic new writer."

—R. A. Scully, author of *The Silvinesh Series*

"Nevins writes with an attention to detail and pace that takes you in and drags you along like a strong undercurrent."

—Craig Hallam, author of *Not Before Bed – and other stories*

"Wow. I actually thought I was out of breath … an excellent read."

—R.W. Goodship, author of *The Camera Guy*

"Kali is a tough, resourceful protagonist, and Tiamat a half-angel tortured by his orders from on high. The sexual tension between the two is palpable. If you enjoy post-apocalyptic tales with a healthy dose of paranormal romance, *Wormwood* will not disappoint."

—Nancy Brauer, author of *Strange Little Band*

WORMWOOD

WORMWOOD

D.H. Nevins

BLACK WRAITH BOOKS

ISBN: 098776120X
ISBN-13: 9780987761200

This is a work of fiction. With the exception of some names and references drawn from biblical, Hindu and Babylonian mythology, names, characters, places and incidents are either all used fictitiously or are products of the author's imagination. No reference to any real person or event is intended or should be inferred.

BLACK WRAITH BOOKS
Kingston, Ontario

To Barry, for without his encouragement
this book would not exist.

The sun will be darkened, and the moon will not give its light;
the stars will fall from the sky, and the heavenly bodies will be shaken

Matthew 24:29-34

Chapter 1

Dappled sunlight danced across the forest floor, as a light breeze cooled my face, making me smile. I always felt so at peace during my morning hike. I fell into my habitual fast stride, nearly lulled by it, as I trekked along Cedar Creek Trail. The bends and dips were so familiar that as I moved, I barely needed to glance down at the network of roots and rocks on the worn, dirt path.

Hiking was a pastime I cherished even as a girl, when my dad would take me on frequent treks through the woods near our home. I always felt whole and in balance when my feet propelled me beneath the trees while I breathed the fresh forest air, and this day was no different. Not at first, anyway.

Everything, however, changed with the wind. Without warning, the pleasant breeze strengthened into a forceful gust, bending the trees and sending flurries of detached green leaves swirling down from above. The forest darkened and I looked up to see ominous grey-black clouds sweeping in to mask the sun. I picked up my pace in alarm. I had no desire to be caught unprepared by a violent storm, and as I rushed along the path, I racked my brain for memories of any appropriate shelters nearby—a small cavern, the gap beneath the root mass of a fallen tree—anything. But I continuously came up empty.

My foot hesitated on the path as I detected another change around me. I stopped, frozen in place, feeling an eerie stillness permeate every inch of the woods. The birds had stopped singing and everything, even the breeze, silenced. Nothing moved. Leaves hung limp on their branches and the entire forest appeared to be momentarily captured in time—like I was suspended in the midst of a still photograph. The very air felt charged and tense. My pulse jumped, my mind screamed to my body to move, but my legs simply weren't responding.

It was then that I heard it, the sound waves raising the hairs on my arms and neck. Something was dreadfully wrong. I could feel the strangeness of it, vibrating wickedly through my bones, and further rooting my feet to the buzzing ground. It began with a low, far away rumbling, rolling ever forward and growling louder by the second. Just as the tumult ripened sickeningly into a deep, primeval roar, I was bucked by violent spasms deep in the earth under my feet. Stumbling to maintain my balance, I spun to look toward the source, and my blood turned to ice. Something was happening, approaching swift as a torrent, as the trees lurched and fell wildly in the too-close distance. It seemed like the earth had become an awakening monster, its body lashing and cresting as it rippled down the hill toward me.

I ran.

The sounds of my feet pounding down the worn path were quickly drowned out by the strengthening uproar behind me. I tried to run faster, my lungs screaming in my chest, as the cacophony suddenly buffeted the air all around me, almost thick in its magnitude. The ground thrust me up, throwing me forcefully onto the sharp stump of a recently splintered tree, and I felt the skin of my arm tear along its edge. At the very next moment, it seemed like the stump itself threw me off and I flew backward. Landing on a soft, rotten log, my fingers sunk into the moist, vibrating moss. I scrabbled across the ground, clutching at roots for support, pulling myself in a vague direction toward Lookout Peak and praying that I was close enough to make it there.

I forced myself up and sprinted drunkenly along the path. It seemed to thrash beneath my feet, as though I was running along the back of a giant, angry snake. Trees reached out and clawed at my body and my face while terrifying, yawning crevasses began to open up in the ground on either side of me. As I leaped over a bush, I realized with a start that I was off the path. Finding it again was useless; the forest was changing all around me. The trees were twisting and falling, rocks were being thrust up from the ground while the earth tilted violently from side to side.

With my panicked senses heightened, everything came into a sharp focus. I took in the violent mess around me as I fled, avoiding all the dangers that I could. I ducked under a thrashing spruce tree and swerved around a birch while clearing a tumbling rock. Then, jumping a tangle of thorns near a ravine edge, a heavy pine branch caught me on the shoulder as the tree crashed down to the ground. It took me with it, but I rolled when I hit the dirt, tumbling down the steep slope into a frothing stream below.

The shallow creek's frigid water swirled around my legs as I lay there for a moment, winded, staring up at the roiling skies above me. I watched as the rain began to fall in large, lazy drops. With foul irony, it reminded me so much of the beloved summer thunderstorms of my youth. The sharp smell of ozone had flashed me back to a childhood memory of sitting on the screened-in porch with my dad, waiting to watch the lightning and counting the seconds before the thunder came. Sometimes the strikes were much closer than we expected, and the heart-stopping *bang!* would make us both jump out of our skins. We would look at each other's reactions, and always burst out laughing, hilarity and relief mingled in our giggles.

A sharp series of numbing flicks on my face quickly brought me back to the chaos of the moment. The rain was pouring down now, mixed with large hailstones that were assailing my body and face as I lay there in my stupor. The ground continued to pitch and lurch, while the stream's flow shifted direction under my back. That terrifying realization was all I needed.

Frantic, I clawed my way up the steep, jerking hillside. Grabbing roots, crumbling ledges and quivering branches, I was once more on level ground and sprinting flat-out without fully being aware of how I even got to the top of the ravine.

Lightning flashed again and again, though I could hear no thunder; not over the roar and groan of the earth that seemed to fill every possible space in my head. The flashing light and tilting ground sent me staggering headlong into a wall of jagged rock. I smashed my knee against the crag, while a piece of crumbling rock fell and hit my shoulder with blinding pain, leaving my arm numb.

As I reeled away from the rock face, however, I finally saw that I made it. Relief flooded through me as I gazed up to see the massive bulk of Lookout Peak leaning protectively overhead. I tripped into a clumsy charge, trying to find the path that would lead me up. It didn't take me long. Amazingly, not only was the path there, but it appeared almost undisturbed by the surrounding disaster.

The shaking ground seemed to calm as I began my ascent. The rocks stilled and the trees merely quivered. Yet I did not slow. One foot in front of the other, up and up I went mechanically, not allowing myself to think about what had happened; not giving myself the chance to fall apart until I was sure it was over.

As I walked, I took a cursory inventory. I prodded with my fingers and bent and rotated my arm and shoulder cautiously. I was relieved to find that neither seemed to be broken. Bad bruising was likely all that would come of it. I had a number of gashes and scrapes, though I knew they should heal well enough. Thankfully, there didn't appear to be anything serious or that needed immediate attention.

The deafening sounds from the ordeal, however, were still with me, ringing in my ears. *Terrific*, I thought absently, *hearing loss would be a great reminder of this fun.* With the ground still vibrating mildly, I felt an almost frantic need to survey the damage and, with any luck, get an idea of how widespread it was. I veered to a lookout point that was about halfway up the climb. But I wasn't prepared for what I saw. I simply couldn't take it in—couldn't believe what my eyes were telling me and what my ears had already registered.

It was still happening. Though the cliff was comparatively still, it was hellish below. For as far as I could see, the forest was a turbulent tempest of angry green as the trees twisted grotesquely and fell. Swirls of shredded emerald leaves eddied in the air under billowing inky clouds that flashed with ready electricity. Though despite this, it was the ground far below that chilled my blood and had me stumbling backward against the rock-cut behind me. *No, it couldn't be. It's impossible,* I told myself, *absolutely impossible. This area isn't active...* Yet even as I formed the thoughts, I could see the lava bubbling and spewing up through great gashes in the earth. Smoke and hot ash rose and twisted with the leaves before ascending to further blacken the fermented clouds.

With my head spinning, I turned and dashed away in blind fear. Up and up I went madly, a pinball bashing into nearly every obstacle as I fought my way up the trail to the leveled rock of the Lookout. Then, as I crashed into the huge blind of rock in front of me, I nearly collapsed with gratitude at having finally reached the main section of The Peak. It would bring me no comfort, but provided safer ground and a vantage point, at least.

I followed the path that wound closely around the edge of the rock blind. As the trail curved to the west side of the towering rocky outcrop, it opened up into a wide swath of fairly level earth, which appeared remarkably unchanged. Surrounding the site were the usual giant-sized boulders—all of which were perfect for sitting on while taking in the once beautiful expanse of lake-speckled forest below. However, that particular view was now so terribly different that I couldn't bring myself to even look at it. Instead, I forced my eyes to the fire pit, flanked by two large logs, worn smooth over the years by use. Many times I sat there, enjoying the warm flames; often by myself, occasionally with friends or routinely with paying groups that I began guiding through these forests just over ten years ago. It was usually a calming sight.

Catching my eye, a spark flew up from the fire pit, which had embers glowing in it from recent use. My heart jumped. *Someone is here.* I raked my gaze quickly around the site, noticing with a start a lone figure standing stark still on the edge of the cliff. He faced the destruction, his arms stretched out before him as though he were giving a benediction over the raving land below.

The recognition hit me like a physical blow. I stared dumbly at him, unable to deal with any more shocks today. Incapable of touching on anything more substantial, his name rose hazily from my memory.

"Tiamat," I whispered to myself.

He spun around, though I have no idea how he could have heard me whisper his name. At that very moment, I heard a horrifying series of sharp cracks coming from the rocky outcrop high above me. As terror shot through my veins, I noticed his face, looking shocked and surprised, with his eyes locked on mine.

I knew I had to get out the way before the crushing rocks fell, even though the effort would likely be futile. I wouldn't be fast enough. As though in slow motion, my muscles bunched to leap out of the way as I set my sights on landing near the worn fire pit logs. Just as I began my desperate jump, something crashed into my side, hard, and I could feel myself being thrown a startling distance from the impact. Though I tried to roll when I smashed into the ground, my head smacked onto the hard-packed dirt, and everything finally went peacefully black.

Chapter 2

Tiamat was not someone who I could easily forget. I could picture the day I met him very clearly, though it was a full ten years ago.

At the time, I was guiding an ill-prepared corporate group along the vast network of trails that veined through Pinecrest National Park. I had led many parties of this type through the woods; their employers so determined to stay ahead in the race, they would happily sign up for almost any initiative that could improve their employees' team-work and productivity—for a reasonable price, of course. Yet even though I grumbled to myself about this particular clientele a little more than was strictly necessary, I tried to have most visitors leave with at least a small appreciation of their wild surroundings.

"The rock under your feet right now is really just the tiniest exposed bit of a much larger rock formation. Amazingly, this formation covers an area that spans thousands of square miles, sometimes buried deep under the soil, but there all the same." I used my loud guide-voice so that Sarah and Mike, a babbling pair of gregarious customer service reps who were always lingering near the back of the group, could hear me. "If you look closely at the rock's surface here, you'll see the striations made from the passage of the glaciers," I continued, leading the group along the ancient ridge of exposed igneous rock.

After I finished giving them their abridged history of the area's terrain, I lead them back to the path that meandered toward a wide stream; the site of their last official team challenge for the day. My eight charges fell into their tired, quiet stride behind me. Two straight days of hiking in the bush turned out to be more grueling than most of them expected it would be.

After not ten steps, I could hear someone pushing his way through the hikers, their muffled curses signaling his closing approach. I cringed in frustration as Brian, a middle-aged sales rep for Logistar, wormed his way to my side yet again.

I knew I wasn't beautiful, though I realized that others sometimes considered me to be pretty. Yet I had been trying to look as plain as possible on this particular outing, due to Brian's unrelenting sleazy approaches. I was wearing the most utilitarian of camping attire: my old hiking shirt, its armholes frayed from the sleeves being ripped off during a previous muggy summer, and my khaki shorts, which had big, practical pockets that bulged unattractively with various useful knickknacks. My long brown hair, streaked with bronze, was tied up into a very sensible ponytail, and probably needed a good wash. For good measure, I reached down and swiped my hand along the tread of my boot. Straightening, I pretended to brush a loose strand of hair from my face, deliberately smearing a streak of muck across my cheek. It wasn't enough.

"For someone that's probably just a sophomore in college, you know a lot of useless information about this area. Is geology your major at...? What's the name of that University, sweetie?" he wheezed, trying to match my fast pace. His legs were long, but he was sorely out of shape, and beads of sweat were forming on his high, balding forehead.

"First of all, Brian," I said, trying to keep a cool head, "this information is not at all useless. If you would care a little more about..."

"Hold on, sweetheart, stop. I'm only making small talk, nothing serious, so let's hold off on the lectures, alright? Not everyone cares about that tree-hugging stuff." Brian flashed me his sleazy version of a flirtatious smile. He was walking far too close for comfort, purposely brushing his sweaty, sticky body against my bare shoulder as he over-dodged low-hanging branches.

I glared back at him before picking up my pace a little more.

"There's no need to be such a cold fish, darling. So tell me again," he said as he lightly touched my arm, sending shivers of revulsion through me, "which college did you say you went to?"

He is such a creep, I thought. Despite the fact that I never told him my age, it was pretty obvious I was way too young for him. And the numerous times I bluntly expressed that I wasn't interested didn't appear to deter him either.

"I didn't say, Brian." I retorted. "And I've never been very good at small talk, so if you want to remain ignorant about your surroundings, I don't have much else to say to you."

I was so sick of his advances, which were getting progressively worse as time wore on. *Damn,* I thought, *it's not my fault that I can't possibly be civil to customers like this. But being rude doesn't frigging work! Maybe if I started singing some 'hippie tree-hugging' song, he would go away,* I stewed. *If only I knew any... or perhaps a good glob of snot...*

Caught up in my brooding, I almost missed the fork in the path that twisted its way down to the rocky stream bed. Turning abruptly, I crashed right into Brian, who caught me solidly under the elbows and swiftly pinned me against a tree. Quickly, he slid his hands under my arms and up my back, holding me in a close, stomach-turning embrace.

"See, I knew you couldn't resist me, honey." He purred, leering at me. "Maybe you'd like me to pin you down tonight as well."

Disgusted, I pushed him away from me forcefully, causing him to stagger backward in surprise. Abruptly turning away from him, I stomped my way down the path. I could feel my face burning scarlet as I hunched my shoulders against the dart-like sniggers coming from select members of the group behind me.

When I reached the rushing, but shallow stream, I examined the five flat stepping-stones that I had left in a pile on the sandy shore. The group was to use these in their team challenge to step on in an attempt to get everyone across to the other side—without getting wet. I considered the stones for a moment, before picking one of them up and flinging it into the bushes. Petty perhaps, but it instantly made me feel better.

"This is our last challenge of the trip, folks." I said when they had all gathered on the stream bank. "Your campsite is set up for you on the other side of this stream. Just get across it and then follow the path over there that leads back up into the woods. You'll notice the site at the top of the ravine."

I pointed the large stones out to them. "You'll need to use these four rocks as stepping-stones to get everyone across the stream. It's shallow, but as you can see it's fairly wide, so you'll all need to work together try to stay dry and figure out how to get everyone to the other side."

Their pathetic, sodden struggles were, so far, the highlight of my day.

Once they finally managed to get everyone across, if a little sodden, I called out my final instructions across the babbling water. This was the point where they had to fend for themselves, I reminded them, filtering water, building a fire safely, cooking their own dinner and breakfast, and finally packing up all their gear in the morning. I told them that I would meet them here one hour after dawn tomorrow to lead them along the rest of the hiking loop, finishing the trip. To respond to their queries about getting back across the stream, I happily revealed the two long planks that I had stashed in the bushes, which I used for a makeshift bridge. I refused, however, to leave the planks spanning the stream, and insisted that they stay on their side of the water until tomorrow.

"But you have the planks, and these four rocks will barely get us halfway across. What if we have an emergency, like if we really need you for something tonight?" Sarah asked, alarmed.

Brian, smirking at me suggestively, muttered something to Mike, who burst out laughing. Chuckling, he leaned over and punched Brian jovially on the shoulder, shaking his head.

It's not about me, it's not about me, I chided myself, thankful all the same that there was a wide stream between me and Brian tonight. I took a calming breath before answering her. "I'll be sleeping right here on the other side of the stream, Sarah. If there are any problems, remember that the point of this excursion is for you to figure things out yourselves through teamwork." I gave her what I hoped was a reassuring smile. "However, I'll be around if you need me for an emergency. If I'm not here, then I'm off on a hike, but I'll never be gone for too long, okay?"

"Hey, don't you worry about us. We'll be just fine, chief," Mike chirped as he steered Sarah up the path to camp. "We'll see you in about 14 hours!" The rest of the pack trailed in fairly good spirits, as though primed by the thought of proving their tenacity.

I warily watched them go, as a mouse would intently watch a cat depart, before I could fully relax. Most members of the party seemed reasonably decent on their own; it was the single rancid personality that soured my opinion of the group. As much as I didn't want to admit it, Brian was more than just creepy; he made me extremely nervous. I stared at the empty path for some time before the tension slowly eased from my body.

After I set up my own camp and had some dinner, I went downstream and hastily washed my face and my hair. The group was leaving first thing in the morning, and I could stand my layer of grime no longer. I tied my hair up again as I made my way back to my tent to change into clean clothing.

Throwing on fresh shorts and a t-shirt and finally feeling human again, my long-anticipated sunset hike could begin. I soaked up the quite solitude as I made my way through the lengthening shadows of the trees. The quiet rhythm of my muted footsteps on the forest floor was soporific and soothing while I made my way unerringly along the winding paths. Eventually, the trail began to lead me steeply upward, ever closer to the most sublime viewing area for sunsets in the entire park. Experiencing a sunset was always the same for me here: from my favorite vantage point, I would silently watch the sun slowly disappear on the horizon, any stresses from the day fading into insignificance under the ignited sky.

It had been far too long since I was last at Lookout Peak. For more than a month, the groups I had been guiding were based out of the park's south-east gate, which was almost as far as one could get from this cliff top. The forest to the south was beautiful enough, with its sharp, rocky hills and sparkling lakes, but it lacked the familiarity of *these* woods. Walking along these trails again felt like a homecoming.

The climb to the Peak's top was invigorating. There was nothing like the feeling of a little exertion out in the rapidly cooling evening air to refresh my mind and work the stress from my body. I slowed when I reached the end of the path, breathing deeply more from a desire to experience the cleansing air than from the exertion of the climb. When I did so, I noticed that there was the scent of wood smoke drifting in the breeze. It couldn't have been smoke from Brian's group that I detected, this smell was much too sharp to be coming from anywhere other than Lookout itself.

I was disappointed when I realized that that meant someone else was likely using the site, and I would be intruding if I barged into their camp simply so I could watch the sun set. There were a few other places on The Peak from which I could watch the sinking sun, but their views weren't nearly as spectacular as the one from here.

I walked slowly around the rock blind, guiltily hoping that whoever had used the site had already moved on, and that they were simply irresponsible with a campfire.

And that's when I saw him.

His image struck me instantly as something beautiful and sad, like a statue I once saw in an old cemetery. True to the likeness, he stood absolutely motionless on the edge of the cliff, staring plaintively up at the stunning sky, which was streaked with fiery oranges as they slowly bled into a deep crimson wash. The entire vision pierced me with unexplainable melancholy. Perhaps it was the unexpected beauty of the scene, like the feelings that can sometimes well up when contemplating truly inspiring art. Something permeated and ignited deep within me, leaving me moved and shaken.

Before I knew what I was doing, I found myself slowly approaching him, circling widely so that I could see him in profile. He was quite tall, with rumpled-looking dark hair and an overall youthful but elegant appearance that was difficult to place; perhaps it was in the way he held himself. He was dressed plainly, in regular hiker's attire: cargo pants and a rough cream button-down shirt. His hands, I noticed now, were balled tightly into fists at his sides, and his stance appeared rigid with tension. I was surprised that I did not see this before. Had his entire demeanor changed from a moment ago without me noticing it, or was I just detecting his tension now that I was closer?

With a surge of panic, I again took in his location at the very edge of the cliff, now alarming in light of the overall mood the man appeared to be in, and I instinctively went closer to him. Though he didn't appear to notice me at all, I was careful to steal toward him slowly and smoothly, terrified that I would startle him into a jump or a fall off the edge. I looked over at his face and took in his staring blue eyes that were still fixed upon the bleeding sky, and I wondered at the root of the apparent anguish that twisted across his handsome features.

"What have you done?" I blurted out in a horrified whisper, before reason was able to stop me. *Stupid, stupid, stupid thing to say to a man who may be about to fling himself off a cliff!* I scolded myself, as he slowly lowered his eyes to look over at me.

He didn't look surprised to see me there, and he held my gaze for a moment before answering. I was transfixed. The unnatural blue of his irises was like nothing I'd ever seen before; it was an incredibly vivid azure, like the color of back-lit sapphires, with each iris rimmed in black. His eyes were remarkable, and I found I was unable to break my gaze.

"It's not what I have done. It's what I must do." His deep, penetrating stare was unnerving, but he spoke with a soft, quiet voice that had the slightest hint of amusement in it. "I must admit, I'm not the most sociable person so perhaps I'm wrong in this, but isn't your question a little direct? Could you not have started with 'Hello'?"

"Oh. Hello," I replied lamely, at last breaking off my stare to glance down at my feet.

When I braved a look back up at him, he smiled at me, if a little sadly, and moved to sit down with his back against a large boulder, facing out over the view. Below us, swaths of model-sized trees blended together into a lush, bumpy green carpet, spreading out under a brilliantly colored sky. He looked over at me and raised an eyebrow inquiringly, flicking a glance at a rock near to him.

I slowly sat on the smooth, sun-warmed rock that he indicated, watching the man warily. He had a kind face, but something about his demeanor seemed dangerous; the haunted look behind his eyes or the determined set of his jaw, perhaps. *Yet he doesn't seem menacing like Brian does*, I thought with disgust as I remembered Brian's lecherous stares.

"It's a stunning sunset tonight," he said, gazing once again toward the skies, "This is why you came up here, is it not? To watch the sun set?"

"How did you know that?" I asked suspiciously.

His initial gaze was frank, but his mouth twitched into an amused smile. "You arrived here shortly before nightfall devoid of any camping gear, so you must be spending the night somewhere nearby. Obviously, you are simply up here to watch the light show. Am I wrong?"

"No. You've pretty much got it exactly," I admitted sheepishly. "What about you?" I asked, glancing back at his gear and tent. I recognized the look of a site that had been used for several days. "How long have you been camped here?"

"A while—a little over a month, in fact."

"Over a month? In this same spot?" I asked, surprised.

"I had some… issues… that I needed to reconcile myself to. This cliff top is…" he paused again, as though searching for the right word, "…inspiring." He shifted his gaze from the surrounding site and stared down at his rigid hands. "I have not had an easy month, to be honest, so it is refreshing to have someone to help me get my mind off things for a bit." He appeared so incredibly wretched when he said this, looking dejectedly down at his clenching hands that my heart immediately went out to him.

Yet I found myself at a loss. What would I say to comfort a complete stranger—a person who is tormented by something completely unknown to me?

"Whatever it is you said you must do," I ventured, "is it possible that it's not worth all the pain it's causing you?"

"Your answer is already in the question. This is something I *must* do. Personal anguish is irrelevant and simply a state I must learn to shoulder—my cross to bear, if you will."

"So then do it," I said, as I watched the last of the sun disappear behind the distant hills. "If your feelings have no bearing either way, it does you no good to stress over it. Just do what you need to and stop obsessing over things you can't control."

He looked at me strangely for a very long moment, holding my gaze steadily. "You have no idea what you are advising me to do."

I shivered as icy waves rippled along my spine, but I stayed the course. "My lack of information doesn't change the fact that you have no choice in whether you do this thing. If you truly have no other options, then our discussing it and you tormenting yourself over it is pointless. I would still advise you to do it."

"Even though you don't know what you're telling me to do?" he asked harshly.

"Would it make a difference?" I countered.

"No,"

"Then my advice is the same."

He turned and looked at me with great interest, studying my face intently. When he responded, he spoke with a gentle voice, but it was firm and insistent. "I want you to understand that this task I must do is already written. I cannot change it. Your advice to me today has no bearing on it and did not make me decide to go through with it. There never was a decision to be made. Do you understand this?" He asked cryptically.

I nodded in response, my head swimming with unformed questions.

"However," he continued, his voice now soft and rich, "you have helped me deal with this more than you could ever know. Thank you for speaking with me." And at this he turned away and resumed watching the colors fade from the sky.

"You're welcome," I answered quietly, conflicted by his warm tone and wondering at his apparent dismissal. "Do you want me to go?"

"You really should," he answered bluntly. "I try not to be around others, if I can help it. It just makes my task more difficult. But..." he paused, looking at me again, "to be honest, I like you being here. Meeting you today was a gift."

After an eternal time, he broke his gaze and looked back out at the scenery as twilight fell. I worked to slow my heart as I concentrated on the shift from day to night, watching the first stars shine softly through the haze of waning light. Probably against my better judgment, I enjoyed being with him too, and found that I was very curious about this bizarre stranger. Yet I knew it was more than just that. I was also attracted to him, and not only to his looks, though they were extraordinary. It was his intensity and his apparent morality; his anguish about having to do something that obviously went against some internal code, which drew me like a moth to a flame. *Don't be an idiot. You don't even know him,* I told myself. With an effort, I pushed my whimsical musings roughly aside, and focused again on the speckled evening sky.

"My name is Tiamat," he said hesitantly, as if he wasn't entirely sure about divulging this information. Giving me a half-smile, he added, "Tiamat La'anah," and he lifted his water bottle for a drink, scrutinizing me over the wide rim.

"I'm Kali Michaels," I replied, smiling as he raised his eyebrows in response to my first name. It was, after all, a common reaction in people who had heard of the Hindu goddess I was named after. "My Dad has a sick sense of humor," I laughed, "I was a bit of a surprise to him."

Water spewed and he snorted as the realization hit him, probably imagining what may have transpired for a man to name his baby after a goddess of destruction. His bottle had upended all over his shirt, and his coughs turned to laughs as he tried to clear out the water he inadvertently snorted. I couldn't help the mirth that bubbled out of me as a result. And as we sat there on the cliff top, two strangers both hooting together in the pale half-light, any tension from our earlier conversation was swept entirely away.

"It is a pleasure to meet you, Kali," he said with sincerity, wiping the tears from the corners of his eyes.

Chapter 3

I glanced down at the growing dark of the forest below and shivered, remembering Brian and worrying about whether he would actually attempt a visit to my tent tonight. The wide stream would likely keep him away, or at the very least, splash in warning at his approach. I wasn't eager to test out that theory, however, and dreaded the coming night.

"You really ought to go, but … would you like to sit by the fire for a bit, first?" Tiamat asked with concern, misinterpreting my shivers for a chill.

I knew that I should be returning to my camp by now, in the rare chance there may be an emergency, but I welcomed the opportunity to put it off a little longer.

"Thanks, Tiamat," I replied, "I'd appreciate warming up before I leave."

He left to put on a dry shirt and I deftly rebuilt the fire from the neglected coals while waiting for him. The flames were already crackling cheerily by the time I noticed him sitting on the log across from me. I started with surprise at seeing him suddenly there, like a silent apparition out of the falling night.

"I take it you've made a fire a few times before?" he asked with a smile. He had changed into a blue fleece jersey, the color augmenting the strange shade of his irises in an almost startling way.

"You could say that," I answered him, tearing my gaze from his unusual eyes with some difficulty. "My dad began taking me hiking when I was quite little and I always loved it; fires and all."

"And did your dad ever try to leave you behind in the woods?" he joked. "He did name you *Kali* after all."

"Believe it or not, he only objected to me in the beginning," I quipped, "and he always said that he got around to liking me rather quickly. He just needed to discover my charming personality." I tried to say this with a straight face, but I wasn't entirely successful at suppressing my smile.

"Actually, he only left me behind in the woods once, and I managed to find him again before he got too far." In fact, my dad had gone for firewood, but he got turned around and ended up wandering lost for a while. I found him on a trail quite close to our campsite. I was only seven. Dad took me with him every time he went for firewood after that, and amazingly, I usually managed to keep him from going too far off-track.

When I told Tiamat this, he seemed to find the latter part of my story quite amusing, and he laughed easily. "So if you're camping with your dad now, Kali," he chuckled, "have you left the poor man to wander around alone in the dark?"

"No, I'm working as a guide now," I answered. "I haven't been camping with my dad for years. Amazingly, he hasn't gotten lost at all without me—recently, anyway." I realized that my humor was dry, and hoped he didn't think I was bragging about myself. "Good thing I taught him so well!" I laughed, trying to make it obvious that I was joking.

"You look young to be a guide. I'm guessing you're about 18. Am I right?"

I looked at him sharply. "Wow, yeah. That's my age exactly." He was good. "And you're right that I'm young to be a guide," I answered, wondering at his age as well. He looked to be in his early twenties, but it was so hard to tell. I couldn't quite put my finger on why that was.

"I just started leading groups this summer to save up some money for college in the fall. If all goes well, I'll do this every summer until I graduate."

"And you enjoy it?" he asked with apparent interest.

"Ninety-nine percent of the time I love it," I responded sincerely. "Though to be honest, I sometimes get the odd client that I want to throttle," I added quietly, thinking of Brian. Just that little reminder made my stomach lurch.

My face must have given something away. Tiamat suddenly leaned forward and looked at me intently. "And who is it that you feel like throttling today?" he asked with a note of severity.

"It's nothing, really, Tiamat. This guy, Brian, makes me kind of uncomfortable; that's all." His gaze was penetrating, and I tried to fluff it off so Tiamat would ease up a little. "But I have it under control. If he bothers me, I really will throttle him," I added with a forced laugh. *Or try to,* I thought. My laugh sounded shaky, but the image of my fist smashing into Brian's face actually did cheer me up a little.

Tiamat leaned back and was quiet for a time, looking agitated. "Fighting is not a good thing, Kali, but necessary, I suppose, if you are left with no other option. Do you know how to protect yourself?"

He was obviously concerned and meant well, but I suddenly felt like I was being interrogated by my father. I tried not to get defensive when explaining to him that I wasn't completely helpless; that I had studied kick boxing for three years.

The impressed look on his face was gratifying, but I knew I had to come clean. "I've worked hard on all the moves and can really pummel the speed bag and heavy bag," I said, focusing on my shoes. "But to be honest, I just do it to keep fit. I've never actually sparred against another person." Glancing up, I noticed his dubious expression, so I continued, hoping to convince him that I could handle myself. "If it came down to it, though, I'm fairly sure I'd be able to land a few solid blows. It'd be enough, at least, to protect myself and get away."

There was a long silence. I felt like a child withering under his contemplative stare. Yet in the end he must have been satisfied with my response, for after a time he nodded and looked away.

Before long, he started up on a new subject. "And what do you do with groups that you guide through here?"

Our conversation went on like this for some time, with Tiamat asking me questions about my job, and laughing at certain things I did or various quirks I had. He peppered the conversation with so many inquiries that he never gave me the slightest opportunity to ask him any questions of my own. Yet I had no idea how to broach the possibly sensitive queries that I had for him, considering his mood when I met him, so the coward in me was happy to let my inquisitive side lie dormant for now.

His light-hearted scrutiny continued unchecked, and when I told him about withholding my group's fifth stepping stone on their stream-crossing challenge, he just shook his head and chuckled.

"You're a force to be reckoned with, Kali, and your dad was right to name you so. I will be careful not to cross you." He shook his head again and began laughing silently, his shoulders shaking in quiet mirth. I was sure he was amusing himself with the prospect of me being even the least bit dangerous.

Deciding that this was probably my cue to leave, I stood up and announced my departure to Tiamat. I was secretly pleased to note that he looked disappointed by this.

"I'd really like to stay longer, but I have an obligation to the group I'm leading. I have to get back in case they need me for anything,"

"I'll walk you back to your camp," he informed me matter-of-factly.

"Really, Tiamat, I know these trails so well, I could probably hike them blindfolded," I countered. "Besides, the moon is up and you can see that it's lighting the paths for me beautifully. I'll be fine."

"I don't doubt your abilities, Kali," he said softly. "In truth, I'm a little sad about parting company. Perhaps you wouldn't mind if I walked with you part of the way?"

"No, of course not, Tiamat... I wouldn't mind, I mean," I floundered, feeling sheepish.

We banked his fire, and walked quietly together down the moonlit trail. We didn't say much for the bulk of the hike, Tiamat seemingly as lost in his own thoughts as I was lost in mine. Then before I knew it, we were entering my campsite. Tiamat had accompanied me the whole way, quietly dogging my footsteps through the moonlit forest. His steadfast presence behind me filled me with gratitude, and I turned to smile at him.

For once, he didn't smile back, and a flicker of his earlier pain crossed his face as he looked at me. "Kali," he said seriously, "will you still be guiding groups through these woods after you graduate from college?"

I grinned wider. "I'll be guiding here in the summer for the next few years, at least. If you want to see me again, Tiamat, you know where to find me," I teased. "Please don't wait until after college, that's much too long."

"You didn't answer me," he said, looking agitated. "When you *are* finished college, will you still be guiding in these woods?"

"I don't know. Probably not. I'm going out-of-state for school, so chances are high that I may get a job far away. A lot can happen in all that time."

Instead of being disappointed that in the future, I may be living a fair distance from here, a look of quiet satisfaction passed over his face. It was maddening. Perhaps I misinterpreted his interest in me.

He paused then, a small crease forming between his brows, looking as though he was deliberating about whether or not to tell me something. I waited a long moment, but he ended up saying nothing, and the silence stretched on.

As I watched Tiamat mull things over, I attempted to distract myself from these little nagging feelings that kept telling me that he couldn't possibly be interested in me; that he was just using me to pass the time. I impatiently pushed these notions away and instead concentrated on his face, trying to guess how old he might be.

Determining his age was a difficult venture. He undeniably had an adult face, chiseled, with none of the roundish facial aspects that most male teenagers had ... yet strangely, he lacked certain features that characterized almost all mature men, even those that were only slightly older. In particular, his face was curiously smooth for someone who had been camping for the past month. He either kept it incredibly clean-shaven or it was virtually hairless. It was also smooth in that it was lacking the fine wrinkles and laugh lines that many men seem to develop shortly after losing their boyish features. Again, I had to place my best guess somewhere in his early twenties, though he had an air about him and a manner of speech that made him seem much older. It was perplexing.

Gaining no further ground in my musings, I couldn't resist the urge to ask him. "How old are you, Tiamat?" I blurted without preamble.

His smile was instantly back, lighting up his features and warming the chill from my heart. But I was unprepared for his response. He stepped close to me before answering, and reached up to touch the tresses in my ponytail. His grin vanished, and was replaced by a look of intensity and thick emotion that stopped my breath and sent butterflies fluttering wildly in my chest.

Reaching around me slowly, he gently freed my hair, taking it down and tenderly smoothing the locks out across my right shoulder. "My real age is meaningless," he replied softly. "Compared to tonight, I feel like I have been half-alive the entire time I've existed."

Everything stopped altogether; the world around us blurred and melted. Despite a look of hesitation in his eyes, he never broke his gaze, while I could feel our closeness charge the very air between us. He leaned toward me tentatively, and I closed my eyes as the forest spun. Very gently, he pressed his lips to my forehead, kissing me light as a breath as he ran his fingers slowly through my loosened hair. Time froze as a feeling like electric energy blazed from where his lips had touched me, burned down my spine and shot out along every nerve ending, leaving my limbs tingling wildly.

"Live well, Kali," he whispered against my skin.

There was a cold breeze, and I opened my eyes to find that I was alone.

* * *

I awoke suddenly, my heart pounding in my chest. The air seemed very close as I kept myself still, my body rigid with tension. Holding my breath, I listened intently for what noises had alarmed me during my sleep, wishing fervently that I could see through the sides of my tent. The thin nylon walls glowed faintly from the bright moon outside, and I felt blind and exposed.

"Oh, darlin'...!" Brian's voice called out, chilling my blood. "Your stud is here," he slurred thickly, like the words formed by a bar fly at closing time. The sound of the chattering stream competed with his somewhat distant voice, and I could ascertain that—for the moment—he was likely on the far side of it.

"'S time fer the hot stallion ta warm the cold fish," he announced. "You'd better be ready for a good pinning, baby, 'cause I know you need it. And this time, I won' take 'no' fer an answer—I know what's good fer ya, you feisty bitch!"

Then I heard it. A faint splashing in the stream sent shocks of terror through me as I realized how negligently naïve I was to put myself into danger like this; sleeping isolated and alone after Brian gave me virtually every indication he might make a move like this tonight. He might have been middle-aged and out of shape, but he was bigger than I was by far, and had looked strong. I was in serious trouble.

My mind reeling with indecision, I quickly went over my options as the splattering in the stream sounded closer and closer. If I came face to face with Brian, I'd have no choice but to try to fight him off. But when it really came down to it, would I even be able to? Frantically considering my options, I immediately realized that any struggle would have to be outside the tent, allowing me a chance, at least, to try to get away. If I could avoid his grasp, I was sure I could outrun him.

The splashing got closer. I *had* to get out of the tent.

Go now! I thought urgently. But if I opened the zipper, the noise would alert him to my escape, possibly ruining my chance to get away unhindered. Should I use my knife to cut my way out the back? I worried, however, that I wouldn't be able to slice my way out quietly without tipping him off to what I was doing.

The splashing stopped. He must be across, I realized with horror. And then the next terrifying sounds came; the unmistakable padding of slow, hushed footsteps on the hard-packed dirt.

Out the back! Use your knife and get out the back! I silently screamed to myself as I jumped into action. My hands shook as I scrabbled for my knife and opened it in the thick gloom. Yet just as I began to slice my way out, working as swiftly and noiselessly as I could, I heard a strange wind-like sound that didn't seem to fit the outside scene—a scene that, in my terror, I had pictured all too vividly in my head. It sounded like someone shaking a large blanket ... or wind snapping the nylon on a giant kite. It just didn't fit. The sound was fleeting, ending as abruptly as it started.

I froze mid-slice, the knife in my clenched fist sticking through the thin nylon. There were no other sounds. No footsteps, no splashing; just the impartial babbling of an apparently vacant stream. Holding my breath, I waited longer. Still, there was nothing. My hand slowly relaxed and I released my breath tentatively, all the while listening carefully for the footsteps to resume. Again: nothing.

Sitting numb and motionless for a time that seemed to extend end-lessly, I sifted through the usual night sounds of the forest around me—over and over—and for every instance, could detect nothing amiss.

I finally fell into a restless sleep sometime in the final hours of the night. Curled up by the small slit I had made at the back of my tent, I slept with my hand wrapped tightly around the hilt of my knife. I would be ready next time, and naïveté be damned.

* * *

"Kali... Kali!" Sarah's panicked voice called out. It carried across the wide, gurgling stream clearly, and I could hear her begin to tromp through the shallows in her rush to get across to me.

I sat up stiffly, prying the knife from my cramped fingers as I shook myself awake. Something was wrong. I hastily zipped back the flaps, stepping into my shoes as I lunged swiftly from the tent opening.

In the pale light of early morning, Sarah splashed clumsily through the last few feet of the water to reach me. She was sopping wet and near hysterics, and I needed to wait for her to catch her breath before I could make any sense of her broken ramblings.

"Calm down and take a breather," I said soothingly, sitting her down on a large, flat stump. "Now when you're ready, first tell me the gist of the problem; we can get to the details later, okay?"

Sarah nodded and took a deep breath before replying. "I'm sorry," she said. "I would have come to get you sooner, but the guys only just told me..." she rambled, apparently deciding to divulge the inconsequentials first. "Mike noticed late last night that Brian wasn't in the tent anymore. At first he thought that Brian just left to relieve himself, but he never came back."

My breath caught in my throat, but thankfully, Sarah didn't appear to notice my reaction.

"For some reason, Mike didn't think much of it. He said he thought Brian might have just curled up by the fire, or that maybe they would find him snoring under a bush this morning. Brian did hit the whiskey pretty hard last night."

"But they couldn't find him?" I asked, unnerved, my stomach twisting in knots.

"No! He wasn't anywhere," she said, her voice rising in fear. "The guys looked all over the area before they told me. He's gone! There's no trace of him!"

I jumped up with cold decision. Regardless of my revulsion for Brian, he was my responsibility. They all were. Walking swiftly toward the bushes, I fished out the planks that were stashed there. I had the boards straddling the stream and was already halfway across before Sarah gathered her wits enough to come trailing behind me.

"What do we do?" she whined nervously.

"Nothing," I snapped back. "The last thing I need is to have more people lost in these woods. I'll look for him alone," I commanded, "and you'll all wait right here until I return."

When I deposited Sarah back at the camp, I gave the rest of the group the same instructions.

"Don't worry," I told them. "If he's out wandering, he'll likely stick to the trails. If he wandered from one, chances are very good that he would have found another one eventually. This park is riddled with them." Noticing that they appeared calmer, I continued. "There are a number of places in the area where the trails cross. He'll likely be stopped at one of these junctions, as people tend to get nervous about choosing the wrong path when they're turned around."

They looked relieved, so I turned to go, reluctant to waste any more time. As I strode away, I called back over my shoulder. "I think I'll find him, folks, so make sure you have everything packed up by the time I return."

I walked quickly along the trails toward a junction that I nick-named The Crossroads, with a strange feeling I would find Brian there. This intersection had four separate trails that bottlenecked together at the base of Lookout Peak before merging into one. There was a good possibility, given the camp's location, that he would have followed one of those four paths and, hopefully, stopped at the junction. It was my best bet.

Luckily, I wasn't wrong. As I neared the spot, I could hear his voice beckoning impatiently, obviously having picked up the sound of my approach and my intermittent calling of his name.

"Hello? I'm here! I'm over here!" he called.

There at The Crossroads stood Brian, looking like an abandoned child. A bewildered expression was on his face and leaves and other debris were stuck in his hair and plastered up one side of his body. His filthy chicken legs appeared rooted to the ground, and he wore only boxers and a dirty-looking t-shirt that was far too small to fully cover his protruding belly.

I was repulsed, but he was shivering noticeably so I pulled out the emergency blanket I brought with me. Rapidly unfolding the thin, reflective plastic film, I scrutinized his face, relieved to see that he only appeared genuinely happy to see me and any traces of sleaze were presently absent. I stepped closer to him and passed him the thin heat shield, indicating that he should wrap it around himself.

"It'll trap your heat so you can warm up," I informed him.

"Thank you, Kali," he said, actually calling me by name. "I don't know what happened. I was going..." he paused, "...just wandering last night and the next thing I knew, I was here. I just woke up here, right on the path. I must have blacked out or sleepwalked or something..."

I looked at him, unconvinced, but he didn't appear to be making it up. I didn't bother asking him where he was wandering before he 'blacked out.'

"Come on, Brian. Let's get back. The others are worried about you."

When we returned to camp a short time later, we found the group entirely packed up and ready to go, apparently having faith that I would find Brian and deciding to follow my instructions in the meantime.

Mike dug some clothes out for Brian who scrambled to put them on.

"Where did you find him?" Mike asked me.

"On a junction near the base of Lookout Peak," I answered. "I didn't have to go far."

"Lookout Peak?" Mike asked incredulously. "But we already checked there this morning before Sarah got you. We should have seen him."

"You went up the Peak?" I asked. "Right to the main lookout?"

"Of course we did. We hoped we'd see a sign of Brian from up there."

"And did you speak to the man who was camped there?" I asked, eager for an update on Tiamat.

But Mike just looked at me curiously. "What man?" he asked. "There was no one at the site when we were there this morning."

"You don't need to look far if you want a man, darling," Brian interjected. "You already found me," he said, stepping closer. Not surprisingly, his demeanor had shifted and I was looking at the old, slimy Brian again. It was probably because he didn't feel so naked and vulnerable in front of everyone now, I guessed briefly, or because the cockroach was no longer relying on me for his safety.

I ignored him, my thoughts shifting rapidly to a more significant person. "The site was empty?" I asked Mike. "You mean he wasn't in his tent?"

"No. I mean the site was deserted. No gear and no tent. There wasn't a soul up there."

I staggered backward. Did Mike mean that Tiamat was *gone*? How could he be gone?

"Hey, don't look so distressed, Baby," Brian said as he slithered closer. "He obviously left because you've got a real man around now. Want to see how manly..."

Almost of its own accord, my fist flashed out and punched him squarely in the face. The force of it knocked him so hard he reeled backward and landed right in the bushes, his legs splayed absurdly apart like he was some silly cartoon character.

"Go to hell," I told his legs triumphantly. "And when you do, don't expect me to come find you ... I *won't* drag your sorry ass back!"

Chapter 4

I awoke slowly, my head throbbing, to a suffocating silence that was so complete it seemed palpable. There was nothing to be heard, nothing at all. The thick, tomblike quiet reminded me of something…

I tasted bile in my throat as the memories flooded back, seizing my heart with terror. Hellish images of crashing trees, splitting earth, and lava spewing hot ash into thunderous skies screamed through my head, threatening to burst it apart. *But it couldn't really have happened*, a part of my mind broke in, attempting rational thought. *I was dreaming; it was just an awful nightmare.*

Venturing to open my eyes minutely, I saw the textured bark of a pine tree floating in the fuzzy haze of my vision. I blinked to clear my eyes, only to confirm that a tree trunk was directly in front of my inert head, and I would see nothing else unless I moved. But the terror lingered from my dreams, and even though I needed to ascertain that my world was still unbroken, I was afraid to move. I closed my eyes and took a deep breath, forcing myself to be rational. "Get a grip, Michaels," I muttered, opening my eyes again.

Listening carefully and detecting no sounds, I cautiously inched my head off the ground. I could feel that there was a thick coating of something encrusting my temple and the side of my face as I peeled myself away from the leaves and packed earth—but I hardly had the attention for it. Determining the safety of my immediate surroundings took precedence over all else.

Peeking around the tree, relief flooded through my body. There appeared to be nothing amiss. Columns of beautiful, firmly grounded tree trunks stretched off into a blur of tranquil green. The forest appeared peaceful and its floor intact. Perhaps I just fell and hit my head, I thought, and my imagined ordeal was a result of the trauma.

Sitting up, I sucked in my breath as twinges of pain shot through my aching limbs and torso, and I touched my sticky temple in wonder. I couldn't fathom what had happened, and worked to recall what had caused my fall as I prodded at the thickened coating of blood that had congealed down my cheek. It was no wonder my head pounded so painfully. As confused as I currently was between nightmares and reality, I was uncertain exactly how I had hit my head. And stranger still, if I had simply had a nightmare, why did my entire body feel so battered? I shuddered with a feeling of foreboding as I sat in the oppressive stillness. Knowing that I was missing some integral piece of information, I very slowly turned to look behind me.

My breath caught. I gazed disbelievingly onto the flat grounds of Lookout Peak, shocked that I was actually there and not somewhere in the woods below. I was near the far western edge of the observation cliffs, sitting a few paces into the forest that stood sentinel around the cleared area of the lookout site. *No way,* I thought, panicked. *If I'm at Lookout, then that means... that means I ran up here when... when...* I stopped, unable to make myself form the thoughts. There was nothing for it but to see for myself. Turning my body a fraction more, I was again thwarted in my attempts to view my surroundings. I was sitting in a slight depression and an enormous mass of exposed rock obstructed my view of the landscape below the cliffs, tormenting me with its concealed knowledge.

I crept toward it, my heart in my throat, hoping desperately that I was nothing more than paranoid, deluded by my vivid imaginings. Yet even as I neared it, my hopes crumbled and drifted away; mirroring the black ash that fell around the look out, drifting toward the earth like tainted snow. My nose was assaulted by the sharp stink of sulfur, prefacing the view that awaited me. I knew what I would see. I stood to face it, and taking a steadying breath, I forced myself to step out from behind the protection of the shielding rock.

The unobstructed view was horrific. Shock ripped through my body as I gazed out over a land of pure devastation, and I saw a world that was completely different from what I had known before. It was a world that didn't fit, which was surreal in its terrifying strangeness.

Stay focused and get the hell out of here, I told myself firmly as I felt my knees weaken at the sight. *I will* not *fall apart... I will* not... I reached blindly for the solidity of the rock beside me, numbly gazing at the cooling lava, blackening over the torn, exposed earth. Fallen, broken matchstick trees lay scattered and jumbled for as far as the eye could see, far outnumbering the forlorn trees that were left standing here and there—like a few remaining soldiers wading through fields of the dead. Lakes, whose locations I knew intimately, were simply gone, in some cases replaced by new protuberances of exposed rock. There were some new lakes—large, silty and debris-laden—that occupied areas which were never before under water. And surrounding everything was the eerie stillness, like I was the last living thing around for miles...

The next memory smashed into me full-force: Tiamat. Tiamat was here...

Spinning around, I nervously scanned the area for any danger. I didn't know if Tiamat was a threat to me; couldn't even fathom what he was doing here, or why my stomach lurched when I remembered him standing over the destruction—if that's what you could call what he was doing—in those moments before I blacked out. I cautiously checked the cliff area, which appeared to be deserted, and moved on to search the campsite.

I didn't need to go far. There, under the shattered cliffs at the opposite end of the site, lay Tiamat. Immense piles of sand, that I was certain were not there before, surrounded and partially overlapped his prone body. Scattered amid the sand were numerous vicious-looking rocks; any of which could have killed me as I stood there earlier. Remembering the terrifying crash of the rocks collapsing overhead, I realized that Tiamat must have pushed me out of the way, only to be struck down as he saved me.

Never in my life had I been so conflicted. For ten years, I had hoped desperately to see Tiamat again, had thought that I would give anything in the world for a reunion … but I was grossly wrong. Not only did the park—and who knows what else—now lay in ruins, I feared terribly for Tiamat. And now, I was also afraid of him. *What was it he was doing when I surprised him today?*

Concern for Tiamat tore at me, clawing angrily at my trepidation, but I wouldn't move. Something was wrong with this scene. Great holes were gouged out of the looming cliff face, but where were the boulders that should have fallen? Why was there only this inexplicable sand mixed with some rather large rocks?

Unable to come up with any plausible explanations, and as the strange piles of sand seemed to be presently harmless, I shifted my focus to the still body that lay among them. I didn't know if he would be a danger to me, but because he risked his life to save mine, I owed him. I knew that I must, at the very least, determine if he was okay. I bypassed my apprehensions as I crept toward Tiamat, my body tense and ready for flight.

He lay on his stomach; his motionless, blood-stained face was toward me, with his left arm flung out beside him. His arm was certainly broken, the skin bulging grotesquely just below the elbow. He looked dreadful, but I was relieved to see that he was breathing evenly and deeply, as though immersed in a restful sleep.

I kneeled down beside him and looked at his tranquil face. He hadn't changed at all since I last saw him ten years ago. His face was still smooth and the lines of his nose and chin held the same note of elegance, like a typical subject one would see in a renaissance painting. Marring the impression, dried blood from a gash on the side of his head had left numerous crisscrossed red trails covering the upper part of his face, creating a gruesome masquerade visage.

"Tiamat…" I said hesitantly.

His eyes fluttered, but remained closed.

"Tiamat, it's me. It's Kali," I said, noticing his face flicker at my name. "You've been hurt. I'm just going to…"

Tiamat's eyes flew open, stabbing with their blue intensity. "Don't touch me!" he cried suddenly, attempting to raise his head.

"It's okay, I won't touch you yet. Not if you don't want me to," I said soothingly. "I'm a trained guide, remember? Yours wouldn't be the first injury I've treated."

He relaxed and closed his eyes again, as though his body wasn't quite ready to keep them open. "Kali, as I told you when we last saw each other, I do not doubt your abilities," he said softly. "Am I bleeding much?" he asked after a pause, opening his eyes a crack.

"From what I can see, you're only bleeding from this cut on your head here," I said as I thoughtlessly reached toward him.

In a flash, he was up on his knees and right arm, scrabbling backward in an attempt to get away from me. But the instant he put weight on his left arm, he roared and fell over in agony. He pressed his forehead into the dirt with a moan of pain.

I was baffled by his behavior, but stayed where I was so as to alarm him no further. It was incredibly strange: shouldn't *I* be backing away from *him* and not the other way around? Unable to help, I impotently watched him struggle into a sitting position as he cradled his left arm. He watched me warily.

"Kali," he began, gritting his teeth and breathing hard from obvious pain, "you must not touch me when I am bleeding. Please, promise me you won't."

I stared at him blankly. "When you're bleeding? But ... why not?"

"Please trust me in this. Will you promise me?"

I was quiet for a moment as I thought over his request. I disliked making promises. The future has a habit of planting landmines when you least expect them, and giving your word always seems to end with that nasty click under your foot; it really limits your options. "Is it just that I shouldn't touch your blood?" I queried.

"Yes,"

"But not that I shouldn't touch *you*?

"Not when I am bleeding."

"What if I just promised to never purposely come into contact with your blood?"

He appeared to ponder this, looking pale. "Alright, Kali. Will you give me your word then? Promise me you will never touch it."

"Okay, Tiamat. I'll never purposely touch your blood. I swear it." I paused. "Do you have Aids?" I blurted tactlessly.

"No," he said. "My blood is far worse than that."

I blinked. Was he joking?

"Are you badly hurt?" he asked me, scrutinizing my probably haggard appearance, my own head caked and crusted from a wound above the temple.

"Mostly bruises, I think." I touched my head gingerly. "I'm pretty sure this isn't deep, and the bleeding has stopped. Like yours, from what I can see."

He touched his own head roughly, and inspected his hand afterward. Appearing satisfied with what he saw, Tiamat stood, staggering a little, and started off toward the woods. "There is a creek in the woods here," he said, turning to me. "I will return shortly, after I have washed this off." He indicated the blood on his head, and began to stride off.

Unwilling to be left behind under the current circumstances, I immediately jumped up and followed him. We walked to the little brook that gurgled happily through the woods before it plunged off the cliff into the devastation below. *A sick parallel to my life*, I thought bitterly, stooping down beside Tiamat to wash my face.

He leveled a look at me.

"Oh, right. Not downstream," I said, trying to look apologetic as I jumped up and walked numerous paces upstream of him.

As I washed, I surreptitiously watched Tiamat struggle to clean the blood from his face and head. A sheen of sweat appeared on his paling neck, and he froze, his jaw tightly clenched, every time he jarred his left arm. He was swaying noticeably by the time he finished, and fresh blood was lightly trickling down his face again.

Using my pocket knife, I quickly cut a strip of fabric off the bottom of my shirt. I gave it a fast rinse in the brook, and wrung it out as I passed it to him. I couldn't stand to see him attempt to wash his face again; he would certainly pass out from the effort.

"Just press this to your head to stop the bleeding," I said. "In a moment you'll be able to splash off the last of the blood from your face."

Taking the cloth, he leaned up against a sturdy poplar that grew on the moist creek bank. A look of warmth spread out across his features when he looked up at me. "Thank you, Kali," he said, pressing the fabric to his head and closing his eyes.

Tenderly feeling my own gashed head, I was pleased to find that the cut had not reopened. I must have been a little gentler cleaning it out than Tiamat had been when scrubbing his wound. Careful not to be too close, I chose to sit on the smooth wood of an old fallen tree that lay a few paces across from him.

"You should let me splint your arm," I told him, knowing it would be a long time before we could get anyone else to look at it, given the situation. "Once your head stops bleeding, of course," I added hastily.

"I would be much obliged," he replied warily, giving me a weak smile, "though I must admit that I am not looking forward to it."

I smiled at him. "I'll go easy on you. But I'll need to do it soon," I said, nodding toward his arm. "It's starting to swell, and I'll have trouble setting the bone if we wait."

Despite needing ties for the splint, he refused to let me cut my clothing more, sending me back to his camp for some rope. I hurried to gather the other supplies I'd need on my way back, and managed to return in a few short minutes.

He was patiently holding his arm up as I had instructed him, to discourage further swelling, and he watched me in silence as I set out my materials: smooth, sturdy sticks for the splint, moss to pack in for cushioning, and short lengths of rope to hold it all together. I was relieved to see that the bleeding on his head had stopped, and he no longer held the cloth to it. Additionally, all traces of blood had again been rinsed from his face and he looked much recovered in the short time I was away. Under normal circumstances, I would have been almost happy.

Yet despite the calming nature of having something purposeful to do, my hands shook. It had been impossible to ignore the view of the devastated landscape when I entered Tiamat's camp, and it was with great difficulty that I suppressed the panic that was bubbling up inside me. I clenched my hands together and tried to focus.

"This is going to hurt, Tiamat," I warned him, wiping my shaking palms on my pants. "But it will be easier if you try to keep your arm relaxed."

He nodded and leaned his head back against the tree, waiting for me to begin.

After shaking my hands out in an attempt to ease the tremors, I reached over and firmly grasped his injured limb, perhaps a little rougher than I should have. Immediately, bizarre ripples of some kind of energy shot savagely through my hands, burning fiercely up my arms. I threw down his injured forearm, leaping away from him in panic.

"Augh!" he grunted in pain, cradling the offending limb. "You certainly have an interesting way to set bones, Kali. And I apologize about the shock; I should have warned you," he added.

"*What*? What do you mean, you 'apologize about the shock?'" I sputtered, the bubbling panic beginning to well over. "What the hell is going on here anyway? None of this can be happening! *It can't*! And your arm... your arm *shocked* me! No, keep it elevated, damn it! It will swell!" I glared at Tiamat as he raised his injured arm again, his expression guarded. "What's happening, Tiamat?" I demanded again, taking in his tight-lipped expression. "I'm losing my mind here and you won't even say anything!"

I stared at him, waiting for him to elaborate on the strange shock that most certainly originated from his arm... waiting for him to elaborate on *anything*. But after a long, drawn-out silence and no change to his guarded expression, I had to resign myself to the fact that I wasn't likely to get any further at this moment.

"Fine!" I huffed. "But at least tell me this. If I touch you again, will I get zapped?"

"You will feel it, but I will not shock you again," he promised. "I was taken by surprise before. You have a very firm grip," he said with mock injury.

Annoyed, I crouched down beside Tiamat again, resolving to get some serious answers from him in the very near future. However, despite my anxiety, curiosity won over, and I hesitantly reached out to touch his skin. Gently this time, I ran my fingers along his broken limb as tingling pins and needles undulated through my hands and crept up the skin of my arms. Feeling carefully for the broken ulna bone, I braced my hands on either side of it and began to pull apart slowly.

Letting out a yelp, Tiamat suddenly writhed. He flung himself on top of me, pinning me down as he stretched his arm high in the air, far away from my grasp. "Ow," he said, as his lips twisted into a surprised, sheepish smile. "Contrary to what you obviously believe, I do have an aversion to pain. Is it not possible for you to be gentle?"

That did it. I had no patience for this crap today. "Maybe I'm just not a gentle person. Deal with it." Taking him with me, I rolled and pinned him in return, surprised by how heavy he was. "Oh, just hold still, Tiamat!" I scolded, scrambling to sit on his chest as I restrained his upper left arm with my hands. I used my left leg to immobilize his uninjured right arm, though he had stopped struggling for the moment. In fact, he looked amused by my response. That only annoyed me further. I continued to hold him down as I finally set the bone, the strange energy that emanated from him crawling like armies of ants all over my skin. Only my irritation with Tiamat—fueled by my occasionally stubborn nature—kept me from leaping up and smacking the creeping sensation away from my flesh.

Looking for my splinting materials, I realized with frustration that they were still over by the tree, where I first attempted to set his arm. They were maddeningly just beyond my reach, and although I shifted my position backward and stretched as far as I could, I was unable to put my hand on them. I would have to release Tiamat if I was going to splint his arm. "Stay put," I told him sternly, flicking a glance at his face.

I stopped, puzzled. Tiamat wore the strangest expression, which smoothly shifted back to that infuriating look of amusement. He slowly raised one eyebrow at me, taking in my current position on top of him.

It only took me a moment.

All at once, in one mortifying flash, I understood the source of his amusement. In my efforts to reach the splints, I had shifted myself much lower down on his body, and was currently straddling Tiamat in a rather compromising position.

Jumping up quickly, I could feel my blush blazing into a beacon of my embarrassment. I was completely at a loss: *how the hell do I save face after this?* I simply stood over him, struggling to find something to say that would help me bounce back from my humiliating blunder.

"Was that okay?" I asked him stupidly. "Um… your arm, I mean. I didn't hurt you too much?"

He looked at me, his mouth twitching, and took a deep breath before answering. "Actually, it was quite bearable after all," he said with an obvious effort to keep his voice even. "Especially that end part…" He snapped his mouth shut before finishing, looking like he was going to burst from the effort of holding in his laughter. Shutting his eyes tight, his shoulders shook while his face turned red with concentrated suppression. I watched in exasperation, waiting for this rather uncomfortable moment to pass. I had to wait a long time.

Finally, as Tiamat's amusement began to subside and I, at long last, finished putting on his splint—a little more roughly than was strictly necessary—I knew that the time had come for some answers.

We exchanged a long look and, without waiting for him to follow, I stalked off to a place I had in mind, a little upstream. Here the creek widened and deepened into a small pool before it swirled out and continued on its merry way. I had always found this place soothing, and I had need of its calming affects now. I sat on the edge of a large rock, which jutted out over the pool, and took off my shoes and socks mechanically. Plunging my toes deep down under the water, I watched them a moment as I worked to steady my breathing. The cool water flowing around my feet was bracing, helping me anchor my hold on reality—a grasp which seemed to be getting more and more tremulous as the day went on.

I looked up to see that he was there, as I knew he would be, standing silently on the other side of the wide pool, his strange blue eyes thoughtful as they locked with mine.

"I think we should talk," I began.

"Yes," he agreed softly. "But weigh your questions carefully, Kali. I am afraid my answers will bring you no comfort."

Chapter 5

It was not difficult to follow Tiamat's advice. I was terrified of the answers I might receive and, as a result, the best strategy I could fathom was to start with a comparatively simple question and work my way up from there.

"Are you happy to see me?" I ventured.

"Yes," he blurted, looking startled by what I asked. But after a few seconds, a shadow crossed his face and he shook his head. "And no."

That amendment didn't matter as much as it should have, and despite the circumstances, I managed an unsteady smile. "Well, Tiamat, it looks like you were wrong," I told him boldly. "You did say something that brought me comfort after all, even if you're only *slightly* happy to see me. And there may be something else too," I added, "another positive thing you can tell me."

He looked at me expectantly, and waited. And though I tried to appear collected, there was something about his demeanor that made me think he could see right through my unruffled façade.

"Earlier today, when we first saw each other, there were some boulders…" I had to pause and hold the edge of the rock I sat on to still my shaking hands, "… falling boulders that were going to crush me. Did you push me out of the way?"

"Yes," he admitted hesitantly. "But Kali, you must face the truth. Though I asked you to weigh your questions carefully, I did not anticipate your avoidance of real answers." He looked at me and shook his head. "I am sorry, but even the mundane questions you selected can't have the soothing responses you expect. So while it is true that I pushed you from that particular path, my exact role in that incident has not yet been addressed."

"What role?" I asked, feigning ignorance. I was under a great deal of stress when I reached the lookout and I must have been imagining things; Tiamat couldn't really have been doing anything... it wasn't possible...

But he interrupted my musings with a harsh shock of reality, one that he appeared to lift straight from my twisted imaginings. "Do you not realize that *I* was the one that caused the cliff to collapse in the first place?" He looked at me steadily, his gaze strengthening the impact of his message and turning my insides into ice.

I gripped the rough, unyielding stone of the ledge, whitening my knuckles and willing my world to stop shifting. Trying to keep my face blank, the implications of what he said whirled in a dizzying vortex of thought and panic. *Somehow, impossibly, he caused that... almost crushing me...* "W-why..." I whispered, "...Why did you try to *kill* me?" I asked, my perspective shifting painfully when I worked to recall the moment. "And then... you almost killed yourself to save me... I don't understand..."

"No," Tiamat said, his voice even. "I did not try to kill you. That was an accident that occurred when you startled me. And when I saw the danger you were in, I pushed you out of the way." Then, almost as an afterthought, he added quietly, "I could not help myself."

"Wait a minute!" I exclaimed, confusion and anger exploding out of me. "You couldn't help almost crushing me, or you couldn't help saving me? There's a big difference, Tiamat!"

"I could help neither one," he said quietly, his eyes steady on my face.

I blinked, surprised. What was he implying? "When you said that you 'couldn't help' saving me, it's like you were insinuating that it went against your better judgment."

"That is exactly what I meant. I *should* have let those rocks crush you, Kali, but I couldn't stand it. And now I don't know what I am going to do. Your presence here has complicated things a great deal."

"I could say the same thing about you, couldn't I? Except 'complicate' is too mild a word to describe your effects on my present life!" I threw back venomously. "Yet in my case, I tried to help you, and I never wished *you* were mashed by boulders..."

"I do not wish that, Kali!"

"...and speaking of boulders, *how*, exactly, did you cause them to fall? And then what the hell happened to them? When I looked afterward, there were only huge piles of sand and some rubble—but there shouldn't be any frigging sand there," I fumed as I reasoned, the fury keeping my mind from crumbling apart.

Tiamat watched me quietly, as though deciding on a course of action. Then, having reached some conclusion, he stooped beside an anvil-sized rock and placed his hand on it, palm down.

I could feel it the moment before it happened; gooseflesh crawled along my arms as the little hairs stood on end, prickling in the swiftly charging air. Then, abruptly, the ground lurched—like someone was blasting with dynamite a short distance away—while thick and forceful, the *fwump* of a shock wave immediately rushed outward, kicking at my eardrums. I grimly recalled hearing, earlier that very day, that exact disturbance while the entire forest became chaos all around me, and I shuddered. And though I knew that I did not take my eyes off that rock, I could not see *how* it happened. One second, there was a rock under his hand, and in the next, it was a great heap of sand, its edges cascading softly under his touch.

"I do not need to touch it," he explained. "But I thought this would be less alarming for you than if I were to crush the rock from a distance."

I nodded, the only response I was currently capable of. My mouth had gone completely dry, as if I had taken a great bite of his newly created sand.

"Falling sand would be less dangerous than the boulders," he explained, as though he were using this information to try to temper my reaction. "But preoccupied as I was with pushing you out of the way, I failed to reduce everything, and was struck by the rubble.

"And as to *how* I am able to do this, that is something that I cannot tell you at this point. The power to do these things does not originate from me, so I am not at liberty to disclose this information to you. I do feel compelled, however, to make you understand what has taken place here." His haunted eyes found my face, and seemed to plead for understanding. "Kali, if you were to remember back to when we first met, could you recall our initial conversation?"

"Yes," I answered softly, looking down at my knees. "I have thought of that day often over the past ten years." I looked up at him as it clicked. "You told me that there was something that you must do, that you had no choice," I said slowly, a horrified understanding creeping into my voice.

"And now we have come to it, haven't we?" he said gravely. "You *know* what I was doing on the cliff today, Kali. I can see it in your eyes, though you are afraid to voice it. You even know how I feel about it, as that was the topic of our conversation ten years ago."

Smooth, fast and graceful, he was suddenly standing in the water, though I saw no specific movement that brought him there. He approached me cautiously, like one would for a frightened animal, across the creek's buffering pool. "Little has changed since that time. I remain in suffering over the task I carried out and the ones that I still must do."

But his tasks were horrific and destructive, and when I thought about this, somehow his *feelings* about them carried little weight when placed in the shadow of his actions.

"Tiamat," I began quietly, watching the water eddying around my feet. "Are you evil?" I asked, glancing up at him. "Or would you say that you're good?"

"That is a very difficult question, that shifts, depending on one's perspective," he responded slowly, stopping mid-stream. He stared off into the trees, his forehead creased and his brow knitted, holding his splinted arm across his chest. "I would have to say that I am good," he said, cautiously stepping toward me again. "But most people would almost certainly consider my actions to be evil."

He was across the pool now, oblivious to his soaked clothes, holding his focus on me. Standing waist-deep in the water that lapped against my ledge of rock, his head was now equal to the height of mine, so we found ourselves eye-to-eye. He reached out slowly, pleading for calm with his eyes, but I recoiled, leaning far back away from him in alarm.

"Do not fear me, Kali," he said soothingly. "I only turn *rocks* to sand," he said with a little smile, "not people." Carefully grasping my hands—giving me the tiniest quiver of shocks—he gently pried them off the stone ledge and examined them.

I was taken aback by what I saw, and realized that I must have clawed aggressively at the rough surface I sat on while I tried to digest what he was telling me—as I worked so hard to remain rooted in reality. My fingers were scraped raw and oozing blood, my short nails deeply split and broken. Yet I had had no recollection of doing such a thing, and I simply stared at them numbly; like they were someone else's hands and not mine at all. Certainly I would not do something so unhinged…

Reaching down, he scooped up a palmful of water and dribbled this over my stinging fingers. He continued this for a moment, while he restrained my wrists in his right hand, as though he was afraid I would injure myself further. A numbing buzz of energy rippled deeply into my skin and crawled unnervingly up my arms, but I fought the urge to pull away, and I watched him closely instead. The ungainly splint on his left arm knocked frequently against the rock, but he ignored this in his tending, doggedly reaching again for the soothing water.

"In spite of how people may feel about me, though, I must conclude that I am good," he said definitively. He bent his head and reached into the pool once more, his dark hair falling forward to obscure his eyes. "Yet, if we had not had this conversation, Kali," he said softly, "I would never have paused to consider the positive, like your question forced me to do just now. You see, even though I understand that my tasks are for the greater good, I have always despised myself. I am nothing but a servant whose requisite duty makes him a monster. And it is torturous for me when my only obligations in life involve causing the pain and suffering of others, while ironically, I truly am merciful by nature," he said heavily. "Yet, though I have little choice about what I do, perhaps these scruples help to make me a better man," he said thoughtfully as he dribbled more water across my bloody fingers. "And you have helped me to see that."

I watched as the blood mixed with the water and dripped gruesomely off my fingertips, splattering onto my rocky sanctuary. As usual, I found his responses cryptic, but something in particular niggled at my mind, not seeming to fit.

"How can destroying the forest be for the greater good, Tiamat?" I asked him searchingly, ripping my eyes away from the grisly red splotches.

He stopped reaching into the creek and smoothly turned to put both of his hands on my wrists, squeezing them firmly. "It wasn't just the forest, Kali," he said, watching me closely.

"What?!" I choked out, "How far, Tiamat? How much land? Tell me!"

"All of it. Everywhere."

No, he can't be saying that, I thought fiercely, as I felt the blood drain from my face. *I can't listen to this...*

"I must tell you," he paused, taking a deep breath, "that I am personally responsible for the catastrophic events, not only in this area, but spanning an area of approximately one million square miles. And I am only one of a hundred of my kind. Every one of my cohorts, each having a task similar to mine, began at precisely the same moment today, and we have all completed this stage now. Do you grasp what I am saying to you?"

"No," I whispered, shaking my head and denying acceptance of his explanation. "This can't be happening." This was something that you saw in the movies for a thrill, and then you left the theatre, all safe and sound, to continue on with your life. This wasn't the sort of thing that people actually experienced. "I can't believe that there are more of you doing this... all over... what is it?... 100 million square miles!" Reason told me that this couldn't be, and it fought against my scattered thoughts as they attempted to focus. "You're saying this is happening all over the *world?*" I demanded, my voice rising in panic.

Releasing my wrists, he placed one hand on either side of my face, anchoring me with his gaze, his energy tingling through my flesh. "Not 'happening,' Kali... *happened.* It is finished. Every inch of land has been cleansed, and some ocean area as well."

My mind recoiled and my vision blurred. I could hear Tiamat's voice echoing through a haze of fuzz, could feel his hands on my face, but it was all coming disconnected, thoughts and senses unraveling and floating off in different directions; seeking solace elsewhere.

"Kali," he said urgently, his distant voice sounding anxious. "Kali, look at me," he said, giving me a mild shake. "This is the way it is," he persisted. "Refusing to accept it will not make it disappear. Now focus. Keep your mind busy and ask me some more questions."

I struggled to gather my shattered thoughts, to salvage whatever reason I could muster. Tiamat was right, I needed to think, to fight against the numbness that was freezing over my brain, threatening to shut everything down. I worked for what seemed like a long time, and finally seized upon a question that seemed integral, but didn't require me to ponder the annihilation of everything I ever knew.

"You said that you were one of a hundred of *your kind*," I forced out. "So, if you're saying you're not human, what exactly are you?" I asked, pulling various disturbing images into somewhat coherent thoughts. "Are you some kind of a devil? ...Or an alien? Who else would want to destroy our planet?"

"To start with, I do not recall saying that I was not human," Tiamat replied, appearing to relax a little. "In fact, my mother was a human woman, flesh and blood. My father, however, was not. And though I am of celestial decent, I am certainly not an alien." He held my gaze with his alarmingly strange eyes, though they were kind now, and calming. He moved his hands from my face and placed one again on my wrists, but he held them gently, stroking my raw fingers with his other hand.

"You guessed closest when you asked if I was a demon," he said softly, firming his grip as I tried to pull away from him. "We came, originally, from the same place. But my father never fell from grace, and neither have I."

"Wait," I said urgently, as a horrible feeling burst open inside me, reminding me... "My father!" I shrieked, tearing my hands away from his grasp. I was immediately on my feet, pacing and stamping like a confined horse, green and wild. "Tiamat, is he dead? Is *everyone dead?*" I asked him desperately.

"I do not know if your father lives, Kali." Tiamat placed his right hand on the rock ledge and leapt effortlessly out of the water before continuing. "There will be some survivors, though the majority of the human race has fallen. I am sorry, but it is unlikely that your father survived."

I turned and ran, frantically needing to flee, desperate to find my dad, but also driven by an acute desire to get away from Tiamat's horrifying revelations. I could take no more. The trees lining the path blurred, though whether it was from speed or tears, I could not have said. And as I ran, an eerie noise floated on the air, high and keening, seeming to pursue me in my flight—until, suddenly, I realized that the din was ripping from my own throat, and I choked it off abruptly, sounding like a murder victim that finally met her end. I exited the trees, raced through the campsite, and tore down the path that would lead me off the Peak.

Yet I did not get far. Rounding a bend, I smashed headlong into Tiamat. He grasped me in a close embrace and held me firmly, though I thrashed and struggled against him. I didn't even pause to consider how he could possibly be on the path *in front* of me. "My dad," I wailed, "Please, Tiamat! I have to know if he is alright! Let me go," I begged him.

But he did not ease his hold. I fought uselessly until the last of my energy was spent, and only then did he venture to hold me at arm's length, so he could look at me as we spoke.

"I cannot let you go, Kali."

"But he's my dad," I cried piteously.

"You must think about this. Even if I did release you, there is *nowhere* to go, and no means for you to get anywhere. Do you not recall seeing the state of the forest from the look out? You will find no intact vehicles and you will find no roads. It is over."

"It is *not* over! Not until I know if he is okay or not. Never until that time." Again I tried to push past him, but he held fast. "You obviously don't know what it means to love someone, Tiamat, or you would understand this!"

He looked suddenly stricken, and blanched noticeably before responding. "Perhaps I do not, then," he said in a soft voice, his thoughts apparently elsewhere. "But regardless of this, I cannot let you run off."

Each of his hands was wrapped firmly around my upper arms, and he looked over to stare critically at his splint, a crease forming between his brows in the silence. The moments stretched on before he brought his gaze back to my face. "I believe I can help you to discern his fate, if you would like me to, Kali," he said, surprising me.

"Do you know where my dad lives? His house is—"

"In Pinecrest, yes."

I opened my mouth to ask how he could know this, but he cut me off before I could begin. "Now is not the time to go into details of how I know. My question remains; would you like me to help you to discern his fate?"

"*How*, exactly?" I asked, unsure of what this may entail.

"I will need you to trust me in this," he said as he raised his hand to my cheek. "As difficult as this may be for you at this moment, it is the only way." My skin prickled and tingled as his fingers trailed leisurely along my cheekbone. "Will you trust me, Kali?"

Locking my eyes with his, I slowly nodded my assent, while his fingers gingerly traced their way up to my forehead. Almost immediately, my entire world was shot with a startling, electric blue, and then—for the second time that day—I felt a crushing dark wave engulf me, pressing me into the black, empty void.

Chapter 6

I was exceptionally uneasy. From all around my prone body came the sinister roar and crackle of fire. There was an intense heat on my face, putrid smoke in the air, while flickering orange specters shifted beyond my closed eyelids.

This was it. My tender fingers, still throbbing from the abuse I had inflicted upon them earlier, moved across the rough surface on which I lay. I made out a number of flat, rough slabs of rock-like material, warm from the heat that surrounded me. It was most likely busted concrete, I reasoned, if I truly was where I both hoped and feared to be.

Yet as I took a deep breath to brace myself for what I would see, a shadow suddenly shielded me from the scorching temperature, and I stiffened defensively in the cool, dark shade.

"Kali, as you requested, I have taken you to Pinecrest. We are in the general area around your father's house," he said, his voice catching as though *he* was upset. "But due to the extensive damage, it's challenging to pinpoint the exact location."

Something inside me hardened at his words and tone. My dread dissipated completely—to be replaced with resolve... and anger.

"I have done what I told you I would do," he continued, "and though I know that this will be incredibly difficult to bear, I believe it is necessary for you to open your eyes and see for yourself." He must have moved then, as I was exposed again to an unrelenting heat, while the harsh brightness resumed flickering through my eyelids.

But it was anger that compelled me now—not my reasoning and not Tiamat's words—and I forced my eyes open. And while my vision was assaulted with images of hell, my mind focused in a rage that shot down my spine and fired through my body. With fury pulsing through my limbs, I planted my hands below me, and raised myself up to face the burning, twisted wasteland around me.

I saw that I had been lying on a small mountain of cinderblocks, which could only have been from someone's basement or foundation, as the houses—when they existed—were almost exclusively timber-framed here. It seemed like the foundation had been inexplicably thrust up into a high mound—in fact, the entire area appeared to have been churned like a massive, rubble-based farmer's field. I stood rigid, my hands balled into fists, as I watched the conflagration blaze everywhere. It raged through a vast rubbish heap that roiled endlessly in every direction, the waves of hot air making the hillocks appear to move and lurch grotesquely.

There was nothing resembling a town here; not a single house, not even so much as a wall was left standing. *Nothing!* There were no telephone poles, no street lamps, no trees, and not even roads to be seen through the scorched piles of broken concrete and brick, jumbled timber and burning debris.

There was no need to ask; I knew that my father was not alive. Nothing at all could have survived this absolute obliteration of the town—of this community where I grew up amid kindly neighbors and childhood friends.

I wondered: did they die in terror, screaming for help and for mercy? I morbidly imagined old Ms. Jones running to save her beloved terrier as her windows shattered and the roof crashed down on top of her. And I pictured my father. What was he doing when Tiamat struck? Was he cooking breakfast in the new kitchen that he painstakingly renovated on his own? I felt slivers of ice in my chest as I pictured him watching his hand-crafted cupboards splinter to bits just before the room imploded in on him. Or maybe he was reading his fishing magazines and plotting to catch the next big one, hoping for leverage in his ongoing wager with his old friend, Tim Coulter. And as he studied his magazine, did he stop when he heard an approaching roar, like I did? Did he try to run? As his world fell down upon him, did he senselessly worry about me? I prayed fervently that my dad's last thoughts were of fish, and not wasted in fear for his life, or in agony, or—I couldn't stand the thought of it—screaming for help that would never come.

I picked up some movement out of the corner of my eye, and I noticed that Tiamat was approaching me cautiously. A renewed flash of rage whipped through me, boiling my blood. *"Don't touch me!"* I hissed through clenched teeth when I saw him tentatively reach out in my direction. "You ... *murderer!*" I spat, rounding on him.

Tiamat reeled backward as though I had physically struck him. But he stopped himself and planted his feet as he faced me. "I am so sorry for what I have done, Kali."

"Just don't ... don't even talk to me!"

"But you know I had no choice. I *told* you this! It is... excruciating... to have to survey the destruction I've caused and imagine the lives and the histories of the people who are dead now because of *me*. And yet, it is almost worse to watch your reactions—to witness what being here is doing to you."

"Jesus Christ! Are you kidding me? You just killed millions of people and you actually have the nerve to tell me that it makes you feel *bad*? I guess you think your conscience puts you right on par with goddamned Mother Teresa!"

"No Kali, listen—"

"To what? Do you think that your regret can somehow make it better? My father never hurt another person. He didn't deserve to die like this!" My voice was shaking with fury now, and I stepped toward him aggressively. "Do you somehow think your pain will erase everyone's suffering or the terror they felt? Because if it can't do that, *then I don't give a shit how you feel!*" I felt like clawing away at his martyred expression, hating the very sight of him.

"Your father should not have suffered at all—no one in this town would have. I hit this area very hard and very fast, making it my first target," Tiamat responded with feeling, fixing his eyes on me strangely. "I ensured that there would be nothing but quick and painless deaths in Pinecrest."

"You..." I said, gasping as I stepped back, "...You thought I might have been here."

"I knew it was a possibility," he replied quietly, almost to himself. "I hoped that you were far away, but I was not willing to take the chance."

My anger flared again. "Am I supposed to be flattered?!" Seething, I turned my face toward the heat of the fires, unthinkingly flicking my gaze over the debris not far from the base of my mound of cinderblocks.

That was a grave mistake. My eyes began to pick out the grisly evidence immediately, and I was unable to stop myself until it was too late. The first thing I noticed was a twisted, shredded blue and brown shirt... no, only blue, but stained with... I ripped my eyes away, but almost of their own accord, they continued to sweep the area, and rested on a dark pool of sticky blood... then I saw splatters of it, gruesomely splashed across some ripped metal ... and then, on a broken board beside that tree branch was... *my God,* I thought, *an arm!* It lay across the board palm-up, the severed limb ending in a pulpy stump just above the elbow. Its dirty, rigid fingers were curled slightly toward the sky, like the hand was waiting expectantly for its due. I had to look away, to get away from these images, but I simply couldn't break my focus. Stained, saturated clothing and shoes, tangled brown hair, barely discernible body parts and stringy flesh seemed to appear throughout the rubble, jumping into my vision as though fiendishly summoned there. "Oh no…" I whispered, horrified, "…No, no, no, no, no…"

My world tilting violently, I staggered backward in a futile attempt to get away and tripped over the uneven blocks on which I stood. I landed hard, winded, my vision mercifully filled with an empty, smoky sky. But simply staring at the sky wasn't enough to help me escape this horror—the knowledge of what surrounded me pressed in on all sides, driving me mad. Eyes opened or closed, all I could see was blood-matted hair and teeth and torn, severed limbs whirling in a tormenting freak show that I could not shut out; that I knew was everywhere… even right under me. "Tiamat… please…!" I said desperately, curling myself into a ball, while keeping my eyes glued to the sooty sky. "Please! I have to get out of here… Tiamat, help me… please…" I begged.

His face like stone, unreadable, Tiamat leaned over me. Reaching his hand out to my forehead, his awesome, unspeakably destructive powers worked in contradiction. I slumped with relief as electric blue incinerated every macabre vision, spiriting my escape into unconsciousness.

* * *

I woke up sobbing and alone, my face pressed into the dirt at the Lookout campsite. Night had fallen while I was out, but no fire burned, so a thick darkness lay over everything, bearing down and smothering me in my loneliness and desolation. I hardly cared. I didn't care about the dark, or my torrent of tears, or the lack of a fire or the grit in my mouth. Grief and despair poured out of me, rancid and black like the oppressive night.

After an endless time, my sobs eventually quieted. I lay in the stillness of the dark, feeling like an empty shell: drained and fragile, but lighter and eased because of it. I would get stronger—if Tiamat would let me live. Though why I was alive at this point was a mystery to me.

Slowly, I started becoming more aware of myself and my surroundings. My arm was pinned painfully underneath me, and I could no longer stand the dirt that was in my mouth and crusted on my lips. The feeling that I was alone lingered and I noticed that the fire remained unlit. Perhaps Tiamat was gone. It was funny; I didn't even know how I felt about that.

Sitting up, I massaged the circulation back into my neglected arm, and spit the dirt out of my mouth the best I could. Using the inside of my shirt—the outside was now filthy—I wiped the grit from my lips while glancing around the site for a sign of Tiamat. I could see none, but it was incredibly dark. There was an eerie blood-red moon that hovered overhead like a wax seal pressed onto the black fabric sky. It gave me the bizarre feeling that it was close enough for me to simply reach up and touch it, and I was almost tempted to do so.

If only the ground would stop shaking…

No, I thought, suddenly panicked, as my mind registered the trembling earth. *No, he can't do this now!* Frantically looking around for some explanation, I tried to understand why Tiamat would torture me with the knowledge of what had happened to my father—of what befell the rest of humanity—just to finish me off immediately afterward. Why would he do that? Yet the vibrating ground was unmistakable; I could feel Tiamat's energy rippling through it, the entire peak shuddering beneath my feet. And he knew that I was on Lookout, of course, as he was the one that set me here, unconscious.

Would I have time to get down off the cliffs before he obliterated them? Not waiting to discover the answer to that particular question, I stumbled through the thick darkness, trying to find the location of the path that would lead me away. But the red moon cast little light, and I feared that I would be about as likely to step off a cliff as I was to find a path to safety.

There was a faint light, I noticed, just on the far side of one of the boulders that flanked the cleared grounds. With a small surge of hope, I clung to the possibility that the light came from a lantern that Tiamat had left behind, and that perhaps I could use it to see my way off the shaking cliffs.

Knowing that time was of the essence here, I swerved toward it quickly, my heart pounding in my chest. I reached the large rock and peeked around it as cautiously as my haste would allow. And I stopped, astonished.

There was a lantern on the ground at the base of the rock, but its feeble glow was not what initially drew me. It was Tiamat. The light I had seen was emanating from him, glowing and shimmering around him in pale blue waves that rippled like a sea anemone in a tidal pool. He appeared unaware of my presence, resembling a cross between a penitent sinner and a man under arrest; he kneeled on the ground with his forehead pressed into the dirt and his hands folded across the back of his head. It was a pose of overwhelming grief; one that I did not expect to witness coming from Tiamat.

As I watched, Tiamat's body wracked and shook, and with each of his tremors, the cliff supporting us shuddered alarmingly. So even though I realized—with some relief—that he was not *intending* to kill me at this moment, the fact remained that if Tiamat didn't rein himself in, he would very likely blow this small mountain to bits—and the result would be the same, intended or not.

The ground lurched again and I grasped the boulder for support. "Tiamat," I said hesitantly, afraid of what he might do if I surprised him in his present state. I watched him warily, but he didn't respond at all.

"Tiamat!" I called out, panicked, as the tumultuous ground pitched violently. Somewhere off to my right, I could hear part of the cliff break off and crash noisily in its long tumble toward the wrecked land below. Still, he did not react, and the ground continued to buzz and vibrate between each terrifying tremor.

I didn't know how I could make him stop. There was *no way* that I was going to touch him—I remembered keenly what even his small shocks were capable of, and now Tiamat was absolutely shimmering and pulsing with energy. So I looked around frantically for some-thing—anything—which I could use to get his attention.

There—a large branch, as thick as my arm and about four feet long, lay a few feet to my right, illuminated by Tiamat's unnerving glow.

Please don't blow me to bits, I thought at him fervently as I grabbed the club-like stick and turned in his direction. "Tiamat," I tried again, hoping I would not have to touch him. Again, there was no response. My nerves jolted as another sharp cracking sound came from some-where nearby. I had to do something.

My heart in my throat, I leaned forward and pressed the butt of the stick carefully against his side. Surges of numbing energy vibrated right through me, but it was bearable, under the circumstances. "Hey," I coaxed over the intensifying rumbles. No reaction. He *had* to stop *now*. The cliffs were going to shatter; I could feel it through every inch of my body.

"Ti-a-*mat!*" I called urgently, ramming the stick forcefully into his ribs. There was an immediate outward blast of blue energy, bursting away from him in every direction with a resounding *wump!* The force of it threw me up and backward, depositing me and my stick on the other side of the boulder. By all rights, I should have been badly hurt, but the heaving ground spurred me on and I noticed nothing. I grabbed my branch and ran back around to Tiamat.

With relief, I saw that I had roused him. He had jumped up, look-ing surprised and alarmed, and was scanning his surroundings with suspicion. Then, noticing me approach him, he turned away quickly. Keeping his back to me, he raised his hands and appeared to be briskly rubbing the traces of his grief from his face. There was tension in his stance and I saw him breathing deeply like he was attempting to calm himself. He stood rigid and quiet for some time, his pale blue aura slowly fading, while the ground tremors faltered and died out.

"Kali," he said finally, his voice calm and even, "I see you have recovered." He turned to face me then, and had the privilege of seeing the reaction on my face.

"*Recovered?*" I hissed. "What a stupid thing to say, Tiamat! Do you think that because I'm standing, I've somehow forgotten that you *leveled* Pinecrest and *murdered my father?*" I was furious, and before I knew what I was doing, I had lunged at him with the stick, swinging it violently at his head.

He jumped out of the way easily, but in doing so, had backed himself up against the cliff's edge, and he tottered there on the brink, looking at me with astonishment.

"Kali," he said placating, "you don't want to do this. Trying to take my life will not bring anyone back."

"*Trying* to? Wouldn't it kill you if you fell?" I asked him, somewhat hopefully.

"No," he admitted, "because I would not allow myself to strike the ground. However, if I did manage to hit the rocks below, it is true that I would die." He lifted his splinted arm in exhibition. "As I am half human, I am mortal," he said, raising an eyebrow at my threatening branch.

"That's good to know," I fumed, raising the stick aggressively. "Did you or did you not kill all those people?"

"I did. But I am under orders, so to speak—"

"And could you have refused?"

He looked uncomfortable. "Technically, I imagine that I could have refused, but—"

That did it. I lashed out at him fiercely, wishing to smash his handsome face to bits, viciously thinking that he should look more like the monster he was.

He leaned back, avoiding my blow. And fell.

"Oh no," I gasped, throwing the offending stick aside. *No. Tiamat can't be gone!*

By all rights, I should not have cared; I should even have been happy. But logic appeared to have no bearing, and I was instantly at the edge of the cliff, looking anxiously for a sign of him.

Yet nothing was there but the yawning blackness of night. I could not see what had happened to him. Was Tiamat, as I hoped, clinging to the cliffs somewhere beneath me? Or did he actually fall and die on the distant rocks below?

I lunged for the lantern and hastily brought it to the edge of the abyss, but it illuminated nothing more than a few feet of sheer rock that plunged down into the darkness. I could drop the light, I thought wildly, but dismissed that notion quickly—it would simply shatter to pieces, likely before I got a chance to see anything.

Hesitating at the cliff's edge, I deliberated anxiously about whether I should hike all the way down the path to have a look below. I didn't know what else to do; I had to determine if he was lying dead at the mountain base or clinging to a rock somewhere lower down.

"Tiamat?" I called into the void.

There was a loud swishing sound nearby, and I leapt away from the edge to face the unknown noise behind me. Stunned, I fell to my knees in terrified awe.

Glowing faintly, Tiamat swooped in from the starless sky at a great speed and landed effortlessly in front of me, his magnificent icy-white wings spread out majestically on either side of him. He stood shirtless, his body shimmering with his light blue haze, flanked by an immense, radiant wingspan at least fifteen feet wide. Like a giant hawk, he shook his wings out briefly before folding them with elegant grace behind him. They were so huge, the bent tops of each folded wing extended far above his shoulders, almost a foot over the height of his head, and the long, pale feather tips nearly touched the ground behind his feet. He was the most beautiful and fearsome thing I had ever laid eyes on, and I could feel my body shaking under his penetrating blue stare.

"Do not be frightened of me, Kali," he said gently.

"Oh my God," I exclaimed, gaping up at him.

He laughed kindly. "He is the one that I obey. I did try to tell you this before, of course, but you were a little too distraught to listen."

"You're an ... *angel?*"

"Just half. I am also half human, remember?"

"I can see which half is your dominant side," I said, trying to speak with a steady voice as I gawked up at his splendor.

"Can you? Well, you must be referring to my human side, Kali," he said with a sad smile. "I have made so many rash mistakes, especially with you. The human in me has run a little rampant, I'm afraid."

He extended his right hand and gestured for me to take it. I hesitated, but after a moment I accepted it, and watched his warm hand gently envelop my battered fingers. Gooseflesh prickled on my skin and static-like tingles crept up my arm as Tiamat raised me to my feet. He carefully released my hand once I was again standing in front of him. "My brothers and I are called the Nephilim."

I stared at him, mulling over this new information, when frightening ramifications of his angelic nature flashed through my mind. "But if it is *God* that you serve, then that means *He* is the one that had you do this. I can't believe that! I thought God loved humankind. Why are we forsaken? Why would he kill us?"

"He does love you. And you must not think of dying in that way. He is killing your mortal forms, true, but you are not really ceasing to be. He is calling you home now, all of you. It is time to be judged."

What did he mean? Was Tiamat going to kill me now? Alarmed, I stepped back a few paces, but found myself backed precariously on the cliff's edge, and threw my arms out to the side in an attempt to keep my balance. I kept it, but just barely.

Tiamat's wings were partly open, and his face looked white. "Please come away from the edge, Kali" he said pleadingly. "It's so dark, if you fall, I don't think I'd be able to see you. I couldn't catch you."

"Why would you care, Tiamat?"

"I just do. Please trust me. Step over here, Kali."

"*Trust* you? Your job is to kill me, remember? If I fall, it'll just make your task easier, won't it?"

"Please *listen,*" he said. "When I said that God was calling 'you' home, I didn't mean you personally, Kali. It's different with you."

"How?"

"Step over here first, then I'll explain," he answered in a voice that was tight and hurried.

Watching him warily, I did as he asked, relief flooding through my limbs at being away from that great, black chasm. I made a point of putting my back right up against the large, hulking boulder, ensuring that any further surprises wouldn't send me unexpectedly over the edge.

"So how is it different with me, Tiamat?" I asked.

He folded his wings up again and took a deep breath, though his face still appeared pale. "It is difficult to explain this to you without a little background, but I will try," he began. "First, however, would it be too alarming for you if I took my wings in? It is almost impossible to sit comfortably with them on my back like this," he said apologetically.

I nodded nervously, not saying anything, and observed his actions closely. Immediately, my breath caught in my throat as my eyes riveted to his body. The change was not frightening; rather, it was remarkable. With the wonder of a child, I watched him transform.

Chapter 7

Tiamat behaved like he was steeling himself for a particularly painful experience, noticeably tightening his jaw and gritting his teeth. Holding his broken arm firmly against his chest, he breathed in deeply, focusing his attention into the black void that loomed beyond us.

Then, slowly, his striking folded wings began to shrink in size, robbing the night of their brilliance. The wings, I noticed, appeared as though they were being gradually sucked into his upper back, but his back did not seem to alter its shape in the least. His body didn't bulge or stretch, yet it could not possibly have accommodated those huge wings. But unless they were disappearing into thin air, I couldn't fathom where else the wings could be going.

Expanding my focus from his wings to his torso, it was then that I realized that his entire appearance was shifting. He grew. It was slight, but Tiamat definitely gained a few inches, and his frame filled and fleshed out all over his body. Appearing closer to the Tiamat I recognized, his face became more robust, and the muscles in his chest and arms enlarged and grew defined. Instead of being bulky, however, his build now seemed cut and solid compared to the lean, wiry look he had when his wings were out.

Yet these were not the only changes he underwent. He also went very pale, and now had a thin sheen of sweat on his brow. And as his wings finally disappeared completely, he swayed and gripped his splinted arm as though it was a source of tremendous pain.

Though my mood was still black, it bothered me to see Tiamat suffering so acutely. "Are you alright?" I asked him. Curious, I began to circle around behind him to have a look at his back. Would there be openings for his wings there?

"Yes, I'll be fine in just a moment," he said. Holding his body very still, he remained quiet for a few seconds before continuing. "Bringing my wings in or out is quite an uncomfortable experience if anything is broken," he explained, examining his splinted arm. "My bones hollow out when I change, and become much like a bird's skeleton—in composition at least."

"To help you fly?"

"Yes. This makes my body lighter, but it also shares out their density, which I use to frame my wings. And my bones—when they are not hollow, at least—are much denser than the average human's. That way they can provide me with enough material for this purpose."

I examined his back as I listened to his explanation. It was completely smooth, devoid of any indication that enormous white pinions had spanned out of it just moments before.

"So you explained the bones, but what about the rest of it? Obviously, your wings are going to need feathers, muscles and skin. And then, what about tendons and nerves," I continued, adding to my list as the thoughts occurred to me, "as well as veins and arteries? I assume that these are also shared out from your body. And if that's the case, would that be why your physical appearance changed—why you got bigger—when you brought the wings back in?"

He smiled to himself, looking amused by my deductions. "I really should remember that you don't miss much, Kali," he laughed. "And you are correct; everything you listed must be generated from my body's existing tissues, nerves and proteins. So changing takes a lot out of me, so to speak." Tiamat turned and looked at me with interest. "Does this not frighten you?"

"No. In fact, I find it fascinating. And it's probably the *least* shocking thing I've learned all day," I replied, keeping my tone cool. Despite his friendly conversation, I refused to let myself be drawn in by his smiles or his laughter. I was willing to speak with him, but it was information that I wanted. "I'm wondering," I continued, my tone sharpening, "if you can change the structure of your bones, why can't you just heal your arm?"

"It doesn't work that way," he replied quietly. The laughter was gone from his voice, likely in response to my confrontational manner. "Just like certain body parts can only perform the functions for which they were designed, my bones can only change in this one way. I cannot alter them to make them heal, nor can they take any other form."

I glanced at his splinted forearm, but my traitorous eyes kept flicking up to his bare arms and chest. It was very disconcerting, and my temper flashed at my juvenile behavior.

"I noticed that you ...uh... lost your shirt when you fell off the cliff," I said, fixing my gaze on a patch of black night just over his right shoulder. "I assume you had to get it off in order to bring out your wings—but how did you have time?"

He shifted uncomfortably before responding, and took a deep breath. "I didn't. My wings had to rip apart my shirt as they opened, and I tore the scraps off once I was safely in flight. I was fortunate that the material was not too thick or tough, or my wings might not have managed to break through."

When he said this, I noticed the red welts on his chest, shoulders and across the front of his neck, caused by the friction and pull of his shirt before it finally ripped away. It looked like it almost strangled him, but I could not bring myself to be remorseful—neither for causing his fall, nor for the minor injuries incurred when he was trying to take flight. I pointedly ignored the fact that he could have easily died on the rocks far below. Despite his angelic lineage, I knew that he was still a monster.

We stared at each other in the still and the quiet, feeling the tension swirl between us. Perhaps there was nothing to be said at that moment. Tiamat dealt a death blow to everyone I ever knew, so any apology from him, due to its sheer inadequacy, could do nothing at that point but injure me further. And there was nothing that I was about to say either. In the silence, he appeared to grasp that I was not the least sorry that I caused him to fall off the cliff—I could see it the moment that stark realization crossed his troubled face.

He watched me evenly for a beat, neither of us speaking, while the silence between us thickened and congealed like spilled blood.

And then, almost robotically, Tiamat turned away. He picked up the lantern—which I must have dropped in the dirt when I saw him swooping in like a bird of prey—and began walking toward the campsite. He moved mechanically, turning back to face me when he reached the boulder.

"There is more to be said tonight," he informed me, his wintry voice formal and detached. "I have promised you an explanation, though I find that I am in need of a shirt. Perhaps we can continue our conversation at the campsite?"

I nodded—fearful that my voice would betray my conflicted emotions—and let him lead me quietly through the darkness.

You're a bitch, Michaels, I chided myself as I followed him the short distance to the site. Tiamat's reaction was suddenly making me feel terrible. He had been nothing but honest and even protective of me from the first time we met. Yet logically, I debated, I really should be fleeing, my escape spurred on by the loathing I *should* have for him and what he had done.

But I could not help the crushing feeling that bore down on me when I looked up at his tall form silently entering the camp. I had to admit it: as ridiculous as it was, I felt ashamed for hurting him.

"I'm sorry, Tiamat," I whispered. And I knew when I said it that I truly was—that deep down, I really did believe that he didn't want to do these terrible things. I suddenly understood that the burden of being obligated to do something that was so unspeakably horrific must be nearly unbearable for him. "I'm sorry," I said again, deep feeling infused in my voice, "for everything."

He stopped. "*You're* sorry?" he asked, incredulous. As he turned, he fixed his unnerving stare on my face. "I have destroyed everything that has ever been dear to you. I have single-handedly caused you more suffering than most people have experienced in their entire lives, and you're telling me that *you are sorry*?!"

He was getting angry; the resulting blue glow became a shimmering warning that rippled along his body. This time, however, the consequence of his runaway emotions was different. The ground vibrated with thunder now, as lightning-charged clouds snuffed out the crimson moon's meager light. A violent wind rushed in and buffeted the Peak with sporadic blasts of aggression while the thunder rolled ominously overhead.

"Kali, by all rights, you should hate me! Do you not understand what I have done?! I don't deserve your pity, your forgiveness or your apologies. Remember that." When he spoke, the words appeared to choke him, and flashing webs of lightning snaked across the black sky.

The storm brewed alarmingly while his abject face twisted and festering emotion shook his body. Tiamat held himself tight and rigid, fighting for control—giving me another glimpse of the anguish that both bound him and tore at him. As though sensing the intrusion, he turned away from me and fixed his stare on the ground as he worked to collect himself once more. Then, as the tense minutes passed, his radiance slowly abated and his breathing and tension eased, silencing the skies back into their restless slumber. The moon again revealed itself, a bloody orb freed from Heaven's cloudy black veil.

I was at a loss again. I should have just let it go, but he looked so miserable that I simply couldn't ignore his suffering. And more than just that, it seemed that in wanting to help Tiamat through his pain, it helped to ease my own as well. I reached my hand out and ignoring the buzz of energy, placed it tenderly on his back, intending to comfort him.

He sucked in his breath abruptly and froze, turning to stone under my fingers.

For a long moment, neither of us moved or made a sound. Had I done something wrong?

"Do not touch me, Kali," he said slowly, infusing every syllable with ice. He held himself very still, as though he was waiting for me to release him.

Staggered and hurt, I removed my offending hand and let it fall to my side. I couldn't imagine the reason for his response. I had simply tried to be kind, and instead, found myself shunned. His acidic rejection stung me more than I would have thought possible.

Once my hand was gone, his body reanimated, and he walked briskly away, depositing the lantern beside the cold fire pit on his way to the tent. He didn't look back at me once.

After a time, Tiamat reemerged from his tent, and joined me by the fire I had built in his absence. His demeanor appeared much improved, and I noticed that the line of tension had eased from his shoulders. He sat quietly for the first few minutes, surreptitiously watching me as I unnecessarily busied myself with poking at the blazing logs.

I refused to be the first one to speak; stubborn resolve surged from the anger that continued to pulse through my veins. And to a lesser extent, I was also fearful of making another blunder, possibly plunging us into discord once again. His sharp rebuke still stung, and I was not eager to recreate that situation. So I kept my eyes on the fire, and let the minutes drag on.

"Here, eat this, Kali," he said, finally breaking the silence. He passed me a granola bar and an apple. "I hope you don't mind the fare, but I doubt either of us is in the mood to cook tonight."

Until now, I hadn't realized how hungry I was. "Thank you, Tiamat," I mumbled without looking at him, and ripped eagerly into the granola bar. I could hear Tiamat crunching on his apple, and after a few moments, glanced over at him.

He sat leaning forward, his elbows on his knees, staring blankly at the half-eaten apple in his hand. His dark hair fell almost into his eyes, nearly concealing the crease of thought that worried between his brows. Then, suddenly, his eyes lifted, seizing me with a forceful, charged stare of vivid indigo. His gaze held me breathless and frozen, and seemed to bore its way into the furthest depths of my soul. And though I felt exposed and naked under his stare, I found that I could not tear my eyes away.

"Kali, I need to apologize," he said, his remorseful eyes riveted on my face. "I am so very sorry for the terrible things I have done today, and I feel wretched about what seeing this has done to you. I know that there is nothing I can say now that will lessen the damage I have caused, but regardless of this, I need you to know how sorry I am so we can move forward from this." He paused, as if to gather his thoughts, but did not look away. "And I am also sorry for the way I behaved when you apologized to me tonight. I have to admit that you took me off guard. I accept your apology, and offer you my thanks for your under-standing—though I still feel I am undeserving of it."

With this he looked away, tipping his head forward once more, and his dark hair obscured his eyes from my view.

A feeling of release washed over me when he shifted his gaze, end-ing an uncomfortable sense of connection with him. I immediately felt relieved, separate, and, strangely … sad.

"Apology accepted, Tiamat," I replied formally, ignoring the bizarre, empty sensation that had spread in my chest. "And thanks for the food," I added, feeling awkward.

He looked up at me and smiled slightly, easing the tension between us. "You are most welcome," he replied, taking a large bite of his apple.

Following his lead, I finished off my granola bar and started in on my apple, before broaching the subject that had been niggling at me since it first came up at the cliff's edge.

"Tiamat...," I began.

"You want to know how you are different," he finished. "Yes, I did tell you I would explain this, didn't I?"

"You did," I agreed. "But can you first tell me if you can read my mind?" I asked him, flustered. "Because it often seems like you do. Not just now, but also earlier today, when you knew where my father lived without needing me to tell you."

"No, I don't read minds, Kali. Only God is omniscient. I am simply observant," he said with an impish grin. "And I must admit that I only knew where your father lived, because you lived there with him when we first met, ten years ago. After you and I parted ways... well ... I knew where to find you. I flew over your house a number of times that summer," he admitted sheepishly. "But do not worry, I gave that up as quickly as I started, and never went again," he added with a distracted note to his voice. He was obviously bothered by a memory of something, and frowned down into the flames, but didn't elaborate.

When he glanced back up at me, the troubled look was gone, and he continued in his explanation. "And a moment ago, I knew that you wanted to ask how you were different, because that subject has been waiting to be aired for a good while now. No mind reading was necessary." And he smiled, looking quietly proud of his deductions.

I simply stared at him, dumbfounded. I found his rollercoaster of moods difficult to keep up with. "Um…" I started, not knowing what to say. "You found out where I lived?"

"You could say that," he replied after a brief hesitation. "And I flew over your house the odd evening ten years ago. But as I said before, I gave that up rather quickly."

"Why did you give it up?" I asked, remembering his troubled look when he said this earlier.

"I cannot say," he responded softly, gazing down into the flames.

"What does that mean?"

"I can't say, Kali. Just leave it, please."

"So then, can you tell me how I am different? Why did I need to get *away* from the cliff's edge, if it's your task to send all the humans 'home?' You should have just let me fall." I said the last in a whisper, as I picked at a clump of dirt on my knee.

"Let us refrain from speaking of falling off cliffs for the remainder of the night, shall we? This does not appear to be a good subject for us," he said conversationally. "And as for how you are different, I will touch on that after I have given you some background on myself. It is necessary to explain one before I can address the other.

"As I said before, there are one hundred of us, and each one is a half-breed like I am. With our lineage comes certain abilities, some of which you are keenly aware of. But there are other traits—knowledge and compulsion, for example—that I wish to explain to you now. My brothers and I all had a vague knowledge about ourselves since the time we were infants. As we grew, this knowledge developed as well, or perhaps, as some of us believe, it was imparted to us incrementally. We all matured with an identical awareness of who we were and a general idea of what we had to do. My full task became clear to me on this very peak ten years ago. Perhaps you remember how I handled it, as you were there to talk with me about it."

"That would explain a lot," I mused, as I remembered his demeanor when we first met. "So, are you saying that God speaks to you in your head?"

"No," he laughed lightly, his eyes sparkling with amusement. "Even among our kind, thinking that we hear His voice would be viewed as an indication of an unsound mind. Instead, we're hardwired to simply *understand* if we are required to do something. Other times, we suddenly find that we have knowledge that was imparted to us from Him—knowledge that we did not have only five minutes before. However, we don't hear voices in our heads, and anyone that ever claims that they hear God's voice is known to be deluded."

His look sobered then, and became serious. "Aside from knowledge, we also feel a compulsion to do certain things, which comes from His will. It's often the way He gives orders, in a manner of speaking. Every one of us, for example, began to tear apart the earth's surface at exactly the same moment today, driven by that same compulsion. But here is the interesting part; we understood that our tasks were related to cleansing the earth of humankind, so we also knew that every one of us would feel compelled to end the lives of *any* human we came across. And for us, direct compulsions are exceedingly difficult to ignore." He leaned forward and looked at me intently, yet there was no aggression or threat to his attitude.

"It is different with you," he said simply.

"How is it different?" I asked, my voice shaking.

"I do not feel compelled to kill you."

He appeared to be telling me the truth, and there was no trace of joking or laughter in his serious tone.

"Why not?" I asked.

"I cannot say."

"You are not *allowed* to say, or you don't *know*, or you don't *want* to say?" I pressed. "Which is it?"

"*I cannot say*," he repeated shortly, looking at me in exasperation. Standing swiftly, he stalked back to his tent, disappearing from sight. Apparently, the matter was closed.

So I sat alone, staring at the flames, trying to digest this new information and glean what I could from it. *Why wouldn't he feel compelled to kill me?* I wondered. Musing fancifully, I imagined that Tiamat had personal feelings for me that interfered with and cancelled out any heaven-sent compulsions to end my life. That thought was appealing for obvious reasons, but I knew that if I was to seriously mull over Tiamat's cryptic explanation, I would have to leave such ridiculous ideas aside. First of all, he already killed millions, even though it didn't align with his wishes; he was *compelled* to do it, and he followed through. It wouldn't be any different with me.

But also, I would be an idiot if I deluded myself into believing that someone like me—a plain misfit from a race his kind was put here to stamp out—would be of any interest at all to a beautiful, powerful creature like Tiamat. In fact, he made it quite clear how he felt about me when I boldly touched his back earlier, in my foolish attempt to comfort him. As I remembered that moment, I shuddered, wondering where I even got the nerve to touch him at all. I knew that I had no right, and suddenly felt ashamed.

Perhaps, after all, that was my answer, I reasoned. Tiamat didn't feel compelled to kill me simply because I was not an important factor in the overall equation. I would die in time, certainly, but I realized that I likely wasn't important enough to bother with—that through my insignificance, I managed to escape God's notice, for the time being.

And as for not wanting me to fall off the cliff, that could be explained as well. Tiamat knew that I would likely die somehow, but as he knew me personally, watching me die in front of him was probably a little much, even for him. At least, I hoped that was the case.

"Kali?" Tiamat said from my immediate right.

I started, not realizing he was there, and looked up at his cautious, half-smiling face. He held a sleeping bag under his splinted arm and was offering me a water bottle with his other hand.

A feeling of ease spread through me at seeing his attempt at a smile. Tiamat often made me feel so comfortable; it was easy to forget that I was not his equal.

"Thanks," I said, accepting the water and smiling back. I reached for the sleeping bag as well, but he just looked at me strangely.

"Oh ... well, there is another one in the tent for you. I was thinking you might sleep there." He gestured over his shoulder before turning away from me, preparing to set out his sleeping area. "And please excuse me," he said, glancing in my direction. "I hope you won't mind if I sleep. It has been a trying day—for both of us."

I had to agree with him there, though I sought to put off sleep for a bit, worrying about what visions would assault me when I closed my eyes. I was hoping Tiamat would be willing to sit with me a little longer, and tried to think of a way to continue the conversation.

"You have *two* sleeping bags?" I asked, smiling. "Do you entertain guests often?"

"No," he replied, looking surprised. "I have two sleeping bags to keep me warm through the coming cold weather. And I have never had anyone sleep with me before—I mean, sleep at the same site as me," he stammered, turning red as he realized what he had said.

Due to its preposterous nature, his comment struck me as something absurdly funny. Trying not to laugh, my resulting snort was likely worse from attempting to hold it in. Tiamat's red face darkened at this, and I worked to rein myself in quickly.

"Good night, Kali," he said forcefully, vigorously shaking out his bed roll and laying it down on the hard-packed earth near the fire.

His grouchy response irked me. "Good night," I grumbled, turning away. "I hope I'll be able to sleep."

"Let me know if you can't. I wouldn't hesitate to black you out, you know," he muttered moodily behind me, "if you think it would help."

I chose to keep silent as I trudged grumpily to his tent, thwarted in my attempts to put off going to sleep. I hoped that if I did slumber, it would be dreamless.

Chapter 8

It was a pristine night—one of those tranquil, cool winter evenings that beckoned with a temperature perfect for walking. Large, delicate snowflakes floated lazily down like fine cold feathers, melting softly on my warm cheeks as I tilted my head back to dissolve one on my tongue. The night felt glorious, silent as a church at midnight, the floating snow seeming to almost suspend time around me, like hovering grains of sand pausing before sifting leisurely through an immense hour glass.

Unable to see very far above me in the darkness, the snow appeared to materialize in scattered white points across the vast, black sky overhead. The flakes were infinitely numerous, yet it was maddeningly difficult to align even one with my open mouth. I grew thirsty as I tried, longing more and more for the cool, wet touch of snow on my dry lips. But despite my efforts, the floating, taunting flakes all eluded my waiting tongue.

Snow drifted down everywhere around me—each and every flake missing me by a wide berth, as though an invisible umbrella was suspended just above me, deflecting my quenching, wet quarry. With growing frustration, I watched the path of a single flake glide idly down from the heavens, first toward me, then veering and swirling a wearisome distance away.

It fell ever so slowly before it came to a rest on a cold, porcelain cheek. Sparkling there like a decorative sequin, the lone flake lay just below wide, blankly staring eyes, rimmed in beautiful black lashes. The woman's mouth was open, as though she, too, were waiting for a taste of snow. But she did not move, and her twisted corpse lay broken on the frozen ground, smashed and bloody in death. A man lay beside her, splayed and crumpled, and a child beside him, her soft, blonde locks matted with blood. There were innumerable human remains behind and all around them—scattered heaps of carnage spanned off into the darkness in all directions, surrounding me completely.

And the snow fell everywhere, blanketing the ground and resting lightly on the bodies. Yet it would not cover them. Regardless of how much snow came down, the death could not be concealed. The deceased stood out starkly instead, gruesomely red, gray and black pop-outs on a canvas of pure white.

Panic swelled, pressed and thumped against my chest as I watched the unsuccessful snow fail to shroud the dead. *Come on... cover them,* I heard myself insist, my voice shaking with dread. But the snow would not listen. *Just bury them!* I screamed to the silent heavens.

Unable to look anymore, I gazed down at the immaculate layer of snow at my feet, and with growing horror, watched spots of crimson dot the pure white surface around me. Anxiously following the source, my eyes rested on my own two hands, drenched with thickening blood, and repugnantly dripping with gore that I knew was not my own.

I screamed. Over and over, horrified shrieks ripped out of my throat as I tried to shake the sopping, sticky blood from my fingers, splattering my face and body with slashes of murderous red.

Then my hands became stuck and bound, and I noticed that the air was suddenly warm and close. I sat up quickly; Tiamat's sleeping bag was tangled tightly around my body, and I realized that I had been dreaming. I was drenched in sweat and shaking miserably, feeling desolate and afraid in the stagnant, shady loneliness of night.

A stirring in the darkness caught my eye, and I noticed a tall shadow moving just outside the door of the tent. It hovered, shifting intermittently from side to side, as though trapped in indecision. After a time the shadow moved off, and left alone with my demons, I eventually fell back into the realm of nightmares.

The remainder of my slumber was crawling with fragments of horrific imagery, pursuing me torturously from one nightmare to another. None were as vivid or as disturbing as the first, but despite this, I woke screaming numerous times. Yet after each nightmare thrust me back into wakefulness, I fell masochistically back asleep, my exhaustion surrendering to the roiling terror of my dreams. And every successive time I thrashed awake, a part of me looked longingly for the comforting advance of a tall shadow, appearing just beyond the tent door. But his dark outline never returned.

Eventually, a gray and washed-out, but merciful sunlight filtered through the thin walls of Tiamat's nylon tent, heralding the arrival of morning. I dozed a while longer, embracing the respite of a dreamless haze, before finally emerging to face the day.

Tiamat was sitting on one of the cliff-side boulders, holding a steaming mug of something—*coffee, perhaps?* I thought wistfully—and gazing critically out at the land below. It was strange to recall yesterday's events in the morning light, especially watching Tiamat lounge so casually on the Lookout. He resembled nothing more than a camper enjoying the morning's solitude—a comfortable delusion, provided I refrained from peering over the cliffs as well.

Veering the other way, I headed for the gurgling creek to wash up. I was filthy from the trials of the day before, and realized with embarrassment that I had slept in Tiamat's tent and sleeping bag in my current grubby state. I would have to do my best to shake out the dirt later.

I hiked my way to my favorite sheltered grove, where the little creek formed a wide, clear pool. *Why, of all places, did I have Tiamat tell me in the grove?* I wondered with annoyance, recalling yesterday's horrifying revelations. How sad that the one place on earth that hadn't been physically altered, should have been tainted so drastically in my mind. This location would be forever linked to abysmal memories, and could never again be a place of peace for me.

Yet there was something different here. There, on the large rock overhanging the creek's modest pool sat a folded towel, and beside that was a new toothbrush, tube of toothpaste, and a bottle of—I laughed when I saw this—biodegradable soap. Right. Like Tiamat wanted to be careful not to damage the earth at all.

Despite my chuckles, gratitude flowed through me at this unexpected kindness. These little gestures were exactly what I needed this morning—that, and a good wash.

After first stealing a quick glance around me to ensure that I was alone, I peeled my torn, soiled clothing from my body with relief, and slipped into the cool, refreshing water. To my dismay, I found that the simple dirt and grime came off much more easily than the smoke and ashes from the ruined town of Pinecrest. I scrubbed and rinsed thoroughly, but could still detect a faint odor of smoke on my skin. Reaching down to the creek's bottom, I scooped up handful after handful of sand and smeared this roughly on my tainted skin. Using the sand along with soap, I scrubbed my body raw, washing away yesterday's horrors as well as I could.

Eventually, once my skin was sore and stinging, I held myself in check, and forced my scrubbing, shaking hands into submission. *Calm down,* I told myself, shutting my eyes and clasping my hands together tightly. *It's over.* I waited until I had my breathing under control before I opened my eyes to peer at my angry-red, sand-encrusted skin. *Nice. Great self-control, Kali,* I thought angrily. I rinsed off, grabbed the toothbrush and scooped some of the clear water into my mouth.

"Augh!" I exclaimed, spitting it out immediately. There was absolutely no odor, but the water had a strong, bitter taste to it, and was altogether undrinkable. This was a concern. In fact, I found the water to be unpalatable to such a degree, that I ended up brushing my teeth dry.

Reaching up to grab the towel, I realized with a start that my dirty, ripped clothes were gone, and new, clean clothing was laid out on the rocks in their place. I scanned the area quickly, but could not see Tiamat anywhere. When had he done this?

"Tiamat?" I called to the empty trees. "Tiamat?" There was no response.

Wrapping the towel around myself, I stepped over to inspect my new attire. The clothing wasn't at all what I might have expected.

Tiamat was, once again, perched on the boulder when I returned to the site. He slipped off it casually when he saw me approaching, and held out a steaming mug in welcome. Despite the warm gesture, however, his face was carefully expressionless.

Tiamat, I recalled, had thrown up barriers since we were first reunited yesterday. For some unfathomable reason, he had locked himself away from me, had hidden behind a wall of distance and detachment. There were instances when he let his guard down slightly, but for the most part, Tiamat's face and demeanor had been deliberately masked. And it was even more noticeable today. This was bothering me much more, however, than a simple cold shoulder should. I found his purposeful distance to be incredibly unnerving—*was he preparing himself for the eventual need to kill me?*

"Kali?" He held out the mug to me which was, until now, still unaccepted.

"Thank you," I said with sincerity, accepting the piping cup of coffee. Trying to ignore the feeling of unease, I held the mug just below my nose so I could inhale the rich scent, and closed my eyes in appreciation. It smelled absolutely wonderful.

"Tiamat," I said suddenly, my eyes shooting back open as it hit me, "where is the cut on your head?"

He looked startled—*did I always do that to him?*—and touched his head instinctively. "Oh," he replied. "It has healed, Kali. Thankfully, I mend much faster than the average human."

"And your arm?" I asked, noticing the splint that was still in place.

"Bones take a little longer to heal than cuts, but I should be able to remove the splint tomorrow." He gazed at me speculatively then, his eyes lingering on my cut and bruised forehead, before resting on my freshly scabbed fingers, wrapped protectively around my morning coffee. "It is a shame that you must nurse your wounds for so long," he said quietly.

I didn't know how to reply, so I simply shrugged my shoulders in response. "Thank you so much for the towel and clothing," I said, changing the subject. "It was really thoughtful of you to leave those things out for me, and what a relief it was to be able to clean up. I must have missed seeing you when you left me theses clothes, though," I said, watching his reaction closely.

His face still maintained the distant expression, but his mouth twitched at this. Perhaps he had watched me bathe after all. "You're welcome, Kali. They appear to fit you well, I see."

"Perfectly. But where did you get these from, Tiamat? And *leather?*" I inquired, indicating the rugged brown leather pants that I wore. The shirt was a close-cut soft doeskin that fit me like it was tailor-made. "Okay, I can see how leather would make sense if I'm going to be alive for a while longer...?" I paused, my half-phrased question hanging in the air.

But Tiamat just stared coolly back at me, waiting for me to continue. Apparently, he would give me no further information about my survival at this point.

"Because of their durability, of course," I continued awkwardly. "I mean, I understand clothing won't be very easy to come by from now on, but..." I paused, confused, "These aren't exactly your size. I can't believe you just had these lying around."

"Actually, I did. I ordered some clothing to be made for myself, knowing that I would have need of it, but there was a mix-up. The tailor ended up giving me some woman's clothing instead of what I ordered. That stubborn man wouldn't take it back, so I decided I would keep it to use for scraps and patches."

He stopped and looked at me appraisingly. "The clothes fit you like a glove. Hmmm... That's amazing," he murmured, continuing to stare. "It is like they were made for you specifically."

Blushing under his close scrutiny, I took a long drink of my coffee, hiding my face behind the delicious brew. Lowering my mug, I noticed that he continued to stare at me; though this time, he was shaking his head in apparent bafflement.

"Ha! Perhaps the tailor knew something I didn't," he said with a dry, humorless laugh. "Now that would be funny, as I considered him to be such a dim-witted man."

"Tiamat! That's not funny at all. And you shouldn't speak ill of the dead, especially seeing how *you're* the one that killed—"

"Okay, enough. I am not perfect, you know, Kali. I am half *human*, after all."

"Yeah, I know you're no angel. And by the way, I really dislike how you keep saying that you're half-human as if it's some excuse for poor behavior. Being human is not synonymous with being depraved.

"And perhaps I can understand how you might have lied to yourself, believing that people are corrupt or immoral so that your *task* would be easier for you to bear," I said with distaste, placing a bitter emphasis on the word 'task.' "But it's over now, so stop dragging humanity through the mud. You've done quite enough already, and frankly, I'm sick of the insults."

"I am sorry. Again," he sighed, looking up at the sky as if seeking some support. "I honestly didn't mean to be insulting. Truly, I have very little experience with people, so I might not always say the right things."

"Yeah, alright," I muttered, dismissing it.

"Now we really should eat this before it gets cold," he said, indicating two plates of scrambled eggs that he had balanced on a rock behind him. I hadn't noticed them at all.

"Thanks, Tiamat," I said with a little smile, shifting my coffee to one hand so I could accept the plate of eggs. "You know, I've never been very good around people either," I admitted, accepting his olive branch and trying again at more civilized dialogue.

We went to sit down on a log near the fire pit to eat our breakfast, and I must have bolted down half of it before I was even seated.

"I never would have guessed that about you," Tiamat said conversationally. His tone was friendly, but I could see that his strange blue eyes remained distant and aloof. "Why would you become a guide if you were not comfortable around other people?"

"Don't get me wrong, I like people. I just feel awkward when I'm with them. At least I did, when there were still people around. And now that they're mostly gone, I would give anything to have them back. It may seem strange, but to feel uncomfortable and out of place again would be a trade-off I would accept in a heartbeat," I said, getting upset. "So don't think for a second that I'm okay with what you've done to humanity—you and your *brothers*. It makes me sick!" I spat at him, realizing as I did so that I got completely off track. I had to focus myself here; dwelling on what occurred yesterday wouldn't get me anywhere, and would only serve to further strain things between us.

I cautiously took in Tiamat's reaction and saw that his jaw was clenched, but he said nothing, and the skies and earth presently remained quiet.

Taking a deep breath, I forced myself back to the conversation at hand, and worked to remember what Tiamat had asked me. "People were almost an afterthought when I was guiding, though," I admitted quietly, feeling somewhat sheepish about my outburst. "It was a love of the outdoors, of camping and hiking through the woods, that was the main draw for me."

"Yes, and you felt like 'throttling' the odd camper, if I am remembering correctly. Funny, that seems so unlike you, Kali," he said, his words thick with sarcasm.

"And the last time we met, I had a camper go missing," I retorted. "I suspected that it was you who took him. But making people disappear is so unlike *you,* isn't it, Tiamat?"

"You found him. Of course, you assaulted him shortly afterward. How incredibly surprising." This time, Tiamat appeared to be fighting back a surge of amusement, but the more he spoke, the less he was able to dam it up. "His intentions toward you were black, and I was worried for you at the time. Perhaps, instead, I should have been worried for *him,*" he snickered. "You have quite the temper!"

"So you *did* take him?" I asked Tiamat eagerly, ignoring his wisecracks. The details of that night had puzzled me for the past ten years.

"He was a threat to you," he answered vaguely. "I have often wondered, though ... how did you find him so quickly the next day? I saw you go straight to him that morning as if you knew exactly where he would be."

"Oh, that was nothing special. I had a hunch, but mostly, I just get lucky with finding people. I've always managed to track down anyone that's gone missing in the park. I just use common sense, really."

Something changed in Tiamat; a subtle difference in his eyes and his posture. He leaned forward slightly and his eyes widened minutely in response to my mundane answer. "What do you mean, Kali?" he asked carefully. "When it came to locating lost campers in these woods, were the other guides always as successful as you?"

"Well, no" I answered, feeling suddenly uncomfortable. "But like I said, I think it was simply luck and common sense. Nothing more."

"How many people went missing over the years, and of those, how many did you find?"

"I'm...I'm not really sure..."

"*How many?*"

"Fifty or sixty, maybe. There must have been at least five each year."

"And?"

"I found every one," I admitted.

"So," Tiamat said, lowering his eyes from me, "you find people."

He sat quietly, staring at his empty plate in the silence. As the minutes melted away, I watched his fine, smooth face flicker with a look of shock, and then slowly drain of color as he raised his eyes to look at me.

What was it? I thought, squirming in alarm under his cold, appraising stare. *Did he have new information now? A new compulsion? Did it have to do with me finding people?*

Shifting his gaze, he next stared hard—almost angrily—at the hazy sky, before bringing his eyes to rest on me once again.

"We must start traveling soon, Kali," he said, his monotone voice contradicting the strange look on his face.

A horrible creeping feeling shivered through me at that look. "Tiamat," I whispered. "I can't lead you to people just so you can finish them off. It would kill me to do it."

"I can find the survivors on my own, Kali," Tiamat replied. "Did I not tell you that? All of the Nephilim possess an ability to sense humans. We can locate them wherever they are."

"What?" I demanded. "No, you didn't tell me that at all." No wonder only a hundred of them were needed to completely obliterate us, I thought despairingly. Humanity, I realized, didn't stand a chance. "That's just so unfair."

"It was never meant to be fair. This is no game we are speaking of."

"Oh, no? Well if it isn't, why didn't your kind just kill everyone off at once? Why leave a few terrified people scattered around, just to be tracked down later? That sounds very much like nothing more than a cruel game of cat and mouse."

"We left some people alive because that is what we were expected to do," Tiamat responded. "The decision was never ours to make. However, these survivors now have the occasion to show their true colors before they go for judgment. For most humans, adversity is the catalyst that either unveils their brilliance or unmasks their corruption. Many will now have the opportunity to prove their merit."

"How kind," I said flatly. "I feel much better, now that I realize we are just lab rats. And I suppose I am alive in order to 'prove my merit' as well?"

"Not exactly," Tiamat said dismissively, as he abruptly stood and gathered the plates. "And do not ask me more about why you are alive, Kali. I cannot elaborate."

I grabbed the plates from his hands, and gathered the mugs as well. I figured that was the least I could do, considering that he provided breakfast. Damned if I was going to be nice about it though. I turned away and started off toward the creek to wash the dishes, and noticed that Tiamat was following close behind me.

"Can you tell me why we need to leave this campsite?" I asked him over my shoulder.

"We will need to travel south, Kali." Tiamat responded as he passed me and stopped, blocking the path.

What was it with him? I wondered. Once again, Tiamat maintained the attitude of a stranger, and his eyes seemed to look right through me as if I didn't exist. *Why?* All I could think of was that he knew that my death was coming soon, and he did not wish to get too close. *Would Tiamat have to be the one to do it?* I speculated as a dark chill stole over me.

"It will be cold here sooner than you may expect," Tiamat said, almost in response to the unrelated frost that was slowly creeping down my spine. He glanced up to the sky as he said this, and I followed his eyes to view the weak, watery sun, veiled behind a sea of haze. "The particles in the atmosphere," he continued, "will cool the earth off rapidly now. We must move to where it will be a little warmer." He turned then, and continued along the path, leading me this time.

"How? Will you fly me?"

"No," he laughed. "I have far too many supplies that I must take, now that you are with me, that is."

We arrived at the little creek then, and he lead me downstream to do the cleaning, closer to the cliff's edge than I would have liked. I noticed that he looked thoughtful, a crease appearing between his brows as he folded his arms and stared hard at the ruined landscape that could be glimpsed between the trees and beyond the cliffs. "Horses would be the logical choice, though I must admit that I have very little practice in that area."

"I could help you with that, Tiamat," I offered as I started to wash up. I wasn't exactly an expert rider myself, but I had had sufficient experience to know how to handle and care for horses proficiently. "But we may have some trouble locating the horses and the gear we'll need. I don't suppose you can sense horses as well?" I asked hopefully.

"Ha! That's an ability I do not possess. And considering how I have no knowledge of how to manage a horse, perhaps riding is not something I am meant to do." He looked pensive at first, before a large grin slowly spread across his face. "That's a pity, because I am quite certain that I will do it anyway." Tiamat looked elated, and his eyes flashed with life.

I was almost completely bowled over. Here, suddenly, was the Tiamat that I remembered meeting so long ago—unrestrained, emotionally intense, and completely mask-less. I knew I had to keep him from locking himself behind his barrier again.

"So how will we find the horses?" I asked with enthusiasm.

"I think you would be amazed by how much ground I can cover when I need to. I will leave right away," he said. "Once you explain to me what gear I will need to locate for the horses. In detail, too, please, as I may not know each item by name." Tiamat sounded excited, and as I told him what I could, he rattled off numerous questions in quick succession, carefully clarifying every piece of information I gave to him.

"I may be gone quite a while. You will please stay right here on the Lookout until I return. Alright?" he said, stepping back as he prepared to bring out his enormous wings.

"Hold on," I said quickly, remembering about the water. "Could you also bring back some potable water? This stuff is undrinkable now." I indicated the little creek, gurgling along through the trees.

"Right." He paused. "I meant to tell you about that, Kali. There is no water I can bring you," Tiamat said, sounding apologetic. "It is like this everywhere."

"What?" I could feel the color draining from my face.

He stepped toward me and touched my arm lightly, leaving it tingling along the trail of his fingertips. "Do not worry. Come with me a moment, so I can show you something."

Tiamat turned and led me several paces upstream, where he stopped on the mossy bank. Placing one foot on a rock in the water, he smoothly crouched down and dipped his hand into the flowing creek. "Scoop up some water from immediately downstream of my hand and drink it," he instructed.

Without the advantage of a rock to step on in the creek, I found that I had to lean way out to reach the water that flowed past his hand. Wobbling to keep my balance, I pooled some in my open palms, and hesitantly brought it to my mouth to drink.

"Tiamat... this water is fine," I said in wonder, amazed at his ability to make the water drinkable. "But how will I drink when you are not around?"

"There are some bottles at the site that I have filled up already. You will not die of thirst today," he said with a kind, teasing voice. He shifted his position, and lifted his hand from the flowing current.

"Wait," I said, stretching out so I could scoop more water. I had hoped for one more sip before he left. But I reached out too rapidly, and losing my balance, grasped clumsily at Tiamat's half-extended hand. This was not an improvement to the situation. Splashing down into the shallow creek, I only succeeded in off balancing Tiamat as well. He tripped and scrabbled for a foothold, but ended up on his knees in the water beside me, his face inches away from mine.

We both froze, trapped inescapably in the other's gaze. Taken completely off guard, Tiamat's face was startled but open, completely devoid of distance or detachment. Quite the opposite, actually. His closeness consuming all other thoughts, fire burned in my chest as I carefully reached up and smoothed a dark lock away from the intensity of his eyes.

Tiamat raised a dripping hand from the water and brushed his fingertips lightly along my lips, the sweet water droplets buzzing enticingly from his touch. I tenderly kissed his fingers, and, running my hand down the back of his neck, hesitantly leaned in toward him.

Then, unexpectedly, he careened away from me, breaking his gaze as he turned his head abruptly. His entire posture was rigid, and when he finally spoke, it was through clenched teeth. "Do not tempt me, Kali. You must keep your distance from me." He shut his eyes tight, and shook his head minutely as a vibrating in the ground started to whip the little creek into froth. "I cannot do it," he said despairingly, throwing his face up toward the heavens.

Tiamat jumped up from the creek then and stomped to the opposite shore. Looking thoroughly angry now, he growled as he stalked off.

"I *can't*!" he suddenly roared to the silent forest. And with a cacophony of thunderous cracks, a great semi-circle of trees toppled at blinding speed like they were nothing more than flattened blades of grass.

The fallen trees lay in broken submission as he stormed past them, their green limbs quivering from the force of the impact.

I sat there, stunned. The choppy creek waters flowed around me, bitter and completely unpalatable; just like I was.

Chapter 9

Stumbling blindly, I splashed my way to the creek's bank as humiliation and resentment seared through my veins, nearly choking me in their ferocity. I simply could not get my mind around what had transpired. *What was so terrible about me,* I thought angrily, *that he should react to me with such aversion?* While I glared mutely at the arc of splintered trees, rivulets of acrid water streamed from my sodden clothes, and formed displaced, brackish pools around my feet. Enviously, I watched the water sink slowly into the ground and disappear from sight. There was little I desired more than to simply hide away; to curl into a tight, protective ball in the impartial solitude of darkness. With this single goal in mind, I stomped back to the campsite, snatched up the lantern and pounded back into the woods.

There was a place I knew nearby that, fittingly, was as close as I could come to actually crawling under a rock. Cutting away from the path, I fought irritably through the thick forest branches to reach the head of the creek. The brook's sullied waters gushed out of a jagged, shin-high cave, which perforated the base of one of the Peak's looming rock faces. About fifty feet to the left of this tiny opening, a yawning gap in a great cleft of rock provided access to the caverns within, and was conveniently concealed by a wall of thick underbrush.

Many years ago, I stumbled upon this cave when I was searching the area for a young girl that had gone missing while visiting Lookout Peak with her family. She hadn't gone far. In fact, shortly after the search began, I discovered that she had scampered up onto the rocks above the campsite and then drifted off to sleep in the warm sun. Overall, that day had turned out very well. The sleepy girl was reunited with her family, safe and sound, and I lucked upon an incredible little cave system that I had been able to scout at my leisure.

Exploring, however, was the last thing I wanted to do today. As I neared the underbrush which masked the opening to the cave, I cast a sharp glance around the surrounding forest to ensure that Tiamat was nowhere in sight. Before he could continue grinding my spirit to dust, I desperately needed to recuperate alone.

Pushing my way past the bushes that concealed the cave's entrance, I flicked on the lantern and hastily ducked inside. I was immediately embraced by the cool, dark solitude of the cavern, and I closed my eyes in relief. *How much longer can I keep myself together?* I wondered grimly. Obviously, I was neither as tough nor as resilient as I once believed myself to be. Preoccupied by these thoughts, I swerved away from the light at the cave's mouth, and began to ease my way into the inky heart of the cavern.

Heading toward the underground stream, it became necessary to pick my footing over the uneven ground, and I forced myself to focus on my surroundings. That was when I noticed it. A subtle gleam, a quick flash of reflection that glinted somewhere in the cold blackness to my left, stopped me short. Holding my breath and staring hard into the thick, murky shadows, I could see nothing but the close darkness of the cavern. The unseen creek chattered loudly in the echo-filled gloom, and it was nearly impossible to detect the existence of any subtler, more sinister sounds.

I raised my light with some trepidation, and with relief, found myself staring at the flat top of a can of corn, lying forlornly on its side in the middle of the rough, earthen floor. Quite the unusual object, in what I—probably naïvely—considered to be an undiscovered cave.

This little mystery spurred me on and, lantern held ready, I started to look around.

Upon further exploration, I was astounded to observe that this can was merely one of an entire wall of cans, gleaming and winking at me as I scrutinized them in the shifting light. And every one of them contained food. Tiamat, I reasoned, had likely stored these here—stockpiling supplies while they were still plentiful.

There were several neat stacks of other items as well. A spare tent and an extra sleeping bag sat tidily together on a folded tarp. Nearby were a crossbow, a saw, axes, shovels, ropes, string, and boxes and crates filled with other unknown supplies. Piles of blankets and clothing rested near the edge of the underground creek, and I sat tiredly on one of these soft heaps, feeling drained. The mystery was solved, and like a deflated balloon, I felt hollow and withered. So I sat quietly for a while, passively watching the lantern beam reflect off the stream's dark surface, showering the cave's ceiling and walls with starbursts of dancing light.

Beside me sat the crossbow and its accessories, though I was uncertain why Tiamat would have need of these items—perhaps to hunt, when it became necessary to augment his food supplies. He had the very best gear: a soft, fitted crossbow case, boxes of bolts and a high-end scope to fit atop his fancy, state-of-the-art, ReCon 175 crossbow. *I bet he doesn't even know how to use this,* I thought irritably, as I picked up the compact weapon.

My dad had just purchased one of these about a month before, and it fired beautifully, considering it was only about half the size of our old crossbow. I remembered how excited he was about his new equipment, and I sullenly turned these images over in my mind as I reached for a crossbow bolt and roughly loaded it. I had felt strangely protective of my dad ever since he first lost his way in the woods so many years ago, and his death was difficult for me to bear. He was a loveable, scatter-brained, decent person, I thought acrimoniously. It wasn't right that his body should be rotting under a mountain of cinderblocks. And if his remains lay among the ruins of Pinecrest, where, then, was his soul? In Heaven?

No, I remembered, Tiamat had said that we were all being called 'home' to be judged. I couldn't help but wonder where a soul waited for this evaluation of their worth. *And what will it be like when I go there?* I thought morosely, as my fingers gripped the crossbow tightly. *Will I see my father?*

Staring blankly at the cocking device, my mind flicked back into action. *What the hell was I doing?* I wondered angrily as I carefully removed the bolt. There was no good reason at all to be loading a crossbow. Who or what would I shoot? I had seen only two possible targets since I ascended this ridge: myself and Tiamat. Beyond a doubt, I knew that I wanted to live, so I couldn't have been thinking of turning it on myself. In fact, I would fight viciously for my life, if it came down to it. Additionally, I had to admit that I didn't desire Tiamat's death either, though I couldn't help smiling to myself when I visualized putting a bolt through his foot.

"You're an idiot, Michaels," I mumbled into the darkness as I shakily set the crossbow down and put the loose bolt back into its box. I was alive, I realized, and fortunate to be so, considering the circumstances. And although it was alright to be out of sorts and require some adjustment time after all the shit I'd been through, fixating on the negative would only serve to spiral myself into a well of depression. That was not how I wanted to spend my last days.

I grabbed the lantern and stood up fluidly. No longer craving the encompassing darkness of the cavern, I gingerly made my way toward the muted light that marked the passage to the cave's entrance. But there was something wrong...a sound filtering in from outside...

It was Tiamat. I could hear him calling my name and yelling something unintelligible; his tone shot with urgency. My mind scrambled for a reason, but I couldn't imagine what might be happening out there.

Whatever it was, I decided, it had to be desperately serious to account for the barely restrained panic in Tiamat's voice.

I launched myself at the cave's entrance, crashed through the protective underbrush, and barreled straight into a very startled half-angel. Tiamat, with his wings spread out behind him, steadied me and grasped me firmly on my shoulders. He stared down at my face, his eyes wide with shock and surprise, while gale-force winds pushed and lashed at us from the swirling skies.

"What is it, Tiamat? Is it a storm?" I asked him as he gaped at me in silence. "What's happening?"

"Kali...I..." he stammered blankly, looking thoroughly dumbfounded. The wind caught his open wings, and he shuffled to keep his balance, planting his feet firmly apart. "You...were..." He shook his head, as though trying to physically clear it. "What happened, Kali? I was worried you were dead."

"What?!" *What the hell was he talking about?* "Why would you think I was *dead*?" I demanded.

"Because I can sense you. Regardless of how far away or where you are, I can sense you all the time," he said, his voice spiked with a quiet intensity. "Do you remember when I explained that my kind could do this?"

I nodded my head mutely, waiting for him to continue.

"I found that I needed some time," he said carefully, "and took to the air. I was a good distance from here when suddenly you were...you were simply...gone. Vanished. You disappeared like the dead, Kali."

It was likely that this could mean any number of things, but the only explanation that would come to me was that I actually was dead... or was about to be. As soon as I exited the cave, Tiamat's face had betrayed the very same conclusions. "You can't sense me anymore?" I asked, my voice shaking.

He peered at me closely, his eyes tracing slowly across my face. "Thankfully, I can sense you again," he said softly. "And I am relieved to discover that you are alive ... now. But I only resumed sensing you the moment before you crashed into me. What happened prior to that—did you have an accident? Where were you?"

"Nothing happened at all, Tiamat," I replied. "And as for where I was, I had gone into the cave system back there," I said, gesturing at the wall of greenery behind me. "I just sat for a while on your stack of blankets by the underground stream." I felt no need to tell him about the crossbow.

His look changed instantly. "You were in the caves?" he asked with interest. "And unhurt?"

When I nodded my assent, Tiamat took a deep breath, and some of the tension appeared to melt from his body through his long exhale. "Would you mind taking a step back into the caves now, Kali? Just so I can see something?"

"I need you to tell me what's going on, Tiamat," I said, pushing his hands off my shoulders.

He took a step back and gritted his teeth in obvious agitation. "I will explain in a moment. But first, I need to ensure that you are not in any danger. *Please*, get in the cave *now*." There was a sharp edge to his voice that would bear no argument.

I could see that Tiamat kept glancing surreptitiously at the skies and the surrounding thicket of trees and I knew, grudgingly, that he was right. Safety first, discussion later. "Fine," I agreed reluctantly. I held his gaze for a beat, then turned and headed briskly back to the open mouth of the cave.

"Oh," I heard him exclaim in surprise as I stepped into the darkness. "Go a little further in," his voice urged from outside. His tone was much calmer now and, no longer as alarmed myself, I took my time doing a round of the front section of the cavern.

"How's that?" I called back loudly. But there was no response. I dashed quickly to the cave's entrance, and cautiously pushed my way through the screen of brush surrounding it. Tiamat stood, leaning with his arm against a birch tree and his wings folded behind him, looking thoroughly absorbed in thought. I wondered if he had even heard me. "I see the storm has passed on," I noted in a friendly way.

He looked up and gave a lopsided, half-smile, so I continued. "What was that all about, Tiamat?"

"Well," he began cautiously, like he was choosing his words with care, "it appears as though I cannot sense you when you are in the cave. It either gives off some kind of interference, or the rock simply blocks me out completely. I do not know which. I find this rather strange. We had no knowledge that there was anything that could impede our ability to sense people."

"So then, when you suddenly couldn't sense me, your immediate conclusion was that I was dead?"

"It seemed to be the only feasible explanation."

"And this bothered you?" I ventured.

"Of course it *bothered* me!" he said with surprise. "What a ridiculous question, Kali."

"So you...you *do* care about me. Don't you, Tiamat?" I pointed out.

His look hardened as he pushed himself away from the tree and took a step backward. "Kali," he said, his voice formal and emotionless, "I wouldn't forgive myself if anything happened to you, but—"

"Why not?" I asked him point blank.

"Do not read anything into it, Kali," he said harshly. "You are my responsibility. There is a reason for you to be alive and a purpose for you here. If you die, I will have failed."

I wasn't buying it. Not anymore. Not after what I knew was between us when we first met, not after what had transpired between us at the creek, and certainly not after observing his reaction when he believed me to be dead. I walked over to him, feeling certain of his feelings for me, but still unsure of how to sway him into admitting to them.

He looked wary and took another step away from me, but I persisted. Boldly reaching out and running my hands lightly along his arms, I stepped intimately close to him. I could feel the caress of the static charge that danced in waves along the tiny shell of air that separated us.

"Kali, *don't*," he said forcefully. He wouldn't even look at me as he said it, and instead kept his head turned sharply away.

I reached up to touch his face, intending to turn it gently in my direction...

"Stop it!" burst out of him, accompanied by a flash of pale blue light. It exploded outward in all directions like a super-sonic bubble, flinging me into a pile of bushes ten feet away.

I slammed down forcefully, the branches snapping like they were toothpicks, as my weight smashed down upon them. Winded from the impact, I lay there, pathetic and vulnerable, while my mouth opened and closed like that of a landed fish. I stared up at Tiamat, whose face, in the blink of an eye, loomed immediately overhead. He wore a blank mask of neutrality, while his eyes raked me over from head to foot; examining, I assume, for any injury. Apparently satisfied, he spun on his heel and stalked a few paces away.

My breath restored to me, I slunk into a sitting position, the crushed branches snapping noisily as I propped myself up in the flattened bush. Speechless, for the moment I could do nothing but glare sullenly at his winged back.

"Kali," he said, exasperated, as he spun around to face me. "Why do you persist? Am I somehow encouraging you?"

"I can't believe this," I breathed. "How can you act like nothing passed between us at the creek today?"

"What happened there was a *mistake*," he snapped. "We were both feeling lonely and we took it too far. Have you somehow blocked the conclusion of that encounter from your memory?"

"I'm not even going to qualify that with an answer, Tiamat," I fumed. It seemed that most of our conversations ended with each of us practically livid…well, one of us, at least. "I'm wondering… are you angry right now?"

"Furious. Kali, I told you not to—"

"Right, I know," I interrupted. "I just noticed that everything's fairly calm; no earthquakes and no storms. So, perhaps you're not really that upset."

"I have been working hard to control that," he said through his teeth. "But I must confess that it is nearly *impossible* to do with you around. Your antics are driving me insane."

"Goddamn it, Tiamat!" I said, jumping up.

"Don't say that," he warned.

"I'll say whatever the hell I want to say. I've had enough of this shit! I'm leaving, which is probably best for both of us. Let me take some supplies—"

"You're not going anywhere—"

"Like hell I'm not!" I threw back. "Forget about the supplies, then, and just give me the crossbow. I'll catch my own bloody food."

"Kali, I'm going to look for the horses now. We will discuss this further when I return."

"I won't be here. I intend to leave as soon as possible."

"Then I will track you down," he said, his voice low and dangerous.

"I'll hide in caves if I need to, Tiamat," I answered. "Even you can't find me there."

"Oh yes, caves may conceal you for a while. But when you emerge, I *will* find you," he promised angrily, his look thunderous. And with a great white swish of his immense wings, he was gone.

* * *

"Damn it, damn it, damn it," I muttered under my breath as I violently bashed the brown, bulky target. Tiamat's sleeping bag, it turned out, didn't get as dirty from my filthy clothing as I initially believed. After a few vigorous smacks and shakes, the sand and dried dirt fell away completely, and I was left with nothing to do. I hated being forced to stick around this campsite; to feel like a prisoner. No, that wasn't correct: to *be* a prisoner. Escaping from Tiamat was impossible.

Immediately after he flew away, I had grabbed the crossbow and its gear, and began to gather some other items that I felt were integral to my survival. I had been in the caves longer than I realized, and if I was going to cover any distance before nightfall, I knew that I would have to be on my way quickly. Yet as I gathered and packed, I found that I moved slower and slower, until eventually, I simply sat listlessly upon the half-packed bag, toying with the crossbow on my lap. *Who are you kidding?* I asked myself bitterly as I put the crossbow down and stood to take my aggression out on Tiamat's sleeping bag.

There was nowhere I could hide, I knew, where Tiamat wouldn't eventually find me. I couldn't stay inside a cave forever. Though perhaps, one of these days, I would take off anyway—just to get away for a little while. *Besides*, I thought, as I reentered his tent to spread the sleeping bag back out, *it would really piss him off to have to chase after me. Escaping would be worth it just for that.*

A noise from outside the tent alerted me, and I froze, listening. It was the sound of footsteps, I realized, and figured that Tiamat must have returned already.

"Did you find the horses, Tiamat?" I said with an edge to my voice, as I turned to exit the tent.

"Horses?" answered an unfamiliar voice. "Perhaps you can explain to me, my dear, why my brother would have need of horses." His strange voice sounded rich and musical, but was marred by the sound of a distinctive sneer.

I peered out of the flap cautiously, to look upon this unexpected visitor.

Chapter 10

A man stood in the centre of the campsite. I would have described him as unspeakably handsome, if not for the look of distaste that twisted his features into an unpleasant scowl. He had the same ageless look as Tiamat, and was tanned and muscular with shiny, golden blond hair that was neatly tied back, revealing a clean jaw line.

For two reasons, I immediately noticed his startling blue eyes. First, his irises were just like Tiamat's, having the eerie appearance of being lit from behind. But it was the open hostility in this man's eyes that truly caught my attention. He held my gaze while, in a moment of obvious decision, he hastily altered his features into a more amiable visage.

"I believe you were going to tell me about the horses," he said in conversational tones while I warily scrutinized him. "Did you not say that my brother went to find some of these creatures?"

He stared at me expectantly for a moment, and when I didn't respond, he shrugged and sat down on one of the logs that flanked the fire pit. "You're Kali, are you not?" he asked.

Surprised, I nodded in response.

"My name is Abel," he said in a smooth voice, introducing himself.

"How did you know my name?" I blurted from the tent opening.

"I would be amazed if you were anyone else," he replied, stretching his legs out in from of him. "You are the only human that … *Tiamat* … has ever connected with."

I must have snorted or made some other sort of disdainful noise at that remark, for Abel stopped and glared at me sharply. "You should not treat this so lightly," he said in a slow, hard voice. "We are not permitted, you see, to develop bonds with any people at all, and my brother slipped when it came to you. Then, when we discovered his transgression, what followed became quite the event," he smirked, and his eyes glazed briefly with the memory. "So in fact, all the Nephilim know *your* name."

I wondered; had Tiamat gotten into some kind of trouble? I remembered him admitting to the habit of flying over my house, but then refusing to explain exactly why he stopped. "What happened?" I heard myself ask. As apprehensive as I was about this stranger, I couldn't help but attempt to find out more—Tiamat was so frustratingly tight-lipped about this subject, I would never get the story from him.

"No," he said in an almost bored voice, "I do not believe I will share that with you." He paused a moment, staring off into the distance with a little smile on his lips. "Are you ready to tell me about the horses now?"

I frowned and backed a touch further into the tent, and with a small surge of pleasure, noted a flicker of annoyance cross his golden face.

"I could hear you from the path as I neared the campsite, Kali," he said with a smile, attempting once again to engage me in conversation. "You were cursing rather passionately. I can only assume that it was Tiamat who made you so angry. My brother tends to have that effect on others," Abel offered with a hearty laugh. "He really can be very moody."

"Tell me about it," I muttered in grudging agreement. "So, if you are Tiamat's brother, you are obviously a…" I trailed off, suddenly afraid of revealing what I knew.

"Of course I am," he answered pleasantly. "Would you like to see my wings?"

I thought I detected a note of mockery in his tone, though he maintained the open, friendly-looking facade.

"Um...no thanks, Abel," I replied as blandly as I could.

Abel was silent for a moment, a small frown tugging at his face as his brow creased in thought. "If Tiamat is indeed searching for horses, it may be quite a while before he returns," he said finally. "Won't you come out and talk with me, Kali? I will not bite."

Biting isn't exactly what I'm worried about, I thought as I hesitantly stepped from the shelter of the tent. Of course, the tent wouldn't offer me a scrap of protection should Abel prove to be unfriendly, so cowering in there, I realized, would do me little good anyway.

As I skirted my bag of half-packed gear, I furtively noted the location of the crossbow and its bolts—four strides, five o'clock—relative to the log I slowly sat upon. I kept my eyes on Abel every second, acutely aware of how quickly these half-angels can move, and made certain that the seat I chose was directly opposite the one he sat upon. I clasped my hands to still the shaking, and made a decision.

I would *not* play the victim. If I had to sit here with this dangerous wolf, I would at least try to best him at his own game—and it appeared that the goal here was information. So, as safely as possible, I would try to exploit any of his weaknesses the best that I could, and his one obvious liability was his pride. Drive a wedge into the slightest flaw, and with the right leverage, anything can be split in two ... in theory, at least.

"I find your story about Tiamat hard to believe, Abel," I said, sounding braver than I felt.

Abel's eyes narrowed visibly as my remark struck home. "What?" he snapped. "Do you think me to be some kind of lowlife that makes up lies to serve his own end?"

"I said nothing of the sort," I replied, trying to sound affronted. "It's just that your story is so hard to believe. It doesn't make any sense."

"Which part, exactly, does your inferior brain have difficulty understanding?" Abel sneered.

Here we go, I thought, and I took a steadying breath. "Your story about the Nephilim shunning any type of closeness with people is a little too far-fetched," I said, monitoring his reactions closely.

"Ha!" he barked humorlessly. "Of course, as you are nothing but a blind little *human*, I can see why you would be confused. People are always so certain that the world revolves around *them*," he scoffed. "Can you even fathom that another being wouldn't want to have anything to do with you?" He shifted his position and shot me a disdainful look. "Personally, I find that your race is revoltingly hypocritical, self-centered and parasitic ... so why would it be far-fetched for us to avoid close contact with the likes of you?"

I refused to rise to his bait, and focused instead on my goal. "I am aware that you were all born here. So as children, I know that you couldn't possibly avoid forming a bond with whomever it was that raised each of you."

His face darkened. He stood abruptly and walked toward me. "You know *nothing*, Kali."

I jumped up and backed away from him, keeping my eyes glued to his every move. But I wasn't paying close enough attention to my surroundings, and found myself backed up against one of the boulders that flanked the campsite.

"Our childhood was the most trying time of our lives," he growled, slowly stalking closer, "because we *did* avoid forming those bonds. Our mothers completely isolated themselves from society, and then died giving birth to us, so we were alone from the start. We were all raised by strangers, and from a very young age we understood that we could not get close to *anyone*. We found a way, each and every one of us, to ensure that first, we were never adopted, and second, that we would be transferred to a different institution as frequently as possible. Often, this meant running away, but it was a necessity if we were to keep from forming bonds with our caregivers."

"Wait—that still doesn't make sense. You must be leaving something out, Abel."

"What?" he demanded, stepping closer. He was only a few paces away from me now, and growing more agitated by the second. "Are you implying that I am hiding something?"

"You could be," I said boldly. "As children, perhaps you were able to avoid adoption, but what about when you were infants? That would have been the most likely time for you to be adopted, and you would have been incapable of avoiding it. How is it possible that not *one* of you—not a single helpless baby—was placed with a family?"

"I truly do not know the answer to that," he answered, looking at me strangely. "Perhaps it was divine intervention, or perhaps not. I simply do not know. In my earliest memory, I was already a toddler, and I was already alone."

He was right in front of me now, his brow furrowed with the shadow of his memories. "You have no idea how agonizing it was. Imagine being a very young child, feeling utterly isolated and alone in this world, and knowing that, not only are you unable to improve your situation, you must perpetuate it. We may have been special and we may have been different, but we were still only children," he said resentfully. "Yet this was what we had to endure if we were to have any hope of fulfilling our purpose here. So we did endure—year after lonely year—we all grew into adults without having developed a single bond with a human. But then," he said, narrowing his eyes at me, "after he finally persevered through this life of hardship, you, like a damned harpy, led Tiamat astray."

I was stunned. I had no idea that they had to suffer through such a lonesome, miserable childhood. I began to picture a young Tiamat, all alone in an orphanage, when my cold voice of reason reeled me back in. I had to focus here, or I would lose any hope of holding the upper hand.

"It is sad, Abel," I said, "that you think you are so intelligent, yet you are unable to see the flaws in your own perceptions," I ventured. "As I am nothing but a simple human, when I first met Tiamat, how could I have known that I was speaking to one of your *breed*? I cannot be blamed for being kind to a stranger that was in obvious distress, now can I?"

Abel reddened, but did not reply.

"And how can you seriously speak of his hardships, when *you* are the ones that *punished* him?"

"We did not punish him, you stupid woman."

Ah, there it is, I thought. "Yeah, right," I scoffed.

"Our second in command, Merodach, assembled a meeting where we discussed Tiamat's indiscretion," he said slowly, like he was speaking to someone who was feeble-minded. "When the matter was aired, Tiamat announced that he would never have contact with you again, and he would maintain his distance at all times. Until now, this was something that he managed to do quite successfully. So perhaps you meant very little to him after all."

"But you said earlier that it was 'quite the event,' didn't you? So, either you were exaggerating before, or you're lying to me now," I told him boldly, planting my feet and sticking my chin out. "You keep contradicting yourself, Abel, and that's what makes your stories so difficult to believe."

Tendons stood out on his neck as he stepped right in front of me, completely closing any distance between us, and I could feel the angry static energy emanating from his too-close body. "The only reason I called it an event is because it was—none of the Nephilim have ever slipped in this way. And it was especially significant because Tiamat, you see, was very well-respected among our kind. This whole affair was quite a shock to us," he said with a spiteful glint to his eye, as though he quite enjoyed the smear to Tiamat's good name. "And now, Kali," he whispered menacingly, "may I ask why, after all of this, I found you in my brother's tent, *you whore?*"

I needed to get him away from me. Immediately. "It looks to me like you are just jealous, Abel," I said, hoping he would step back in revulsion.

"I told you that I am not a liar," he said quietly, as he placed his hands on the boulder, one on each side of my head, and leaned in toward me. "So, if I am to be honest," he breathed, his face inches from mine, "I must admit that you are ... enticing." He shuddered, but maintained his closeness, like he was sharing a terrible secret. "Yet all the while, I also have a strong compulsion to kill you," he whispered, bending over so that his lips brushed my ear. "So I confess, Kali, that I find myself torn. All the more reason, I suppose, to end your life immediately, before you can do any more damage."

He pulled his head back from my ear and stared hard at my face, lust and hatred written plainly across his arrogant features. Then his eyes opened wide in a mixture of shock and pleasure as I raised my hands up to his smooth cheeks and caressed them lightly.

"Mmmm..." he breathed and closed his eyes, while I ran my fingers along his jaw and stroked them down his neck, tangling them into a firm grip on his collar. Then, grasping him tightly, I brought my knee swiftly up into his groin, completely taking him off guard. As Abel doubled over in pain, I smashed my right elbow into the side of his face, and then kicked him squarely on the chest, forcing him to fall backward.

Not bothering with the unloaded crossbow, I turned in an attempt to race back to the caves, hoping that once I was there, Abel would be unable to find or sense me until Tiamat returned. But only three paces into my sprint, Abel, unbelievably fast, clamped onto my ankle and I fell flat, smacking my chin on the hard dirt path.

I struggled and thrashed, but he grasped both my ankles tightly and pulled me roughly toward him. As I was dragged across the ground, I clawed at the dirt uselessly, searching for a handhold or a weapon, but found nothing but clumps of sandy soil.

Abel roughly flipped me over and, his expression dark and murderous, he crawled on top of me, pinning my legs with the weight of his own. His hands, bearing the mass of his upper torso, pressed down on my arms, rendering my upper body immobile.

"Out of respect for Tiamat, I shall tell him you didn't suffer," he growled into my face.

"No! Stop," I shrieked. "Aren't you supposed to be merciful?" I asked in desperation.

"You will find no Angels of Mercy here, Kali," he snapped like a rabid dog. "We are Destruction and Death. We are God's Vengeance, unleashed upon the wickedness of humanity. On *you*. I should have killed you when I first—"

Thwump! The huge stick that I had used on Tiamat last night came up in a wide arc, and with terrific force, it smacked Abel squarely in the face. The impact sent him crashing into the dirt beside me, where he rolled into a wary crouch.

Tiamat leapt past me and, brandishing the stick menacingly, loomed over Abel. "Kali is not to be touched," he said, his voice hard with anger. "She has a purpose here."

"Hello, *brother*," Abel sneered, spitting blood. "Open your eyes. If she truly had a purpose, why would I feel such an overwhelming desire to kill her?" He stood up and dragged his arm across his bloody mouth, leaving his shirt stained with a long, red smear. "There is only one fool here, and it isn't me, nor is it that dirty siren." He made a move to get by Tiamat, but was blocked by the stick. "She will die today, one way or the other."

"Not by your hand."

"What the hell does that mean?" I interjected, scrambling to my feet.

"Be quiet, Kali," Tiamat warned, not taking his eyes off his brother. "I think it would be best if you would *disappear*," he hinted. "Quickly."

I knew that he was referring to the caves and I had already intended to go there, but only after first grabbing a weapon. If this should go badly, I was going to need any protection I could get. I raced the few steps around the huge boulder, and listened intently while I hastily picked up the crossbow and bolts.

"Now you have the right idea, Brother," I could hear Abel say. "But I am afraid it is too late to simply send the tramp away. Later, you will need to answer for this. But first, I must—"

"No, Abel ... *Stop!*" Tiamat shouted.

Sounds of a violent scuffle immediately came from the far side of the boulder, spiked with grunts of pain and exertion. With my weapon in hand, I dashed away from the rock, just as it smashed to pieces from the force of a great impact. As I leapt the boulder fragments and made a wide arc around the scene, I could finally see what was happening. Abel was pulling off his shirt as he ran for the cliff's edge, pursued belatedly by Tiamat, who staggered as he extracted himself from the boulder's rubble.

The air itself seemed alive with angry, pent-up energy, crackling through the negative spaces on the lookout. In a rush, I could feel it dance past and through me as it sped to gather in a great blue light around Tiamat. Then, with a loud *whump* and a thunderous crack, a huge boulder—that was right beside Abel—flew to pieces. Two of the fragments hit him solidly as he ran, knocking him on his face. He was up in a flash, but by this time, Tiamat—his blue glow fading—had nearly caught up with him. Tiamat had torn off his shirt as he ran, and his wings burst out in a blur of startling white.

During Tiamat's fast approach, Abel had also brought out his wings, though the process was comparatively jerky and slow. He had barely stretched them out when Tiamat launched himself at Abel, throwing them both over the edge of the cliff.

Yet they did not fall for long. Exploding upward in flight, Tiamat suddenly shot high overhead, but Abel was following close behind, slicing through the sky, looking fast and deadly. Carving the air in a swift, tight loop, Tiamat changed direction and dove down straight at Abel, causing a collision that sent rings of brilliant blue light pounding out in all directions, leveling me—and a few more trees—in their wake.

I jumped up quickly; relieved to discover that I was relatively uninjured, I ensured I was a safe distance from the surrounding trees. But standing wasn't as easy as it should have been, and I stumbled as the ground suddenly lurched in an all-too-familiar way. Vibrations buzzed up through my legs as little rocks and pebbles began to bounce in warning across the unstable ground. The wind, breathing viciously across the Peak, towed in a maelstrom of swirling black clouds, buffeting God's two servants as they fought, tumbling and circling beneath the savage sky.

Entering the caves at this point would be suicidal, I realized. I would very likely be crushed by falling rocks or buried alive in rubble. I looked frantically for somewhere I could hide, but to no avail. The caves were too risky, the trees were treacherous and the boulders were deadly when they shattered. If I stayed in the open, Abel would kill me as soon as he got the chance. I knew he could sense me anyway, but standing in a clearing felt like flourishing a red cape at a raging bull. So I wiggled my way into some scrubby brush—its branches waving in surrender to the raging wind—and with mingled horror and awe, watched the deadly conflict unfold high above me.

Like two giant raptors, Tiamat and Abel swooped at each other, smashed and then plummeted toward the earth, grasping and punching as they fell. Then, when it looked as though they would smash into the cliff top, they broke apart and swooped tightly upward. Tiamat, however, quickly changed direction again and flew straight into Abel. Grasping him around the neck, Tiamat dove straight back toward the lookout, with Abel splayed helplessly in front of him. The ground rocked when Tiamat drove Abel into it, and narrow fissures snaked outward in all directions, making the point of impact resemble a giant smashed window.

In haste, Tiamat leapt backward off of his brother, who sat up slowly from the dust and stones, his now dirty and powdered face twisted with disdain. Seeing that Abel was alright, he reached a hand down to him and said forcefully, "Now that is enough, Abel! We must talk about this before one of us gets hurt."

"You are deluded, Brother, and unable to carry out what is expected of you," Abel replied, grasping Tiamat's proffered hand. "So I find," he said, standing swiftly, "that I must relieve you from duty." A knife flashed in Abel's hand as he pulled Tiamat in toward him, slashing viciously at his chest.

Tiamat lunged back quickly, but the blade sliced into his side as he twisted to avoid it. He grunted in pain and smashed the heel of his free hand up under Abel's chin, sending him flying back into the dirt. Then, with a flash of his wings, Tiamat launched himself back into the air, but he floundered, having trouble gaining altitude.

Abel, however, had taken flight quickly, and came up in a wide arc above Tiamat. Blade in fist, he tucked into a fierce dive, aimed directly for Tiamat's back. But mid-dive, Abel suddenly squawked and fell clumsily—tumbling straight downward like a large, golden stone. Missing Tiamat by inches, he landed heavily on the cliff's edge, his eyes wide with shock as he looked down at the crossbow bolt protruding from his chest. He raised his hands to examine it, and blood suddenly poured from the wound, flowing in ghastly red rivers down the skin of his paling torso.

Tiamat landed heavily near his brother, and stared down at him in silence. The two of them watched the blood spill across the cliff top, yet neither of them stirred.

Abel's eyes lifted and immediately met mine. They were no longer hostile—they simply stared at me with incredulity.

The crossbow felt unnaturally heavy in my hands. "I'm sorry," I whispered, staggered by the gravity of what I had done.

His eyes then glazed over, as he slid backward off the cliff.

Tiamat, I noticed, made no move to save him.

Chapter 11

It was silent. The earth stilled and the heavens ceased breathing; there wasn't so much as an errant puff of air to stir the inky black clouds that hung ominously overhead.

Tiamat, again resembling a graceful, solemn statue, stood precisely where he did when I first met him. His tormented expression was almost exact, and on both occasions he stared transfixed on the spread of crimson before him—though ten years ago, it was simply a sunset, and not his brother's blood, growing cold on the dirty ground.

And though he stood of his own volition, Tiamat appeared significantly worse for wear. His face was bloodied from cuts on both his jaw and above his right eyebrow, the splint was broken and hung off his arm in tatters, and a long, straight knife wound appeared to twist in an evil grin across his right side. Even his magnificent wings had smears of blood marring the pristine white of the feathers.

Tiamat, very slowly, turned and raised his eyes to meet mine, unfathomable expressions flickering and twisting across his features. For the life of me, I was completely incapable of reading them. He drew a series of deep, ragged breaths, and the spell of stillness ended abruptly. Wind immediately surged across the ridge, and the clouds swirled angrily. Tiamat staggered slightly and, holding his side, started walking toward the shattered woods.

"Tiamat..." I begun, not knowing what I could say. "Wait... You know I had to... He was going to kill you!" I said desperately. But he continued on, appearing not to hear me. "Tiamat," I tried again. "Listen to me..."

Without looking up at me once, he continued on into the woods, stalking his way through the numerous fallen trees, ripping the remnants of the splint off as he went. Despite his injuries, he navigated the twisted mass of limbs and branches almost effortlessly, his folded wings fluttering half-open now and again to help maintain his balance.

Taking the crossbow, I started chasing after him as several large, heavy drops of rain fell from the sky, smacking onto the dirt and rocks with increasing rapidity. "Tiamat?" I called, having lost sight of him among the maze of branches. "Are you there?"

There was no reply but the steady splatter of raindrops on the surrounding foliage. The rhythm quickly increased until the clouds finally burst open, inundating the cliff top under sheets of heavy water.

I veered abruptly and made my way toward the caves. There was a chance that Tiamat may have headed there, I decided, and if I was wrong, at least I could take shelter until the downpour passed over—or until Tiamat was in control again, if he was the reason behind this foul weather.

The day's events reeled through my head as I haltingly trudged through the crippled woods. Why would Abel have felt a compulsion to kill me when Tiamat didn't? Could one of them have been dishonest about this? That didn't seem plausible; both half-angels seemed particularly averse to lying. Quickly dismissing that notion, I was forced to accept that they definitely had differing opinions about whether or not they were obligated to end my life. Tiamat, in fact, appeared to believe strongly that I had some purpose, and that I *needed* to live.

So then, if these compulsions came from only one source—God— why would they be conflicting? I knew that I was supposed to have faith and trust that there was some reason behind this, but even if that were the case, then that would mean Tiamat and Abel were simply being set up … and for what? I simply couldn't reason that one out. Perhaps this was another one of God's tests; a test which we just failed…

Now that was a disturbing theory, and despite my immediate attempts to dismiss it, I felt the rancidness of the idea begin to burrow its way into the depths of my being, slowly spreading feelings of doubt and despondency like a cancer. I couldn't, however, allow these cynical thoughts to take hold and drag me down. Finding and speaking to Tiamat was vital right now… hopefully, he would set me straight, or at the very least, provide a new perspective on the matter.

Luckily, he had gone into the caves as I hoped he would, and I found him kneeling in a circle of lantern light beside the underground stream, his wings half-open behind him, which gave him the striking appearance of a great, injured bird. The presence of the lantern seemed strange, and I wondered why Tiamat had need of it, if he could just emanate light on demand. As I neared him, I could see that he appeared haggard of body and spirit, and he gleamed from the wetness of the rain, while the blood ran freely from his wounds. The gash on his eyebrow spilled blood in two thin rivulets down his face, neck and chest, but the blood from his knife wound was the worst. There was so much of it that his entire right side was slick and red, and small, dark pools were forming on the rocks next to his blood-spattered right leg.

"For someone that heals quickly, you certainly do bleed a lot," I remarked in a soft voice, breaking the tomblike silence of the place.

"It is just the rainwater. When any water comes into contact with an open cut on my body, it prevents the blood from clotting." He didn't look up at me as he spoke, keeping his eyes fixed instead on the creek that tumbled across the rocks in front of him.

"And if your wounds stay wet, you'll just keep bleeding until you die? Is that it?"

He didn't say anything, but nodded minutely; the only movement from his still figure.

"So dry it off!" I gasped, rushing to grab a blanket from the nearby pile. He looked as though he had lost too much blood already.

"No," he said forcefully, raising his head to meet my eyes. "The state of my body hardly matters now, Kali."

I stopped. What did he mean by *that*? "That's not true."

"It is. One of my brothers is now dead, and it is my fault. The knowledge of that alone is almost impossible to bear. But it is far worse than even that." He paused and took a deep breath, before continuing in a voice that shook with the resentment of finality. "What I have done tonight has damned us both. We're finished."

"Tiamat, you can't believe that," I countered. "We were only protecting ourselves. Abel's persistence left us no choice."

But Tiamat's face was hard and determined, his jaw clenching with tension at the mention of his brother. "That may be," he said in a carefully leveled voice, "but God's laws are clear, regardless of circumstance."

"I thought it was also clear that God was merciful. Could we not repent and ask for forgiveness?"

"I am one of the Nephilim, remember?" he said bitterly. "Because humans must rely on faith alone, the penitent can be absolved of their transgressions. But angels have knowledge of the divine, so forgiveness is not possible for us. Our sins are irreversible."

"But I am the one that killed Abel. Not you."

"That is a problem as well. You are now unique in that you have knowledge you should not possess, thanks to me." His voice was hard and bitter as his eyes locked fast with mine. "And you killed a celestial being, having full understanding of his true nature. I wonder, then, if *you* can be forgiven, Kali."

My blood ran cold, but I pushed on. "I'm not convinced of that," I said as stoically as I could. "Nor am I convinced about your case. You may have divine knowledge, but you did nothing wrong. And you did not kill him. I did," I reminded him.

"You would not have found it necessary if I handled the situation better. I should have been able to reason with him, but I failed on that account."

"I was there, remember? Abel was single-minded about killing me. There was no way you could have reasoned with him." I knelt down beside him and looked up into his troubled face. "You did all you could have done in that situation. After all, if I truly have a purpose, I'm sure you would have been expected to stop Abel somehow. So perhaps you can be forgiven," I said. "Maybe we both can be. There's still hope, isn't there?"

An odd look flashed across his face, and his eyes turned to steel. "Hope is a crutch for the ignorant or the powerless, Kali. And I would like to believe that I am neither."

"So then... if you don't think you're powerless in this case, are you saying that there is something we can do? Can we redeem ourselves, Tiamat?"

His eyes widened and raked across me, before he flicked them back down to the creek. Then without looking up, he spoke, his voice softening like the wind playing across a field of tall grass. "Perhaps there is..."

He didn't elaborate further, and in the silence that followed, as nonchalantly as I could, I lifted a blanket from the stack and smoothly knelt back down beside him. I wished fervently that I had never made that promise about not touching his blood—tending his wounds would be a tricky business without coming into contact with some of it. Nevertheless, I would have to try.

Moving cautiously, I leaned forward and carefully pressed the folded blanket against his side. He made no move to stop me, so I increased the pressure, raising my eyes to gage his reaction... and froze. He was gazing down at me, the look on his face heartbreakingly tender. I was afraid to react, move or even breathe; the fear of rejection was so acute. So I held my breath and waited.

"Do not worry, Kali. The cut isn't deep, and will heal quickly now that you have kindly dried it off." He placed his hand over mine and smoothly lifted it from his side, the blanket falling to the ground between us. But he didn't break his gaze, and his hand lingered on mine, his thumb tracing light, tingling circles on my skin.

He raised his other hand and gently touched my face, following the line of cheekbone and jaw, while I struggled to keep from reacting. Yet with our eyes locked as they were, I felt my breath stop, and a force stronger than anything I had ever known worked to draw me toward him. But I kept still. Our touching fingers were now intertwined, and Tiamat's hand was gripping mine with increasing force, while his other hand continued to trace my face. I could feel my resolve weakening by the second as his fingertips slowly circled behind my ear and ran gently down the curve of my neck.

And then, just as my willpower was about to give out, Tiamat acted. All at once, he leaned in abruptly, his hands suddenly tangled in my hair. Flooding my body and mind with blinding white light, Tiamat pressed his lips to mine and kissed me fiercely. He gasped as I clutched myself tight against him in response, and with my hands firmly in his hair and on the back of his neck, I brushed my lips against his partly open mouth, and he lost control again.

We pressed together and grabbed at each other in an almost frenzied passion, neither of us capable of restraint any longer. I felt his wings wrap around the two of us and I could taste the forbidden blood from his face, but I didn't care. And several heartbeats later, I could also taste salt, though whether it was from sweat or tears, I couldn't have said; I didn't even know if it originated from me or from him. Again, it didn't matter.

I was vaguely aware of the stack of blankets spilling across the rocky floor, which then cushioned us from the cold, rough surface beneath; and of the shimmering blues and greens that rippled along the cave's ceiling and walls like the aurora borealis. But besides these hazy

126

memories, I knew of no further external details—because at the centre of it all was Tiamat; and truly, nothing else existed that night but him.

* * *

I awoke much later to the sound of a soft groan, and sat up to see Tiamat lying on his back beside me, with his hands pressed up against his face. I assumed he must be mourning for his brother, and I gently reached down to ease him up to me. He sat up willingly, and buried his face into my shoulder. As I tenderly stroked the dark locks of his hair, he wept silently, wrapping his arms tightly around my waist, and it occurred to me that we must look like a classical painting done backward—the mortal comforting the angel. Aside from when he was an infant, this was likely the only time in his life he had ever been held or comforted, and the knowledge of that nearly broke my heart.

* * *

The next morning, I awoke wrapped in numerous blankets and saw that a wonderful smelling breakfast rested on a nearby rock. I thought about these little gestures and smiled dreamily; Tiamat was a good man—if that's what I could call him. This new, bleak world suddenly didn't seem so hard to bear, knowing we could face it together.

The lantern had burned itself out, but a soft light filtered in from the cave opening on the far side of the large cavern room, and would be sufficient to guide my morning routine. I ate, washed up and dressed, and just as I was leaving the cave, it struck me that the creek's water hadn't tasted bitter today. Surprisingly, that important detail had almost completely slipped my attention. Could the waters be back to normal already? I went back to check, and hastily knelt down by the water's edge. Dipping my hands into the creek, I brought the cold water to my lips, and took a hesitant sip. I wasn't mistaken. The water had a crisp, clean taste that was almost sweet. I wondered if this meant that the worst was over. Was it premature to believe that things were beginning to improve already?

Yes, it is, I told myself. *Don't be a fool.* Regardless of where I stood with Tiamat, I knew where my road ended. Like people were some faulty product, God was recalling his entire human line, and there was no escaping it. It wouldn't do to delude myself about that.

Despite these sobering thoughts, as I tromped through the roughly beaten woods, I felt lighter and more energetic than I had in a long time. My feet practically flew over the irregular, obstacle-laden ground on my way toward the campsite; to where I hoped to find Tiamat.

But when I emerged from the woods, I found the site empty. Deserted. No evidence of Tiamat's camp remained... except for me. The shock of it completely blindsided me, and I simply stood there, dumbfounded, staring at the stark, open ground.

Chapter 12

"Tiamat?" I called into the empty air. "Have you left...?" It came out as a ragged whisper, and was all I was capable of as panic and misery squeezed my chest in a crushing embrace. Unsure of what to do, I sprinted to the head of the path and began a hasty descent from the ridge, hoping desperately that Tiamat would still be somewhere nearby.

I barely watched my footing as I charged down the steep, winding trail of rock and dirt, preoccupied with finding a feasible explanation for his disappearance. But all my arguments on his behalf were less substantial than whispers. My delusions dissipated and slipped from my grasp, as cold reason's steel talons bit into my heart. *It was lust, not love*, my reason told me. *He was torn up and grieving last night and I was simply a warm body to comfort him. And now he probably looks back at our intimacy with nothing but shame.*

Defeated and broken, I stumbled blindly down the path, my mind whipping my spirit relentlessly with harsh truths. *The majority of the time, Tiamat was cold and distant,* I reminded myself. *And he told me numerous times to keep away from him. Of course he did—he is one of the Nephilim; beautiful, strong and deadly, and I am nothing.* My throat constricted as the words suddenly rang true in my head. *I'm only a human, and Tiamat could barely disguise his contempt for my inferior race,*

I remembered, choking on the idea. *I was nothing but a prisoner and a burden to him.*

But then, why did he leave me breakfast this morning? I wondered. *Was it out of guilt?* Then a thought occurred to me that twisted my stomach into knots. *Or, more likely,* I realized, *he left it to keep me occupied while he finished with his packing and took off. Now he has left. And I am alone.*

As I carried on descending the steep trail, I was lost in such a fog of self-loathing and hopelessness, that I hardly noticed the passage of time, or the familiar twist near the end of the path. I would not have noticed my surroundings at all, had an inconsistency not snatched at my attention.

It was a distinctive sound that dragged me from my stupor; conspicuous and completely unexpected. On the gentle, upward breeze floated the characteristic puffing and soft snorting of horses, though it was several moments before I was able to place the drifting sounds, and grasp their significance. Yet when I did, it was as though the noises themselves pumped through my heart and surged in my muscles, propelling my body down the remainder of the path as though I, too, was simply a sound carried on the wind. My mind, still unwilling to entertain hope—for fear of what it would do to me, should that hope be in vain—was utterly powerless to stop my body's reaction, and from a remote corner of myself, I watched with an almost morbid fascination as my body trotted heedlessly down the trail.

After half-running around the bend, I stopped in wide-eyed disbelief, gaping at Tiamat securing a large sack behind the saddle of a beautiful palomino. A chestnut mare stood impatiently behind him, laden with bulging bags and small sacks that were strapped firmly to her back. A number of the bags were ingeniously fashioned—the bottom straps from a large backpack had been detached, so that the now-free padded portions, which were still attached to the top of the pack, could be slung across the horse's back. A second pack was then secured to the ends of these straps, creating a set of backpack saddlebags that hung down on either side of the horse's body. Normally, I would have been impressed. Yet today, my mind was elsewhere.

Tiamat stiffened at the sound of my footsteps and turned toward me slowly, his face carefully neutral. I could see his eyes take in my look of relief and then linger on an escaped tear, rolling traitorously down my cheek. His jaw clenched noticeably before he turned to the horses again, checking and pulling at fastenings that appeared to already be secured.

"With events as they were last night, I failed to tell you that I succeeded in finding horses yesterday. These two even had some of the tack you described, but just the basics, I'm afraid—halters, saddles, reigns," he poked at the various tack. "They obviously lost their riders in The Cleansing. If there ever were any saddlebags on them, they are long gone now." His voice was detached and flat, and Tiamat spoke to the packs and straps, keeping his back to me. "So I was forced to create my own from the bags I had. I hope these will serve?" he asked, raising his eyebrow to me. Yet his expression wasn't playful. It was all cold inquiry.

I nodded my head, his behavior making my stomach drop.

Tiamat broke eye contact immediately and turned back to the animals. "And I suppose the timing was fortunate, as you will need both of these horses today."

"Both?" I blurted in surprise. It was only then that I realized the chestnut mare was loaded in the capacity of a pack horse, and would not be carrying any passengers. "What about you, Tiamat? Will you be flying?"

He kept his face turned away from me, as his hands worked at a loose piece of strapping, tucking and weaving it vigorously among two flanking straps. "I am not going with you, Kali. We simply cannot be near each other anymore."

His words hit me like a fist to the stomach. *"What?"* I sputtered, as possible reasons seared through my mind. "If it's because of our...

intimacy… then I'm sorry, Tiamat. I'll keep my distance so it won't happen again. It really won't," I promised, unsure of *how* I would accomplish this, but certain that I would try if he would only give me the chance. "And I'm sorry that by being with me, you had to sink so low last night."

"First of all, I am not speaking of emotional distance, and I believe you know this. You need to take the horses and leave, Kali," he muttered, staring down at the thrice-tied strap. "And as for your second statement, you have surprised me again by how perceptive you are. Still," he mused, pulling absently at the over-tied fastenings, "you have no idea about the depths to which I sunk when I lay with you—"

"Enough; *stop!*" I could feel the hot, fresh tears, spilling unbidden down my cheeks. "I think I get the point, okay?"

"But, Kali—" he said, spinning to look at me in exasperation.

"I can't do this anymore, Tiamat!" I yelled over him, unable to hear anything further. "This…" I said, flinging an arm at the torn-up wasteland around us, "this is already a living hell you have created for me here. But to top it off, you have slowly and steadily been tearing the remnants of my soul apart, and I simply can't stand another second of it," I said miserably.

The distance in Tiamat's face appeared to crumble, and he stepped toward me, reaching out a hand…

"I don't want your pity!" I cried vehemently. "I don't want anything from you again."

"Kali, I am so sorry that I hurt you."

"You're *sorry?* Tiamat, you've hurt me so painfully and precisely, that I don't think you could have planned it better," I said, almost sobbing now. "And you must even be pleased—I mean, look at how perfectly it's worked out for you. Yesterday, I wasn't allowed to leave, even though you admitted that I was driving you insane. It's quite a coincidence that suddenly I can leave today, after you got what you wanted from me last night."

"No, that isn't exactly true. I didn't *want* for that to happen between us...no wait...what I mean to say is that I had to—"

"God, Tiamat! Just stop!" I said, pressing my hands to my face. "I'm leaving now, get it? You've won. So you can stop using this pretense that you care as a means to wound me."

I pushed past him and grasped the saddle of the tall, caramel horse. I mounted the palomino smoothly, while Tiamat stood motionless; his hands hanging limp at his sides. From my peripheral vision, I could see him tilt his head up toward me, so I turned down to face him. Yet I couldn't stand to meet his eyes, so I kept my own unfocused, and made myself gaze right through him.

"I have a feeling that, eventually, you will be the one that'll have to kill me, Tiamat. Maybe that's why I must leave now. But if it's not too much to ask, I'd like a semblance of peace before I die," I choked out, my throat constricted and raw from emotion. "If you ever cared for me at all, please allow me this small mercy."

"I do care for you, Kali," I heard him whisper quietly.

I paused to take a deep breath, and had to fight to maintain control before continuing. "Then leave me alone," I answered evenly. "And when you feel the compulsion, kill me if you must. I won't resist you. But until that time, just keep the hell away from me."

With all the resolve I could muster, I set my eyes firmly ahead, and kicked my horse into the fastest trot possible, given the broken terrain. I managed to ride steadily for nearly a full hour, firmly resisting the impulse to look back the entire time, while a soft rain fell endlessly from the gray, overcast sky. A gentle blowing and clomp of hooves behind me indicated that the mare was following closely, and was almost certainly tethered to our lead, though I did not turn to look at her.

My gaze remained locked onto a forlorn stand of trees on the distant horizon, and I left my horse to pick his way around crevasses and gorges, and over the raw, exposed rock and churned, blackened earth.

And although I provided the palomino with very little direction, that ride sapped the last of the tenacity and focus that I had, so after that first hour finally crawled by, my strength left me. With barely sufficient time to slide off and tether my horse, I puddled onto the ground, sobbing.

* * *

The days blurred into each other as I worked my way south. Everywhere, the terrain looked unfamiliar and alien, though occasionally I would come across a remnant of our ruined civilization; the twisted wreckage of a car; scattered, burned material from a home or structure of some sort; and one time, a segment of untouched road, crumbling and disappearing under rock and debris after 30 yards or so. I was incredibly thankful that I had not yet hit the ruins of a town or a city, or stumbled across any human remains that I could see. And though I was aware that it was simply a matter of time, I was terrified by the prospect of it.

In the depths of night, I was still awakened by nightmares; brutal visions of creeping, reaching shadows through a world of rubble that was once the sleepy town of Pinecrest. What Tiamat had done to that town—to this entire area—was absolutely staggering.

In fact, I wouldn't have believed I was on the same planet if I hadn't experienced the changes personally. I knew, firsthand, that the landscape here was once filled with rolling hills, ridges and valleys, all of which were thickly forested and segmented by a large network of lakes, rivers and streams. But now the land was harsh and angular. Rivers and streams flowed along different, unknown paths, and silty, displaced lakes were all that were left of the original, sparkling blue waters. The majority of trees lay half-buried or in splintered green masses, and bare, broken rock towered menacingly out of the ripped, crevasse-laden ground. Ridges and valleys still abounded, but these were fresh and new, consisting of sharp, recently chiseled rock, strong with the smell of the earthly wombs from whence they came.

For a period of five days, I rode by a series of limestone cliffs where numerous underground caves had been thrust into view. I investigated the more accessible ones, and though many turned out to have collapsed within their twisting tunnels and caverns, a surprising number of caves, I found, were largely intact.

As evening fell on each of those days, I would set up camp adjacent to one of the exposed cave openings, remembering keenly how a similar cavern had blocked Tiamat's ability to sense me. Yet although I was tempted to spend the night within the secrecy and security of rock, I always ended up sleeping out in the open. I had Tiamat's tent, but I chose not to pitch it by the caves, simply drifting off beside the embers of my lonely fire, the horses and thick, black night my only companions.

And every night, after my nightmares had subsided and I drifted in the fog of restless sleep, I would dream of Tiamat. These imaginings were unbidden, unwanted, and proved to be the most vicious dreams of all. In them, he was always unbearably tender, and would hold me, kiss me and laugh with me until the dawn came. I would wake, happily muddled in ignorant bliss, only to brutally plunge into reality a few short moments later. Every morning I was forced to relive his humiliating rejection of me, and feel the wounds of his betrayal opened fresh and new.

It became almost habitual to force down this misery, and then continue on following the routine of travel that I had fallen into as one day bled into the next.

Water, however, tended to throw a bit of a wrench into the general routine. Wherever we went, I found the water to be not only potable, but clean-tasting and incredibly refreshing. Yet the horses didn't share my opinion. Early on, during that heart-wrenching first day of travel, I had feared I would lose the horses as well. They were exhausted and tired, and though they appeared extremely interested in the stream I had brought them to, they would not have any of the water. Coaxing them didn't work, and neither did attempting to force them—they would have none of it.

Only when I tried to entice them by example, kneeling at the stream's edge right in front of them, did I have some success. I had scooped some water into my hands and was slurping it loudly, when the mare curtly nudged my face out of the way and drank the water from my hands. I scooped up some more, and she drank it voraciously. The palomino appeared just as anxious to drink the water from my cupped palms, though neither one could be made to drink water straight out of that particular stream nor any other one I came across. It was either out of my hands, or not at all. Needless to say then, that our water-drinking routine became a lengthy, time-consuming process.

One cool, gray afternoon, I stopped by a wide, shallow stream for a water break, and led the horses down to the stony shore. Again, they would not drink from the stream itself, so I sighed and knelt down to scoop water into my palms. This time, however, I kept my hands hovering just over the moving water, so I wouldn't have to keep reaching back and forth.

The mare was willing to risk a drink that close to the offending stream, and despite leaning down hesitantly, she drank willingly enough from my palms. I lowered my hands for a refill, and the mare's nose dipped also, following them right into the flowing water. I kept my hands partially encircling her mouth, so as not to spook her with the change, but she drank directly from the stream, and seemed content to do so. When she had finished, the palomino eagerly took her place, and drank from the stream in the same way.

I was beginning to get cramped up by this time, and risked moving my hands slowly from the stream so that I could shift position. But the moment my fingers ceased touching the water, the palomino snorted and jerked his head immediately upward, shaking it vigorously.

"Holy crap," I whispered, amazed. *No, I must be mistaken...*

I scooped water into my palms, and slowly enticed him back down toward the stream. Once he was again drinking from the flowing water, I very gradually removed my hands until only my fingertips were dangling in the water, just upstream of where the horse was drinking. Then, without making an obvious movement, I balled my hands into fists, which lifted my fingers completely out of the water. At the exact moment that my fingers ceased contact with the stream, the palomino yanked backward like he had been stung, and kicked his forelegs in frustration.

"Shit!" I yelped in surprise as I stumbled away from the stream and the horse's flashing hooves. In my haste, I tripped on some driftwood, reeled backward over a mound of small, round pebbles and sat heavily in a heap of them. The horse started and shied back from the stream's edge, looking like he was ready to bolt, and I had to jump up quickly to grab his headstall and steady him. The mare simply stood haughtily nearby, calmly watching the two of us like we were mentally unbalanced.

"Easy, boy," I said, stroking the horse around his halter. "It's okay. Everything's okay. I'm sure the mare still thinks you're a very manly horse," I joked, while I tried to ease my breathing and calm my own frazzled nerves.

But I was strung tighter than a bowstring. I wondered; did I now have the ability to make the water drinkable? I knew it shouldn't be possible, yet the horses were clearly indicating that that was the case. How on earth could that have happened?

It took a little longer this time to coax the wary horse into drinking from the stream again, but I steadily lured him back down to the flowing water, and eventually had him drinking with just my hands half-circling his mouth on the upstream side.

Yet as I did this, my mind buzzed with questions and speculations, and I couldn't wait for the horse to ease his thirst so I could try a few things out. As I sat there, idly dangling my hands into the water, I wondered when and how this had happened. The first time I thought the streams were drinkable again was the morning after I slept with Tiamat. It was also the morning after I killed Abel. Yet there was another event that preceded it, which I had not thought of until now…I had come into contact with Tiamat's blood.

There were too many factors here, any of which might be linked to my new ability. And then again, none of them may be. Then, there was another consideration: when Tiamat sent me away, did he know that I would be able to drink the water? Looking at the mare, I scrutinized the two measly canteens of water he had packed me, hanging next to a rolled up sleeping bag on her back. At a glance, it appeared Tiamat knew when he loaded the horses that I would not have any problem with water—but if he thought that the water was still unpalatable to me, he had knowingly set me up to run out of water nearly two weeks ago. And Tiamat's intentions aside, perhaps, I thought, I will eventually lose this ability, and possibly die of thirst anyway.

"Damn it," I muttered, incensed. Even when Tiamat wasn't around, he still had me wound up and guessing at his motives. It had to stop; Tiamat had to stop being the focus of my energy and attention. And to do that, I needed to face up to the fact that he was gone, and concentrate on surviving.

The first thing I had to do, then, was figure out as much as I could about this water thing.

"Are you all finished there, hero?" I asked the horse as he lifted his head and began to back away from the stream. I hobbled him next to the mare, and left them both to graze on a lawn-sized chunk of grass nearby.

Then I returned to the bank, and knelt down by the edge. I decided to see what would happen if I tried to drink without touching the water with my hands, so I leaned forward and sipped some water directly from the stream. But there was no difference—the water tasted fine.

"Technically, I guess I'm still touching it," I sighed as I sat back on my heels to think. A snort from the horses, however, gave me an idea. I returned to the stream a moment later with one of the canteens, which I emptied onto the stones as I walked.

Careful not to touch the water, I dipped the mouth of the canteen into the current and partially filled it, then walked over to the mare and poured a little of it over her mouth as she tried to graze. She immediately snorted and tossed her head, hopping in agitation and straining at the hobble that restrained her front legs.

"Okay, easy girl," I cooed as I worked to settle her. "I just had to see something. And besides, Hero needed a little cheering up," I said, realizing that I had just named the palomino. "Hero," I repeated, liking the name, "if you think that was funny, watch this," I said, lifting the canteen in the air.

I proceeded to pour the water straight into my open mouth, and as I should have expected, it was palatable. Maybe a bit of an anti-climax for the horse, but at least I learned that I could drink water in any fashion, and that with this ability, I should be able to keep the horses alive as well.

Next, I had to see if there was anything else that I was capable of doing. I walked back down to the stream bank and sat myself beside one of the mounds of round river stones. Picking a small one up in my hand, I tried to clear my mind and focus solely on pulverizing the stone; thereby reducing it to sand. But nothing happened. I concentrated on sending energy into the little stone, in an attempt to simply crack it, but again, I was unsuccessful. Over and over I tried as the pale afternoon light slowly faded into evening. I attempted to gather energy from around me and centre it on the rock; I tried with my eyes open and closed, both while holding the rock or while I rested my hand over top of it; but nothing seemed to work in the slightest.

"Forget it," I fumed, forcefully throwing the stone away. "I obviously have no destructive abilities, though I know my dad would never have believed *that* one."

Resigned to the fact that I would not have time to do any more traveling today, I removed the hobbles from the horses and looked around for something secure to tether them to for the night.

But as I glanced up, a gray smudge immediately caught my eye, and I was furious with myself that I hadn't noticed any sign earlier, absorbed as I was in my attempts to break the tiny stone. There, above a scraggly stand of trees a little downstream from my location, a thin wisp of smoke twisted and rose into the rapidly darkening sky.

Chapter 13

It was a campfire...it had to be. There was no lightning at all today, and due to the amount of particulate in the sky, there never was a single moment of direct sunlight, so any chance of a fire starting from a concentrated beam—say through broken glass—was absolutely impossible. Additionally, too much time had passed from when Tiamat had 'cleansed' the area for there to be any fires remaining from that pivotal day. Those blazes had long been cold, and to the horses' delight, a sparse peppering of feathery grass sprouts had even begun to spread across the bleak landscape since that time.

And that wasn't the only change. A few days ago, a robin was singing sweetly from the branch of a gnarled, old maple. It was, to my ears, the most beautiful music I had ever heard. And shortly following the sounds of the robin, I had noticed numerous other birds, calling and flitting happily through the air. It was as though they were heralding the appearance of other small animals, seen in blurs of movement through the bushes and fallen trees. It seemed as though the days of destruction were finished, and that nature was slowly rebounding and reclaiming the land. So in these cool, gray days of growth, any fire that was not from lightning, had to have been started by *someone*.

But who? It seemed unlikely that Tiamat would announce himself in such a way, though I had already learned the hard way that I was better off not attempting to guess at his intentions or predict his actions. Yet if it wasn't Tiamat, I could be in serious trouble. Should this 'camper' be one of the Nephilim, he was almost certainly sitting and biding his time, having sensed my presence long ago. There would be no escaping—confrontation, I thought grimly, would be my only chance of survival. And it would be a slim chance, at that.

I tethered the horses to the stout limb of a fallen tree, and removed the crossbow from its soft, protective case, weighing it in my hand as I deliberated its usefulness. If it was Tiamat, I certainly wouldn't need a weapon, would I? But if it wasn't him...

I maintained my hold on the crossbow and grabbed a few bolts, tucking them into a small carrying case that was attached to my belt. I draped the bow's cocking rope loosely around my neck and crept silently downstream, trying to step only on bare ground or rock to allow for the quietest possible approach.

Halfway there, I paused to cock the bow, deciding that it would be best to be prepared, particularly after my encounter with Abel. Ducking behind a blind of felled trees so as to not be caught out in the open, I tipped the front end of the crossbow onto the ground. Then I quickly placed my right foot on the bow's stirrup, to hold the front of the bow firmly down. Swiftly feeding the cocking rope around the drawstring, I then pulled up hard on the two rope handles, expecting the usual strain that always accompanied the cocking of a crossbow— for me, at least.

But not this time. The drawstring came up quickly and with relatively little effort, and had me examining the crossbow to see if something was wrong with it. Yet the weapon appeared to be in perfect working order, and its finish didn't bear so much as a scratch.

Perplexed, I removed the cocking rope and decided I would try to cock the drawstring manually. This, I knew, should take about 175 pounds of force, and was a feat that went way beyond the capabilities of my strong, but slight frame. Yet something was off here, and I needed to determine how badly the crossbow might be damaged.

Again, I put the end of the bow onto the ground and placed my foot on the stirrup to hold it in place. With two hands, I grasped the drawstring and began to pull up carefully, watching the bow closely for any obvious defects. It did require some effort, but to my annoyance, I was able to pull the string into the exact position, without noticing the slightest flaw anywhere.

"Shit," I muttered angrily as I finished cocking the bow and loaded a bolt. What was I going to do if it was broken? I couldn't begin to think of how I would fix it. Yet without it, how would I hunt? And worse yet, how would I defend myself against the Nephilim? "You're screwed, Michaels," I whispered as I took aim and fired at a large pine tree, testing to see if the bolt would even make the distance.

But the shot was perfect. The bolt slammed into the trunk precisely where I had aimed it and I could see that I'd need my knife to get it out again. My mind went perfectly blank for a moment as I stood there, stunned, staring first at the bolt, then at the crossbow, and finally to my hands and arms.

They looked the same as they always had; there were no bulging muscles anywhere, and my hands, as usual, appeared small and unremarkable. *I couldn't possibly have gotten stronger, could I?* I thought, as I glanced around for a way to test this. My eyes rested on a large rock, one that would normally be a little too heavy for me to lift, but that I should be able to roll if I needed to move it. I knew that this would be an imperfect test, as I never attempted to move that exact rock before, but it seemed to be a passable experiment for the time being.

Crouching down beside the substantial rock, I placed my fingers firmly beneath it and slowly tried to stand up. It was almost easy.

"Oh," I squeaked in surprise as I stood there holding the rock at my waist. While it was possible that this stone was simply much lighter than it looked, it wasn't likely—especially in light of the surprising ease with which I cocked the crossbow. Why hadn't I noticed this before?

Careful not to alert whoever might be at the fire, I gently placed the rock back down on the ground, promising myself that I would need to experiment with this more fully at another time. The diffused light of dusk was already fading from the surrounding land, and the darkness was deepening.

As soundlessly and swiftly as I could, I went to the pine and dug the bolt out, quickly reloading it in the crossbow after first sheathing my knife. Then, alert and silent, I continued on toward the mysterious fire.

Before long, I could see the warm, orange glow of the flames between the silhouetted trunks and branches of the surrounding trees. I hung back in the shadows, my feet purposely frozen in place, as I peered through the brush and into the campsite.

A lone man sat by the fire, young, but gaunt and ragged-looking. The clothing he wore was dirty and torn, and his features were rather plain, with a short, scraggly beard sprouting over the lower part of his face. He had brown hair that was in need of a wash, a wide nose, and pleasant-looking eyes that eagerly watched what I assumed was his dinner, cooking on the fire. This consisted of one medium gray lump and two small brownish lumps that were sizzling on a rough-edged, square sheet of metal. The makeshift pan rested on a bed of glowing coals, which he had obviously scraped to one side of the fire for this purpose.

I saw that there was little else at the empty-looking site. He was a human survivor, and had almost certainly lost everything he'd ever known. The ground would be his only bed, and the scrap of metal may very well be his only possession—useful, perhaps, for digging, cutting (if it was sharp enough) and, evidently, cooking food.

Food, I thought. *What is he doing for food?* I craned my neck to get a closer look at the man's much-anticipated meal, and recoiled in surprise. The gray lump had rounded ears on a small, triangular head, and a long, hairless tail; and the two light brown lumps appeared to be slugs of some sort. Not my preferred type of fare, but I supposed I would eat a similar meal myself, if I had nothing else and was otherwise faced with starvation.

I realized, belatedly, that I must have made some sort of noise when I noticed the nature of his meal, because he lifted his head abruptly and stared hard in my direction.

"Hello?" he called uncertainly. His eyes darted anxiously between his meager meal and the dark trees, like he was afraid someone would emerge and steal his much-needed food. "Who's there?"

I paused a moment and took a deep breath; then stepped quickly from the shadows. "My name's Kali," I replied. I held the crossbow loosely at my side, cocked, but aimed down at the ground. I hoped to indicate that I meant him no harm, but that I was armed, should he decide to try anything stupid.

His eyes went wide when he saw me, materializing like an apparition from the dark fringe of trees. He blinked and shook his head minutely, as his surprised expression melted into one of speculation. I saw his gaze linger on my crossbow, his countenance alternating between wariness and envy, then look wonderingly at my leather clothes, before resting finally on my face. His eyes seemed kind, if a little suspicious of my intentions.

"I'm Eric," he answered carefully, "and—no offence—but I really don't think I have enough food here to share with you. And seeing how you can hunt with that crossbow there, you probably don't want any of this disgusting stuff, right? So maybe you'd be kind and let me eat my grub?" He barked a forced laugh at his own bad pun, while he made a poor show of casually grabbing a steaming slug and throwing it into his mouth. It was obviously blisteringly hot, and his eyes popped wide before he sputtered and spit it back into his hand. Unfortunately, it appeared to be too hot for his hand as well, and I watched him bite his lip as he quickly upended his appetizer onto his lap to cool.

"I've already eaten, Eric," I lied, "and I only came to investigate the fire; I have no intention of taking anything from you."

He was quiet for a moment as we sized each other up. Then, apparently deciding to believe what I said, he broke into a huge grin. "It's

really great to see someone else, you know. You just looked a little...
um...hostile...appearing out of the night with your crossbow there."
He turned to his meal after he spoke, and used some sticks to slide the
metal plate off the coals.

"Uh...you said you were Kali...right? Is that your name?" he said
looking up and pausing in the retrieval of his meal in order to verify
that detail.

I nodded to him, waiting for him to continue.

"Would you like to sit down?" he asked, setting his sticks back
onto the ground beside him. "I'd really appreciate it if you would," he
said earnestly. "I've been searching for someone that may have some
information—anything—about what's been going on here. You see,
the only others I've found knew nothing. They seemed just as destitute
as me and even more confused." He stared at me closely before continuing. "But you're not the least bit like them."

"What do you mean?"

"Well, just look at you. You don't appear lost or needy at all. And
you waltzed up to my fire as confident as anything. Mind you, you have
that crossbow, but it's something more than that. You don't have that
bewildered, half-mad expression that the other two had."

"So you've really come across others?" I asked, my voice rising in
excitement. Until now, I hadn't realized how much I had missed the
company of other people. It was strange, as I always considered myself
to be a bit of a loner. But I supposed that old adage was true; perhaps
one doesn't realize the worth of something until faced with its absolute
loss. "Where are they?"

"C'mon, Kali, please sit down. Unlike you, I'm unarmed, so I'm
obviously no threat to you," he said as he lifted the cooled slug from his
pants and threw it into his mouth.

I watched him closely as I lowered myself onto the ground on the
opposite side of the fire. He seemed sincere enough, but for the time
being at least, I continued to hold the crossbow—this time on my

lap—and was careful to ensure it was pointed toward the woods; well away from his vicinity.

"So you've come across other people?" I repeated.

"Sure. I'm a scout for the camp—"

"What camp?"

"It's just a small group of people that have survived the disaster, you know? Everyone just wants to stay together, so when some help finally finds us, no one will accidentally get left behind." He popped the second slug into his mouth, and seemed to be trying to swallow it without chewing, looking much like a pelican trying to down an oversized fish.

"But you're out scouting, so for some reason, you're not afraid of missing a rescue team," I observed. "Why?"

Eric swallowed soberly and immediately looked uncomfortable, shifting his weight and changing his position while he stared into the flames. "I volunteered to scout. They need me to find out anything I can about what's going on, and see if I can get some help."

He moved his eyes to me then and looked at me frankly. "And we've gotta find it soon. People are starving, and half of them are going crazy. We've got Nellie that keeps ranting about complete nonsense, and Greg—he's pretty much gone nuts. He thinks everyone's trying to steal his food, and he killed a guy for it a few days ago—freaked out and kicked his head in. And then there's the water. You know how bad it is…I gag every time I have to choke some back. So that's it. That's why I'm out scouting instead of staying back and going insane with the rest of them. I've gotta get out of here. We all have to. So you have to tell me what you can. Please," he said pleadingly. "Like for starters, where did you come from?"

"I'm from the town of Pinecrest, but I was in the park when it hit."

"Pinecrest…? You mean you were in *Pinecrest National Park*?" he asked, incredulous.

"Yes. I was lucky to escape with my life—"

"Shit—you were all the way in Pinecrest... This is way bigger than I thought it was," he said, sounding worried. "How did you get here so quickly?"

"Oh—well, I..." I stammered, unsure I wanted to let him know at this point that I had some extremely valuable horses with me.

"I can't believe it!" he exclaimed as his face lit up. "You had transportation ... like a ... a helicopter, right? That'd mean you're with a rescue team, or a crew of some sort... You can get me outta here!" He jumped up and peered excitedly around him, as though he was expecting a rescue squad to step from the trees as I had.

"Oh, Eric, no ... No, there's no one with me and there is no help," I said feebly, setting my crossbow down and walking around the campfire to him when I saw his reaction.

"There's no one? No help...?" he echoed softly, looking confused and stricken.

"No. I'm so sorry," I said, putting my hand on his shoulder to console him.

"I thought ... I thought, maybe this time..." he choked. He pressed his hands to his face as his head slumped down in despair. "I don't know how much longer I can stand this..."

I awkwardly held onto him as his shoulders started to shake and he quietly came unraveled in my arms. But though Eric obviously needed consoling, I had no desire to be this close to him—misery, I found, was like a great, voracious black hole, devouring anything in its vicinity. So in an effort to stave it off, I desperately cast around for something else to think about instead. My eyes shot around the fringe of dark woods as I searched for inspiration for another train of thought—but it wasn't to be. What caught my eye made me jump, and Eric, sensing my reaction, lifted his head and looked around warily, though he didn't appear to see anything amiss.

"I thought you were going to leave me be," I breathed angrily, ignoring Eric's questioning look.

"What?" Eric asked me in confusion. "I don't know what you're talking about."

Tiamat stood at the edge of the trees, his bearing as dark as the surrounding shadows. "You shouldn't have touched her," he said to Eric, a soft menace to his voice.

Eric spun around and yelped in surprise when he saw Tiamat, whose sudden appearance was far more frightening than my own entrance. "Whoa—hey, man, it's not like you think." He raised his hands defensively and backed a step away. "I won't go near her again. I swear."

"It is too late for that," Tiamat said in barely a whisper, stepping on Eric's cooked mouse as he swiftly approached him.

"No, stop!" I screeched impotently, my crossbow sitting in the dirt on the far side of the flames. Unable to even fire a warning shot, I could only watch in horror as Tiamat thrust his hand onto Eric's chest. The young, weary man lurched and convulsed grotesquely, and when Tiamat removed his hand, he fell in a limp heap on the ground.

"Oh no," I gasped, falling to my knees beside his still body. "Eric?" I called desperately, shaking him, "Can you hear me?"

He wasn't breathing, and I clutched his wrist to check for a pulse ... but there was nothing. I double-checked at his neck, but again, nothing. Tilting his head to open his airway, I gave him a rescue breath, watching his chest rise artificially as my own constricted in sorrow. I gave him a second breath and began compressions, watching my hands through a blur of tears as I rhythmically pressed onto his chest and counted to thirty in a thick, cracking voice. Then: two rescue breaths; next: chest compressions—thirty of them, before returning to the breaths again. And I repeated these steps, over and over—stopping at intervals to check for breathing that would never come—for what felt like a hollow, spiraling eternity.

Finally, my hands slowed, and I sat back and stared at the surrounding emptiness that echoed my feelings within. I was alone once again.

Tiamat had long since disappeared into the night and Eric's body was nothing but a lifeless corpse. I slumped next to his graying remains, wondering absently how his lonely fire would possibly keep the creeping night from enveloping me. But then I realized that it couldn't—the black had already penetrated my empty body, and I felt it try to take hold, beginning to cloud my senses with unwelcome despair.

I had to take control: I snatched up Eric's scrap of metal and began to dig. But its jagged edges were sharp and bit into my hands, so I threw it aside and ripped some shreds of fabric from the fringes of his ragged shirt. Using these to cushion my palms, I grabbed the fragment of metal and resumed digging.

I broke up and scooped the earth with a frenzied intensity, though the progress itself was frustratingly slow and labored. For hours I worked, not easing my pace for even a moment's rest. The cushioning scraps of fabric added some protection for my hands, but as I continually struck into the dirt, the repeated pressure and occasional slip of fabric left my hands bloody and torn. I gripped the makeshift shovel tightly, swinging it down to dig some more—grunting in agony as metal and dirt pounded into the open wounds on my hands; but even then, I did not stop. I struck down again and again as tears of pain, rage, sorrow and release fell into the deepening pit—a pit that was growing under the sheer force of my will alone, as my arms had long since gone rubbery with exhaustion, and my hands now blazed and throbbed.

Finally, in the deepest black of the night, I scooped the last pile of dirt from Eric's grave. I was utterly spent, but I crawled from the hole and stumbled to the far side of his body. Half-laying across him, I forced my quivering muscles to work once more, and I rolled him into the earthy pit.

The mountain of displaced soil loomed beside me, and I crawled to its heaping mass, flinging myself into the side of it. Using my arms and body, I scooped and pulled the cascading soil into the hole, watching it pile and mound on his feet, then chest, then face. When all the earth was finally mounded up on his grave, I collapsed a few paces from it, and let the spreading despair overtake me.

Chapter 14

As I slowly drifted toward consciousness, I marveled at and relished the elusive sense of contentment that had permeated deep within me. A stream babbled somewhere nearby, and my mind drifted like a spiraling leaf, floating within the watery, chattering sounds. I imagined dazzling ribbons of sunshine, sparkling in dancing reflections off the clear, rippling water, filling my body with warmth and light. And underlying this, I had a lingering notion that someone had been stroking my hair, and I basked in the security of the feeling and the intimacy of the action; I hadn't felt this peaceful in a long time.

I began to stretch my sore muscles as I leisurely came to, and as I did so, I felt my body shift strangely. I wondered absently if I was lying on an unstable surface. The surface, however, wasn't the only thing that shifted—as I became fully awake, my mood and sense of reality began to alter drastically. Memories of the night before bubbled to the surface like a noxious gas, and any remaining sense of contentment withered and died. Reality had eclipsed the sunlight of my dreams, exposing me to the cold, gray truth of consciousness.

I opened my eyes to find that I was lying on a bank of round stones next to the stream where I had tethered the horses yesterday. There was no sunlight gleaming off the dull surface of the water, and my waking world remained dim. The sun, as always, was masked behind a veil of cloud and dust—its brilliance likely hidden for the short remainder of my life.

I was not surprised to feel a deep, dull throbbing in my hands, and with some trepidation, I shifted my head to glance down at the mess I had made of them. However, my hands, I saw, had been cleaned and bandaged, and like a mindless marionette, I sat straight up and stared at them in astonishment.

The horses blew noises of welcome from behind me, and I turned to see Tiamat stroking the mare's nose and watching me in an offhand way. I did my best to not look startled when I saw him, but his presence always knocked me off balance for so many different reasons, and every one of them had a matching, contradictory mate. It sickened me that I continued to crave his presence, despite the emotional torture that always followed.

"Did you do this?" I inquired in a small voice as I held my bandaged hands up in front of me.

"Yes," he answered carefully, his hands slowing as he stroked the horse's neck.

"Why?" I asked. "You heartlessly kill one and then tend to the other. I don't understand you, Tiamat."

"You have a purpose, Kali. I have told you this before," he pointed out. "You must take care of yourself so that you can fulfill it. And it … saddens me … to have to patch you up."

I let my hands fall back down limply, and the action reminded me painfully of the manner in which Eric died … of the way Tiamat killed him personally and brutally: face to face, while I stood watching. "You told me that you're merciful by nature, Tiamat," I whispered. "And I believed you. But what you did last night demonstrated something else entirely."

"You already know what I am and what I must do here, and I already told you that the very thought of it tears at me in ways you can't understand. I do what I must, and I will not explain myself to you anymore."

"You're right; you won't," I answered, "because you're going to leave me alone, like I asked you to." I stood up and walked a few paces toward him as he watched me coolly. "Please, Tiamat. Please promise me that you'll keep your distance," I pleaded. "Just let me die in peace."

Tiamat looked off to the horizon for a long moment before responding, and appeared as though he was fighting with something internally—though what thoughts he grappled with, I could not guess. He finally turned his face back to me and, in contradiction to his expression, spoke in an almost bored manner. "I will grant your request for a short time. It so happens that there is something that I must do, so I will be gone for a while and you may have a few moments of peace." Once again, he turned his face away from me and resumed stroking the mare. "I will, however, return when I have finished this particular task, and I fully intend to check in on you from time to time, Kali. You will simply have to accept that."

I bit my lip in frustration. The idea that I wouldn't be left completely alone wasn't altogether unexpected, though I was pleased to learn that Tiamat would be absent for a time. "So how much longer will I be alive, Tiamat? Can't you tell me what's going to happen with me, or what I'm supposed to do here?"

"Not exactly, no. I regret that I can't be more specific, but I assure you that you will be alive for a good while yet."

Relief flooded through me at his words, despite the fact that I felt like I was nothing but a walking curse. "But what kind of a miserable life will I be clinging to, if you're going to dog my footsteps and kill any poor soul I come across?"

"Remember, Kali. I do not need you to find people for me. I can sense them on my own. When it becomes necessary for a man to leave this life, I will ensure that he goes, regardless of whether or not you have made his acquaintance."

"I know there's more to it!" I huffed, glaring at his collected, taciturn exterior. "Then at least tell me why you killed Eric right in front of me. Why not do it before I met him or wait until after I left? You must have realized what that would do to me—it's like you're *trying* to hurt me, Tiamat."

His hand dropped from the horse and he spun to face me. "That's not true ... I have never *wanted* to hurt you ... all those times ... but ... I..." he trailed off. "I'm sorry," he said, sounding frustrated. "I'm completely unable to explain why I must behave this way with you, but what I *can* say is that, last night, I didn't originally intend to kill that man in front of you, Kali. I had planned to send him on after you left, but as I waited, I saw that circumstances changed somewhat..."

"Wait a minute," I breathed as I remembered in a flash what he had uttered last night. "You were upset because he touched me... That's what you said," I recalled, incredulous, my mind racing with the possible implications of that statement. "You *killed* him because you were *jealous?*" I asked in shock.

"I would never do such a thing!" he fumed, stalking past me to reach the stream bank. "There was an entirely different problem that arose out of his contact with you. And *please*, do not ask me what it is." He picked up a handful of stones and, one by one, threw them out into the water, watching each one splash into the surface before tossing the next. After a long moment, he said more gently, "I won't divulge this because I am not able to, Kali."

Frustrated, I quietly smoldered, watching his careful, deliberate movements as he threw each stone into the water. As I studied him, however, I was struck by a number of rather alarming changes that I was surprised I didn't notice before, and my annoyance dissipated like a lifting fog. He was thinner, pale, and had dark smudges under his eyes that made it look like he hadn't slept in days. Tension virtually hummed through his body, and I was surprised he didn't crush each stone that he handled...

"Tiamat," I gasped, suddenly noticing the thick bandages that encircled each of his wrists. I went straight over to him and—ignoring the ripple of energy that buzzed over my hands—gently grasped his left arm, examining his wrist as though I could see through the dressing. "What ... what happened?" I asked, casting a look up at his face.

I had taken him off guard again, and our gazes locked for the briefest of moments, his vivid blue eyes searing down into my soul, freezing my limbs and breaking my heart. Then, in an instant, the intensity was gone, and his eyes were veiled with that look of false indifference.

"It is nothing, Kali." He broke his gaze and stalked a few paces away, crossing his two bandaged wrists behind his back. "I am aware of how this looks, but I most certainly did not attempt to take my own life. In fact, I have had to spill my own blood a number of times in order to fulfill what is required of me—and I will need to do so again," he admitted. "To be honest, it is fortunate that I heal quickly, as I am required to do this ... rather frequently." His mouth twisted as he spoke, making it fairly obvious how he felt about this work.

Out of concern for him, I clenched my bandaged hands—only to receive a stab of pain—and immediately rubbed them against my thighs to ease the resulting ache. I wished he would tell me more, but I knew better than to inquire about it. I cast about for a different subject, and like a magnet to buried lead, my mind fixed back on the strange circumstances surrounding Eric's death.

Leaving Tiamat by the stream bank, I paced back up toward the horses as I wondered: why would it be so bad for a guy to touch me ... if it wasn't jealousy, what was it? Procreation? That seemed somewhat plausible, but was still an unlikely reason to suddenly kill a man that I was simply comforting. Yet my procreation theory made me think of something, and I stared hard at Tiamat. "Could I be pregnant?" I asked him bluntly. "From you, of course," I added quickly.

His eyes widened as a look of surprise—and then alarm—flashed across his face, immediately animating him. He marched over to me and put his hands on my arms, his static energy surging across my skin.

His left hand slid down my arm and he shifted it over, placing it gently on my abdomen. He paused then, his brow knit in concentration.

"You are not," he responded in a tone of quiet relief, his pent-up breath coming out in a rush. "I know this for a certainty."

I was wracked by contradictory feelings yet again, but I did my best to conceal them. In doing so, another thought occurred to me.

"You said I would live for a while yet. So what would you do if I met someone else and became pregnant by him?" I asked.

Tiamat flinched like he had been struck, but did not reply. He simply stood as he was, with one hand on my abdomen and the other tightening on my arm.

"Would you slaughter my child after you've done away with my new partner? Is that what you would do?"

The wounded look on his face persisted, but I noticed something else there, hidden deep in his eyes, that alarmed me. "You would do it, wouldn't you?" I whispered; my face inches from his.

"You needn't worry, Kali," he said in a hard voice. "That particular scenario will *never* happen."

"Why not? I suppose you'll kill anyone I might ever get close to, is that it?"

"Stop antagonizing me, Kali," he said through his teeth in frustration, "or you'll think I am doing this out of retribution... but believe me, I am not."

"Doing what? I don't understand..."

"In fact," he continued, not listening, "this conversation just made me think of it. And I understand now that I must follow through... But I apologize—this will be terrible."

"What?" I asked, now panicked. I struggled to get away, but he held me firmly. My new strength was no match for his.

"I am so sorry," he whispered fervently. From under his hand, an itching buzz penetrated down into my body, and I looked at him in horror.

"What are you doing?" I gasped.

He didn't meet my gaze, but released his hold on me and backed a few paces away, riveting his eyes to the ground. "Something appalling... but necessary, all the same."

As I glared at him, the itching sensation within my abdomen quickly progressed to one of burning; a feeling of searing, licking flames that forced me to the ground in desperate agony.

"Tiamat ... stop it ... *please!*" I screamed. But it kept coming: the burning, the pain; it wouldn't stop, like my insides were scorching, blistering, blackening under my hands and within my writhing body. I shrieked and moaned, clawed at the dirt and scrabbled at my clothing as I twisted on the ground, my insides screeching with pain. "Please, please ... oh, please make it stop ... stop it..." I sobbed frantically. "I won't ... be with anyone else ... I promise ... I won't ... please stop ... Tiamat ... please..."

He paced beside my thrashing form, and looked down at me with a face that was twisting with emotion. "It's almost over," he said, his voice sounding strangled and raw. "Hang on, Kali, it's nearly done."

And it was; almost. I writhed and gasped and screamed out a few times more, and then, slowly, the blistering fires began to ebb, easing the torturous pain by degrees at a time. When the burning had stopped, I moaned and wrapped myself into a tight ball, whimpering at the severe ache that repeatedly seized my abdomen in a series of crushing waves.

I felt Tiamat pick me up and carry me a short distance, before setting me gently down on that same bank of rounded rocks.

"You should be more comfortable here—the thick layers of pebbles have more give than solid ground," he said, sounding awkward. "And after a while, I expect you will feel much improved."

"Did you just ... *sterilize* me?" I moaned.

"Kali ... I ... I did what I had to," he protested. "But there are more reasons then the obvious, I assure you," he said, his voice pleading for understanding. "Besides, I can't believe that you would even think of bringing a new life into this world. Humankind is finished, Kali. Remember that."

"*Bastard*," I whispered into the rocks.

"Yes—I am the worst kind," he agreed quietly, kneeling down beside me and pensively brushing a damp lock of hair from my face. "And the situation will not improve. I am afraid that you will truly hate me before the end, and I am eternally sorry for it ... for everything."

"Oh no," I moaned. "Please ... just leave me alone—I really can't take anymore."

"You are stronger than you know, Kali," Tiamat said fiercely. "And you *can* take more. So be ready, because *you will*." He stood then and began to leave, but stopped himself almost immediately, and turned back to face me. "Know that ... that I wish there was some other way..."

Tiamat hesitated, then swiftly brought out his wings and lunged into the air. With a succession of ever-quieting swishes, he flew off to the west, on and on toward the distant horizon, until he was nothing but a speck in the dreary, gray sky.

* * *

After an hour or so, I found that I could get up again, though my abdomen was incredibly tender and sore, and ripples of burning pain seared across it if I twisted the wrong way. I didn't, however, want to waste any more time than I already had, so with a great deal of care, I got to my feet and gingerly made my way toward the horses.

Tiamat, I reflected, was correct to insist that I was strong enough to weather these weeks of abuse, horror and desolation—but only by the thinnest of margins, and not without that insidious ache, which wormed further into my soul by the moment. He was wrong, however, if he believed that I was about to accept more of the same. I would not.

And even though I knew I might not be able to stop whatever could be coming, I would *not* just sit and take it…and neither should any other survivors. Not if I could help it.

As far as I knew, Tiamat wouldn't lie about being away for a while, so that meant that I had at least a narrow window of freedom—days or even weeks, I hoped—which I had no intention of squandering. I would try to find Eric's camp, and help those people however I could; even if that meant warning them, and arming them with whatever knowledge they might need. They shouldn't have to be lambs waiting to be slaughtered—they deserved a fighting chance.

Maybe I can direct them to those caves I passed earlier, I thought. *If the camp is close, it should only take them a little over a week, on foot.*

The knowledge of what I was about to do was like a tonic for the spirit, and I felt almost elated at having this purpose; an objective that could help others, and hopefully lend some meaning to my time here.

I was beginning to form a plan in my head, and I approached the tethered horses with an outlook that was more positive than it had been in some time. "C'mon, Hero," I said, untethering him so I could lead him down to the stream for a drink. I had decided to lead the palomino down first for a change, but once we started walking away, the mare began fussing and stamping behind us.

"What is it?" I asked as I gingerly started back toward her, minding my tender stomach. "Are we not paying enough attention to you, girl?" Holding Hero's lead in one hand, I stroked the mare's head and neck with the other, and spoke to her softly. "Do you want to come with us?" I asked as she nudged my shoulder with her nose, driving me back slightly and making me laugh. "Oh—aren't we pushy," I chuckled. "You are such an irritable, spoiled prima donna," I said, scratching her around the ears. "And I have the perfect name for you."

In a fitting manner, she tossed her head abruptly, and I laughed in response. "No point shaking that beautiful mane for me, Paris. There are no paparazzi here," I grinned at her. "It's perfect," I chuckled, tethering her to Hero's saddle so I could lead them both down for a drink together. "And yes, you can come too, but don't think you're drinking first, princess," I said to her. "Now come on you two mollycoddled twits."

I was relieved to see that I retained the ability to make the water drinkable, and once the horses were finished, I drank some myself before hobbling them on a nearby patch of grass. I was forced to move carefully, but found that I was able to get around fairly well, and with only a few instances of breath-sucking pain, I managed to eat some food and pack up for departure in fairly good time.

I rode for the remainder of the day, always keeping a sharp lookout for tracks or signs of any sort that might indicate people could be nearby. I followed the stream, as I noticed Eric had done, by the footsteps he left that led to his last, lonely campsite, coming from the south. I lost sight of his tracks after the first few hours, but kept on following the stream, determined that I was on the right path.

And I was. Shortly before nightfall, I smelled wood smoke, and soon afterward, I detected a pungent odor that wafted to me on the westerly breeze: the unmistakable, heady stink of a latrine. I continued on around a bend in the stream, and just past it I could see that the far bank was trampled and muddy, riddled with the dents and impressions of many feet. A packed, dirt trail wound away to the right, where it climbed an embankment and circled around a thicket of fallen trees before disappearing from view.

I was exhilarated—yet extremely nervous. I couldn't imagine how they would take the news that I was about to impart to them. And what, exactly, should I tell them about myself? Certainly nothing about my abilities, I decided. That wouldn't be wise at this point. But at the same time, I couldn't just let them continue to drink that awful water as it was...

As I puzzled over these things, I started riding Hero across the shallow stream, with Paris trailing closely behind. But I stopped halfway.

How would a large group of desperate, starving people react to a lone woman, riding into their midst, with two horses and more supplies than they'd seen in weeks? *They'd probably mob me before I could even explain myself,* I thought grimly, turning the horse around. *Perhaps it would be better to leave the horses somewhere more secure for the time being—just while I assess the situation…*

I selected a thick copse of trees, which I had passed earlier, as a temporary hideout for the horses. There were almost no tracks in the area, which was a good indication that few people from the camp ever went there.

Additionally, some of the trees overhung the stream, so I could tether the horses close enough to the water that they would be able to reach it for a drink. I wasn't sure if the spoiled nitwits would stoop to drink the rancid stuff, even if they were incredibly thirsty, but it was the best I could do for them at the moment. Besides, I thought, the other animals must be drinking it, the humans certainly were, and now so can my pampered little horses—if only for a short while.

I ripped up and gathered a few armloads of grass, and made sure I left a separate pile which only Hero would be able to reach, thereby thwarting Paris' usual attempts to push him out of the way and devour his share. However, once she saw the food, Paris naturally went for Hero's share instead of her own, stretching out her neck and baring her teeth. But she couldn't quite reach it, and so pulled her head back and shook it, her mane dancing wildly in her mini temper tantrum.

"Just eat your own, Paris," I said to the horse unnecessarily, knowing I was truly stalling now. I hated to admit it, but I was incredibly apprehensive about this visit.

According to Eric, other survivors had joined their group, so I should have no reason to think they might be hostile toward me …

until I tell them the last thing they'll want to hear, that is. *So should I go there weaponless?* I wondered, imagining that even the knife—let alone the crossbow—might be too much of a temptation to those desperate people. It would be better if I appeared non-aggressive, I decided, with nothing in my possession that could provoke envy, fear or hostility. Besides, these people needed help, which I hoped to give them; and I craved their company, which they could give me. Nothing more was required at the moment.

So I said goodbye to the horses, and without allowing myself another moment's hesitation, briskly made my way toward the camp.

Chapter 15

In some aspects, the physical camp itself was more developed than I had imagined it would be. I didn't know what I was expecting to see: perhaps a jumble of dirty people huddled together on the barren earth, or even a number of poorly constructed lean-tos, scattered here and there around a debris-laden clearing—but I soon saw that these notions were an underestimation of their coping skills.

Two rough buildings had been erected, each loosely resembling a Native American longhouse, though they were much smaller in scale; the narrow, rectangular structures probably only capable of housing about ten people each. They were crudely built, and looked like they would leak and ooze terribly in even the lightest rain, as the roof and walls were made of nothing more substantial than rows of lashed sticks with mud and leaf matter packed between them. Yet the shelters themselves were a testament to someone's ingenuity and determination, as the group likely had little in the way of building materials or tools at hand. And these were people that were expecting rescue at any moment, so the additional investment of time and precious energy to make the buildings more permanent would likely not have been a consideration.

Each of the buildings had a single hole in the roof, from which wisps of smoke stretched and spiraled into the air. And in a flat, central area of packed dirt, about halfway between the two structures, a small fire crackled invitingly. Though I couldn't see anyone when I first glanced around, a number of nearby voices drifted across the clearing from various unseen locations. The pitch and volume indicated clusters of regular conversation, with the exception of a high little shriek, which originated from behind one of the buildings.

Spilling around the far corner of the structure on my right, two boys tumbled and fell, rolling, twisting and grabbing at each other. They both wore dirty, tattered clothing, and like Eric, didn't look like they had bathed since the Nephilim hit. One of them, perhaps ten years old with shaggy red hair and a long, black smudge on his face, wriggled free of his captor's grasp, leapt up and ran full-tilt toward the central fire. He had half-circled it by the time the other boy made it to his feet, and used the flames as a buffer between the two of them.

"Give it back!" screeched the smaller, olive-skinned boy that had been left on the far side of the fire. He had two defined, expressive eyebrows that shot about his brow, punctuating his dismay. "I caught it ... I caught it! It's mine," he pleaded, his voice cracking through his tears.

"I'm bigger than you. I need more food," the redhead mocked.

"But I already gave you—"

His rebuttal stopped abruptly when a large hand swept in and pulled the smaller child into a friendly, but restrictive, embrace. "What's going on, my little cockroaches?" the hand's owner inquired. He was a short, stocky man with an unruly black beard that obscured the lower half of his face, though two kind, dark eyes that were augmented by a series of laugh lines were his dominant feature. "Didn't you already promise t'stop fighting with each other...? Now, when was that?" he asked, while he scratched his beard thoughtfully with his free hand. "Seems to me, it was maybe just a few hours ago."

"I'm sorry, Tony," the smaller boy said contritely, still enclosed in Tony's left arm.

"And what did you promise t'do if Randy here bothered you again?"

"Ask for help," the child said quietly, his dirty black hair tumbling forward as his eyes turned down to his dusty feet.

Tony released the boy and started around the fire toward the red-headed child, while his charge followed him timidly. "Randy," the man said with a note of disappointment in his voice, "you need t'be helpin' the younger ones. You hear me? Now what did you take?" he asked the freckled boy.

But Randy was frozen, his eyes staring hard at a point behind Tony and across the clearing, with his lips parted slightly in surprise. His booty—which appeared to be a frog—fell to the ground, forgotten, and the small boy rushed in and reclaimed it. His meal back in hand, the child scampered out of sight, never noticing what had so engrossed the older boy's attention.

"Randy," Tony said firmly, trying to compel the older child to look at him. He crouched down in front of the boy, and gently put his hands on his shoulders to turn him, so that Randy would be facing him. Nevertheless, Randy's head swiveled on his body, so that even though his frame twisted under Tony's direction, the position of his head didn't alter in the least. Tony huffed in quiet exasperation, and looked over his shoulder to see what, if anything, Randy was staring at.

But his look mirrored that of Randy's the moment his eyes found me, standing quietly by the broken branches of a large felled tree. Tony stood up slowly and, never taking his eyes off me, backed toward the far end of the clearing.

"Hanna, Maurice ... everyone ...?" he called, keeping his eyes on me as if he wished to keep me in place with his stare, "I think you'd better come over here. Now."

Within moments, the small clearing buzzed with activity. Over a dozen people arrived with anxious expressions, talking to and questioning each other, in response to the apparent agitation in Tony's summons. Then, little by little, the clearing froze into silence, as though icy tendrils penetrated each person in turn, turning them to stone the instant they saw me.

I walked closer to them, my heart in my throat and my hands sweaty and trembling, and tried to remind myself that I spoke to groups of people all the time; it had been a part of my job for years. But no, this was different. So terrifyingly, heart-breakingly different.

"Are you ..." Tony began, his voice hoarse. He cleared it and tried again. "Are you stranded like us, or are you here to help us?"

"I did come here to help you," I replied in a surprisingly steady voice, "but I'm sorry to say that I'm not a relief worker."

The group seemed to reanimate all at once, shifting or mumbling in confusion. "I don't care who you are, so long as you get us the hell out of here," growled a thin man with sharp, weasel-like features.

"I'm sure that is everyone's first priority, and I agree that you need to leave," I said to the rapidly quieting group, "but you need to hear about the situation first—about what caused this, and what might happen next. To start with, I have to tell you that I bring you information only, and—I'm sorry—but this news that I have is about as bad as it gets." The clearing, I noticed, swiftly returned to a deathly silence, its occupants' expressions shifting from disappointment to dread. All was quiet, and they looked expectantly at me, waiting to hear the worst.

"The ... uh ... *disaster* is so much bigger than what you may have been imagining, and this is why you haven't seen any sign of a rescue effort." I took a deep breath, while I wracked my brain, trying to think of the best way to approach this.

"How much longer, then?" called out a young woman, wearing tattered business attire. "Because we have an injured man here that really can't wait, so you go tell your people that they need to take care of him now," she demanded. "And the rest of us will wait if we have to, but we'll need food and supplies immediately or there'll be hell to pay."

"How big is it?" another voice called out, almost simultaneously. "Did it hit Lyndentown?"

"Goddamn bureaucrats!" spat the weasel-faced man. "You all think we're not important enough, don't you? Well, if you can get to us here, then we can get out of here, too. I'll just follow you—I won't stay here and rot."

"You tell her, Greg," goaded a tall man with a smooth, deep voice. This man didn't appear quite as ragged as the rest; his dark brown hair was somewhat neat, and though the rough green shirt that he wore was frayed and rumpled, his clothes were relatively intact. Both in the way he looked and in his manner, he simply reminded me of a spoiled prince from some generic fairytale, casually lording over his men.

"Some of us will just tag along with you," the tall man said, watching me with a look of cold speculation in his eyes. "The able bodied should not have to stay behind because of the few that are too weak to go. Why should everyone suffer because of them?" He leaned over then, his stature commanding and aristocratic, and murmured something unintelligible to the man he called Greg, the faintest of smiles playing across his lips.

Greg nodded vigorously, and squared his shoulders defiantly when he looked back at me. "There are many of us and—from what I can see—only one of you. I'd like to see you try to keep us from following along."

I could hear the man with the smooth voice chuckle quietly as Greg said this, as though he found the whole situation rather amusing. *Who the hell* was *this guy?*

"Quiet," I insisted firmly. "Like I said before: I *do* want you to leave. But if you want to know what's happening, you have to listen!" I had to take a deep breath and close my eyes for a moment to ease my frustration. But when I opened them, I saw that amazingly, each one of them had stilled; including Greg, who glared at me with a sullen expression, and his apparent puppeteer, who simply watched me with a look of mild interest, his silken voice presently silent.

"To answer one of your questions, yes, it did hit Lyndentown, and I don't even know where that is," I continued, my hands balled into fists from the tension, pulling the bandages painfully tight against my throbbing palms. "The truth is, there isn't a place on earth that hasn't been hit. It's happened everywhere ... across every speck of land of every country in the world ... and each one of these places has been affected just as bad, or even worse, than here."

I saw their faces pale, and three or four of them sat down abruptly, like someone had knocked their legs out from under them. "I think that there are very few survivors, overall. So there will be no rescue effort and no trip back to a city, because there are none left standing," I reported, pitying the horrified expressions on their faces. "And it's not over yet." I warned them. "You aren't safe here, out in the open. I can direct you to a more secure place, but you'll need to leave soon. There isn't much time."

"It's God's wrath!" a shrill, female voice wailed, shattering the silence that had solidified around them.

"Oh, shut the hell up, Nellie," snapped the business woman, rounding on her. "Why the fuck did YOU have to survive? You're such a tiresome piece of shit."

I had decided earlier that ranting about half-angels and the end of the world would only make it look like I had lost my mind. But against my better judgment, a prickle of irritation pierced through my waning patience, and before I could think twice about it, I had spoken.

"No, actually ... Nellie's uh ... she's right," I admitted, knowing as I said it that I was undoubtedly undermining the strength of my earlier statements. I could almost see the words, suspended in the air like they were incased in a cartoon speech bubble, and I wished fervently that I could wrench them back.

"Listen to that! She's a believer, unlike the rest of you heathens!" Nellie evangelized in an ever-loudening voice. "She's always known it would come; that the almighty God would reach down from the heavens and rip open our corrupt earth, spilling Satan and his legions out across the land—"

"Well, I don't really think—" I tried to counter.

"—so that they can burn our infested planet to cinders with their fire and their brimstone. Beware, you heathens; soon the flames will come to burn you all alive! I have seen—"

"No ... listen, everyone. I'm not—"

"—that she speaks the truth! Soon little demons will come to rip apart your bodies and feast on your limbs. The end is here! It is just as I always said—"

Tony, thankfully, had taken hold of Nellie and forcefully led her away before she could say anything more. But the damage was done; I could see the dark looks full of doubt and anger, and the crowd began muttering in a strengthening staccato of sound.

"To think that some of us actually listened to you!" growled Greg, his dark, rodent-like eyes sparkling at the group's discontent. "If, as you claim, the entire surface of the earth has been destroyed, how could you possibly know? Do you have your own personal helicopter that's capable of circumnavigation at warp speed, or did you see this in a vision?" he mocked.

Most people seemed to agree with what he said, and many shifted position, nodded their heads or folded their arms in anger.

"I have heard about the extent of it first-hand, from one of the ... people ... responsible for this devastation. And I have seen it happening with my own eyes—I watched him as he did it. But for the record," I added quickly, "I had no part in it, and I was powerless to stop him."

There was interest there. I noticed that a few people still appeared to be listening to me, despite their apparent skepticism.

"Oh, I see now," began the smooth-voiced man. "You agreed with Nellie when she said that it was God's wrath, and now you are telling us that you watched the one responsible wreak this havoc. So obviously, you're telling us that you had a talk with God, and then personally watched The Almighty destroy the earth. Makes perfect sense."

Shit.

I had to think fast...

"I *never* claimed to see or speak to God, and you *know* it." I replied forcefully, infusing some authority into my voice as I looked disdainfully at my antagonist. Then turning my attention to the rest of the group, I continued. "The ones responsible believe that they are acting out God's wishes. That is what one of them told me."

"So what do you propose we do?" asked Tony, who had returned after depositing Nellie somewhere—presumably a place where she would agitate fewer people. He seemed to be an intelligent, selfless person, and from what I had seen in the short time I'd been here, I would have to assume that he was a kind of undeclared authority: the originator of an underlying cohesiveness, holding the group together. Perhaps if I convinced *him*...

I turned to look at Tony. "You must leave here immediately—"

"Why?" demanded Greg. "Because you say so, with no proof and no evidence? I'm willing to bet that you don't really know anything."

"I know that you killed a man, Greg," I said in a low voice, staring at him hard. He dropped his eyes under my stare, and I felt a small thrill of triumph.

There was a collective gasp at my knowledge, and each of them gaped at me in wonder.

"It isn't remarkable that I know," I admitted to them, "because I learned this information yesterday from a man named Eric."

"And did he believe your nonsense?" asked the man with the voice like dark silk. "Is that why Eric failed to come back here with you ... because he knew you were talking shit?"

"He didn't have time to hear it," I told them. "Eric is now dead." The group's mutters stopped abruptly, and the looks of shock and horror returned. "He was killed by one of the men I told you about. And it's just a matter of time before they decide to come after you. Whether or not you believe me, everyone must leave here. Immediately."

"Our spot here in the woods seems pretty safe to me," said Tony, sounding shaken. "We'll have t'be smarter about burnin' fires, though … don't want anyone to notice the smoke."

"It doesn't matter what you do—they have ways to find you *wherever* you are," I countered. "With the exception of one type of place, and that's where I want you to go. They cannot locate people through rock."

"Through rock? How will that help us?" asked a large, stocky woman with bright, hawk-like eyes.

"She might mean caves, Hanna," Tony said to her. "But if that's what you're getting at," he said, turning to me, "I only know of one 'round here—and it would only fit about one person. That just won't work." Tony was beginning to sound agitated.

Does this mean he believes me?

"I found some caverns, north of here, which are large and extensive. They would make decent living quarters, and one section even has an underground stream that runs through it," I told them, pointing in a northerly direction. "It should take you about a week to reach them on foot. You should be safe there, and hopefully, you'll make it before your presence is noticed."

"Very encouraging," Tony muttered.

"I'm sorry," I said, "but it's the best chance you have."

In the brief silence that followed, the crowd came to life.

"What do these men look like?" Hanna asked. "And how many of them are there?"

"How can they find us?" called another voice.

"Can't we stop them?" a woman asked.

"How can *anyone* have done this to the earth? It isn't possible! We don't have weapons that are capable of this."

"So you expect us to all just pack up and leave, is that it?"

"She's crazy!"

"Hold on!" I yelled over them. I chose to ignore most of their questions—they wouldn't believe the answers anyway—and tried another tactic. "I know that this is hard for you to believe, and that's okay. Even if you think I'm insane, you'll still get a very decent shelter out of agreeing to go—one that won't deteriorate, leak or fall apart. And when *he* comes, you'll all see soon enough that I'm telling you the truth. Honestly, you won't want to be out in the open when you find that out for certain."

The large woman that Tony called Hanna hesitantly stepped forward. "You'll take us to these caverns?" she asked.

My stomach twisted into knots ... there was no way I could take them. The chances of Tiamat showing up rose almost exponentially the longer I stayed with them. "I ... I'm sorry," I stuttered. "But I can only give you directions. I can't take you there."

Everything pretty much degenerated after that. I was accused of being crazy, of trying to trick them out of their shelters, and even of being a prophet, of all things. The latter was by Nellie who unfortunately returned for a repeat performance, which turned out to be even grander and more colorful than the first. Anyone that listened to me, she told them, would be given powers by God that enabled them to transform into any creature they wished—with the exception of a mouse, which apparently was the epitome of evil.

By the time the dark began to set in, my case had been completely lost. People drifted off in small clusters, giving me looks that varied between ones of pity and outright disgust. *It was worth a try,* I sighed to myself as I walked slowly toward the felled tree where I first made my appearance. The adrenalin abandoning my system, I sat heavily on the trunk and let my head fall into my carefully bandaged hands. I didn't know what else I could do here.

"Can we talk?" came a muted voice from nearby.

I looked up to see Hanna standing with Tony and another man, who both looked very much alike, except that the second man was taller with a lean build, and his eyes were a light shade of hazel. Black, curly hair puffed out like a halo around his head, and his arms were heavily tattooed with a myriad of images.

"You've got to understand that it's easier for them to call you crazy than it is to accept what you've been saying," the tall man said in a low voice. "The implications are a little much for most of us to handle all at once, you know." One of those busily decorated arms reached out to me casually, in an apparent attempt to tap my shoulder consolingly.

"Don't touch me—" I gasped, ducking away from his reaching hand. But I leaned too far, and started to slide backward off the fallen tree. Grasping a branch that dangled to my right, I managed to steady myself quickly, and with my other hand on the rough trunk, I smoothly swung my legs over to the far side of the tree. Nothing, however, seems to pan out exactly as planned, and true to that sentiment, my new position had a branch that pressed into my upper back and prevented me from standing upright, so I was forced to bow forward awkwardly. *Great. Really smooth,* I thought, embarrassed.

Without looking, I twisted, reached behind me and grasped the offending branch, hoping to snap it off so that I could stand properly. Thankfully, it broke easily. With one hand, I made a motion to toss it casually to the side, but the branch felt like it was snagged. Casual was out, then. I glanced back to determine the source of the problem, and my heart jumped into my throat. In my hand was an impossibly long limb that I had ripped with freakish ease from the tree—its long branches twisting into the tree's withered green mass—and I was handling it as though it was no more than a twig. I dropped it quickly, turning to peer over the trunk at my surprised visitors.

"Anyone that can do *that* has my vote," the man said, sounding completely surprised. Without thinking, he reached over and offered me his hand. "I'm Maurice."

Hanna muscled her way in front of him and gave him a look; one that was laced with fondness, but appeared to scold him in an almost maternal way. "I don't think she wants us to touch her, Maurice.

175

Remember?" she gently chided. Hanna looked at me frankly and pursed her lip. "I'm Hanna and this is Tony," she said curtly. "Look, to be honest, I don't know if I believe you, but you have me spooked enough that I'm willing to talk about this a little more. Will you talk?"

"That's why I came here, Hanna," I said. "And I'm Kali." I nodded to them, keeping myself on the other side of the tree. Maybe they would be safe if they didn't touch me.

"Why can't you take us to the caves?" Tony asked me directly.

I took a deep breath and explained that one of the men would come to find me soon, and should he find me with them, everyone would probably be killed. Their eyes widened at this, and I saw Hanna grab and squeeze Tony's hand in silent communication.

"It's still important that you take us then," Tony said, his voice resigned. "If these men are goin' to track us down, I'd rather not be wanderin' around lost, blindly searching for these caverns of yours. Time's a factor, right?"

"We'd rather have you take us straight there, Kali." Hanna interjected. "We know there's a lot more going on here than you're divulging, so if you won't tell us, I'd rather at least have you with us."

"But you might be fine for weeks—even months—before they decide to come after you," I protested. "That's plenty of time to get to the caves. But this man I told you about will come and find me *soon*; guaranteed. Really—you don't want to be anywhere near me then. And I don't know how soon he'll show up. It's too great a risk for you."

"If you'd just agree to take us yourself, I know I can convince everyone to go," Tony said. "Please consider that."

I bit my lip and rubbed the bandages that covered my torn palms, the memories of Eric's graying corpse flashing across my mind. If they dug in and refused to go anywhere, they would certainly die ... it was just a matter of time. I would have to take the chance...

"I'll take you."

"Okay," Maurice said, looking pleased, if a little anxious. "Good. We'll talk to them. I'm sure we can get them to agree to leave at first light. Don't you think?" he asked, glancing over at Tony.

"Yeah. She's got 'em scared enough that they'll wanna have a look around." Tony shifted uncomfortably as he said this, darting his eyes from side to side and making it clear that he felt exactly the same way. "Come on, we'd better get started," he told them, beginning to walk off.

Hanna lingered behind a moment and looked at me appraisingly. "I think it'd be better if you stayed away for now, Kali," she informed me. "Just so we can talk to them."

I agreed. "I'll meet you again at first light," I said, wanting to get away. "Good luck."

I felt like I was endangering them every moment I was near. I turned abruptly and weaved my way out of the surrounding tree branches, then walked as casually as I could toward the stream. The camp disappeared behind the embankment, and little by little, my fists unclenched with each passing step. Glancing down, I could see that Tiamat's white bandages were now stained a dirty red.

* * *

It was still very dark when I awoke, and something wasn't quite right; I could hear Hero stamping and blowing nervously, and the jingle of Paris shaking her head in agitation. There was other movement too: the sound of hushed footsteps across the dirt, moving in the direction of the horses. It couldn't be Tiamat, I realized with mixed relief, as the horses both seemed comfortable around him, and wouldn't be fussing as they were.

The steps changed direction now, and sounded like they were coming toward me, deliberate and slow. I opened my eyes and stared into the empty darkness, the soft footfalls approaching from behind me, and wished that I was lying on my other side so I could see the intruder. I let my eyes adjust to the murky dark as I slowly reached for the knife at my belt. But my hand found nothing, and I remembered with a jolt that I had left all my weapons on the horses when I went up to the village, and hadn't re-armed myself before lying down to sleep.

"Who's there?" I called out, my voice causing the footsteps to stop abruptly.

There was no response.

I flipped around as fast as I could and found myself staring straight into my own crossbow, held at the ready by a familiar shadowy form. It was Greg—the one that Eric had said killed a man in a dispute over some food; the man with the weaselish face, sharp tongue and angry glare. But it was his friend that I found more dangerous overall, the tall, calculating man with the silken voice that directed and controlled from the background. I could see him, standing in the shadows well behind Greg, watching the scene with that slight twist of amusement to his lips. His expression now—as earlier today—just seemed wrong, and sent chills of revulsion down my spine.

"It would have been better to kill you in your sleep," Greg hissed. "Easier for me and easier for you."

I stood up slowly; keeping my eyes glued to his, and hoping his nerve would falter.

"Why'd you have to wake up, you stupid bitch?" His hands were shaking, and I could see the sweat begin to gleam on his forehead.

"Even if you kill me, I'm sure the group will still go," I told him, trying to make my voice clear and strong. "I told Tony how to get to the caves last night, so he doesn't need me to show him the way," I said, hoping he wouldn't see through the lie. "He sounded pretty determined to leave no matter what, so you'd be killing me for nothing."

"You're wrong, sweetheart." Greg smiled despite the evidence of his wavering nerve, and seemed buoyed by my misunderstanding. "You think I give a shit about what those losers do? I'd be happier if they left—Richard and I could have this whole area and the shelters to ourselves. With these horses and this nice loot you have here, I think I'd be pretty comfortable."

"So ... you're *robbing* me?"

"Actually, I'm gonna kill you. What do you care what I do with your stuff afterwards?" He grinned evilly, but the sweat was running down his temples and his dark weasel eyes kept darting around, as though seeking an escape.

"Look," I reasoned, "if you just leave me with my knife, you can take the rest; the horses ... everything. You have my word that I won't cause a problem for you. We'll all be leaving at first light anyway. There's no need to kill me."

Greg paused and licked his lips nervously, frozen by indecision. "You're trying to trick me. I ... I can't trust you." The crossbow was beginning to shake, and he tightened his grip on it.

"Of course you cannot trust her," purred the tall man from the shadows. "Listening to her would be a mistake, Greg. You are smarter than that. How do you think she gathered all of this equipment in the first place? Trickery, I'm sure. She fooled some other poor sods—just like she's now trying to trick everyone here out of their shelters—she's just looking for a nice, cozy place to live. But now you can be the smarter one. Kill her, and you will beat her at her little game. Let her live, and she will probably kill you in your sleep."

*Shit, shit, shit...*I thought, casting around desperately for something compelling to say. "That's not true—" I started.

But as I spoke, Greg aimed the crossbow and stepped forward, practically jamming the thing down my throat, while Richard chuckled low and said casually, "Remember my warning, Greg. Do not get too close or you'll be a dead man. And if you touch her—"

"What did you say?" I blurted, blindsided.

Greg, however, wasn't listening to either of us. With a wild look in his eyes, he pressed the end of the bow onto my cheek, and I saw him steel himself for the squeeze of the trigger. He was going to do it.

Without thinking, I bashed the crossbow away with my left arm, feeling something sharp tear painfully across my cheek, ducked, and punched Greg squarely in the diaphragm. Winded, he doubled over immediately, and I grabbed the back of his head, brought my knee up sharply, and cracked him in the face with it. Thankfully, while I was doing this, I managed to keep my body in control, and ensure I didn't use too much force on my weaker adversary. I didn't want to kill him.

With Greg now disarmed and stunned, I grasped him by the shoulders and flung him away like a rag doll. He tumbled in the dirt, and raised his blood soaked face with a look of fury in his eyes. "You *bitch*," he hissed, rearing himself up like a cornered animal.

It had to end here. I scooped up the fallen crossbow and pointed it at him, glancing around warily for Richard. But he appeared to be gone.

"Your friend deserted you," I told him. "You're on your own."

Greg looked around wildly, but didn't appear to see Richard either. His bloodied face fell, and he instantly looked defeated and frightened.

"Go back to the camp, Greg, and I'll forget about what happened here."

"Right, like I'm going to go with *them*; wandering around looking for some fictional caves while I slowly starve to death. I'm not that stupid," he said, snorting back some of the blood that flowed from his nose. "I'm staying around here. And once you've gotten rid of those gullible idiots, you'll have to fight me for the shelters if you want them. But we'll do it straight up—no weapons and none of your dirty tricks."

"I'm not coming back," I told his retreating form. "You'll die if you stay, Greg. I'm telling you the truth."

But Greg had gone. And as I stared after him into the surrounding gloom, a niggling thought about Richard surfaced in my mind. Unlike every other man at the camp, Richard, I realized, had no facial hair.

Chapter 16

I lay awake for what seemed like hours after the men disappeared—
my crossbow at my side and my blade returned to my belt—and
finally fell into a restless, disorienting sleep a fathomless time later.
The past few days had been grinding me down, and a heavy weariness
inevitably dragged me into the consuming depths of slumber.

And like every other night, when I slipped into oblivion, my sub-
conscious cruelly returned me to Tiamat's arms. We were sitting in the
sun near the precipice of Lookout Peak; Tiamat rested with his back
against a large boulder, and I sat reclining against his chest, feeling the
warmth of his arms enclose me. Everything was as it should have been;
spread out below us was the familiar green swath of healthy, sturdy
trees, bejewelled intermittently by sparkling, sapphire-blue lakes.
They were, I thought, almost the exact color of Tiamat's eyes.

I felt him gently kiss the top of my head, and relished the sensation of his energy tickling its way down my spine. "I need to tell you
something, Kali," he murmured into my hair.

"Mmm," I answered, closing my eyes and leaning my head back
against him.

"You need to abandon this plan of yours." He lightly stroked my
hair, and his voice sounded thoughtful. "You know full well that if I
catch you, it will force my hand. You already hate me enough as it is."

"I don't hate you," I answered without hesitation. "I love you."

"And loving me is even worse." Tiamat slowly ran his hands down my sides, and let them linger at the small of my back. "That is why it is far too easy to make you miserable," he whispered into my ear. "You need to wake up and realize this." And as he spoke those last words, Tiamat gave me a hard shove, sending me tumbling off the edge of the cliff.

I sat bolt upright in the velvet silence of deep night, a fresh knife of betrayal sharp in my chest, and the slow march of tears sliding warmly down my cheeks. *Don't concern yourself, Tiamat,* I thought earnestly. *I already loathe you from the depths of my being. I doubt it's possible to despise you more.* Gritting my teeth in frustration, I scrubbed my knuckles across my forehead, working to physically banish any lingering vestiges from the dream.

Please leave me alone, I moaned as I flopped back down onto my cold earthen bed; it would be a trying day tomorrow, and I was already grossly lacking in sleep. I would have to get some rest. I closed my tear-blurred eyes, and let the darkness overtake me once again.

It felt like I had been out for only a matter of minutes when a warm, glowing light touched upon my face. I relished the feel of it; having always enjoyed waking up to the first rays of dawn touching my eyelids like a morning kiss. I wondered—in a muddled, half-asleep sort of way—how long it had been since I was awakened this way. But there was something I was missing in that reflection—something about the sunlight ... about the world—and with that same fraying will that had miraculously propelled me this far, I laboriously dragged my consciousness back to the surface.

As I did each morning, I gave myself a minute to get oriented, went over what I knew had happened to our planet, and made myself accept this new reality before I opened my eyes to face it. And now there was a new puzzle to consider; wasn't this altered world indefinitely shaded? I tentatively opened my eyes and blinked in disbelief, gazing through a straggly stand of saplings at the radiant arc of the sun, flaring gloriously over the horizon.

I was stunned. It was one of the most beautiful sights I had ever seen; striking in its own right, its colors blazed across the surrounding clouds and haze, painting everything in gold, crimson and vibrant orange. But it was wondrous also, in that it was like a forbidden visitor, blasting into our dreary prison, once morosely enclosed by incessant walls of cloud. I remembered that Tiamat had spoken as though the sun would be blocked out for months—even years—plunging the planet into a dark, cold hell. I didn't think I'd ever lay eyes on it again.

I stood up, dreamlike, and wandered to the edge of the sparse stand of brush, staring in awe at the gift of beauty before me. But then, almost like a curtain was being drawn, the brilliant orb was obscured again, and the land returned to its muted gray.

Yet deep within me, a smoldering warmth remained. I hurriedly packed the crossbow, untethered the horses, and mounted Hero with a flash of optimism in my heart. For the first time in what felt like ages, I believed there was a chance. For all of us.

When I arrived at the camp, I could see a large group of people milling around the cold fire pit, looking excited and anxious. The children were there also, and off to the side someone was laid out on what looked like an impromptu stretcher. The assembly silenced immediately when they noticed me ride up from the stream, and they stared with childlike openness between me, my horses, and the gear on Paris' back.

I rode up to them, heartened by their ready appearance, and dismounted before speaking. "I can't tell you how relieved I am that so many of you have agreed to come," I said with sincerity. "And I'm willing to share everything that I have with you; including use of the horses."

"I *told* you the sunrise was a good sign, cockroach," Maurice beamed, tousling the dark hair on the small olive-skinned boy, who stood beside him looking rather wide-eyed at my appearance.

I gave what I hoped was a reassuring smile as I walked past them, on my way toward the stretcher. Bundled onto it was a middle-aged man; thin, glassy-eyed and fevered. Hanna was on his opposite side, securing loose fastenings on the rickety stretcher and sighing as she did so.

"I hope this holds him," she muttered, shaking her head dubiously.

I knelt down and checked his pulse. It was weak, but steady. "I have some rope and leather strapping that we can use if these supports start to give out," I told her. "But I think we'd better get going for now. We can always reinforce this later." The stretcher looked passable, and with any luck, would serve us until nightfall.

Hanna nodded. "I can't imagine he'll put too much strain on it, he's so light now," she sighed. "I'm afraid we're going to lose him soon. He was already injured when Eric found him, but it wasn't as serious as this. Every day, he's been getting worse, and there hasn't been a damned thing we could do about it."

I could see the man's problem plainly. His swollen legs were battered and twisted, wrapped in ripped, blood-soaked cloth, and so inflamed that his ballooning skin was straining tight against its wrappings. Yet it was the odor that was the worst; the reek of festering flesh, thick and putrid in the still air. The legs would have to be amputated if we were to have any hope of saving him, but even that was impossible. I didn't have the expertise or the instruments that would be necessary for such an operation. And even if I did, it was unlikely he would be strong enough to survive it. All we could do at this point, I realized, was to try to offer him what small comfort we could—and this trip would be the farthest thing from that.

I sighed and worked to loosen the straining bandages, feeling Hanna's eyes watching me critically. "It seems a shame to put him through all this." I could hear the regret in my voice, and as I spoke, the man's eyes slid in my direction, focusing with obvious clarity. "I'm sorry," I told him. "It's my fault you're being moved."

"Forget it. We should thank you. Don't apologize." He was breathing shallowly, and seemed to expend a great deal of energy for speech. "I'm going to die soon anyway. I can't let them ... stay here on my account."

"Thank you." I gently placed my hand on his burning, sunken cheek; the only comfort I could give the poor man. "And I *am* sorry, all the same."

The man's eyes closed. "It's okay," he assured me, his body relaxing and voice growing quiet. "Your hand feels ... so strange. Like it's ... buzzing..."

Hanna's head jerked up and her eyes narrowed in speculation. "Why—?"

I didn't wait for her to finish, but jumped up like I had been burned. How could I have been so careless? In my haste to check on and comfort the man, I completely forgot about maintaining my distance. But Tiamat wouldn't bother showing up to kill *this* man, would he? It wouldn't be long until he was dead anyway, considering the poor man's condition. Perhaps I needn't be concerned in this case.

And then, what was it the man said about my hands? I wondered, gazing at them critically. He said they were *buzzing*!

"Why couldn't Maurice touch you yesterday?" Hanna asked me sharply, jerking me out of my shocked deductions.

I hesitated, not certain I should articulate my suspicions at this point—I didn't even know if my fears of contact were anything more than mere paranoia. "I don't know, really," I answered slowly, thinking it over. "In trying to be safe, I could be seeing risks where there are none. As for contact with me, I'm worried that ... something, um... bad ... might happen if anyone touches me. There might not be any danger in it at all, but I can't say for certain. It's just a precaution."

Yet as I said those words, a creeping feeling of horror uncoiled from my spine as visions of last night's encounter with Greg resurfaced. Without a doubt, I had touched him, too.

"What is it?" Hanna asked, alarmed. The change in my face must have been telling.

"Have you seen Greg this morning?" I asked, attempting to sound casual while my heart hammered in my ears. "Or Richard?"

"No. Why? What's happened?" Hanna stood, abandoning her work on the stretcher.

It's probably just a coincidence, I told myself. *He said last night that he was going to stay behind. That's why Greg's not here. Certainly Tiamat is still far away...* "It's nothing, Hanna. Sorry to alarm you," I told her. "Greg told me that he and Richard didn't trust me and weren't planning to go. I was just wondering if either of them changed their minds."

"We're putting a lot of faith in you, Kali." Tony walked over to join Hanna, and had obviously been following our conversation. "I know you're trying t' help us, but there's so much you're not sayin'." He looked at me evenly, but when I didn't offer anything more, he added, "We need t' get going, right? So perhaps we can discuss this some more along the way?"

I nodded. "We have to cover as much ground as possible today, so I'll be taking you a more direct route—away from the stream. We'll meet back up with it before noon, but it'll be a good hike before we see water again." I paused only briefly before continuing. I would have no choice but to show them. "Everyone should drink some water first. Then we can go."

"I've already had some of that swamp water, Kali," Maurice said pleasantly. "I'll meet everyone back up here."

"Please come with us anyway," I called over my shoulder, leading the majority of the group to the stream's edge. There was a strange confidence to my voice that I felt was grossly unfounded. "You just may change your mind about the water, Maurice."

* * *

The morning's exodus was charged and tense. I kept a constant, nervous watch upon the muted skies, expecting one of the Nephilim to appear at any moment. And though the group worked to match the brisk pace I insisted upon, it never felt fast enough. The feeling of raw exposure consistently prickled across my skin, and wouldn't dissipate.

And to top it off, the group was buzzing like a hive as we traveled. Despite this, however, I felt like I was trapped in a personal bubble of silence. Every time I drifted near someone, the pervasive whispering would stop, and an anxious quiet would prevail. Most people wouldn't meet my eyes, and kept their own downcast when I looked at them. I wasn't sure how I had expected them to act after they witnessed what I could do to the water—but I certainly didn't anticipate this show of outright fear. At least, not directed at me.

Tony and I—separately, and without communicating directly—ensured that the children and those in the group that were flagging took turns riding Hero, and I would walk the skittish horse with his reins in hand if the rider was the least bit inexperienced. This proved to be the majority of the riders, but I didn't mind. I found it calming to walk with my old equine companion, and welcomed the relief from the surreptitious stares and speculative whispers. Besides, my presence also helped to keep Paris' antics in check, who seized—literally—every opportunity to trot up to Hero's unsuspecting riders and attempt to chomp down on their fleshy thighs. Apparently, the fleshier the thigh, the greater the appeal.

When managing the horses wasn't necessary, I would busy myself by carrying one end of the stretcher. At first, the men who were taking turns hauling it chivalrously refused my offers of help, but when I insisted, they then agreed with embarrassing deference.

"Trust me. I'm not anyone special," I had tried to tell them. But they wouldn't even meet my eyes, so I let it rest for the time being. Now wasn't the time to explain to everyone what was happening. Not yet. We had far too much ground to cover, and I couldn't risk slowing our progress for anything.

The stretcher's makeshift handles—which were simply the elongated ends of the two main support branches—were splintered and jagged, and I had to ensure that I didn't accidentally catch myself against the sharp slivers of wood. This wasn't too difficult. Like Hanna had feared, the stretcher was morbidly light; the poor man had wasted to little more than skin and bones. He dozed in a fitful, fevered sleep, and appeared so incredibly out of touch that I began to doubt if I really did hear him speak to me that very morning.

Nellie, throughout our hours of travel, said nothing, but appeared infuriatingly smug. In the early afternoon, she was, as I grudgingly expected, the one that approached me first. The young woman that wore the tattered business attire had mounted Hero and was managing both horses relatively well, so I had just relinquished the lead and had started back toward the stretcher. Not five paces away, however, Nellie intercepted me.

"I've been watchin' them," she wheezed conspiringly, waving her arm at the ragged group. "All of 'em. Not a holy bone to be found in the whole stinkin' lot. Except for me. And maybe Richard. He knows the bible, that one." I looked at her sharply but apparently oblivious to my reaction, she plowed on. "I would make a great judge. You know, to help on Judgment Day. You tell Him. I judge others all the time."

"Next time I see Him, I'll be sure to pass that on," I said blandly, and with a nod to end the conversation, I increased my pace, intending to join Tony at the front of the group. The sooner I distanced myself from Nellie, the slimmer the chance I would say something that I'd regret. Besides, I needed to speak to Tony. During the last few minutes, it had seemed like we were losing momentum, and with that, my fear of discovery heightened exponentially.

"We don't have much time, Tony," I said as I reached him. "Please don't slow down."

"Showin' us that thing with the water this morning was smart, Kali. It's the only reason we've kept this pace for as long as we have." He stopped walking altogether and turned to face me directly, swaying slightly where he stood. "We're all half-starved. No one's had a drink or even a rest for almost seven hours. We'll start dropping soon, you know. Awe of you will take us no further."

Embarrassed, I ducked my head in acquiescence, and could feel my cheeks flush with heat. "I'm … I'm sorry…" I stammered. "I'm just so afraid of what will happen if we're found. I wasn't thinking—"

"I understand. But if we don't rest, we won't be able t' go any further at all. Most of us have nothin' left."

"Okay, Tony. But can we just push on to the stream? We're nearly there."

He looked at me evenly, and I glanced back to see that everyone was already sprawled in exhausted heaps on the ground, having sat or collapsed in the brief moments since Tony and I stopped walking. I realized that it would be pointless to try to get them back to their feet now. He was right; we wouldn't cover another inch until they'd rested a moment.

I sent Tony and Hanna around with my two canteens, leaving them to distribute the water as fairly as they could. Trying to conjure up images of the food I had to hand, I remembered that there was a large bag of trail mix in one of the sacks on Paris' back. It would be easy to share out, and thankfully required no preparation. Retrieving the mix, I pressed Maurice to pass it out, leaving me free from accidental contact with any of the people in our ragged little group.

News of the coming snack, meager as it was, undulated through the wilting party like a rogue current. The anticipation became almost tangible, animating each person like the tightening strings on a fallen puppet. This short break, then, would cost us little in lost time. In fact, I hoped this fresh wind of energy might be sufficient to get us moving in short order.

As might be expected, it didn't take long for the group to finish off their small portions of trail mix and water, which allowed me to begin packing back up almost immediately. The party looked tired but luckily remained animated; they could be mobilized immediately, I realized with relief.

"How much farther till we get t' the stream, Kali?" Tony asked as I secured the empty canteens to Paris' back. He looked exhausted, and I wondered if he gave away his share of food and water, like I had. Actually, I didn't doubt it. And chances were high that Maurice and Hanna did the same.

"It's hard to tell." I scanned the landscape to try to glean some clue as to our exact location. From following the gurgling waters on my way south, I knew that the stream curved in a wide arc. Instead of having the group trudge along the deep, long curve, we were cutting across land to save time. I had been careful to ensure we were always travelling toward the stream, though the necessity of circumnavigating gaping crevasses and masses of heaved rock and earth lengthened our trip more than I had expected. Still, we had to be close now. "We'll be there soon," I said to him kindly. "You look like you could use a drink."

He barked a tired laugh. "Yeah, and a good stiff one, too. Now if you could do *that* with the water, I'd be really impressed."

It turned out that we had been very close indeed. Not twenty minutes later, we arrived at the stream, and everyone all but lunged into the water in relief. Then, after the group was satiated, and after a great deal of prodding and coaxing, they finally picked themselves up from the muddy banks and forced themselves to continue on along the path of the river—though it was at a much reduced pace.

We made camp close to nightfall, when most people had become little more than the walking dead. Fires were made, and I set a few of the group to the task of making bannock and heating water to reconstitute some dehydrated packets of chili. Needless to say, dinner was appreciated, though many of them seemed akin to slathering wolves surrounding a fallen deer, their hollow eyes sharp on my movements as I kept them from lunging upon the cooking food. And when they finally ate, it was like standing in a circle of animals; simple creatures who, through necessity, had completely surrendered to one of their basest needs. It was almost beautiful, in a raw sort of way, and heartbreaking.

* * *

"So tell us," Tony said quietly, "tell us everything you can." The fire was burning low, a lean stew simmering for tomorrow's breakfast over its glowing coals. The majority of the group was sprawled about, having fallen asleep shortly after finishing dinner and variations of low snores and deep breathing hovered in the evening air. Tony's eyes were rimmed with red, as were Hanna's and Maurice's, but none of them showed the slightest inclination to retire yet.

I knew, as did they, that they were ready to hear the truth. After seeing what I could do to the water, believing the rest of it wouldn't be too much of a stretch, I supposed. Though I knew that wasn't the real issue anymore. They needed answers; craved to know what was happening, even if that meant having to face an unbelievable and devastating truth.

So, only leaving out the details of my intimacy with Tiamat, I told them. I told them everything.

Chapter 17

Tony, Hanna and Maurice took the news far better than I had, though I supposed they were better prepared to hear it. They had survived for weeks seeing no indication that any civilization still existed. There was hope of rescue, of course, shortly after the disaster, but as time wore on, expectations thinned. They knew something was wrong, and tried to send out scouts to see if any information could be gleaned from exploring the surrounding wasteland. Eric had been the only one to volunteer, preferring action and solitude over remaining close to camp in the anticipation that help might arrive. And through his forays, it became clear that not only was there no sign of any rescue efforts, there was likely no one else that was alive in the area. The group was getting increasingly anxious, their hope nearly extinguished, when I had arrived.

Then, after witnessing the impossible with the fouled water at the stream that morning, they had the entire day to mull over what I had initially told them about the extent of the disaster. So when the time came that I finally revealed what I knew, the three of them were calm, inquisitive and rather grave. Though they did not immediately accept everything I relayed—shifting uncomfortably and shooting wary glances at each other when I told them of the Nephilim—as my story progressed, a cautious acceptance of this reality appeared to progress along with it.

"We'll need t' tell the rest of 'em tomorrow. Perhaps over breakfast, so we don't waste travelin' time over it." Tony's voice was quiet and resigned, and together with his solemn expression, I had a startling image of him speaking condolences to friends at a wake. Hanna's hand was clasped tightly in his, and Tony hadn't let go of it since we began our conversation.

"They'll have lots of questions," Hanna sighed, fixing her stare on their linked fingers. "It'll take too long to tell them all this. Even now, I feel like a sitting duck." She shivered visibly and raised her eyes to meet mine. "You think we should be moving already, don't you, Kali? I can see it in your expression, and could read it in the way you told us of all this. And my nerves are telling me the same thing. But we really have to wait for morning. Someone could get hurt or killed if we attempt it in this dark. However," she added, looking into Tony's face, "we'll need to be ready to go as soon as it's light enough to see. We shouldn't waste a moment."

Maurice had been staring silently into the darkening coals, their light and warmth leaching out into the surrounding black. "I know it will cost us time, Hanna" he said quietly. "But they still must be told." He picked up a stick and stirred the coals, their dark forms bursting forth into a swirl of hot, orange fireflies. "Just think; as soon as everyone understands what's coming, we'll probably be hard pressed to keep them from stampeding from the camp. We might even make better time than yesterday." He looked around at us, and smiled at Hanna. "But yes, let's be completely packed and ready to go by first light. Then, as soon as they're told, we can go."

Once this was decided, we finally lay down to sleep. Hanna trudged off to do the first watch over Carl, which, I learned, was the name of the unfortunate man in the stretcher. Sadly, he had not regained consciousness since that morning. We also agreed that the person on watch would need to keep an eye out for any Nephilim, though if one of them should show up, there would be little any of us could do.

As we had decided to take turns with the watch, I was surprised when I woke up the next morning and realized that no one had roused me in the night to take over their shift. I scrubbed a hand over my face and slowly stood up, glancing around the silent, slumbering camp. Carl lay upon his stretcher a short distance away, and appeared to have died sometime since last evening. His skin was very pale, and blowflies were already swarming over his open eyes and mouth.

I picked my way toward him, stepping around various sprawled, sleeping limbs, trying not to wake anyone unnecessarily. Tony, Maurice and Hanna didn't appear to be anywhere nearby, and I assumed that they must be off somewhere, trying to decide what to do about Carl's body. It would be best to bury him, of course, but everyone could lose their lives if we didn't get to the caves fast enough. Perhaps we'd have time if they had already started digging...

Crouching down beside his body, I reached over to gingerly lift his wrist, but found that his arm was already stiffening. No need to check for a pulse, then. He had a shredded rag that partially covered his prone torso, and I used it to brush the insects away from his face before closing his empty, staring eyes with my hand. As I spread the cloth gently over his sunken features, I wondered why one of the others didn't think to cover him like this before walking off. In fact, why didn't they think to move his body out of the campsite? It seemed a little out of character for them to leave Carl in the middle of everyone like this; a shocking, morbid greeting for the early risers.

With no one else awake or nearby to help me, I forwent the stretcher and picked Carl up as if he were a child, slipping one arm under his back and the other behind his legs. His stiffening muscles kept his corpse taught and rendered his slight, wasted remains relatively easy to lift. However, holding his body in front of me made it difficult to see my feet—rendering navigating my way around the many sleeping forms a torturously slow process. Flies were hovering all around us, buzzing and landing on his body and crawling on my arms, face and neck. And together with the swarming insects and the fact that I had never carried a corpse before, I had to fight with my desire to step on and run right over anyone in my path in order to clear the camp and be rid of him. But I had almost made it around the fleshy obstacles, and after enduring a few more unshakably long moments, I was finally able to walk freely.

Like many of the mounds of upturned soil and rock I had seen in my past weeks of travel, there was a particularly large embankment of heaved earth looming at the far side of the camp. I headed straight toward it, intending to use it as a partition between his corpse and the sleeping group. In fact, if the soil was soft enough from being churned up, it might be relatively easy to bury him within it, I thought. I set him down behind the gigantic mound, and pressed my foot into the mountain of raw soil. Just as I expected, it was soft and yielding, sliding and crumbling beneath the mild pressure from my boot. Despite the fact that it wasn't an ideal grave site, if the others hadn't already prepared something more suitable, this one would have to do under the circumstances.

I left Carl where he was, and went off in search of Hanna, Maurice and Tony. I felt certain that I would find them by the stream, and as I strode quickly toward the gurgling chatter of its waters, I wondered how each of them had slept. Despite their fatigue, were any of them able to drift off after hearing all I'd said? If they hadn't, that would likely explain why no one had roused me to take over their watch. But this was bothersome. Today would be another physically exhausting day, and was likely to be emotionally draining as well. Slogging through it after having no sleep would surely stretch them to their limits. And considering that they were likely at the stream now, splashing a good dose of cold water on their faces might be a good start...

When I reached the bank, however, I was surprised to find it deserted. I had been almost certain that they would be here—there were few other possibilities. Besides the large hillock behind which I left Carl, there was little more than open wasteland that stretched for a good distance in all directions. The landscape had numerous chasms and incredibly uneven ground, but one would likely need to enter a crevasse or crouch behind an embankment to keep out of sight. I could think of no reason why they would do that. So then, where were they?

Trying to remain calm, I knelt by the water's edge and used wet sand to scrub where Carl's corpse had rested upon my hands and arms, while feelings of panic squeezed like metal bands tightening around my chest. I had to search around more thoroughly, I told myself. Surely I was simply overlooking something. I briskly rinsed the sand from my arms and immediately started a quick circuit of the camp. Looking over the group's sleeping forms, I not only confirmed that they were indeed absent, but with a shock, I also discovered that the small, dark haired boy was missing as well.

The burgeoning panic immediately welled up and surged through my veins. I dashed to the far side of the hillock and, standing over Carl's body, scanned the surrounding wasteland for any sign of them.

"Tony!" I called, heedless of the sleeping group behind me. "Hanna! Maurice, where are you?" There was no response but the soft, background murmurs of a waking camp.

Running over to where Hero and Paris were tethered, I looked around in all directions, but could see nothing. There didn't appear to be any supplies missing from the sacks that I had left in a pile near the horses, and my crossbow was exactly where I had left it. If they had indeed deserted us in the night, why had they not taken any supplies with them? It didn't add up.

I hastily threw the saddle on Hero, and was up and riding before anyone in the group had a chance to ask me what was wrong. With my pulse thundering in my ears, I pushed the horse, leapt over crevasses and rode hard in a wide circle around the camp, scouring both sides of the stream and looking fiercely for anything that might indicate where they had gone. But after a thorough, fruitless scout of the countryside,

I began to slow my pace, the gravity of what may have transpired sinking in like a corrosive poison.

"Tiamat!" I screamed, my voice laced with venom. "What have you done with them? Where are they?" I turned the horse and scanned the gray skies, but could see nothing. "Show yourself, you son-of-a-bitch!"

And he did.

Tiamat appeared as a speck on the western horizon, growing larger by the second as he neared our location. And all around him, pacing his approach and stretching wide across the sky, rolled towering black clouds, thick and heavy with impending rain.

With my heart hammering in my chest, I kicked Hero into motion and raced back to the camp, watching Death approach on silent wings. He was incredibly fast—we reached the camp at almost the same moment—Tiamat, a vulture circling overhead while I thundered in like a conquering soldier.

There was a loud clang as the stew pot fell and splattered into the dirt, the group's hunger forgotten under awe of this heavenly sign. They stood frozen, gawking at Tiamat in wonder and ignorance. Obviously unaware of the danger they faced, they looked expectantly at him, believing perhaps, that mercy would come from above.

It did not. Like a warning, rain began to fall in a steady drizzle. It gathered and beaded on our upturned faces, and dripped from Tiamat's wings and body as he circled overhead.

I watched him closely, my limbs shaking from anger and adrenalin. Keeping my eyes glued to his still passive movements, I slid from Hero's saddle and scooped up the crossbow—Tiamat's crossbow, actually. But while I loaded a bolt and cocked it, Tiamat matched my ante and calmly pulled out a knife. I was confused by this move at first. He could kill us in any number of ways; quickly and effortlessly. Why put himself at risk by resorting to a blade? Yet perhaps, I thought, he had to avoid harming me if I was meant to fulfill some purpose. I hoped that was indeed true. It could prove to be the only defense this group had.

I moved to the center of the throng, trying to protect the others by maintaining a simple proximity to them. "Keep close to me," I told them. "He's come here to kill us." A few of the group moved in toward me, but most looked at me like I was insane. Nellie and the tattered-looking business woman, whose name I had learned was Jennifer, actually stepped a few paces away, as if to show this celestial being that they did not share my sentiment.

"Damn it," I muttered under my breath. What was I to do? Did they think he was going to *bless* them with his knife? "If you want to slaughter them, you'll have to kill me too!" I shouted at him. My hands shaking, I aimed the crossbow up into the drizzle.

Tiamat didn't respond and made no move toward us, but instead brought the edge of the knife to his bared wrist. He held it there for a moment, appearing to exert pressure with the blade, and I lowered the crossbow in shock. "Tiamat, don't..." I gasped.

With a swift, violent movement, he slashed his left wrist deeply and the blood pumped out like a river, running down his arm as he held his gashed limb above his head. Wasting no time, Tiamat flew straight up into the drizzling sky, gaining height at an incredible speed. Then he ceased flying and immediately began tumbling downward, plummeting as he deliberately smeared the gore from his wrist across the feathers of his right wing. At the last moment, he pulled out of the free fall and swooped above our heads, scattering bloody water droplets onto our upturned faces.

"Oh ... *oh shit*!" I cried, realizing what he was doing. There was something with his blood ... what was it about his blood? I raised the crossbow again, watching as he tightly bound his wounded left wrist while he circled us, flinging blood from his wings with every beat. I had to shoot him ... I *had* to...

My hands were slippery on the crossbow and my eyes blurred with tears. With quick, angry swipes, I dragged my arm across my eyes to clear them, and tried to aim again. I had him in my sights; he was about to slice into his right wrist—all I had to do was pull the trigger. I could feel the tears running freely now as a sob escaped my throat. The crossbow shook, but I fought to hold it steady, and focused my aim at his chest, the only way I could be sure...

I began to squeeze the trigger just as he finished his cut, and I saw him grit his teeth against the pain of it. That was all it took; anguish stabbed through me like a red-hot spike, robbing me of the last of my resolve. My finger froze on the trigger, and I dropped the crossbow on the ground before I could fire. I couldn't do it, I just couldn't. My chest squeezed tight and I doubled over, listening to the sound of the sobs escaping from my throat. The ground seemed to come up beneath me as I sat down heavily, and I put my head onto my knees in misery while Tiamat bathed us in his blood.

I didn't know for certain when it was that Tiamat left, though the rain ceased shortly after I failed in my resolve to stop him; when I had dropped to the ground like a spineless rag doll. Despite the panic that reigned around me for some time afterward, I knew that Tiamat had likely cleared off before the rain did. From my prone state, I had heard voices begging God for mercy and crying in confusion. Some muttered lifelessly that they were going down to the stream to wash, while others simply prayed. I felt someone's hand shaking my shoulder, and looked up to see Nellie hovering over me, still streaked in watery blood, and with an expression that was dark with anger.

"Didn't you speak to Him?" she demanded of me. "I should've been taken as a judge! I always knew I was to be a judge when the time came. You cheated me! You sent your no-good friends instead!"

I looked at her blankly, not able to fix upon what she meant.

"Didn't you hear me, you bitch?" she snarled, sticking her face close to mine. "I shouldn't be here right now! I was to be taken in the Rapture! Not Hanna! Not Tony! And certainly not that joker, Maurice, or the useless *child*! A *child*, Kali! You suggested a child over *me*?! What kind of a judge could a *boy* be? Useless! You're a god-damned whore and a cheat, Kali," she spat. "If I were a judge, I'd make you rot in hell!"

"Then it's a good thing I didn't recommend you," I muttered, turning over what she had said in my mind. It wasn't really a lie, I supposed.

I heard Nellie stomp off as I thought about the content of her tirade. Rapture... I had heard of that, though I wasn't certain what it was. It seemed as though it involved God taking people to be judges. That would fit with what Nellie said, but could that really be where they had gone? It seemed more likely that Tiamat had taken them. But if he hadn't, what other options were there? At least Nellie's version of events was more comforting to consider, even if I would sooner believe the delusions of a hardened criminal over any of her self-righteous rants.

I got up slowly, picked up the crossbow, and started back toward the horses. Amazingly, Hero, skittish as he was, hadn't wandered off. Not wanting to push my luck, I grabbed his lead and tethered him next to Paris. Both animals were shifting uneasily, surrounded as they were by the chaos of the camp, and I knew that the sooner we were moving, the better it would be for all of us.

After setting the crossbow down by my packs, I started toward the stream to wash Tiamat's blood from myself. I was afraid to imagine what the result of today's bloodbath would be. It was highly doubtful that these people would now share my ability to cleanse the taste of the fouled water, or realize increased strength. Whatever the outcome, I was certain it wouldn't be good.

There were a number of other people at the stream, their faces white with shock, washing themselves with either absent-minded, robotic movements or scouring with a similar preoccupied ferocity. I considered our situation as I joined them in the water, and began to scrub Tiamat's blood from my face and hair. Our flight now felt hopeless. After all, what was the point of hiding if your pursuer could just follow you to your hole, and then obliterate you once you were inside? But with a lack of other options, it still remained the only path for us to follow. What else could we do? *Perhaps*, I thought, *he's done with us for now. With luck, we might have time to make it to the caves before he returns.* As this seemed the only plausible course, I knew we would need to continue on as soon as possible.

While sparing the group a little time to recover from the shock, I busied myself with cleaning up the pot from the spilled stew, and packing and watering the horses for departure. Once this was done, I asked the group to assemble, and told them of the Nephilim.

My description was cursory and to the point, and without allowing a discussion on the matter, I continued the trek toward the cave. I lead Hero and Paris out of the camp, and as I hoped they would, the group followed. Then, only an hour into our journey, I realized that I had forgotten to bury Carl.

* * *

Randy, the tall, red-headed child, had been riding Hero for some time when he began to sway alarmingly. I hadn't been paying much attention to him, lost as I was in contemplation of our situation, and hadn't noticed the change in his skin and color. I stopped the horses the moment I saw him totter, and with concern, pulled the child down from saddle. But when I looked at the boy's face, I was shocked. What I had thought before was simply a rash had ballooned into large pustules that covered his face and neck. His skin was incredibly hot to the touch, and his eyes were glazed and staring.

I grabbed my canteen, and raised his head so I could pour a little water into his mouth. He coughed and sputtered, but otherwise seemed unaware of my presence.

"Randy," I said to him, sticking one of my sacks under his head to serve as a pillow. "Can you hear me?" But there was no indication that he had, and his eyes continued to stare sightlessly into the cloudy sky.

The rest of the group had assembled around us by that point, and stood looking down at the boy.

"We have to keep going," a man named Eugene put in, sounding anxious and afraid. "Can't we just carry him? Or tie him to the horse, maybe?"

I spun around in disgust, and noticed with horror that every single one of them had a bumpy red rash covering their necks and faces. I touched my own in alarm, but with a guilty relief, felt only smooth skin under my fingertips.

"We're going to make camp here," I said, trying to hide the desperation in my voice. The progression of symptoms from a minor rash to a serious illness happened remarkably fast in the boy. There would be no hope of making it to safety before the entire group became too ill to move. I estimated an hour, tops. This location would be as good as any then; we were close to the stream, and there were arches formed by the branches of fallen trees that would provide minimal shelter if it should rain. The screen of trees gave the illusion of cover and safety as well, though I knew in reality they would make no difference.

* * *

My scrap of cloth was full of blood. It smeared a streak of gore across Randy's pale skin as I attempted to wipe the sweat from his brow, and keep the red fluid from pooling in his eyes. I knew that I should stop trying to mop at him; it was impossible to do so without disturbing the virtual minefield of sores, many of which were now ooz-ing blood, seeping steadily like a flow of tears. It soaked the boy's clothes and hair, and now saturated my cloth. I would have to rinse it out, I knew, so then I could continue daubing his tender skin. There was nothing else I could do ... nothing...

I found myself at the stream then, watching Randy's blood cloud the water with red, as my tears blurred the image into a shimmering haze. There was no one else to help me—all the others were slumped around the site, suffering through the various stages of the illness. Everyone was now fevered, and had developed the pustules in varying degrees of severity. But they would all progress to the boy's stage, I knew. And I didn't know how to stop it; could do nothing but watch them slowly die.

I should have known better. They were here because of me; dying because of me. If they had stayed at their camp, they might have sur-vived longer, might even have gone unnoticed for a while. Perhaps when their time came, they would have experienced deaths that were faster than this. They might have even died painlessly. But not like this ... It was my fault they were dying like this ... Suffering to prove their worth or some sanctimonious bullshit like that. I keenly remembered Tiamat explaining to me why the Nephilim were ordered to leave some humans alive. He had spoken of adversity as being the catalyst that unveils either radiance or corruption; the vehicle through which survi-vors could prove their merit. But these people had suffered enough; it wasn't right that I went and led them into more misery. And to think that they trusted me...

I was lost in the grip of self-loathing when I felt the hair prickle on the back of my neck, and had an overwhelming notion that I was being watched. I quickly spun around to see a tall, lean fig-ure standing directly behind me. He still wore that annoying smirk, like he knew something that I didn't, and I could almost see it glow as he looked around at the sick that lay sprawled across the ground.

"Tisk, tisk, Kali," Richard said solemnly, sounding like he was reprimanding a naughty child. "Just look at what you have done."

Chapter 18

My mind went utterly blank. I stared at Richard, fury catching like a lump in my throat, while my mouth opened and closed in mute astonishment. "What ...?" was all I managed.

"Be kind now, my dear. I'm hurt that you don't appear happy to see me," he said in a smooth voice, "and I am *very* easily offended." He leaned forward at this, and his eyes took on a malicious gleam—eyes that were a muted gray like the cursed veil of clouds that blocked out the sun's warming rays.

My breath froze in my chest as I stared back at his hairless face. He wasn't human; I could see clearly that he wasn't. And my gut warned me that whatever he might be, he was almost certainly dangerous.

But knowing exactly *what* he was, or whether or not he posed a threat did not concern me at that moment. If Richard possessed some power, then these people might have a shred of hope yet, and that was all that mattered. They were in a desperate situation, fading faster by the second, each one wilting into oblivion on their solitary patch of hard, bare ground. Without warning, I was vividly experiencing a childhood memory; I had wandered off to gather some wild flowers from a nearby meadow, which I had intended to give as a special gift to my dad. But when I returned, he was furious with worry. We both said things we didn't mean and I ended up flinging the delicate blossoms onto the rocky ground, where they were left scattered and forgotten under the glaring sun. When I returned for them a short time later, they had withered and wasted, their petals baked onto the searing hot rocks. From a whim, the flowers turned out to be innocent victims of my stubborn impulsivity.

"Are you able to help us?" I blurted at Richard with characteristic impetuousness. "They're dying! There must be something that can be done."

He laughed and walked toward a fallen tree, stepping squarely on Nellie's hand on his way over there. There was a sound like snapping twigs and Nellie cried out in agony, writhing and twisting into a ball to cradle her crushed hand. He took a moment to size up the tree's bough before casually perching himself on it, and gazed at me evenly. "I'm really not the helping sort," he said with quiet malevolence, rubbing his hairless jaw with the back of his hand. "You have nothing at all to offer me, Kali. I will make no deals with a woman who is already damned."

My mouth went dry. *Was I damned?* I tried not to let his words affect me, but it was impossible. The night I shot Abel, Tiamat wondered at that very thing, and now here it was, staring me in the face. But nearly everything about Richard alarmed me from the moment I met him. He used tainted words that corroded subversively, words which I should never take at face value. Yet he had an obvious knowledge of things that humans would have no way of knowing—so there was a remote chance that his words could occasionally ring true. There was no way to be certain, however, and I reminded myself of this as I turned to face him.

"You're not one of the Nephilim, are you?" Confident of this fact, I said it like a statement while I walked over to Nellie and knelt by her side. Her hand was twisted and gnarled, having apparently suffered numerous compound fractures; a considerable amount of damage to have endured from a single footstep. She whimpered quietly so I gingerly picked up her injured hand and cradled it in my own—there would be no point in doing much else. She was so far gone from the illness, the poor woman wouldn't survive much longer. I glanced up at Richard, but could see nothing but disdain in his steely eyes. "And I doubt you're any angel."

"Ah," he said, his eyes flashing with life. "I was, once. But now, things are different. Do not think less of me, Kali," he said in his silken voice. "I may have fallen, but I still serve God's plan. Of course," he chuckled, "there are many that wouldn't see it that way."

"But then everything you say could be a lie—including your tale about serving God's plan," I said flatly. "You're evil."

"Humanity's antiquated notion of evil is so subjective, Kali," he sighed, feigning exasperation. "Our influences are necessary in the grand scheme of things. It is easy to have faith and be righteous when everything is going your way, isn't it? That is where I come in... Someone needs to stir things up a bit. Kind of like what you have done with these poor souls here, Kali. Well done, by the way. Well done. And don't fret. You are just helping to maintain the balance, that's all. Remember, where there is light, there must also be dark."

"But it's *all* dark, Richard! Where is the balance in that? How can I believe that a merciful and just God would perpetuate all this suffering; especially at the end like this, when we're all going to die anyway? I feel like we're all ants getting burned for the amusement of a child with a magnifying glass!"

"That's a valid point, my dear. Merciful and just, indeed! Perhaps He is not all you think He is ... He enables your suffering, after all. Because, simply put, dim lights shine more brightly in the darkness, do they not?"

"So I suppose I'm one of the 'dim lights', am I?"

Richard simply smirked. "But you have been told a variation of this already, haven't you?" he asked, leaning toward me with intense interest.

I didn't answer. My earlier conversations with Tiamat felt like they had no place here with this creature. Despite what he had done to me, there was too much that had passed between us, and I wasn't about to speak of him with his probable enemy.

"What's the matter?" he growled at my reticence. "Didn't you believe it when you were given this information the first time? You were already told—perhaps in slightly different words—that we are all being manipulated as part of a greater plan. Are you having trouble trusting the words of that great betrayer that you came to know so intimately?"

He leaned back with exaggerated indifference when I continued my silence, but I noted the tight line of his mouth, and the clenched fist resting casually on his leg.

"Not that I can blame you, Kali. That half-breed *has* been awful to you, hasn't he?"

"And you expect me to trust *you?*"

Richard just smiled, but didn't reply immediately. "He's damned, you know. And so are you." He leaned forward, his eyes glinting with malice. "Good deeds can't negate that, Kali. Even *if* you could call *this* a good deed," he added, sweeping his hand to indicate the many scattered bodies of the ill.

"I know you don't want to help me, but if you cured them, don't you think that would really piss God off? You did say that you were here to stir things up a bit. Well, if undoing this planned suffering wouldn't throw a wrench in things, I don't know what would! What do you say? Can you help me?"

"I am *not* here to help."

"Please," I begged, my voice catching in desperation. "They have been through too much already. I know you can prevent it from continuing." I looked down at Nellie's crushed hand, and heard her moan softly, mixed in with a discordance of quiet gurgles, gasps and sobs from the surrounding sick. Little Randy was just behind me, his weak, jagged breaths coming at uneven intervals now, and signaling the beginning of the end for his small body. The sound of every gulp of air lashed at my soul with stinging precision, tearing it ragged. "There must be something I can do for you to stop their suffering. Please end this. I'll do ... anything."

"Agreed," he said in a voice dripping with quiet triumph. "I will think on what you can do to repay me."

"No!" growled Tiamat, springing out from behind a screen of fallen trees. "Don't even think of negotiating with him, Kali."

Anger flared up at the sight of him, blurring my vision in its intensity. "What the hell gives you the right to advise me? It's because of *you* that they're suffering like this, you bastard!" I snapped at Tiamat, glaring at him furiously and hating him for what he had done.

Yet my livid glare went unnoticed. Tiamat appeared rooted to the ground, with his eyes locked on Richard.

"Eavesdropping, were we," said Richard, standing, "Wormwood?"

I shivered at the name. *Wormwood. Where had I heard that?*

"Do not call me that," Tiamat warned in a low voice. "And listening to another's conversation is obviously something you are familiar with yourself ... Iz—"

"Silence!" Richard let out his breath in a hiss. "You know better than to use my true name, Tiamat *La'anah*." His voice became rough and primeval, like a monster awakened from its slumber. "You, unlike me, are not entitled to veil your identity. Is it not considered subversive for your kind to hide from their true station? And your surname remains *Wormwood*, whether you conceal it in Hebrew or not." Richard slowly circled Tiamat, his stance shifting to resemble a stalking beast more than that of a man. "You know who you really are—you know you cannot escape it—yet you continue to hide from it with disgrace," he said through clenched teeth. "And even though you may be the true destroyer among your brothers, do not dare to weigh yourself against me, Wormwood. I am superior. And my true name is NOT to be uttered by the likes of *you*." Richard stepped closer to Tiamat; his face contorted and mottled with rage, and he spoke in a thunderous voice. "And *never* should you *dare* to speak it in front of any humans!"

There was a flash of blue. The air crackled around us, and with it, a dense black smoke seemed to rise from the very earth. As though alive, it crept swiftly toward the ill and swirled about them, entering their ears and snaking up their nostrils. It pushed into their mouths and entwined their bodies, making every one of them convulse violently upon the ground.

I dropped Nellie's hand and scrabbled away from her, should I be struck by a flinging limb or afflicted by the power of Richard's rage. And I hadn't backed off a moment too soon; surrounding me, the dozen shaking bodies began to lift, and they hovered a foot above the earth, flopping and flailing in the air like electrified rag dolls. Their eyes rolled back into their heads while all over them, the massive amounts of bloody pustules burst open. A cluster of horrific fountain heads, they scattered chunky, crimson gore everywhere, as though the people were rejecting the blood Tiamat had flung upon them earlier that morning. It sprayed the campsite and coated their bodies, turning their faces into lumpy, inhuman masks of red, gruesomely contrasted by the whites of their rolled back eyes. Then, all at once, the smoke disappeared in a pulse of blue light, and the shaking ceased. Their limp forms fell abruptly to the ground, landing with a series of sickening *thunks*, and lay deathly still.

Fighting back my horror and dread, I crawled back to Nellie's still figure, terrified of what I would find, and looked down into her lifeless, staring eyes. There was no doubt that she was dead. Without giving another thought to what was happening, I was on my feet and running from one corpse to another, frantically checking each person for vital signs that I knew would no longer be there.

I was hovering over Randy's ravaged little body, my shaking hand sweeping across his bloodied face to close his eyes, when I heard the soft rustle of a foot fall behind me. I didn't care who it was or what they wanted;

didn't care about anything anymore, and could do nothing but stare listlessly down at this dead child while I felt my will to survive ebb away.

Though I didn't want it, a soft pressure came down on my right shoulder. I felt a gentle squeeze, while energy buzzed and tingled into my deadened interior. "This is your fault, you know," I muttered lifelessly.

"Yes," Tiamat murmured, placing his other hand on my left shoulder so that he clasped both of them from behind me. Then, speaking into my hair, he added softly, "I am the one to blame, Kali. You were only trying to help them. It wasn't your fault and I know they wouldn't blame you," he said with quiet feeling. "You gave them a chance. You gave them hope. I am the one that took that away. Not you. Remember that."

Relief closed my eyes as the meaning of his words sunk in. *I wasn't responsible for their deaths.* I swallowed down the lump in my throat and put my hand over his, nodding my head in acceptance. I couldn't believe it yet, but it helped to hear him say it, all the same.

He kept his hands on me for another beat, his face close behind my ear, and then the open breeze wisped around me once more.

But despite the coolness of it, I became keenly aware of a charge in the air, the tension behind my back growing palpable. I turned to see Richard glaring at me, with Tiamat watching him warily, his stance rigid as a coiled spring.

"It has been done. Their suffering has ended, Kali, and you are now indebted to me," Richard said through his teeth, looking at me as if I were a worm. "Do not forget that, because you can be certain that I will hold you to it."

"No, Richard—there's no bargain," Tiamat interjected. "You cannot ... their deaths are not what she asked you for."

"It may not be what she intended to request," Richard said with a ruthless smile, "but she did specifically ask for me to *stop their suffering.* And that is exactly what I did."

Tiamat went red and silently removed his shirt with tense hands, while a faint, blue glow began to shimmer around him. Then, in a swift, fluid movement, he tossed his shirt away as his enormous wings unfolded, likening the scene to an agitated eagle looming before a pitiful field mouse.

But Richard only chuckled. "I could humble you without lifting a finger, half-breed. You wouldn't stand a chance against me."

"There is always a possibility, even if it is a remote one." Tiamat was breathing heavily, his entire body tense with anger.

"You had best temper those emotions, Wormwood, or you'll have those interfering *brothers* of yours poking around again. You always try so hard to avoid that, do you not? And when they arrive, they will discover that Kali is the cause once again. That should go over well."

"What do you mean?" I asked. "What's he talking about, Tiamat?"

"Didn't you know, Kali?" Richard said in his smooth, silken voice. "The Nephilim can sense each other's emotions—but only if their feelings are particularly strong. That's how they originally found out about you, and how Wormwood here was shamed. A beautiful day, that was."

Tiamat froze, appearing to hover in indecision. Then, slowly, he folded his wings and brought himself under control. His shoulders remained rigid with tension, though the shimmering blue haze faded with his resolve and his wrath.

My mind was racing; could it be true, then? Was this the reason behind Tiamat's seemingly cruel behavior? If he felt strongly about me, if he loved me, he would have had to constantly suppress any feelings for me so as to not alert the other Nephilim by inadvertently sharing his emotions with them. Remembering Abel, I understood the risk to my life should they discover Tiamat and me together.

My mind went over a series of interactions in a blinding flash of insight; his frequent detachment and frosty exterior—constantly shutting me out and acting devoid of feeling, despite the numerous actions that continually contradicted this façade. We had, for example, shared moments of tenderness that I knew to be genuine, only for Tiamat to suddenly freeze up and either storm off or coldly push me away. I recalled our intimacy in the cave, the evening after we discovered that the cavern blocked the Nephilim's honing sense—and likely their sharing of powerful emotions as well—only to be followed by Tiamat sending me away the next morning. He had suffered a moment of weakness then, and must have concluded that a relapse would likely get me killed. He had to send me away. If he loved me, he would have had no choice. Distance between us would have obviously been the only way to ensure his emotions remained even-keeled. Could that be why Tiamat wept that night? It didn't explain everything, but Richard, in a moment of spite, had answered so much...

"Tiamat..." I began, stumbling toward him before I could think.

"No, Kali," he protested roughly, backing away quickly and stopping me in my tracks. "There is much you do not know, and don't yet understand. Everything he says suits his purpose," he spat, shooting a cold glance at Richard. "And most of it is a twisted version of the truth, at best. Are you failing to remember everything that I have done to you? Do you forget what I did to you by the edge of this very stream?"

"There must have been a reason for it, like there was a reason for everything else, Tiamat. I know that in time, you will explain it to me."

"I will explain this; my surname is Wormwood, though I prefer La'anah, which is the scriptural form of the name. He rested his hands on the limb of a fallen tree, looking ready to crush it to sawdust.

I just stared after him, feeling like I was missing something. "So?"

He turned his head, raising an eyebrow. Then slowly shook it before focusing again on the tree.

It was Richard that answered, appearing to enjoy this game. "It is written that Wormwood comes down from the heavens to bring destruction to the earth." He slunk closer to me, leaning forward to take in my expression. "So you see? It wasn't his brothers that shattered the planet. It was him."

"What?" It came out like a strangled gasp of air as I stumbled a few clumsy steps backward. My body seemed to be going numb.

"I was the one that initiated the destruction." Tiamat spoke to the tree, his voice barely a whisper. "My brothers linked with me and used my power to assist in the process, but *I* was the one that did it."

Tiamat then turned to stare right at me, and his tortured eyes bored into mine. "And that's not everything, Kali. Do you know what 'Wormwood' itself means?" he asked, holding me like a prisoner in his eerie blue gaze. "La'anah is an Israeli shrub, though in scripture, it indicates *evil*, Kali. And furthermore, it labels the drinking of the liquid extracted from it as evil. You saw what my blood did to these people, so perhaps you understand now why it is so dangerous." He glanced away then, releasing me from his stare, and riveted his eyes to the ground. "Remember, that night we were together in the cave, you tasted my blood—ingested it—and I am to blame. There is much that has happened as a result of that action."

I turned, confused, and sat heavily on one of the tree boughs, working to gather my thoughts. *It couldn't be... Tiamat couldn't be responsible for* everything... Yet before I could ponder it any further, Richard stepped forward and fixed his cold steel eyes upon my face.

"My task for you is simple, Kali. You must bring about the death of one of the Nephilim—again. You already disposed of Abel, and you have gained more power since then, so I know you are capable. Perhaps this one here would be your best bet, hmm?" he asked with false amicability, indicating Tiamat. "He certainly has it coming; after all he has done to you, you deserve a little restitution."

"No, please. Isn't there something else I could do?"

"This is not negotiable!" Richard flared. "I did what you asked, and now you must do what I ask. Do not presume to think I am flexible—or it will be your ruin." Richard shook himself like he had just eaten something distasteful, and then smoothed his hair as he gathered his composure. Then he smiled—slowly. "As I told you before, you're both damned. Uphold your end of the deal and you two will be guaranteed a place in Achaia—which, before we made our little deal, is where you were originally meant to go, by the way."

Tiamat started visibly at this, and in the short instant that he let his guard down, his eyes flashed with hope.

"It is truly miserable there, but if you fail me," he continued, "I will see that you both go much deeper."

Richard smirked as Tiamat's look darkened. *What was this place?* I wracked my brain, but was certain I had never heard of Achaia before.

"I can see this half-breed has grasped the magnitude of what exactly is at stake," Richard said with a gnash of his teeth. "Is it hard for you, you bastard of Heaven, to learn that you were bound for Achaia, and in the same breath, realize this woman has likely lost it for you?" he sneered at Tiamat. "Your chance to escape hell could be gone, simply because she bartered with me over the lives of people that were going to die anyway. What a waste," Richard chuckled, looking expectantly at his counterpart.

But Tiamat, though his jaw was clenched, stared back at him quietly, and didn't rise to the bait.

His face again hardening, Richard rounded on me, spearing me through with his vicious stare. "Let me make myself perfectly clear; if you fail to carry out what I have ordered, I will bar your way to Achaia and both your souls will fester forever in the depths of Hell. You can use your imagination to try to deduce what it is that we will do to you, but I assure you that whatever images you conjure up, what will be waiting for you will be beyond reckoning. And rest assured that our treatment of your beloved Tiamat will be infinitely more vicious than that," he said with quiet malice. "I will guarantee that his screams will be heard in Heaven; over and over and over again. That is what you will both face if you do not fulfill your end of the bargain," he breathed, thrusting his face close to mine. "Do we understand each other, you pathetic bitch?"

I nodded my head, scrabbling backward away from him, putting the limb of the tree between us. He smirked at Tiamat, bowed condescendingly to me, and spun to go, roughly kicking Eugene's lifeless arm out of his way as he went.

"Oh, and Tiamat," Richard added, turning to glare at him meaningfully, "here's a tip. The death of any Nephilim will do. And as long as this woman somehow brings it about, I will ensure that you are both sent to Achaia ... regardless of what *type* of death it may be. You have my word," he grinned. "Food for thought." With a wink, he started on his way again, chuckling under his breath in his low, silken voice, "Oh, the perils of love ... someone *always* gets screwed over on an exponential scale."

"This is not the end of it!" Tiamat bellowed after him, his wings towering above him in his rage. But he was obviously shaken, because when Richard had departed and Tiamat folded his wings and looked at me, his skin was pale, and his expression held a look of bitter finality.

"We need to talk," he said gently as he held his hand out to me. "But we should leave this place, befouled as it is by the dead and Richard's stink."

I stepped out from behind the tree limb, but did not accept his proffered hand. Without looking at him, I walked over to the horses and began untethering them, my fingers as numb from shock as my mind was. *Yes, we certainly do need to talk. There is much to be explained.* But I couldn't face it right then; not yet. "What about all these people? We can't just leave them here like this."

"They are no longer here themselves, Kali. Billions have perished all over the world in the past month. You cannot bury them all, and nor is there any need. Their souls have moved on. And so should we."

But I disagreed. They had trusted me to lead them to safety; the least I could do now was deliver their bodies from the indignity of being left scattered across the ground like this. I owed it to them. "When I die, will you leave my body to rot where it falls?" I asked him.

"No ... I ..." he began, flustered. "You mean something to me. I would need the closure," he said softly.

"Well so do I. These people meant something to me too, Tiamat."

It didn't take much more to convince him, and once I conceded that cremation would be acceptable, we made a huge pyre, ripping off the limbs and branches of two fallen trees to stack along the remains of another. After their bodies were placed atop its length, we set it ablaze, with Tiamat commending their souls to heaven. It was a formality for my sake, I assumed, as I knew we had no bearing on where it was they were to go—heaven, hell, or to judgment. Though the thought of deciding the fate of one's soul brought a significant question to mind...

"What do you know about the Rapture?" I asked Tiamat, as I watched the flames take hold.

"So you have some knowledge of it?" he asked, surprised. But in seeing that I hadn't, he ceased that line of questioning. "The Rapture is a divine act;" he replied, "an event that is almost unilaterally misunderstood by mortals. During the Great Tribulation—that is this time now, by the way, a time of great trials that lead up to the last judgment—a number of mortal humans are selected and taken bodily into heaven. There they are to assist with the final judgment of humanity's souls." He looked at me strangely then. "Is that why you believe you are still alive, Kali? So that you can be taken in the Rapture? I am sorry to tell you this, but that is not your purpose here."

"Oh ... No, Tiamat," I responded, taken aback. "No. Four members of our group disappeared last night, and I could find no trace of them this morning. They couldn't have run off; they had a child with them and took no supplies. One of the women from the camp seemed convinced that they were taken in the Rapture, but I wasn't sure what that meant," I told him, watching him closely. "I thought you had taken them."

"I can assure you that I did not," he said, affronted. "What did you think I would do with them?" I had no response for him, so he tried a different question. "Do you believe they were good, moral people?"

"Yes, they were exemplary."

"Then perhaps it has happened," he mused, speaking almost to himself. "The corruptible have been made incorruptible, and the mortal have put on immortality."

It was a fanciful thought, imagining Hanna, Maurice, Tony and the dark-haired boy up in heaven, helping to weigh the deeds of the souls that came before them. And then, picturing Nellie's expression when she saw who her judges were, I felt a small smile of amusement spread across my lips. Now that would be an exchange I would have liked to have seen.

And at that, I finally let Tiamat lead me and the horses away. We turned our backs on the enormous blaze, and a weight lifted from my shoulders like the shedding of an iron cloak. I understood then; what happened was not my fault—I had tried so hard to protect those people and I did everything I could. At long last, I had closure.

Tiamat walked just ahead of me, lost in his own train of thought. Yet he didn't need to say anything at the moment. Without needing to ask, I could see where we were going. We were headed north, I noticed, toward the caves.

Chapter 19

We hadn't been walking for long when Tiamat broke the silence between us.

"I wouldn't believe him, Kali," he said, looking thoughtfully down at the shirt he carried in his hands. "It was presumptuous of Richard to simply proclaim that you're damned. Contrary to what some may believe, these things are not written in stone." Tiamat had brought his wings back in as we walked, and he now shrugged back into his shirt in a slow, deliberate manner, his face a mirror of preoccupation. With a look of concern creasing his brows, he turned his hawk-like blue eyes onto my face. "It is true that you shot Abel, but for you, I do believe redemption is possible. You have not grown up with an intimate knowledge of the divine," he said, stopping. "Unlike me. As I mentioned before, regardless of any penance, my sins will always be irreversible."

He looked miserable by the thought, which reminded me painfully of the cost to him—to us both—should I fail to fulfill my end of the bargain with Richard. "Tiamat," I said, leveling a look at him, "What is Achaia?"

His eyes remained distant, but he reached toward me and lightly brushed his hand over a lock of my hair before responding. "A place for which you are too good," he said, letting his hand drop back down.

"If you can truly and honestly repent, perhaps you will know nothing of it."

I knew I would consider this carefully later, but for the moment, I was not to be misdirected so easily. Remembering the look on Tiamat's face when Richard mentioned Achaia, I pressed my point. "Were you hoping to go there?"

"Achaia is a terrible place of personal grief and anguish—it is hell," he said simply, stepping closer to me and speaking as though he were sharing a secret. "It is the only level of hell, however, where there is the possibility of transcendence through penance. So if we *are* to be damned—if pre-death penance somehow doesn't work for you—we must ensure that Achaia is the place to which we are sent."

The thought of languishing in hell prickled across my skin, like a monster breathing rancid air on the back of my neck. But I couldn't turn to face it. Not yet. There was something about what Tiamat had said... "But if your sins can't be forgiven," I said, looking up into his troubled face, "wouldn't that mean that you'd be stuck in Achaia forever?"

"I do not know," he said pensively. "I am half-human, so perhaps once I have wasted in that plane long enough, I may be granted release. It is possible that our time there can be finite. Remember Kali, if you are to be damned, it is the best you can hope for."

"But now, the only way we can be sure we'll be sent there—"

"—is through the death of another of my kind," Tiamat finished gravely.

Without another word, he took the reins from my hand and turned to tether the horses to the exposed root of an enormous felled willow tree. Then he walked purposefully to the stream bank and unsheathed his knife. He sat quietly, turning it over in his hands as he stared at the flashing metal.

I cautiously approached him, but saw that he appeared much like he did on that first night that I met him; tormented and alone. Quietly, I sat down near him and looked over at his sharp blade, moving between his hands as though it sought one to wield it. His wrists were still bandaged from this morning, and it sickened me to remember the amount of blood that very blade had already spilled today.

"Richard just said that you needed to bring about a Nephilim's death, not that you had to do it personally," he mused softly, gazing down at the glinting knife in his hands. "If I took my own life, it would end your obligation to that snake."

"But Tiamat—you can't!" I responded, alarmed. "Please. There has to be another way," I pressed, trying to quickly conjure up arguments to dissuade him. "You won't die on my account. I'll kill one of the other Nephilim—using the crossbow," I said, my lips numb from the very idea of it.

"No!" he said forcefully, putting down the knife and turning toward me. "I think you can be forgiven for Abel, and all of this will be nothing but a bad memory. But killing another in cold blood will almost certainly damn you." He looked fiercely at me as he said this, then reached over and grabbed my arm in his fervor. "And on top of that, if you mess up in the attempt and fail to kill a Nephilim, he will certainly kill you instead. You will not get a second chance and the deal will be broken. Achaia will be lost to *both* of us. Forget it," he said turning from me and picking the knife back up. "This is the only way."

"But it's a terrible idea! If we can think of something else, maybe we can *both* avoid going to *any* level of hell. Remember, Richard could be lying; you don't know that you're damned either," I argued. "You didn't kill Abel, remember? You were only trying to reason with him. You did nothing wrong there, Tiamat, and you know it." I reached over, took the knife from his hands and jammed it into the ground. "But if you kill yourself, you're completely screwed. Suicide is a major sin! Even if you go to Achaia, you might never get out. How could I possibly let you do that?"

"At this point, it really isn't of consequence that suicide is a sin. Abel's death is not the only item that lies on my conscience, Kali," he said, looking away from me. "You have no idea about the things that I have done. Suicide or not, I already know where I am going when I die, whether it's Achaia or deeper. No," he continued, fixing his gaze on me once more and hardening his voice. "There is no alternative. And at least this way, you will have fulfilled your end of the deal—indirect as that may be."

"But I can kill a different—"

"No! If I leave it in your hands, I'm liable to have my own special welcoming committee in the seventh level of hell," he flared, sounding more agitated by the moment. "Then on top of that, after your blundered attempted murder, I will be forced to spend eternal damnation with you!" He stood abruptly, his body rigid with anger, and the ground shook as though to punctuate his next statement. "You are not welcome down there with me!"

He huffed and began to pace, attempting to bring his temper back under control.

"Nice," I muttered when the ground stilled.

"You know what I intended by that remark," he said through his teeth.

I sighed. "I don't even know why we're having this conversation right now."

He stopped pacing and raised an eyebrow at me. "Do you not?" he asked dryly.

"I don't!" I said, getting to my feet to face him. "Why do we have to stand here and decide our fate the moment after Richard dropped this shit on us? We're talking about the possibility of burning in hell *forever* here—I think that should take a little bit of consideration on our part. There's no need to be rash, Tiamat."

He stared at the stream in silence, then reached down for his knife and moodily pulled it from the ground. The waters clouded with dirt as he cleansed the blade, and when it was unsoiled, he dried it off and put it away.

"And if you should die before we have settled on what to do?" he asked quietly. "What then?"

"So ... it will be soon? That might be important to know."

He faced me straight on and simply stated, "I cannot say."

"Damn you, Tiamat!"

"Under the circumstances, Kali, that's really not a nice thing to say, you know."

"Well seeing how that's where you're going, maybe you should ensure that I *don't* die before we've come up with a plan. Not if you're hoping to land yourself in Achaia. Think you can manage that?"

"So long as I do not strangle you myself, I believe you may survive for a while longer," he said evenly, walking back toward the horses.

He was quick to untie Hero, and stroked the skittish horse's neck while waiting for me to join him. Paris nickered in agitation, apparently peeved about her lack of attention, and I ran my hands around her long face to calm her.

"Would you care to ride? I believe I should take to the skies for a time," Tiamat said.

"Is that to keep watch?"

"Look, to be honest with you, Kali, it is exceedingly difficult to be in command of my emotions with you around. Truly, you're driving me insane."

"So what Richard said was right?" I asked, nearly choking on a quick intake of breath. "You can feel each other's emotions?"

"We do, but only if they are nearly overwhelming. And I know what you are deducing from that, Kali, so stop it," he said, throwing Hero's reins at me. "You need to think harder about our time together and realize that I am not the loving person you think me to be."

"Aren't you?" I inquired, picking at the leather reins. "You were willing to sacrifice your life for me just a moment ago. Or was that simply my imagination?"

"I was planning to sacrifice my life for *me!*" he fumed, sticking his face close to mine. "Do you not understand? I am already damned. But a Nephilim death—by *any* means—will close your cursed bargain. Can you see the importance of that? Taking my own life would have been my insurance for keeping well out of the lower levels of that appalling place. Maybe I would even have a chance to get out of there eventually. And that alone is everything! This is an *eternity* we're talking about. Get it?" he asked, pacing away.

I ignored his moody retort, and tried a different angle. "I know you care about me. I've seen it in the way you look at me sometimes. And I know how you feel because I've *experienced* it. Firsthand."

He stopped pacing and sighed. "I know you hate it when I say this, but I have human qualities and am fallible. I struggle with the same needs and desires that any man does. You had tempted me so many times, Kali, and I faltered. I am so sorry for that, and I apologize for making you think that night was more than it was."

"But ... you were the one that initiated it."

"What I did was unforgivable. You have my deepest regrets," he murmured as he removed his shirt and brought out his wings. He tucked the shirt into one of Paris' sacks and without another word, took off into the skies.

I stared after him, his words stinging like a slap in the face. But I wasn't sure if I believed him...

I briskly mounted Hero and continued riding north, keeping my back straight and my head up, hopeful that my posture would hide the turmoil that clouded my thoughts and ran through my veins like ice. *If I don't repent, I'm going to hell,* I thought, gripping the reins and saddle until my hands were white. *And now it seems that whatever I do—whether I kill a Nephilim or not—I'm set to go to some level of it. I'm set to go there...* Prickling and crawling, monstrous thoughts whispered again across my skin as the ground opened black beneath my feet, yawning and falling away in my imagination. I felt myself teetering on a precipice, about to tumble in.

"I'm sorry," I whispered fervently, clinging to the horse's reins like a lifeline, "I am sorry that Abel had to die." Looking up, my eyes fastened on Tiamat's celestial form, flying gracefully overhead, and I felt myself steady. How remarkable it was that he could be so frightening at one moment, and so sublimely beautiful in the next. "But I'm *not* sorry that I did it," I continued in an almost horrified whisper. "I would do the same thing again if it meant saving him. If I am forced to choose a life, it will always be his. Always. I ... I can't be sorry for that choice. Please ... have mercy on me."

* * *

We continued north for the rest of the day and stopped to make camp shortly before evening fell. It was apparent that my food supplies were running out, though neither of us mentioned it. We sat in a strained silence as we ate; both of us focusing on the fire like it was our only anchor in this vast void of quiet.

"Are we headed for the caves?" I asked, keeping my eyes riveted on the flames.

"Yes," he answered simply.

"What for? I thought you said before that I should travel south."

"I did. But I need to speak with you frankly, Kali, and the caves provide the best accommodation for just that."

"Oh," I replied, feeling my hopes lift and hating myself for allowing it. Tiamat's head turned sharply toward me, as he had likely detected the note of optimism in my voice. I waited for his rebuke, though after a time he ended up looking away and saying nothing.

We turned in shortly afterward, neither of us contributing to the conversation any further. We both slept on opposite sides of the fire and the moment Tiamat lay down, he rolled away from me, ensuring that he faced into the dark night instead.

* * *

The next day began much the same between the two of us. We ate breakfast and packed up our camp in relative silence, with Tiamat bursting into the lightening gray skies as soon as I began untethering the horses.

The morning was long and uneventful. Both Hero and Paris plodded along mechanically, while I again lapsed into brooding thoughts about our situation. There seemed to be very few options available to us, yet the more I thought about it, the more ridiculous Tiamat's proposal appeared. Regardless of what he thought, I simply couldn't believe that he was damned. My gut told me that he wasn't, and I intended to keep it that way.

It was approaching noon when Tiamat dove from the sky with such speed that it alarmed the horses and made Hero bolt, dragging an agitated Paris along behind us. I managed to regain control quickly, and turned the horses back toward their aggressor. He had pulled out of his dive and landed safely, and was now running full-tilt toward me, further alarming my barely-restrained coward of a horse.

"Easy ... easy, baby," I cooed into his ear, stroking his neck to calm him while keeping him under a tight rein.

"Kali, get down," Tiamat said in a hushed voice. "Get off the horse."

Surprised by his uncharacteristic panic, I did so immediately. "What's wrong?"

"They're here," he whispered, reaching over to my forehead. "Sorry about this, but I can't let you do anything stupid."

"Stupid? Who—" was all I managed before Tiamat engulfed my world in blackness.

* * *

I opened my eyes to a spread of dried green leaves, rattling gently in a mild breeze. Moving only my head, I took a cursory look around, noting the horizontal splay of branches that arched around my prone form, their dead leaves encasing me reasonably well on all sides. Only a few feet from my back was a rock cut, so it would be exceedingly difficult for anyone to sneak up on me from behind. The drooping puce cover would adequately screen me from human eyes, though I knew it would do nothing to block the senses of any Nephilim...

"Commander," sounded a voice near at hand.

As quietly as I could, I slid my body forward an inch, and peered through a gap under a large, partially-grounded branch that spread from the fallen tree that enclosed me. Tiamat stood about twenty feet away, facing two winged Nephilim, both of whom appeared to be jubilant by the reunion.

"I cannot tell you how it pleases me to see you here, Commander," said the slight, sandy haired one.

I swallowed hard, certain my breathing was far too loud, echoing as it did among the fluttering leaves. Digging my fingers into the dirt to steady myself, I wondered anxiously, how soon would they sense that I was here? Why had they not detected my presence already?

"You are well-met, Nathanial." Tiamat responded kindly, as he and his brother grasped each other's forearms in greeting and, pulling close, smacked the other's shoulder in a single, jovial pat with their free hands. "As are you, Cephas," Tiamat said with a smile, turning toward the dark-haired Nephilim. He grabbed the other's muscular arm and bestowed the same greeting on him.

When he stepped back, Tiamat noted blandly, "I was not informed of any gathering."

"Then I am much relieved you are here, sir," replied Cephas in a deep, resonant voice. "Merodach has called an assembly, and though we were not told the reason, there are rumblings that he works to further discredit you. It is no surprise, then, that you did not receive the summons."

"What Merodach has to say about me is not my concern," Tiamat replied. "I receive my orders from one source only, and that source has never been Merodach."

"But Commander," Nathanial interjected, "he claims your judgment has been impaired. He alleges that you are harboring and protecting a human woman—that *same* human woman that you ... uh ... that caused those problems before— and that she has poisoned your mind. Excuse me for saying this sir, but he no longer believes you are capable of command."

"It is not his place to question your authority," grumbled Cephas. "And it disturbs me to think of Merodach in command instead of you. He covets the position too much." He stepped closer to Tiamat and said seriously, "Your presence here is no mistake, sir. It is my hope that you will confront Merodach and end these repeated insults."

"That is not my purpose here, Cephas," Tiamat stated patiently. "Not in this place nor on this earth. And as such, I will not attend his gathering. I do not answer to Merodach." Both Nephilim looked incredibly deflated by hearing Tiamat's refusal, so he added, "Take heart, brothers, and do not cause strife on my account. I appreciate your loyalty, but I still maintain that we are not here to fight amongst ourselves. Remember that, and follow Merodach if it will keep the peace."

"But—" Nathanial began.

"Enough!" interjected Tiamat. "Attend this fiasco of Merodach's and then continue with the tasks you were put on this earth to do.

Waste no more time on this attempted shift of command. Let him take it if he wants; it bothers me not, and nor should it concern you."

"But sir! He cannot assume command unless you submit to—"

"I am fully aware of how it is done," Tiamat interrupted. "Let us speak no more of it."

"Yes, sir," they both muttered, nodding contritely.

Tiamat stepped up to them and placed a hand on each of their shoulders. "Live well, brothers," he said kindly.

"Live well, Commander," they responded, each putting a hand on Tiamat's shoulder in return. After a brief pause, the three separated and his visitors turned to go.

I breathed a sigh of relief, amazed that they didn't sense my presence, and began to wonder at their exchange. I had no idea Tiamat was so highly ranked; was this what Richard meant when he said that Wormwood was the 'true destroyer'? And why was one of his brothers bent on usurping his command? I had thought they were all working together toward a common purpose—obliterating humankind.

"Well, now," sounded a booming voice from just above me. "What have we here?"

I turned my head to see a rather large Nephilim standing on a rocky outcrop that thrust out of the ground just behind me. He squinted down at me, the breeze playing with long strands of red hair that had escaped from a tie behind his head. *Oh no,* I thought, *Oh no, not now...*

His mouth twisted into an impish grin as he scrutinized me, obviously pleased with his discovery. Large, tawny wings opened wide and slowed his fall as he leapt playfully from the outcrop onto the main trunk of the fallen tree.

I stood up quickly, ripping a large branch from the tree to use in defense, and backed away from him as smoothly as I could, out from the shelter of the arching boughs.

"Not just pretty, but talented too, I see," he jeered, leaping from the trunk and approaching me as he would a wild animal. "What a fine pet you have here, Commander," he said with a tilt of his head in Tiamat's direction, while keeping his vivid blue eyes glued to me. "Though it is a shame I will have to put her down. We have a strict no-pet policy around here," he said with a flash of his teeth.

"I know the reason you have all gathered here, Daniel," Tiamat interjected, his voice full of authority. "And it looks like I will be addressing Merodach's accusations, after all. Take her with you, but do not harm her until you have heard what I have to say. It is time that everyone here learned why I have kept this woman alive."

I shot a look at Tiamat, unsure of what he was planning, and in that brief second, Daniel had managed to make it to my side. He swiftly knocked the branch from my hands before I could even raise it, effectively disarming me in two seconds flat. Fast, they were so very fast. I would have to remember that, I chided myself, as Daniel pulled me close, restrained my arms, and launched into the air. It was a humbling lesson, but one I vowed I would learn from.

The ground fell away and I ceased my struggles, dangling as I was in the open air. Up ahead, I could see large clusters of Nephilim standing in wait by the extensive bank of limestone caves.

My breath stopped cold. We were headed for the gathering.

Chapter 20

Far below us, in the shadow of a wall of limestone cliffs, was a large swarm of half-angels, milling around like winged ants across the raw, exposed earth by the cliff's base. Then just above them, on a low, rocky ridge that jutted out over their subordinates, stood a small faction of Nephilim. One of these minute figures pointed in our direction, and in apparent response to this, a gray-winged form detached himself from the group and sauntered to the edge of the platform. He raised his arms to the crowd that buzzed on the torn ground about fifteen feet below him, and with clockwork precision, the waiting assembly reacted by shifting fluidly into a military-like formation.

I couldn't pick out any particular words from our altitude, though the speaker's melodious voice drifted around us on the wind. It rose and fell in turn, and assuming it was Merodach who spoke, my vivid imagination easily composed the general content of his speech. As we drew closer, I listened as it alternated between punctuated tones ringing of indignation, only to then lull with softer notes that smacked of a call for consensus.

Then, in an apparent response to something the speaker said, the crowd began rumbling and muttering amongst themselves. The gray-winged figure raised his arms in an appeal for order, and as we neared the gathering, his words gradually became clearer.

"...was truly shocked, myself. To think that one in such a position of trust and responsibility would behave so inappropriately is appalling. And what are we to do about it, I ask you?" he demanded, raising his voice self-righteously in a television evangelist lilt. "Are we expected to sit idly by and watch while this abuse of power is flaunted before us? And then, knowing that his priorities are so skewed, how can we possibly believe that the commands we are given are legitimate?"

Daniel angled in for a landing and the platform rushed up beneath us like a drunken, tilting ship deck. The rocky surface slammed up under my legs just as Daniel roughly pushed me away, leaving me to tumble toward the speaker's feet in a grand entrance of indignity. I did my best to maintain some control by tucking into a roll and fortunately managed to end up on my hands and knees, instead of the intended tangled heap. Keenly aware that any one of them could kill me in an effortless instant, I rose smoothly to my feet and bowed politely to the surprised half-angel that stood before me.

"Sir," I said deferentially, and watched as his dark gray eyebrows shot upward on his pale, otherwise unlined forehead. Despite the silvered gray color of his closely cropped hair, his face held the ageless, youthful appearance shared by all the Nephilim I had seen thus far. He took a step closer to me—his eyes, sparkling with interest, were sharp as an owl's—and looked me over almost indecently.

My hands twitched nervously, but I kept them hanging casually at my sides as I pictured the exact placement of the knives I carried; one at my right hip, and the other strapped to the outside of my left calf. Stabbing one of the Nephilim would be the end of me, but if I could obtain a quick, fast kill, that would fulfill my end of the deal with Richard. And if the one who died was Merodach, it would simply be a bonus.

Knowing these things and acting upon them were entirely different entities, however. I could feel my heart hammering in my chest at the thought of what I needed to do, while my skin prickled with perspiration.

"I'm Kali," I told him politely, but I was careful that my tone clearly indicated that I expected his name in return.

He raised an eyebrow at my impertinence, though there was a twitch of amusement on his lips, and after only a moment's hesitation, he bowed grandly to me. "I am Merodach."

His head was bent low just inches away from me; he wasn't looking, and my hand was right on the knife at my hip. I would just need to slide it out and...

"We are not at court, Merodach," Tiamat said impatiently as he pushed between us, ruining my chance. Then, keeping his body firmly between Merodach and me, he turned his attention to the waiting assembly. The group had fallen eerily still, listening intently to the exchange between us, their eyes riveted upon our every move.

"It was not my intention to speak with you today." Tiamat's strong voice carried personably to the formation below, though many of their faces appeared hard with suspicion, their opinions likely swayed by Merodach's speech. "Yet it seems that many of you, despite consistently being true to the nature of your duties, are now being *coerced* into questioning the authority that *God* has set before you. By attending this slanderous meeting, you are thereby neglecting the tasks you were sent forth to complete. You should not be here," he said sternly, his eyes moving pointedly around the group, making eye contact with one after another as he scanned their faces.

This seemed to hit home. There were a number of red faces, and many of them lowered their eyes in shame. "Though it is my understanding that many of you were led to believe that you were doing the right thing," he said almost sympathetically. "So, in good faith, I will explain myself to you—this *one* time. Yet you receive this explanation only because these rumors have been extremely counterproductive for our kind. Let us dispel them now so you can get back to your work. But *do not* expect me to be so indulgent should a similar situation ever arise again."

He then grabbed me by the arm and roughly thrust me to the very front of the platform. "This, as I imagine you overheard a moment before, is Kali," he said emotionlessly, maintaining a hold on my arm like a captor would with a prisoner. After allowing them sufficient gawking time, he thrust me back behind him and released his hold. I stumbled, but fortunately maintained my balance by a hair.

Standing near me were my captor, Daniel, and Tiamat's friends, Nathaniel and Cephas, who lingered together a few respectful feet back. Though all eyes were riveted on Tiamat, they appeared to differ in their reactions to his speech; Daniel's mouth was drawn into a tight line, while Cephas and Nathaniel looked mildly pleased. Behind them stood a disciplined line of five other Nephilim, who I took to be Merodach's cronies due to the look of displeasure frozen on their hard faces.

"How many of you feel a compulsion to kill this woman?" Tiamat demanded of the crowd, making it clear he expected their full honesty. Strangely, only about half the hands went up, despite Tiamat's earlier insistence to me that all Nephilim would instantly feel a compulsion to kill *any* human they came across—including me. Amazingly, only a few of the half-angels that were with us on the platform joined their hands in the count, indicating that they all seemed to be following Tiamat's command in spite of where their loyalties obviously lay. Near me, Daniel's hand went up, though Cephas and Nathaniel remained still. A rumble of surprised speculation rolled through the assembly in reaction to the census.

"How can this be?" a dark-winged Nephilim that stood behind us on the platform demanded. "Our compulsions are orders from God. Why would He give us conflicting ones?"

"We should *all* feel compelled to kill her. Some of you are being false!" bellowed one from the crowd below.

"We cannot accuse our brothers of being false," placated a Nephilim with large brown wings that stepped forward from the orderly line behind me. "We will need to think on what is happening here."

Tiamat raised his hands and the crowd grew silent immediately. "You can see that this woman is special, though I cannot yet share her full purpose," he told them. "And I cannot tell you why some of us feel compelled to end her life and some do not, but I assure you that it has been revealed to me that she *does* have a purpose here." He spoke to them sternly, in a tone that brokered no argument. "So although this may be confusing to you at the moment, it has *never* been requisite to fully understand why certain things unfold as they do. You all know very clearly that it is not our place to question His methods. Not for *any* of us," he said, leveling a hard look at Merodach, and making a number of them wither under his scrutiny.

"Now you all have tasks to do, which you have neglected in order to attend this *meeting*. So that you are not considered to be insubordinate, I strongly suggest you disband now and attend to them." I could see many nod their heads in agreement, and all of them, including those on the platform with us, appeared relieved to put an end to the confrontation and go on their own way immediately.

I started to relax, and let my hand move away from the knife at my side. Thankfully, Tiamat and I would now have some more time to decide how we can fulfill my deal with Richard without engaging in too much risk to either of us. This would have been the deadliest, stupidest place imaginable to make an attempt on one of them, though for a time I feared I would have no other choice.

I glanced over at Merodach, and saw him nod his head slightly, as though he were responding to someone speaking to him. But Tiamat had stepped away to speak with Cephas and there was no one else nearby. Merodach's strong, square jaw clenched and released, and a crease formed between his brows. Shifting his weight slightly, he nodded again, inclining his head just the slightest fraction. And there, in the empty space immediately behind him, was a slight disturbance. It wavered like sweltering heat rising from hot asphalt in the summertime—just the barest of shimmers in the otherwise cool, breezy air.

"Now wait a moment, Wormwood," Merodach said, halting everyone's retreat. "You must allow me to apologize for this ... misunderstanding. However, you yourself must admit that the situation looked very suspicious indeed. In fact," he said, almost laughing, "I wouldn't have let this go so easily if it were not for ... well, you know."

"What are you getting at, Merodach?" Tiamat asked in a short, clipped manner. "We all have things to do."

"Well, you did maintain that this woman was around for a reason. I do not know how many here actually noticed it, but any one of us should have immediately detected something different about her. And now that I have sensed it, I can clearly see the purpose you had in mind for her. Tell me, Kali," Merodach said to me, a nasty smile curving his lips, "did you consent to being a host?"

I felt my skin prickle at the negative emphasis he put on the word. "A host?" I asked, confused. I knew the Roman Catholics had something called a host in church, but I didn't see how that applied here. "What does he mean?" I asked Tiamat.

But instead of responding, Tiamat looked extremely uncomfortable, while the disbanding crowd of half-angels immediately resumed their previous formation, their interest renewed ten-fold.

Merodach laughed in a light, melodious chuckle. "Does she not know?" he enquired, sounding delighted. "We are meant to send the humans on, not toy with them in such a fashion! I am impressed, Wormwood. This is truly cruel, even for you. It seems you have lived up to your calling at long last."

A reaction to his words rippled through the crowd like a current. First, in response to hearing that I knew nothing about being a host, whatever that was, and second, at Merodach's insolent remarks to his commander. Many appeared to be outraged, though there were numerous grins of pride at Merodach's gall.

"Why is it cruel to make me a host? What have you done, Tiamat?" I demanded, despite being terrified of the answer I might receive.

But still, Tiamat remained silent. It was Merodach that answered instead. "Has Wormwood left you to wander the land, my dear, and have you perhaps come into contact with any people on the way?" I nodded my head yes, and as I did so, the intended meaning of 'host' slammed into me full force, knocking the breath out of me. "Ah ... I believe you understand now," Merodach continued after observing the look on my face. "You see, you have been set loose to carry a deadly disease to some of the final survivors, thereby unwittingly helping us with the task of sending all humans to their judgment. But here is the cruel part, Kali. Only women can be made into hosts, and then, there is *only one way* to make you a carrier."

Tiamat kept quiet, but blushed considerably at this statement, and the assembly erupted into a chorus of excited chatter. The noise echoed like a deafening roar in my ears and the world tilted violently as I understood, finally, much of what had been happening in these past few weeks of misery. I suddenly realized the futility of my existence here— my suffering, my relationship with Tiamat; it was all for nothing, all based on nothing—my knees buckled and I felt my legs collapse as the knowledge of what he did shattered the last of the will I had left. *He used me,* I thought bitterly, feeling the hard rock scrape my knees and palms as I instinctively braced myself when I went down. *Oh god, how could I have been so stupid?*

"This whole time, you never cared for me at all," I whispered, staring sightlessly at the hard rock under my hands. "And those poor people ... you let me believe I was helping them." I looked up at him then, but he wouldn't meet my eyes. "I killed them!" I yelled at him, feeling the tears run down my face. "*I'm* the one that made them sick, *I* made them suffer, and you let me believe that it was you! Did you spray them with your blood as an elaborate way to trick me? Why would you do that, you sick, twisted bastard?"

"Yes, Wormwood, why *would* you do that?" Merodach echoed, sounding intensely interested. "They would have been dead from her virus within a week. Could you not have let nature take its course?"

When Tiamat answered, he ignored me completely and spoke to the other Nephilim only, in a voice as rigid with tightly controlled anger as I had ever heard it. "The deception was necessary. This woman has a remarkable knack for locating stray people. I needed her to see that I was the one causing their deaths; otherwise, I was certain Kali would refuse to search out any further humans if she knew that she was also making them ill. As you can observe," he said, indicating my kneeling form with a sweep of his arm, "she finds the thought rather distasteful, and was much more obliging when she was ignorant of the virus." His glare roved slowly across the silent faces as though blaming all of them for exposing his plan.

"The ones she found so far could have been easily located by us, so I needed to keep her in the dark so we would still be able to use her later—I had hoped to have her infect those humans to the south that are proving to be more elusive." He looked pointedly at Merodach when he said this, and the man actually appeared to squirm under Tiamat's glare. "Your folly has cost us an important weapon, Merodach, and lost us much time. It will be difficult to obtain her cooperation now."

Merodach obviously did not take public embarrassment well, and appeared to boil with rage under Tiamat's reprimand. His face reddened noticeably, and bulbous veins surfaced like sea snakes along his forehead and neck. "What you did is forbidden, Wormwood, even if making her a host serves a purpose," Merodach said through his teeth.

"We will all remember this transgression, make no mistake about that," Merodach warned.

Tiamat simply looked mildly back, appearing unperturbed by the warning. "As you know," he continued as though Merodach had said nothing, "there are large pockets of people about 50 miles south of here, but locating them outright has been problematic." He glanced around at the attentive assembly, and a good number of them nodded their heads or murmured in agreement. "At times, we can sense many of them, and then the next day, there are none. This cycle leads me to believe that they are somehow blocking our ability to locate them. We could send these people on as we find them, but chances are high that many will be overlooked. However, sending Kali and her virus into their midst would take care of that problem, thereby allowing us to focus our attentions elsewhere."

"I won't do it," I breathed angrily, wishing I could kill him with my glare. "If you want them, why don't you just tear the earth up around them, like you did to kill most of us off in the first place? You don't even need me."

"The Nephilim no longer retain that ability on such a grand scale," Tiamat replied coldly, looking right through me as though I didn't exist. "It was a one-time deal, so to speak. The planet must be left to heal itself now, so any remaining stragglers need to be sought out individually. For the most part, we can locate and kill them quite easily," he said, rubbing a bandaged arm as a reminder, "though there are some that are proving difficult to find." He fixed his gaze on me now, and his vivid eyes were piercingly sharp. "That is where you must come in."

"No!"

He ignored me and turned instead to Cephas and Nathaniel. "Take her to the Mokarabi region south of here. She has horses and supplies that are just beyond that ridge. These must go with her if we expect her to survive."

"Yes, Commander," Cephas answered heartily.

"I think not," interrupted Merodach, his voice carrying loudly. "You have explained everything satisfactorily, but in order to prove, finally, that you have no ties to this woman, I am certain you will consent to having different guards accompany her—ones of my own choosing."

"I do not find it necessary to prove anything to you, Merodach," Tiamat growled. "But if you insist on having your own guards take her, I care not."

I looked from one to the other, listening with black resentment as they discussed whose guards would take me to end the lives of more innocent people. Tiamat was about to be sorely disappointed if he really believed that I would consent to spreading that virus again, simply because he told me to.

"I will have Daniel escort her," Merodach responded. "I do not see why I should waste two of my men on that woman."

"Very well. Ensure she has her horses," Tiamat said curtly. And with a cursory nod to Merodach, he turned to go.

"I won't do it, damn you!" I spat angrily, jumping to my feet.

Tiamat stopped in his tracks and rounded on me. "Oh, I believe you will, Kali, because if you do not, you will no longer serve a purpose on this earth. And you know where you could be bound after that if you have not yet *prepared*," he said, giving me a meaningful look. "No, I do not think you are ready to die just yet."

Without another word or glance, he turned abruptly and leapt off the edge of the platform, his icy white wings thrusting him straight up into the dismal sky above. I watched him as he disappeared into the distance, a shrinking white speck swallowed whole by the immediate gray oblivion.

Merodach turned to me and smiled slowly. "Well, now," he began, his honeyed voice dripping with false amicability, "I doubt anyone here will object now if we send you on your way."

That didn't sound right. Despite Tiamat's obvious authority, it was plain that Merodach made his own rules. "You mean south? With Daniel?"

"I am afraid that Daniel will not be going to the same place you are, my dear," he responded with a curl of his lip. "Wormwood's judgment is jaded—we can all see that you are nothing but trouble, woman. It would serve us better, I think, if we send you on as soon as possible."

"You were given orders, Merodach," Cephas growled. "Your opinions on the matter mean nothing."

"On the contrary, Cephas, *you* were given orders, not me. He agreed to let me send her with Daniel, but never ordered me to do so."

"They were implied, nevertheless."

"That's all perspective, my friend. Besides, surely you can appreciate the benefit of having her out of the way. You must admit that your commander has not been himself lately."

Cephas fixed his jaw and stepped forward angrily. "He is your commander as well. Do not forget it."

"Think about what I am saying," Merodach implored. He turned to ensure all that were still nearby could hear him. Approximately twenty Nephilim remained, perhaps waiting to see if anything further would happen. It looked as though they would not be disappointed. "We know that some of us feel compelled to kill her and some do not. Could it be that it is only permitted for certain ones to end her life? That makes so much more sense! If we were meant to keep her alive, no one would feel the drive to kill her at all."

"This is wrong, Merodach. I will have no part of it," said Cephas, spreading his wings.

"Nor will I," echoed Nathanial. "But I believe I should remain, brother," he said to Cephas, "to bear witness." He faced his friend and the two clapped each other heartily on the shoulder, seconds before Cephas burst into the air and flew out of sight.

"You dirty manipulator," I said to Merodach. "You don't give a shit about what happens to me. It's so obvious that your only agenda is to aggravate Tiamat as much as possible—even though I can't imagine what you might hope to gain from my death. Can't you see that he doesn't care about me at all?" My mouth twisted as I said it, the bitterness of the statement nearly choking me.

There had to be some way to buy myself some more time. I couldn't die yet, I thought, letting my hand once again hover near the blade at my belt. I would have to either talk my way out of this, or take one of them down before I died. "Your existence is kind of pathetic, don't you think?"

This time I noticed that Merodach shook his head the slightest bit, though once again, there was no one near enough that he could be responding to. Then his lips curved and he gave a quick nod, fixing his eyes on my right hand. "Are you hoping to stab me with that, Kali?" he asked with a smile. "Perhaps liberating me from this 'pathetic existence' of mine?"

"Better you than me." Wrought with indecision, I kept my hand suspended where it was, failing to either move it away or commit to unsheathing the knife. "Though it looks like you're not my only opponent right now—and I'm not talking about the other Nephilim here," I said loudly. "Who is it that's hiding in the air just behind your back, giving you instructions, Merodach?"

My accusation appeared to have the affect I had hoped for; by the general tone of the muttering surrounding us, the remaining Nephilim sounded shocked and immediately suspicious—though I didn't dare take my eyes from Merodach to confirm it. "If I were you," I said, speaking to the cluster of Nephilim nearby, "I would keep a close watch on this one. Not only is he being advised by someone he doesn't want you to see, he's blatantly defying orders from your commander, right before your very eyes."

Merodach's mouth had gone into a hard line. "There is no secret advisor, you stupid, delusional woman. There's no one!" He stepped toward me, his face reddening from anger. "I've had enough of you!"

"Then put an end to it, you two-faced liar," I challenged. "And even though there are many ways you can kill me, don't do it like a cowardly bureaucrat. Face me and fight."

Merodach took a step back, looking surprised. "I'm not going to fight a woman."

"Oh, you won't? Do you think it's somehow more gentlemanly to murder me outright using powers I don't possess and can't compete with?" I snapped.

Merodach's mouth opened and closed in surprise, but no sound escaped him.

"And if it will ease your delicate conscience, then give me better odds and be done with it," I told him curtly. "If I win, you leave me alive and allow Nathaniel to escort me to the Mokarabi region, as Tiamat ordered. If I lose, I die. Either way, you're rid of me, and you can look like less of a slime ball by at least giving me a fighting chance."

"And your knives?"

In response, I unsheathed both blades and threw them to the side. My mouth was dry and my hands shaking, but there was no going back. If I was going to die now, this would be my only chance to try to take one of them with me. Without my knives, it was almost hopeless, but I knew I had to take whatever opportunity I could right now, no matter how lean.

Merodach watched me quietly for a moment, before a grin slowly spread across his face.

"Jared," Merodach said to a brown-winged Nephilim. "Fight her." He dismissively waved his hand in my direction—a spitefully flippant gesture—while taking a large step back, apparently removing himself from the pending brawl.

Jared's jaw fell open in astonishment. He looked from Merodach to me and back to Merodach again. "I ... I do not believe this to be right," he stuttered. "Nothing you are doing here is—"

"I will do it," interrupted a tall one with large, cream-colored wings.

Merodach simply folded his arms and smiled broadly.

Apparently, the fight was on.

Chapter 21

The Nephilim clustered around us in a wide circle—my own personally-orchestrated ring of folly from which I had only two means of escape; and the prospect of either one of them scared the hell out of me.

I took a deep breath, trying to clear my mind of extraneous clutter, and faced the tall opponent across from me. The Nephilim were faster than me and likely stronger, too—my only possible advantage was the hope that they had no actual training in hand-to-hand fighting. As far as I knew, they would have had no reason to ever expect to engage in what they likely considered to be a dirty, excessively-personal form of combat.

I watched him closely, noting the smug, overly confident look on his face and the lack of readiness in his posture. Despite his ability for incredible speed, I had to take the chance. I lunged in with a jab and a cross—he dipped his head to avoid my jab, but in doing so, practically plunged his face directly into my left fist, which slammed toward him with a force backed by wild desperation. I connected with his nose and heard the crunch, cracked him with my elbow and kicked him squarely in the chest to send him stumbling back from me.

Once again, I underestimated the strength I now had; he flew several feet backward and landed heavily, blinking like a dazed owl while two red rivulets streamed out of his nose to drip off the smooth skin of his jaw. It wasn't long, however, before his stunned countenance dissipated and his strange blue eyes fixed themselves on me once more. It seemed like they practically pulsed from his anger and it was with a focused effort that I tore myself from their pull, urgently needing to spread my awareness to his entire body.

He kept his intense eyes locked on me as he unhurriedly swiped the back of his hand under his flowing nose, carelessly smearing blood upward across his pale cheek. Without blinking, he rose to his feet, smirking at me with bloodied teeth. "This is akin to sparring with a wild dog," he taunted, and spit a gob of blood onto the ground. "You so perfectly illuminate one of the reasons we were directed to wipe out your kind. Violence is just instinctual to you humans, is it not?"

"How dare you lecture me about violence after what you and your brothers have done?" I flared back at him. "If you're looking to validate your existence by belittling ours, you're no better than the worst of us. Do you actually think that by putting us down and exaggerating our worst qualities, it might somehow negate the fact that you're nothing but a murdering, sociopathic asshole?"

He appeared to be taken aback by my passionate response, and his eyebrows rose in response. The eyes, however, remained locked on my every move. "Oh, I see. Humans, of course, would never sink so low as to stamp out other forms of life on this earth. Nor would you ever actively try to obliterate another of your kind based on things like differences in race or religion. Is this what you are telling me?"

The smug look on his face, as he paced over the ground across from me, was maddening. It was staggering that he truly seemed to believe what he said. "I never claimed that humans weren't fallible or destructive or even prone to violence sometimes. In truth, we are. But—as you well know—we are also compassionate beings and usually try to fix the mistakes we have made. Unlike the Nephilim; you've destroyed life across an entire planet!" I pointed out, circling him carefully. "And you're acting like this is okay simply because some humans are occasionally violent? Only a weak-minded, ignorant fool would fail to see the absurdity of that argument."

"Enough chatter," he snapped as I saw his muscles bunch to lunge at me. Wary of his speed, I noted the spot on which he focused his eyes—precisely on the left side of my face—and counted on his movements to take him there.

The instant he acted, I dashed to my right, giving a powerful side kick with my left foot, aimed at the air where I hoped his head would be a brief moment in the future.

I was lucky. As my leg extended, I felt the blow connect with something solid. The half-angel flew to the side, slamming with dead weight into the hard ground a few paces to my left. He laid still, his head tilted awkwardly backward, like he was craning to see something just behind him.

Not certain if he was alive or dead, I ran to his side and righted his head, checking for a pulse just under his chin. It was there, beating strongly under my fingertips, an unheeded warning of what was to come.

The Nephilim's eyes opened suddenly, just as his hand flashed out and firmly grasped my upper arm. With his other hand, he swiftly backhanded me across the face, making random black spots pop and spread across my vision. The hand that restrained me then began to emanate a painful buzz, causing a slow surge of electricity to move maliciously up my arm and toward my torso.

I panicked. Taking him by surprise, I grasped his hair with both my hands, and with savage force, pulled his head down toward my right knee, which I slammed up into his face. After it connected, I threw his head backward, causing the half-angel to sprawl in a rather undignified manner across the ground. Free of his grasp, I jumped clear of him, and stood staring at his still form from a respectful distance away.

With a muffled thud, something then fell to the ground at my feet, and I stared down to see what it was. Yet I was dazed, my mind strangely disconnected, and I simply stood there, gazing uncomprehendingly at the appearance of one of my blades, gleaming in the dust by my right foot. Unable to attain further meaning at ground level, I raised my eyes to see Merodach glaring at me expectantly.

"Pick it up, Kali, and finish what you intended to do here," he said in a spiteful voice. "And if you do not, then I cannot say that you have won this fight."

My head still spinning, I slowly reached down and grasped the blade, staring at it in my hand like it was some strange, foreign object. If I killed this Nephilim, I was free; free from both Merodach and Richard at once. Almost of their own accord, my feet propelled me toward the prone Nephilim, while my thoughts begun to spin wildly in my head. After only a few steps, however, my hands started to shake, and I could feel a prickle of sweat break out across my skin. I stopped, inches away from his still body, and could make myself go no further. I had to do it; I knew there was no other way, yet despite that small voice of insistence, my legs and arms resisted wholeheartedly. I turned and looked at Merodach curiously, as rational thought finally surfaced clearly in my head.

"But why would you want me to kill him? Isn't he one of your brothers?"

"This is a fight to the death, is it not?" Merodach responded coldly. "And if it's a fight to *your* death, would it not need to be a fight to your opponent's death as well? A bargain is a bargain, after all."

There was no way. I couldn't kill a Nephilim in cold blood like this, slicing into him as he lay unconscious on the ground. Debt to Richard or not, how could murdering someone in such a defenseless position possibly keep me *out* of hell? It didn't add up, and neither did Merodach's insistence that I needlessly kill one of his own men.

"No," I told him, raising my chin defiantly. "Unlike you, I wasn't put on this earth to end lives."

"How unfortunate for you," Merodach sneered, taking a step closer to me despite the knife I held in my hand. "Your only purpose now is to kill, my dear. You need to kill one of us with the blade so you can be released to exterminate your kind with the virus. Otherwise," he gloated, his lips curling unattractively, "you have no reason to be here."

"But he's completely out! Regardless of whether he's unconscious or dead, I still won the fight," I tried. "You agreed that I could go if I won—the fact that he still breathes is totally irrelevant."

But Merodach only turned a deeper shade of red, his impatience apparently boiling closer to the surface. "I already told you what you must do in order to win," he said through clenched teeth. "So finish it!"

"I won't." Shaking my head, I threw the knife to the ground, imagining that my lifeless body would soon fall in a crumpled heap beside it. "Do as you promised and let Nathaniel take me to the Mokarabi region."

"I will only release you when the fight is truly over—and not before that time!" He stepped back then and raked his eyes around the clustered Nephilim. "Who wishes to take Benjamin's place?" he demanded of the crowd, likely referring to my unconscious opponent. "We need to finish here so that we may resume God's tasks. Who among you will lend your strength to ensure His work is done?"

I couldn't believe it. I was speechless, my chest leaden with dread, as I watched a second Nephilim step forward.

"Sir," he began in a rough voice. "With all due respect, I feel we have been far too indulgent here, and I am anxious to be done with this business."

"As am I, Damien. Are you offering your services?"

"This woman is a dangerous distraction, so yes; I would be pleased to send her on."

"Remember our promise to her," Merodach added in a tone that was likely meant to mock me. "You must fight as a human would, and it is to the death. Fair is fair after all, my friend."

"Not to worry; she will receive the treatment she deserves."

It hit me then, standing there listening helplessly to my fate being decided, that they were *never* going to let me survive. No bartering, reasoning, or convincing of any sort would secure my life at this point. Merodach never expected me to actually take the blade and kill the unconscious Benjamin. My refusal to end his life simply provided the snake with a justification to renege on his promise to me. I felt the realization take hold and spread like a disease, while my mind worked to counter it, to focus, to keep myself alive so I could try to figure a way out of this mess ... if there was a way.

Damien turned to face me then, and a look of sick pleasure stole across his elegant features. I should have been watching him, and should have been trying to anticipate his movements. But I wasn't. It was almost as an outside observer that I lackadaisically noted Damien stopping and fixing his hawk-like eyes on me.

Idiot! I thought, chastising myself to further distraction. Of course I expected that Merodach would try to weasel out of letting me go—he made it clear that he was both underhanded *and* loath to lose at his little game with my life. Sulking about my lot wouldn't help me.

I have to do something, I thought frantically, *or say something to outsmart—*

I didn't even see it coming. A sudden, walloping blow crushed into my stomach, knocking the air from my lungs and causing me to double over as the pain ricocheted through my torso. But the moment I bent over myself, a white-hot force exploded on the right side of my face, blinding me with its shattering intensity. I felt my body sail sideways through the air and land with a jarring impact. My world flashed from white to black, and finally to fuzzy gray as I struggled blindly onto my hands and knees. Blurred and tilting as he was, Damien came into relative focus, gloating over his prowess a few paces in front of me. My vision compromised, I watched him as carefully as I could while I shakily staggered to my feet, feeling a warm wetness slide down my cheek like tears.

I was running out of chances. Convincing them to let me live was likely my only hope at this point. I tried to focus my mind, but it, like my body, felt jumbled and shaken and I worried whether my arguments would even make sense. I had to try, however.

"Look at what Merodach is doing! Do you really want a Commander who so openly deceives?" I asked the faceless shapes around me, my voice sounding dull through the thick fog that seemed to encase me. "One who craves power and takes advice from a concealed stranger?" Unfortunately, my ears were ringing so badly that I couldn't tell if my words were having any effect.

Attempting to glance quickly to the side, my world tilted and I staggered slightly. Yet somehow I managed to stay on my feet, and I fixed my eyes back on Damien. "You are defying your true Commander if you let me die," I told them. "Regardless of whether you agree with him, he left orders that were meant to be followed."

"Quiet, woman," Damien snarled, lowering his eyes at me. "No one cares about what you have to say."

Before I could react, I was suddenly being battered by a barrage of rock-hard fists, slamming me all about my body as I helplessly used my arms to protect my face and head. Damien hit me with such force and speed; it was like being attacked on all sides by an angry mob. I couldn't avoid him, had no way of anticipating his moves, and aside from one lucky blow to his head with my elbow, I was utterly incapable of countering him. One of his hits landed solidly on my temple, and in a sea of red and stars, I felt my body scrape and sprawl across the rocky ground. I knew what was coming next, and tried to curl into a ball to protect my head and my organs. But there was no real protection, and when he began to kick me—one shuddering, vicious blow after another—I simply wished I would die.

There was a brief pause in his assault, and I shifted my throbbing head to chance a terrified peek between my arms. I saw that Damien had stalked a few paces away and was now turning with a determination in his step that sent alarm bells screaming in my ears. A charging bull, he launched himself at me with deadly speed, allowing me time to do nothing more than tighten into my pathetic defensive ball and wait for the force of his kick to either shatter my head or rupture an organ. Then it would finally be over, and he could hurt me no more.

But the kick never came. It was as though he simply disappeared, or chose instead to launch himself into the air. Terrified of exposing my vulnerable head, I remained still for a moment, breathing shallowly as any movement of my ribs—likely broken—caused the fire in my chest to explode when I attempted to gulp the much-needed air. Yet in the lapse of action and my sudden stillness, I noticed—with the faintest stirring of hope—that there was a great deal going on here besides our immediate fight. A stir of commotion came from the surrounding Nephilim, with notes of surprise intermingled among their hastily shuffling feet. It was only moments later that a fierce rumbling deep within the ground reverberated through my battered body, the sound of it humming and growling within the raging winds that swirled with increasing intensity around my balled-up form.

Chancing a peek, I raised my head to see a surprised-looking Damien sitting on the ground like a four year old, with his legs splayed apart in front of him and his arms braced awkwardly behind his back. He gaped up at Tiamat who loomed impressively over him, practically crackling with fury and backed by churning purplish clouds which looked ready to engulf the lot of us. The Nephilim stumbled to regain their footing as the ground shook and lurched unpredictably, while large rocks began to dislodge themselves from the surrounding cliffs and tumble down all around us.

"As you can see my brothers," Merodach called over the surrounding roar, "the Almighty is angry at Tiamat for interfering. It is clear, then, that the woman must die."

"You're such an idiot," I responded with disgust, trying to ignore the agony in my chest as the wind whipped the words away from me, and the shaking earth savagely jarred my tender ribs. "It's Tiamat that's doing this."

"Again, you speak nothing but lies! The Nephilim no longer retain such power—"

"ENOUGH!" Tiamat bellowed, and his voice, bursting with rage, seemed to blast through all of us, while immediately, the floor of the valley ripped violently in two. A huge, gaping chasm now yawned hungrily just below the platform on which we stood, breathing upon us the scent of damp, grave-like earth.

The eyes of the half-angels grew wide as they gazed between the deep black of the gorge and their Commander. Yet little by little, their expressions shifted like the light fades after a sunset, and neutralized into a wall of guarded masks.

"I expected that my orders regarding Kali would have been followed," he began, his voice shaking with anger. "Never before have I witnessed such mutinous behavior! Never!" he said thunderously. "Despite anything that Merodach might say, I am the highest rank among you. This position, and the abilities that come with it, were granted by God, as you can plainly see!" He flung his arm to indicate the gaping chasm, and a number of Nephilim actually lunged to get out of the path of his pointing limb, as though expecting lightning bolts to explode from the end of it. "The next command I will give you *must* be followed, or you will *prove* to be insubordinate. Many an angel has fallen over much less! *Am I making myself clear?*"

Like frightened, scolded children, the crowd mumbled their assent, their eyes fixed upon the ground.

"Listen," he said in a fierce, persuasive voice, staring fixedly at each of his brothers in turn. "Any Nephilim that feel a compulsion to kill Kali *must* depart when we are finished here. You are not to have any further contact with her—ever. Despite what is transpiring here, she *does have a purpose* and it is not your place to question it. Nathaniel is to safely escort Kali and the horses to the Mokarabi region immediately.

In time, when her task there is completed, it will be Nathaniel that will decide when and if Kali is to be sent on. Do you understand these orders?"

The Nephilim again grunted their assent, and Tiamat immediately rounded on them.

"I asked you a direct question! *Do you understand these orders?*" The ground began to shake once again, and thunder rumbled ominously in the distance, underscoring the immense power that had been granted only to him, and serving as a stark reminder of his authority.

"Yes, Commander!" they responded immediately, standing stock straight.

"Merodach," Tiamat barked, snapping his eyes to the gray-winged half-angel. "I expect your full compliance in this. If you ensure these orders are carried out, you have my word that I will surrender myself to a release of command."

Merodach scrutinized him like he suspected a trick; but after a moment of consideration, his entire face altered to one of elation and scantily concealed greed. "If you truly do step down; I will personally see that these last orders are followed, Commander Wormwood."

"You will be held to that," he said, staring Merodach down. The gray-winged Nephilim bowed his head and took a respectful step back, his deference barely masking his oozing glee. Tiamat shot his eyes around the ragtag assembly and continued, "Before we proceed, I need a moment to speak with Kali alone. Only after I have finished, will I submit to your discharge of my authority. Now leave us."

At a nod from Tiamat, the Nephilim turned away and walked just out of earshot in order to give their commander some privacy, while still maintaining proximity to their high-status detainees.

It was then that Tiamat finally looked at me, his straight back and stern face melting as his eyes raked me over. He closed the distance between us in two quick strides and fell to his knees, gently grasping at my shoulder with one hand and carefully lifting my chin with the other. I felt his fingers tremble as they touched the stickiness on my cheek, and he pulled his hand back to stare at his bloodied fingers in dismay. "Kali ... oh Kali, I am so sorry," he said quietly, his voice now shaking with emotion. "Are you alright?"

"What do you care?" I muttered, staring back down at the ground and ignoring the pains that seared in my chest every time I spoke or moved.

"You know what you mean to me," he replied gently, lifting my chin back up and cupping my face with his hands. "You have always known, haven't you?" he said with a sad laugh. "And you were right, Kali. I ... I have always loved you. I tried so hard to protect you—I buried my feelings so I could keep you a secret from my brothers, and pushed you away so you would not tempt me. And it ... tore me apart ... to see what my cruelty was doing to you."

I couldn't believe my ears. More than anything, I wished he was speaking the truth, but after everything he had done to me, how could I hear this and not be skeptical of his motives? "But ... didn't you trust me, Tiamat? If you had explained everything to me before, I wouldn't have tempted you. If you truly loved me, you would have trusted me as well," I said quietly.

"I do trust you. But, Kali, telling you how I felt would have served no purpose—there is no future for us. Look around you. The Nephilim are nothing but vultures lording over a dying planet. *That* is the only future there is." There was a bitter note to his voice and I could feel his regret palpably. "And the truth is, I thought it would be safer for you if you hated me," he whispered with distaste, lowering his eyes so I wouldn't see the pain it caused him. "I did so much to earn your hate," he continued, keeping his eyes downcast. "Then there was the virus I gave you."

"Yes," I murmured, feeling the malice of his betrayal rip through my chest more keenly than the searing pain of my broken ribs.

His face briefly twisted as he fought to maintain control over his emotions, but he continued on in an urgent, low voice, "I didn't want to do it, Kali! As soon as you revealed that you could find people, I felt the compulsion to give you the virus, and I fought it with everything I had. But after Abel appeared, I was forced to accept that if I wanted to keep you protected, I ... I would have to make you a carrier." After a brief moment, he fixed his tortured eyes on me again, reaching up to very gently smooth away the bloodied hair that was beginning to stick to my throbbing temple. "You see, the virus makes you nearly invisible; we can't ... feel you ... anymore." He was looking at me intently, his eyes pleading for understanding.

Despite my skepticism, his story was falling into place, and I felt my heart skip in response; if Tiamat truly loved me, he would have needed to find ways to protect me ... even distasteful ones... "They really can't sense me now?" I asked, glancing around at the surrounding half-angels and realizing the vast implications of his actions. I no longer needed to hide in caves to keep from being detected; if I could just stay out of sight...

"Perhaps it's because the virus kills in such a short time, the Nephilim have no need to track or locate anyone infected with it," he continued. "Even though you are a host and virtually unaffected by the virus, we are still unable to sense you."

"But ... those other things..." I said, remembering. "You killed Eric, and then sprayed those people with your blood, killing them first so I wouldn't know that I was the one that got them sick. Why—"

"So you would blame me and not yourself. Think about it! I never meant for you to come across other people. The chances, I thought, were nearly impossible. Then, when you did, I knew it would tear you up if you realized you were responsible for their deaths. I ... couldn't do that to you. I wanted you to be certain in your mind that they were dead because of me."

"You would actually rather that I hated you," I whispered in astonishment, imagining the pain his charade must have caused him. "You did all that—you sliced into your arms and let me blame you for their deaths; loathing you—so that I could have a *clear conscience?* That's insane!"

"Look, it was my fault, Kali. I am the one that made you a host ... and I had put you through so much already ... too much," he said quietly, running his hands lightly along my arms while he shook his head sadly. "And that brings me to my next point. The Mokarabi region truly does have people there, and they will die from the disease you carry. The disease your friends got from my blood is a variation of the same virus you carry—the potency of my blood simply brings the sickness on faster. Keep away from any other people; avoid them, because I know what killing them would do to you."

He spoke like he wouldn't be going with me—and I remembered his orders that it was not only Nathaniel that would take me, but that Nathaniel was also to be the one to decide my fate when my 'task' was done. I felt a surge of panic. Tiamat didn't include himself in the future at all. "But—"

"Listen to me, Kali. There isn't much time. There are caves there as well, where I have stockpiled supplies. Keep out of sight and be safe, because you will be on your own now. And for what it's worth," he said, swallowing hard, "I am so sorry ... so very sorry for what I have done to you—for how I have been treating you." His eyes were haunted. He reached up with both hands and traced his fingers down my neck, leaving my skin burning in their wake. "With all my heart, I wish that things could have been different between us." His voice was fervent, but the sad note of finality pierced me through. "I love you." He let his hands fall limply to his sides, and moved to go.

"Wait!" I said desperately, grabbing at his hands as an onslaught of searing hot pains shot through my chest. "What will they do to you when you hand over command to Merodach?" But even as I said it, I realized I knew. Despite the heat of my injuries, I could feel my insides turn to cold, hard ice. "Tell me they won't kill you, Tiamat," I demanded in a horrified whisper. "Tell me."

Not meeting my eyes, he simply looked away, his silence a glaring affirmation for an answer, and I realized with horror what kind of an agreement he had made in order to secure my life. "Please don't do this," I begged, my voice cracking. "Please. I'm going to die anyway. Just let them kill me, Tiamat."

"There is no turning back from this now, Kali. Just a moment ago," he said, his jaw clenching in anger, "when I saw ... when I saw what they were *doing* to you, I nearly lost my mind. Keeping my emotions buried was no longer an option—*they all know how I feel about you now*," he stressed. "It is a secret no longer."

"I don't care if they know!" I answered impulsively, knowing full well what a revelation like this would do to Tiamat's credibility. "There must be *some* way out of this for you. Please, Tiamat. Surely if I'm out of the way, you can all move on from this."

"You know," he said, ignoring my pleas and running his tingling fingers down my cheek, "despite the circumstances, it is a relief to finally share with you how I feel. I just wish ... well..." The sentence hung unfinished, his words unnecessary in the waning gray light. He smiled sadly and leaned in to brush his lips against my own. "I am yours eternally," he murmured, his breath warm and alive against my face.

I choked back a sob. He was set on his course, and we both knew that the die had already been cast. It was over. "I love you, too," I whispered back and pressed my lips to his, kissing him fiercely. His mouth opened in surprise and he kissed me heartily in return, slipping his hands behind my back and pulling me close against him. I ignored the pain in my body, insubstantial compared to the wrenching loss I faced, and grabbed at him blindly. His grip tightened as I stroked his hair, touched his charged skin, and all the while I felt my heart tearing apart from the finality of the embrace.

He broke away abruptly, and reached up to touch my face again. Leaning in, he pressed his forehead to mine, breathing heavily while he ran his fingers lightly along my cheeks, wiping away the tears that trailed there. "I was dead inside before I met you. But you changed all that. Please, let me keep it that way for these last few moments. When I give myself up to them, you have to let me go. You must not say or do anything. Do not try to stop them. Please, *please* let me die knowing that you will be safe. Please, Kali. For me," he begged, his voice thick.

Unable to respond, I nodded my head, and tried to swallow back the misery that was threatening to overcome me.

Just like he did on the evening we first met, he gently pressed his lips to my forehead, and I savored the feel of his energy shooting down through my body for the very last time, tingling through my broken bones and shattering my spirit to pieces. "Live well," he whispered against my skin, running his hands through my hair. "Just ... live..." His voice cracked and he paused to regain control, keeping his hands frozen in my hair, while his warm breath caressed my forehead like a last embrace. When he moved again, he slowly stood up and backed a few paces away from me, keeping his warm eyes focused on my face the entire time.

"Merodach," he called out in a clear, even voice. "It is time."

Chapter 22

I had the strangest surrealistic sensation; like everything around us was too contrasted or overly sharp—illusory compared to the vibrant life that stood before me. Tiamat and I had our eyes locked, the world around us crystallizing into slow motion, while the feel of a cold, black void spread like spilt ink under my breastbone. A small voice inside me whispered weakly that this couldn't be happening, dwarfed by my logic which impotently registered countless details that confirmed otherwise. I wished I could say or do something to reverse the inevitable, but my body was frozen in place, stuck in one of those nightmares where you can neither run nor speak, as I waited for the unfolding of events which would sweep Tiamat forever away from me.

He gave me a sad, almost apologetic smile and while he whispered the words, "For you, Kali," he flicked his eyes toward the dismal sky. Curiosity taking hold, I followed his gaze and watched in amazement as the blanket of gray thinned and parted. Immediately bursting upon us was a saturation of spectacular rays, emanating from the brilliant, yellow-orange sun. The large, fiery orb floated over the horizon, its beams bathing our small area in a dazzling pool of light. The sun's rays illuminated everything and compounded the feeling of surrealism as it gleamed starkly off a rock, the sweat on Merodach's brow, and a small depression near my foot that was half-filled with stagnant water.

Like children at their first magic show, the half-angels stared around themselves in unrestrained, open-mouthed awe, alternating wide eyes between their Commander and the radiant exposed orb shining through an impossible cloud break high above the horizon.

His bitter-sweet gift of the sun burned away the dark fibers of my soul, wrenching it painfully apart in the process. It was the last time either of us would bask in its resplendent rays; parted forever under its vivid light, just as our relationship dawned beneath its waning glow ten years before.

Tiamat, looking vaguely uncomfortable, gave a slight shrug of his shoulders and flashed me a lopsided smile. In spontaneous response, I croaked out a combination of a laugh and sob tumbled together—making me sound more like I was choking on a hiccup than anything else. I covered my mouth as tears spilled unhindered down my cheeks, released the instant I lost the focus necessary to restrain them. Stopping myself, I wiped away the errant tears and—in an effort to share with Tiamat whatever strength I had left—I managed to gather myself enough to return a warm, but shaky smile. I felt the numbness in my lips, and realized that I was likely sending him a grin that appeared as sad and lopsided as his own.

Then, like an unwanted guest, there was Merodach, suddenly kneeling at Tiamat's feet, licking nervous lips as he looked up at his Commander expectantly. Following my eyes, Tiamat, as if in a dream, gazed over at him slowly, appearing almost surprised to see Merodach kneeling there, and paused for a long while, staring with disconnect down at his usually vocal adversary.

Merodach continued to sweat, and though he appeared incredibly uncomfortable under Tiamat's unregistering gaze, he said nothing. Eyes unfocused, Tiamat mechanically reached his arms out toward Merodach, one hand in a fist and the other enclosed around it. The kneeling half-angel then placed his own hands over Tiamat's, appearing, by the bulge of his muscles and the redoubled gleam of his perspiration in the overly bright beams of sun, to be grasping his hands with excessive vigor.

Despite the obvious pressure on his hands, Tiamat was unresponsive. Without acknowledging Merodach in the slightest, he instead turned his face away and raised his eyes to gaze back at me. However, in complete contrast to the odd look he had given Merodach, the vivid blue eyes that found my face were as clear, immediate and warm as the sunlight that surrounded us. He smiled at me once more—his look laced with regret—and took a deep breath, as though stealing himself for what was to come. Then in a very deliberate movement, he closed his eyes, and an aura of tranquility settled upon him. The unfolding scene moved like a movie in slow motion, as Tiamat turned back to face Merodach and, eyes remaining shut, carefully spread out his magnificent wings, the sun's rays turning his pure white feathers to gilded silver.

The Nephilim, their astonishment at the sun's appearance beginning to wear off, seemed to again realize their duty and moved stiffly into their tasks. Two stepped forward to restrain Tiamat's arms and another four reluctantly advanced to seize his immense wings—two to each one. They dragged their feet as they approached their shimmering whiteness, shooting nervous looks to each other as they reached up to grasp his span of pristine white feathers. Yet the four eventually overcame their apprehensions and, gently at first, placed their hands on his wings while looking wildly about them as though they expected to be swiftly struck down from the heavens. When no recourse occurred, however, their manner switched abruptly, their looks turning almost gleeful as they grappled to secure their hold, breaking and snapping his feathers in the process. Flickers of pain crossed Tiamat's peaceful face, but he neither moved nor opened his eyes as his subordinates roughly defiled his remarkable wingspan.

Daniel approached Tiamat from behind, the cheery sunlight flashing wickedly off an enormous blade that he held firmly in his right hand. The weapon was deadly; its blade looked to be 10 inches long with an unusual serrated edge better suited to sawing than slicing. *What would they need a blade like that for?* I wondered anxiously, watching the glint of cold steel as it moved callously through the barely warmed air. Feeling myself go light-headed, I crawled a few feet and grasped a nearby boulder for support, leaning on it as the last of my strength ebbed away. *Oh, please don't let them cut him to pieces,* I prayed in desperation as the bright world around me clouded through the haze of my waning vision, *please, please, please...*

There was a flash off this wing and that feather as I dimly noted Nathaniel struggling against another Nephilim in an effort to reach his friend. I imagine there was a cacophony of warnings and yelling, but at that moment, any noise there was echoed in an ocean of muffled peripheral sounds, circling my body along with a visual of disjointed, stark images.

Tiamat's gift of sunlight illuminated the worst things for me—the shimmer off Daniel's blade as it sawed mercilessly into the base of one of Tiamat's wings; the gleam of a broken white feather, appearing to be suspended in mid-air as it drifted slowly downward; glittering rubies of blood falling to splatter against the sun-warmed rocks; and glistening red snakes slithering down Tiamat's convulsing back.

I wished I could close my eyes against the stark images—the beckoning dark behind my lids offering a welcome, guilty respite—but felt that the act would be akin to abandoning Tiamat. And so, sickened, I continued watching the bright, horrifying spectacle, as bits and pieces of a gleaming, visual barrage burned themselves forever into my memory. I glimpsed a flash of white as Tiamat's left wing fell abruptly to the ground, and a renewed spattering of red jewels as Daniel's gleaming knife jittered and worked over the base of Tiamat's other wing.

When it was done, Tiamat, now no longer restrained, swayed drunkenly where he stood, his head drooping limply and his wingless back drenched in slick, red blood. Nathaniel and the others stood stock still, their faces as pale as the disembodied wings that lay in the dirt, and as one, we all watched mutely—our looks varying between ones of open-mouthed horror and fascination—as Daniel ceremoniously passed the knife, hilt first, to Merodach.

Merodach, firming his jaw, enclosed his hand around the blood-soaked hilt and raised himself to stand in front of Tiamat. Gazing insolently at his Commander, he dusted himself off with an air of distaste, and spit upon the ground at his feet. No one moved or made a sound of protest, all eyes glued as they were to the glimmering red of the knife. We watched as it flashed through the air in a swift upward arc before its blade buried itself under the bottom of Tiamat's ribcage, thrust there in a fatal, upward angle.

"No!" I shrieked, helplessly watching Tiamat's body convulse as Merodach's blade hit home. "No, please..." I sobbed into the rock. "No ... no ... please, no..."

Not satisfied with the initial strike, Merodach threw his body weight behind the knife, bending his legs to press forcefully upward, ensuring the wound was mortal.

And so it was. Tiamat's lifeless body crumpled as Merodach withdrew the knife, falling to the ground with an unearthly thunk. He lay in a pool of weakening light, his blood spreading darkly as the familiar, dismal shadows engulfed the ridge once more, blocking out the last of the world's sunshine.

It was at that moment I imagined I felt him; the touch of his lips, the warmth of his arms around me, and the stroke of his fingers in my hair. I cherished the feel of him, wishing with all my being that his closeness would linger with me forever. But it was not to be. The sensation vanished with the breath of a breeze, and I gazed down to see that the only thing I held was a hard, rough rock, rapidly cooling after being robbed of its brief spell of warming sunlight.

"Don't go," I whispered softly to the empty air. "You can't leave me alone here," I quietly cried. "I have no reason to be here without you." But there was no response, and the cool breeze was nothing more than vacant wind.

I looked over to see a circle of grim-looking Nephilim surrounding Tiamat's body; many appearing almost shocked to see him sprawled there. It was as if some other force was responsible, and they, unable to stop it, were now gazing gravely down at the inevitable result.

"He is dead," I heard one of them mutter. "I can no longer sense his presence here."

Yet I already knew this before it was so candidly announced; felt it in my bones and in the black, wrenching emptiness that gnawed hungrily through my entire being. Tiamat was gone.

"Yes," agreed another, glancing up at the bleak sky where the sun had been moments before.

Nathaniel stepped forward, closer to his friend's prone form, his face twitching from suppressed grief. After a step, he paused. Then, without lifting his eyes, he raised his hand to the sky, palm up. There he stood, alone, his eyes fixed on his friend and his arm suspended above him.

Yet he was not unaccompanied for long. With the exception of Merodach—who stood gazing out over the cliff's edge—the rest of the Nephilim soundlessly joined Nathaniel, forming a close circle around Tiamat's body. And without a word, one by one, each of the half-angels raised a single hand to the sky, Daniel included.

"Death has come for thee," Nathaniel uttered. "A roar of silence is thy speech."

"Never again will you hunger," they echoed, their voices flat and hushed.

"Never again will you thirst."

"Yet thee are not forgotten," they finished.

I could feel the static before I saw anything, tingling past my body as it seemed to sweep toward the circle of Nephilim. A soft blue then gathered in their upturned palms, gradually increasing in intensity.

The energy built and built—until all at once, it released from their hands with a shockwave that burst outward in all directions, as surges of blue shot up into the sky. Together, the bright orbs collided into the cloud cover directly above us, sending out a second shockwave that rippled across the sky in brilliant rings of blue. And just above the rings, the clouds lit up with vibrant forks of azure lightning. It flashed and flowed away from the point of impact, illuminating the sky with its florescent web. It was bright and hauntingly beautiful; then faded into the mass of endless gray.

Slowly, their hands all lowered, and they stood in silence. It was some time before they turned to look at Merodach once more.

"Mors ultima linea rerum est," muttered a dark-winged angel. "Death is everything's final limit. It is Merodach that commands us now." His lips twisted as he spoke.

Their new leader stood facing the land that stretched out below the cliff. His face was turning red as he glared fixedly at a spot in the distance, his body seeming to strain with effort. Down in the valley, a grouping of about five boulders trembled and shattered in a violent spray of splintered rock, apparently the hapless victims of Merodach's scrutiny.

Seeing this, Merodach rounded on the Nephilim in a rage. "Why can I not control the weather?" he demanded of his men. "And the earth will not quake or split—regardless of my efforts! Boulders! All I can smash are boulders! Why, I ask you, are my abilities unchanged? Wormwood is now dead—and a full shift of command has taken place—so all of his gifts should have been bestowed upon me. I am the new Commander, am I not?"

Daniel walked toward him. "Perhaps it takes some time," he placated. "Or it could be that you must first prove your qualities as our leader before a Commander's powers are imparted to you."

"I have been cheated," Merodach continued as though Daniel had never spoken. "Wormwood has betrayed us!" Merodach looked wildly about him, overcome by his indignation. "Her!" he shouted, pointing in my direction. "Kill her! The traitor's false orders are no longer valid."

A handful of the Nephilim looked appalled, shooting wide-eyed glances at each other as they shuffled discreetly backward, attempting to distance themselves from the entire sordid incident.

"I will do it," answered Damien with a sigh. "Sir," he added as an afterthought. The large half-angel that had nearly killed me a short time before, once again stepped forward. His look, however, was not nearly as predatory now, with his slouched stance making him appear more resigned to fulfilling an unpleasant duty than anything else.

"You will not," a voice answered forcefully as the most unlikely of advocates stepped in front of my shaking body. Surprise and relief surged through my veins at seeing Daniel standing there guarding me, spawning a flood of fresh tears to flow onto the rough rock under my cheek.

"Commander," Daniel said, addressing Merodach. "Your position is such only under conditions from our previous leader. He specified that the woman was to be delivered south—unharmed—in return for his surrender of command. In case you cannot recall, you agreed to this. Like many of you," Daniel continued, looking around at his comrades, "I feel a compulsion to send this woman on. But if we are to be just, that compulsion must be ignored."

"Wormwood is gone!" Merodach fumed, taking a menacing step toward Daniel. "I am your Commander now, and you are bound to follow *my* orders. It makes no difference whether you believe them to be just or not."

"That may be," agreed a tawny-winged Nephilim as he, too, stepped protectively in front of me. "But you lead us only because Wormwood stepped down. And he did so on the condition that his final orders would be followed," he maintained, reiterating Daniel's point. "So the way I see it, if you do not obey those stipulations, then the exchange of power is not valid and therefore, *you are not our Commander.*"

Merodach's mouth shut like a trap, his face reddening as he watched the faces of his once equivocal subordinates. Through the silence, the tension in the air became almost palpable as one by one, every last Nephilim moved in to shield my body from Merodach's wrath.

I couldn't believe it. My eyes welled with tears once more, as my emotions threatened to sweep me away. This was why Tiamat died, I realized. He finally found a way to keep me safe, and yet, I would have given anything to reverse that. The thought of it was almost too much. I quietly wept as I witnessed the respect for Tiamat's final orders, and the Nephilim's resolve to see them through—orders that he bought with his blood. Reality flashed through me once more and, dizzy and sick, I and pressed my forehead down onto the rock.

"As Wormwood made clear," Nathaniel said loudly, "any of those that feel a compulsion to kill this woman should depart immediately."

"Starting with you, Commander," Damien's rough voice prompted. "The rest of us will follow."

Adrenalin abandoning my battered frame, I let my body slump onto the boulder I held, listening to the flurry and swish of a dozen pairs of giant wings, departing according to Tiamat's final orders. And then: silence. I turned my head. My cheek pressed into the rock, I stared blankly at his lifeless form, wishing my tears would bring him back, or that my love would somehow transcend the void that separated us. But I knew that neither would, and so I continued to lay still and stare, hoping that my body and senses would eventually go numb and release me from the pain of reality.

"Kali," sounded a voice from just above me. "I ... I am sorry for your loss," Nathaniel said, sounding uncomfortable. "He meant a great deal to me also, and I feel the weight of his passing. But we can grieve Wormwood as we travel. He wanted us to be away from this place."

"Burn him," I heard myself mutter through dry lips. "Or bury him. We can't leave him lying here like this. We owe him—" I choked on the words, a sob escaping my throat, "...we owe him that much at least."

"We do," he agreed softly. "I will see to it, Kali."

At first, Nathaniel suggested a cairn of rocks, taken from smashed boulders and piled up over Tiamat's laid out form. But dead or not, I couldn't fathom the thought of heavy rocks being piled on top of Tiamat's head and face, and from my prone position on the boulder, told Nathaniel so.

He turned away to return to his deliberations, and as Nathaniel fretted and paced, I kept my eyes glued to Tiamat's face. I followed the lines of cheek, nose and chin, desperately trying to commit his features to memory, lest they, too, fade forever away from me.

Nathaniel finally settled upon a solution that worked for both of us. Laying his hands upon the platform's solid floor, he moved them back and forth in a sweeping motion, shattering the rock that lay under them in even and calculated chunks. He stopped and lifted out the pieces to reveal the creation of a shallow grave, just large enough to fit Tiamat with his two enormous wings placed lengthwise over the top of his body.

Yet when Nathaniel had only just laid Tiamat to rest, the feathers of his wings obscuring his peaceful face, feelings of irrational panic began to boil inside me. Desperate to touch him one last time, I anxiously crawled to his open burial pit, my ribs screaming in painful protest. *You have to let go, Michaels,* I told myself as I reached in to touch his white face beneath the shroud of feathers. *He's dead. Let him go.* In confirmation, the skin I touched was cold and slack, and my eyes blurred as tears of farewell fell into his hard, stony grave.

"Oh, Tiamat..." I sputtered miserably, barely keeping from breaking down. "You were everything to me. I wish I had told you that."

Nathaniel placed his hands upon the stack of rocks he had lifted from the grave and turned them to innocuous piles of cascading sand. He paused before continuing, and looking at me, raised an eyebrow in question.

Understanding immediately, I reached over and grasped a shaking handful, suspending it hesitantly over the grave. "Goodbye, Tiamat," I whispered, and sprinkled the sand gently over his beautiful white feathers.

Not able to bear the sight of Tiamat's face and body being covered over in sand, I forced my legs up under me and stumbled toward the edge of the platform. Blocking my way, however, lay the dark pools of Tiamat's blood, a horrific reminder of the brutal end he endured for my sake—to keep me alive in a cold, empty world where my time was already starkly limited.

"Good night, brother," I heard Nathaniel say in a low voice.

My legs gave out and I sat heavily on the periphery of the red-black pool, letting my head fall into my hands in dark misery.

* * *

The next few days passed in a muddled haze of movement and sleep. Nathaniel, unable to coax me to my feet after burying Tiamat, had simply lifted me up and flown to the spot where Daniel had discovered me hidden in the fallen tree earlier that very day. Leaving me propped up against its branches, he left to find the horses, and after returning with them some unspecified time later, made a brisk camp. Refusing his offers of food, I turned my back on the fire and closed my eyes to the world.

It was the first night in recent memory that I didn't dream of Tiamat, the images from my sleep consisting of nothing but dark and clouded shapes that dissipated into obscurity.

I awoke in the gray light of dawn, and apathetically discovered that the gash on my head had healed completely. *So I'm a fast healer now too,* I thought. My bones, I figured numbly, would mend shortly thereafter, and then I would have nothing to keep my mind off the voracious emptiness that gnawed at my core. And aside from that, I thought nothing more of this new ability. I let my body fall into the routine of packing up the camp, and rode away on Hero while Nathaniel glided overhead like a circling raptor.

As the days wore on and my mind slowly began to work once more, I started to wonder about Nathaniel. Although he was distant, he had a quiet manner about him and had treated me kindly. On the third day, he had even inadvertently given me a gift; some further knowledge behind one of Tiamat's perceived acts of cruelty, and a possible motive underlying it.

We were sitting by the fire when Nathaniel asked me, quite unexpectedly, if I was barren.

"I ... don't know," I responded in surprise, realizing as I said it that I hadn't menstruated at all since before the Nephilim struck. There was only one time that I bled, and that was immediately after Tiamat did something to my abdomen by the stream that day... "I believe I may have lost the ability to bear children."

"Hmm," he murmured, rubbing his hand on his chin. "Wormwood was fortunate in that instance."

"What?" I demanded. "Why would you say that?"

Nathaniel explained that even if carrying the virus, women in their child-bearing years could still be detected at close range. "A woman, even a host, can still be impregnated. Though her mate would die from the virus, it's possible that the child could be immune—and undetectable to us. We cannot have that. Our ability to sense a fertile female—host or not—assists us in our task."

"The task of extermination?" I asked him pointedly. He didn't answer, but inclined his head in affirmation.

"So because I'm a host *and barren*, you can't sense me at all?" I looked at him closely, but his vivid blue eyes were steady and his face open. "If I truly am sterile, that is."

"You must be. You are completely invisible to me," he confirmed. "But only if I have my eyes closed, you know," he joked in an apparent attempt to lighten the mood. "Tell me, did Wormwood do this to you as well? Did he make you so?"

"Yes," I answered quietly, staring down at my hands as I remembered. *When he was hurting me like that, why didn't he just tell me?*

"How?" he inquired, his manner completely guileless.

"I really don't know, Nathaniel," I whispered abjectly. "He just put his hands on me and did it. He didn't explain anything."

Nathaniel, likely sensing my mood, nodded wordlessly and once again let the crackle of the fire fill the sounds between us, leaving me alone with my grief. We turned in shortly afterward, neither of us speaking another word about it.

I was thankful for the knowledge gleaned from this exchange, and even for Nathaniel's quiet presence. But during that fateful afternoon on the ridge, despite his apparent allegiance to Tiamat, I had noticed that Nathaniel was one of the last ones to side against Merodach. In fact, he was the second last one to step up to protect me, taking his place with his brothers only moments before Damien did. Why?

It wasn't the sort of thing I could simply ask him, but as luck would have it, the answer presented itself two evenings later. Once again, we were sitting by the fire in relative silence, the crackle and glow of it comforting as it filled the dead air between us.

"Kali," Nathaniel said tentatively, poking the coals with a stick, "I cannot let you go into the Mokarabi Region."

I jerked my head up in surprise; this was completely unexpected. "But ... you have orders," I responded, unable to imagine why he, of all the Nephilim, would seek to defy one of Tiamat's direct orders. "I didn't think you had the option of not following them."

"You have it exactly right," he sighed. "But you, unlike me, are not bound by any such restrictions. You are protected by free will, and I thought, because you were so strongly against going there to kill those people..."

Immediately, I understood. From the first time Tiamat gave the order, Nathaniel, I realized, never wanted to see me fulfill it. "You're protecting someone that's there, aren't you?" In spite of his loyalties to Tiamat, the spread of my virus meant a death sentence to whoever Nathaniel had hidden there. If Merodach had killed me, it would have solved his dilemma.

Nathaniel took a deep breath and gazed into the dark past the fire, refusing to answer. After a length of strained silence, he looked back at me, his eyes pleading. "I have no choice but to take you there. But I was hoping that, once I leave you at the outermost boundary, you will decide to leave again ... on your own."

There were few things I could hear at that moment that would make me happier. I remembered about Tiamat's hidden supplies, however, and mentioned the complication to Nathaniel.

"Oh," he said in surprise. "So Wormwood and I have both hidden supplies there," he responded, almost laughing. "That area is well-stocked.

"I have an idea," he said, leaning forward. "There are some cliffs just outside the northern boundary; we shall pass near to them tomorrow. I have some emergency items stored there that will see you through for some time. If you agree to go straight back to the cliffs after officially stepping into the region, and promise to stay out of Mokarabi from that time on, I will find Wormwood's supplies and deliver them to you in about a month's time." He looked at me eagerly then, gripping his poking stick tightly as he waited for my response.

I had a thing about making promises. Was there a way I could put his mind at ease without committing? "You have nothing to worry about, Nathaniel," I began carefully. "And really, I'm so relieved! You know it would kill me if I had to be the cause of any more deaths," I told him honestly. "I want nothing more than to stay far away from those borders."

Nathaniel appeared overjoyed by my response. "Oh, Kali ... that is ... that is ... simply fantastic!" he beamed in relief, enthusiastically throwing his poking stick into the meager flames and smacking the dirt off his hands.

We worked out the final details that night, and only two days later, I found myself standing alone within the borders of the Mokarabi Region, Nathaniel having only just recently departed south, into the heart of the area.

"In a month, then," he had said to me before jumping into flight.

"I will be at the caves," I replied in earnest, gaining a departing smile in response.

As I said I would, I turned Hero's nose north, and headed toward the cliffs that loomed barely outside the Northern boundary, trying to ignore the feeling that from somewhere up ahead of me, I was being closely watched.

Chapter 23

The awareness came like a prickling across the skin, writhing and crawling along the fine hairs at the base of my neck. *There is someone here with me ... watching.* Stopping the horses, I anxiously raked my eyes over the terrain ahead of me, scrutinizing suspect mounds of earth, rocks and fallen trees... anything that could conceal someone from sight. Nothing moved. I quickly spun in the saddle and looked behind me, but there was no one there either.

Yet the feeling persisted like a creeping finger of cold working slowly along my spine. *Someone is here...* Keeping my eyes flicking around me, I kicked Hero back into motion, needing to move—to do something. But the route in which I was headed was precisely the direction that was causing the chill to spread through my blood. The horses nickered nervously as I slowly reached behind me, feeling for the crossbow. Paying the animals no mind, my hand brushed across the weapon and without lifting my gaze from the surrounding landscape, I brought the bow to the front of my body so I could determine if it was loaded and cocked. Finding that it was, I breathed a sigh of relief that I had had the foresight this morning to set the bolt. I had been keenly aware that Nathaniel and I would soon be parting company, and I was loathe to be caught alone and unprepared.

My heart beating loudly, I steered Hero around a massive knoll of twisted, exposed tree root, the bulb's extensive bulk resembling a horde of entangled wooden snakes. And there, just on the far side of it, a quick flash of movement caught my eye, and my nerves jumped in response.

I swiftly aimed the crossbow, just as Richard stepped boldly out from behind the obstruction, meeting my eyes with a defiant sneer. Completely without fear, he stood directly in Hero's path, and the spooked horse shied back and stomped his hooves uneasily. My stalwart steed was likely preparing to bolt, the coward.

Seeing Richard appear so suddenly, dripping with that pompous, insolent air of his, sparked emotions I had no idea still existed within me. The heavy blanket of numbness that had engulfed my being since Tiamat's death fell off completely as red-hot fury surged like wildfire through my body. Grinding my teeth, I tightened my left hand on Hero's reigns, and with my right, aimed the crossbow directly at Richard's chest. A bolt had killed Abel; it should work on Richard as well.

"I see no reason why I shouldn't shoot you right now, Richard, or run you down with my horse, you manipulative piece of shit." My voice sounded low to my ears and shook with barely restrained anger. It was a wonder that I spoke to him at all and didn't simply shoot him down where he stood.

"Temper, temper, my dear," he chided condescendingly. "Believe me; you wouldn't want to do either of those things."

"Oh, I think I really would, after everything you have done to me and to ... to Tiamat." My finger tightened fractionally on the trigger, while I hoped that he missed the thickening of my voice. "Your absence would improve this hellhole immensely."

"Do it then," he challenged in a mocking tone, spreading his arms wide. "Perhaps you are willing to gamble with your life that you are indeed faster than me. And after, when nothing but your leaking, mangled body is left upon the ground, you can tell me how that worked out for you, hmm?"

I stared at him in indecision, my finger tight upon the trigger, and my body as rigid as a spring. I wasn't sure I really cared if he should kill me; I simply had to decide if my probable death was worth the chance of seeing my crossbow bolt imbed itself in his chest. It was tempting...

Noticing my hesitation, he raised an eyebrow in question, daring me. The hard steel of the trigger felt so pliable under my finger, waiting to be moved and squeezed into the release. It seemed so simple, so easy...

Letting my breath out in a rush of defeat, I lowered the bow. Even though I had every reason to shoot Richard, I simply couldn't do it like this. Despite what he was and what he had done, I was no killer, and didn't have the callousness needed to shoot him down where he stood. I wished I did; but it just wasn't there.

"A wise decision, Kali," he jeered. "But had you foolishly attempted to kill me and died yourself in consequence, it wouldn't have been such a bad thing. Not anymore."

"I don't have time for your riddles," I snapped impatiently. "You obviously came to tell me something; so spit it out or leave."

A flicker of amusement crossed his features. "Your insolence is astounding," he chuckled.

"What a coincidence. I was thinking the same thing about you."

Richard didn't respond immediately. Eyes fixed on me, he crept close to my side—his body next to my foot where it rested within the horse's stirrup. I tried to suppress the resulting shudder, and viciously fought the urge to lash out and kick him in the face. "I only came to share some good news with you, sweetheart. Would you not like to hear it?"

"What is it Richard?" I asked in the most civil voice I could muster. It came out sounding clipped and short.

"I simply wished to congratulate you on Tiamat's death," he hissed.

Like a reflex, my leg flashed out toward his head, while I simultaneously raised the crossbow and squeezed the trigger, firing into a space of empty air that was a little behind him. Amazingly, I felt my boot connect, but before I could determine the success of my bolt, Richard retaliated and I was walloped by a numbing, unseen force. I flew violently from Hero's back and smashed down upon the rocky soil. *Oh,* I thought calmly. *Is it over for me? Have I been blown to pieces now, like Richard had threatened?*

Cautiously, I attempted to wiggle my fingers, and found that I could. Fingers, feet, legs arms ... all seemed to be intact. I lifted my hands up into my line of sight and gazed blankly at my undamaged digits before letting my arms flop back down to the ground, each one landing with a dull thud. Surprising myself, I wondered if I was actually disappointed that I was whole and alive.

Pondering this, I lay there listlessly—allowing the leaden blanket of apathy and gloom to press upon me once more, settling all across my body in numbing comfort. *No,* I realized. *I don't want to die. I just don't want ... anything.* I found that I couldn't even muster the desire to sit up to determine if my bolt had found its target. *Why should I bother?* I thought dully. *What does it matter anymore?*

A shadow fell across my face and my eyes reluctantly refocused. I couldn't fathom why there would be a shadow—the sky remained a thick dull gray—but darkness fell over me nonetheless.

"One of these days, I will take great pleasure in squashing you like the infuriating little insect you are," whispered a voice that was rough with barely-restrained anger.

I blinked my eyes just as Richard loomed over my prone form, looking furious. There was a gash on his cheek where either my boot or stirrup had cut him, and the crossbow bolt had firmly embedded itself in his right shoulder. It was oozing blood that was leaking down his chest, causing his rough, green shirt to stick to him along a gradually spreading splotch of red.

"Why didn't you just kill me, Richard?" I asked the hovering demon in a dry voice. "You told me that you would."

My question appeared to calm his rage, and he glowered at me for a long moment before answering. "And rob you of all the fun you're having? I shouldn't think so, doll."

I slid my eyes away from him despondently. Maybe if I ignored him, he would just go away.

Instead of leaving, however, Richard crouched down by my side and leaned directly over me, waiting for me to look at him. I could feel soft puffs of breath on my cheek while fat drops of his blood splattered sickeningly onto my chest. With my head facing a mound of churned earth that was about twenty paces to my left, I stubbornly kept my eyes riveted on a half-buried, twisted bit of metal that looked suspiciously like the hood of a car. *Where was the rest of it?* I wondered, struggling to ignore the *splat ... splat* of his warm blood.

He waited. But so did I. *What kind of car could it have been? Was there anyone inside it when it was decimated like that?*

Finally losing patience, Richard grabbed my face and turned it roughly toward him, squeezing my jaw hard in the process. "Kali," he said through clenched teeth, almost as though he was grasping his own jaw and not mine. "Tell me about your father."

I was stunned. Why would he ask about my dad? "Uh... he raised me on his own..." I began, so surprised by Richard's question that I forgot my seething anger. "He was an avid hunter and loved to fish—"

"Enough. I don't really care—"

"But you asked!" I could feel my face flush with frustration. *I shouldn't even be speaking to him at all,* I silently reminded myself.

Richard ignored this and began another line of questioning. "You saw me behind Merodach when the others could not. How?"

I didn't answer him. Even if I knew the reason why, I wouldn't have told him. He was a filthy schemer, the driving force behind Tiamat's death, and I absolutely hated him. I stared up into his smooth, stubble-free face, marred by the long gash along his left cheek, and wished that my bolt had pierced him directly through the chest.

"Let me begin by telling you," he said, squeezing harder, "that revealing my concealed form is not acceptable. It is my right to influence others in this way and you are *not* to interfere! Do you understand this?"

Yet I simply stared passively back at him, neither responding nor showing Richard any indication that I had even heard him.

"You are maddening, woman," he exclaimed, letting go of my face so he could pound the ground with his fist. "Maddening! You nearly ruined everything with Merodach, and now ... this! You shot me, you bloody bitch!"

I could feel the smile spread across my lips, not even caring what his response might be. "Oops." This time I did not look away, and held his gaze defiantly. "Looks like I did." I wondered if he would just kill me now; I certainly seemed to annoy him enough.

But strangely, he didn't. Instead, he smiled at me in return, his lips twisting cruelly. "Ah, I know what you are doing, even if you do not realize it yourself. Deep down, in a place you dare not look, you are hoping that I will be the one to end your life, and relieve you of your misery. But I am not merciful, Kali, and would much rather watch you suffer through the last of your lonely, pitiful life. And it is no wonder you feel so terrible. Your beloved is dead;" he breathed, each word hitting me like a physical force, "brutally killed before your very eyes while you did absolutely *nothing* to stop it."

The words were said slowly and harshly, each emphasized so as to have the maximum effect. Their impact extinguished all desire to smile or even argue. I was done. Yet he was wrong in one respect; I didn't want to die. Not really. If it came down to it, I knew I would fight viciously for my life. It was all I had left.

"Oh dear, have I upset you, darling?" He leaned back with a cool smirk and raked his eyes over my face. "You look so pale. But do not worry; like I told you before, I have good news to share."

"What?" I mumbled, hardly caring about what he might have to say. I'd had enough of his games.

"There was an agreement between us, remember? And now a very special half-angel is dead because of you," he reminded me, his words gouging deeper into my open wounds. "As a result, you and Wormwood are both guaranteed Achaia; the only layer of hell that can be transcended. Does this not please you?"

Like a flash of light in a dark mine, my mind latched onto that thought and snapped awake. "So Tiamat has a chance to go to heaven?"

"If that chance exists for the Nephilim, then Wormwood has it," he answered cryptically. "And here is something else for your vexatious little brain to ponder; Achaia is now the very worst you can do, I personally promise it. So whenever or *however* you might choose to die, you will sink no lower than the first circle." He stood up then and turned on his heel to go. "Think about that," he called over his wounded shoulder in his silken voice, "and perhaps you might understand how greatly I have assisted you today."

He disappeared as abruptly as he came, and I simply lay there, stunned by so many of the things that had recently transpired. It had to be a trick—Richard would never willingly help me, I knew. But as I slowly got up and bumbled my way back to the horses, my jaw throbbing from Richard's grasp, I couldn't stop wondering about the implications of his words.

I absently picked up handfuls of dead leaves and used them to wipe Richard's blood from my chest, while my familiar wall of numbness slowly shut out the insidious promise that Richard had planted in my mind. It wouldn't do to dwell on that, I realized. It wouldn't do to dwell on anything.

Without another thought on the matter, I scooped up the crossbow and mounted Hero. Checking that Paris was still tethered securely to our lead, I passively let the horses resume their journey toward Nathaniel's caves, which lay a short ride ahead. There were no thoughts needed, no decisions to be made—just a cavern and supplies to locate for the time being. With the reassurance of this knowledge, I could allow numbness and despair to keep my mind carefully blank, while I bounced absently forward on Hero's solid back.

* * *

The supplies that Nathaniel had stored appeared to be abundant. Stacks of boxes, crates and casks stood in tall, crammed rows between towering shelves of various sundry that lined the walls of the rambling, dark cavern. The extensive clutter of stockpiled supplies was so plentiful, it would likely be sufficient to carry a small army.

But I couldn't really find myself caring. Without stepping further into the cave, I turned and strode back into the diffused light of day. The caverns I had been investigating were just above a wide ridge about a third of the way up the cliff, accessible on foot—or even by horse, as I discovered—by way of a long, narrow path that wound back and forth below me. Hero and Paris had traveled up the long trail fairly easily and were currently tethered nearby, munching contentedly on a wide swath of bright green grass shoots. They tossed their heads in greeting as I approached them.

"You've been a good boy, Hero," I murmured as I pulled off his saddle, packs and all tack. I did the same for Paris, and watched the two horses for a moment, unrestrained and free, lingering hungrily over the new grass. "Tiamat ... couldn't have found better horses for me." It escaped as a whisper, hanging like a ragged vapor in the air before dissipating into nothingness.

The cliff's face consisted of pocked, worn limestone, and without hesitation, I turned toward it and reached up. Grasping a bulbous lip of rock, I hauled myself upward, easily finding the cracks and depressions I required for foot and handholds. The numbness encasing my mind steadily dissolved as I worked, and remembered moments with Tiamat surfaced cruelly—consoling and tormenting me to the point that tears blurred my view of the crumbling limestone before me. All those times that I had assumed he was being cruel or aloof, I was completely wrong. He had loved me always, and was forced to remain silent and distant—impotently watching me suffer, or to even cause my suffering himself in an attempt to protect me. It must have been almost unbearable for him, and I knew that I had only made the situation more trying.

With a deep clunk, a large rock I had stepped on shifted abruptly and my foot slipped off into the empty air. I tightened my grip on the crumbling shelf of limestone above me and pushed upward with my other foot, raising my centre of gravity and stabilizing my balance.

I paused only a moment, and then continued to propel my body further and further above the receding ledge that spanned wide and rocky far beneath my feet. Hero and Paris were still down where I had left them, their once reassuring presence growing ever smaller as I neared the crest of my climb.

Finally reaching the top, I easily pulled my body over the last lip and staggered into an irresolute, half-ready stand. I glanced around, searching for inspiration—but I didn't know what I was looking for. It seemed that there was nothing that could take away my pain, or ease my sense of loss.

The rocky ridge that topped the cliff was large and partially forested, throwing my thoughts back to the Lookout where Tiamat and I first met. This place appeared pristine, and must have been purposefully spared when the rest of the world was decimated. Were all the Nephilim able to protect such a minute area so precisely, or did Tiamat shield these cliffs as a favor to his friend?

"I don't care!" I yelled out in response to my thoughts. "It doesn't matter anymore." I struck out along the edge of the cliff, walking angrily toward an immense outcropping of bare rock, dwarfed by a majestic expanse of towering pines that stood solidly behind it.

But the entire area reminded me too much of Tiamat—I almost expected to see him standing solemnly on the smooth rock at the cliff's edge, gazing out at the sunset beyond. But he wasn't there—he would never be there. Ever. There was no sunset, and no Tiamat; nothing but bleak, gray emptiness filled all the spaces around me.

Despair overwhelmed me, and I was forced to put my hand onto the rough bark of a large pine in order to steady myself. My other hand clapped down upon my knee as I doubled over, drawing in quick successions of ragged breaths—each of which only served to fuel the feelings of guilt and worthlessness. Like acid, these emotions inexorably corroded their way through my chest.

I forced myself to ignore the burning in my chest, and think critically about my situation. "How could you leave me like this?" I whispered angrily, pushing myself away from the tree. But of course, there was no answer.

I paced to the very edge of the cliff, and saw that I was now looking out toward the western horizon. A turbulent, blue river snaked past the escarpment's base far below me, speckled on both sides by patches of new, green grass. I stared out at the terrain for a long while, until slowly, the blush of green that dappled the land began to penetrate through my haze of despair. Shifting my view, I now noticed fresh swaths of emerald growth all over the once-sullied landscape, a gentle herald that nature was finally reclaiming the earth. It brought a weak smile to my lips, seeing it. Life was returning, and with a shaky resolve, I realized that I was thankful I was here to see it.

Letting my eyes follow the river, I saw that it twisted and frothed its way into the Mokarabi region to the south, which left me wondering when I would see Nathaniel again. He was the last friend—the last of any living connection—that I had.

As if in answer to my question, I heard a soft cough behind me, and spun around in surprise. I hadn't expected to see him so soon, but I was grateful for the distraction.

"Kali," Nathaniel said, stepping toward me. His look was serious. "Please accept my apology for this."

I grinned at him, hoping he would gather from my expression that I was always happy to see him. "Don't apologize, Nathaniel. You are welcome any time. Of course, I do have a very busy schedule here, but I'm sure I can fit you in," I said, feigning a light heartedness that I didn't feel.

But Nathaniel didn't smile back. Instead, I saw his mouth draw up in a tight line, and he shifted his weight awkwardly.

"I think he means to apologize about me," came another voice from the trees.

Shock ripped through my body as I stepped from Nathaniel in disgust. I turned my head toward the trees just in time to see Merodach emerge from their thick cover.

I glared back at Nathaniel, intending to question him, but I was so surprised and so furious, I wasn't able to say anything. I could feel my mouth falling open and then snapping shut, but no sound came out.

"Don't worry, Kali," Nathaniel said, grabbing my hands and squeezing them in an apparent attempt at reassurance. "Merodach is unable to hurt you now. Remember, he risks losing his rank as our commander if he causes you any harm."

"Actually," I countered, "Tiamat forbade anyone but you to *kill* me; he never said that the others couldn't *harm* me." I looked up at Nathaniel, and when I saw that he didn't disagree, it was clear that he remembered this. "But aside from that, any Nephilim that feel a compulsion to end my life were also ordered to stay well away. Merodach is violating that order just by being here."

Merodach walked a few paces toward us before stopping stiffly. He appeared undecided about joining the conversation.

"I asked him the same thing," Nathaniel said in an undertone, "and as crazy as this may sound, he maintains that he never had any such compulsion."

"Bullshit!" I blurted. But as soon as I said it, I started to second-guess myself. I was faced with a vivid recollection of that day on the cliff, when Tiamat ordered the Nephilim to reveal if they felt any compulsion to kill me. And as I pictured it, I very clearly remembered that Merodach did not, in fact, raise his hand to be counted among them. At the time, I assumed that Merodach simply thought he was above the poll, but now I wasn't so sure.

"That's okay, Nathaniel," I said, looking up at his worried expression. "I'm sure you had your reasons for doing this."

He blushed considerably at my words, confirming my suspicions. He brought Merodach here himself, I concluded. And I believed I could guess the reason.

His face, still crimson, twitched with his unease. "Kali," he tried in a horse whisper, "I have betrayed your trust terribly." He kept his eyes riveted to the ground, and appeared to be almost on the verge of tears. "Please forgive me."

This time, I was the one to offer reassurance. I stepped up to him and grasped his arm in a firm hold. "I'm certain you had no choice but to bring Merodach here," I began, piecing it together as I spoke. "There is no need to tell me that you only did it as a way to protect something dear to you; something that is in the Mokarabi region. I'm ... disappointed ..." I continued, attempting to find the right words, "but ... but I'm not angry with you, Nathaniel. I just hope that Merodach will respect whatever bargain you made with him."

Nathaniel began to look even more uncomfortable, his red face having drained to white as I spoke. "I have made a huge mistake," he whispered quickly. "I acted impulsively, consumed by the need to protect ... that one thing. I simply wasn't thinking," he muttered, looking away.

Nathaniel's eyes narrowed and his mouth twisted in sudden scorn. "And Merodach has proven to be untrustworthy. He will never stay away from ... from that place ... like he promised. Of course he will not!" He took my hand off his arm and held it in both of his, squeezing earnestly. "And I can't let him stay here with you."

"Nathaniel—"

"No, listen. This is my mistake to fix, Kali. And your kindness and understanding only make me feel that much more wretched for not considering your safety. I will make him go and ensure he stays well away from you." He loosened his grip on my hand as he prepared to confront Merodach, who was now pacing impatiently just out of our earshot.

I squeezed back harder, keeping Nathaniel with me. All I could think of was Tiamat and how he died because of his association with me. No good could come from Nathaniel standing up to Merodach on my behalf. I couldn't let that happen.

"You did me a favor," I lied. "I wanted to speak with him. And I don't want you interfering, alright?"

"But—"

"He'll lose his command if he kills me, right?"

"Well ... that is our belief."

"So, no matter what, he won't risk me dying by his hand. The command is too important to him." I put my hands on his arms again, grasping him tightly to press my point home. "Nathaniel, if you stand up to him, you risk the Mokarabi region as well as your own life. Stay well away, and let me speak to him. Please." I looked up at his face and saw interest there. He seemed to be listening. "Remember, I want this, so it's between me and Merodach now. No matter what happens, don't come back and don't interfere. It's no longer your affair. Okay?"

He let his breath out in a rush, looking intensely relieved, but his eyes held a note of disbelief. "So—you actually *wish* to speak with Merodach?"

"Yes," I lied again. "So really, this meeting benefits us both, Nathaniel. Perhaps it really will help you to keep ... whatever you're protecting ... safe. And at the same time, I finally get a chance to speak with Merodach, without worrying about him trying to kill me. Honestly, I'll be fine."

Nathaniel leaned forward and gave me a brotherly kiss on the cheek. "Yes, I saw first-hand how well you can hold your own," he confirmed with a wink. "You're much smarter than him, you know. It's almost like Wormwood blasted Merodach's brain when he blasted the rest of the rocks on this planet. He should be easy enough to deal with."

"He will be. So there is no need to worry," I pressed. "Now— remember to stay away, or I'll lose my focus by worrying about you, alright? This is now between Merodach and me."

"Take care of yourself, Kali."

"You too, Nathaniel." I kissed his cheek in return, and stepped away from him. As I walked toward Merodach, I could hear the departing sweep of Nathaniel's wings behind me. Hopefully, he would keep out of it, and I wouldn't have another person that I cared about die on my account.

Merodach stopped his pacing and looked at me with interest. His manner was almost ... deferential, I noticed. "I simply wish to speak with you, my child," he began. "It is true that I do not have any heaven-sent compulsion to kill you. I never did."

"And you showed that by doing everything you could to end my life."

"Compulsion or not, I know my purpose on this earth, and I will follow it through as well as I can. You cannot fault me for this." He resumed his pacing as he spoke, gesturing with his arms in an animated, theatrical manner. "And truly, you should no longer be here. All humans must move on." He spun to look at me, raising an eyebrow. "You know this, do you not?"

"I've heard it."

He stared at me for a moment, deliberating. Then, crossing his arms, he leaned back against a tree. "Believe me, I did not intend for you to suffer so," he said carelessly. "We would have sent you on quickly and easily, but you are the one that insisted we fight you. It sickened me to see such brutality. It would not have been our choice to engage in something so vicious."

I snorted. "So that whole fighting business offended your kind nature, did it, Merodach?"

His mouth twitched. "I must concede that calling us kind is a significant stretch. But when it comes to causing suffering, I speak truthfully when I say that we will avoid it if possible. We simply must ensure that you all go to your judgment. It needn't be painful." He unfolded his arms and stepped away from the trunk of the tree. Holding his hands out in an imploring gesture, he walked toward me. "That is why I am here, Kali. I must ask you to do a most difficult deed."

I wondered what it was. Was he going to use me to double-cross Nathaniel, and ask me to seek out the people in the Mokarabi region? That wouldn't surprise me in the least. I folded my arms. "My answer is no, to whatever it is you're going to ask."

"Be reasonable, Kali, and hear me out first," he implored. "I know that you do not wish to be the cause of any more human deaths. But if you go near so much as a small child, you will cause her to die from an unspeakably horrific and gruesome disease. You have seen this first-hand. There is only one way you can be certain you will never spread this illness again."

That had me. I still had nightmares about little Randy, Nellie and the rest of them dying under masks of their own gore—and I knew that I would be forever weighed down by the guilt of having done that to them, unwittingly or not. It was a feeling that I would never overcome. "How?" I asked warily, certain that I couldn't trust him. Perhaps, however, his information could be useful to me.

"It is simple, really. You must die. That is the only way." He shrugged his shoulders, like he was proposing the most straightforward of options. "I cannot do it, due to—certain limitations—of which you are well aware. You will need to do it yourself."

I was disappointed. That was it? "No."

"Think of it, Kali. As a human, you must leave here. It is not really death; you are simply moving on. And if you go, you can be assured that no one else will die on your account." He resumed his pacing as he spoke, arms gesturing as he outlined the benefits of my death. "Then, perhaps after you have left, you will be reunited with Wormwood. I imagine he is waiting for you."

I could feel the anger burning through my veins like fire. "No."

"But God wishes it!" he blurted, his voice rising in his fervor. "At the Gathering, when we faced you, I heard His very voice, speaking to me of the necessity of your death. It was a miracle, and as you know, we must all heed God's wishes."

I couldn't help it; I laughed. It simply bubbled out, completely unheeded. Merodach froze and narrowed his eyes.

"How dare you—"

"Do you know who Richard is, Merodach?" I interrupted. "He's a *demon* that you probably know well." I actually looked forward to seeing Merodach's face when he learned exactly *who* was giving him directions.

"Richard?" he asked, taken off guard. He looked around quickly, like he half-expected the demon to step from the shadows. "Believe me; it would be prudent to not mention Izeil again."

Izeil. That must be Richard's true name, I thought.

Like a flash of lightning, something in Merodach's comment triggered a long dormant memory inside me—one that I had forgotten even existed. Instantly, I was transported back to my early childhood.

I couldn't have been much more than six years old when my father sat me down on our soft, but nearly threadbare chesterfield. He had a crumpled letter in his hand and a serious expression on his face.

"Kali, there is something you need to know," he told me, opening the letter.

I was fearful of that letter. Whatever it contained took the light from my father's eyes. It made him look worried. But I only nodded my head, waiting for him to continue.

"This is from your mother," he said, gazing down at the battered page. "She was a wonderful woman. Intelligent. Full of life. We got along really well. Then, years ago, she told me that she was leaving." He swallowed hard, the memory of it seeming to choke him. "It was about nine months later that I got a call from the hospital, asking if I could come to pick up my baby. It was a very difficult birth, and your mother didn't survive it." He paused to clear his throat. "This is why I am raising you on my own.

I only had you home for a few days when this letter arrived in the mail. Your mother must have mailed it just before she gave birth to you. Maybe she sent it as soon as her labor started." He smoothed it out, and I saw that not only had this letter been crumpled badly, it had also been torn apart and carefully taped back together, the short segments of clear tape zig-zagging numerous lines down and across the battered page.

Suddenly, standing there facing Merodach, with the flood of memories swirling back, I wondered why this moment had been buried so deeply in my memory. Had I suppressed it? ...

"She wrote here that she met someone else; that's why she left me. But she says that she made a huge mistake; that she still loves me and loves you too, Kali. The man she was with left her after only a few weeks. But she felt so terrible about hurting me, she decided to stay away." His voice was getting thick. He cleared it again. "But then the letter gets really strange. She explains here," he said, pointing to a place on the letter, "that she knows—but she doesn't say how she knows—that the childbirth will kill her, but she isn't afraid.

The birth will bring you into this world, which makes her very happy."
He paused and put his arm around me, squeezing me affectionately.
"And it makes me happy too, squirt," he added, kissing the top of
my head. He was quiet for a moment, but I could tell that there was
something else.

I looked up at him, waiting for him to continue.

He slid his eyes away from me, and focused down on the letter
instead. "But... well ... listen, Kiddo, that other man that she met...
he ... well ... he's your real father, Kali. Not me," he finally blurted.

He looked so miserable and uncomfortable when he said it, that
I felt terrible for him. And I didn't really care that some other guy
fathered me. This lovely person with the rumpled letter was the man
that raised me. He was the only father I ever knew. He was the only
dad I ever wanted. "That's okay," I told him. "You're my dad, and
I love you. I don't care about him."

He looked so relieved when I said it. I almost laughed with delight.
He mussed my hair with a big hand. "Thanks, Kiddo. I love you too."

"Let's not talk about this anymore, okay, Dad?" I wanted to
forget it. I wanted things to be back to normal with my dad.

"Well, sure, Squirt. But ... uh ... don't you at least want to know
his name? Then, I promise, we won't mention him ever again."

And we didn't, I remembered. We never mentioned him again. I
ended up forgetting about the entire conversation.

I looked up at my father's face. His eyes sparkled again. He
wouldn't mind telling me the other man's name. I nodded my head
to him.

My father pointed down to the name, written by my late mother's
hand. "She says it's Izeil."

Chapter 24

Merodach's feminine chuckle jolted me back to the present—somewhat. I couldn't focus. Chaos screamed through my head, and my world seemed to tilt violently beneath my feet. Through my confused haze, I could hear my breath rasping rapidly like that of a frightened animal. *Focus!* I thought to myself, shaking my head to clear it.

Thankfully, my footing remained—I had had the sense to brace myself against something and hang on. I could feel a rough texture under my hands. With a cursory glance behind me, I saw that I had backed myself up against a tree and was grasping its rough bark. My fingers were actually imbedded within it.

"Finally, you show some sense and cower like a human should," Merodach said, laughing from the mistaken belief that I was actually recoiling from him. "Now, it would be prudent to do exactly as I say."

My temper flared; it launched me from a state of confusion into one of focused anger. Working to keep myself under control, I pulled my fingers from the trunk and shook them out. I was careful, however, to keep my back firmly against the rough bark—my world still spun. With a grounding breath, I leveled a look at him. "No."

His face reddened. Without hesitation, he pulled out the large blade with which he butchered Tiamat, and held it up in what he obviously believed to be a threatening pose. Along with the knife, he also raised his eyebrow to me, apparently expecting me to tremble at the sight of him.

He looked ridiculous. Another laugh unexpectedly escaped my lips, and his brow furrowed. As soul-shattering as the revelation of my lineage was, it did at least illuminate one useful thing. I was, somehow, his equal. Emboldened by this knowledge, I pulled out my knives and faced him, raising my eyebrow at him in response. Strangely, mocking him seemed the only logical thing to do.

We stood poised and ready for a long moment. Neither of us was willing to call the other's bluff. "Do it," I muttered.

Merodach hesitated. A bead of sweat formed on his brow. I wondered if he was agitated enough to fight me, even if it meant risking his command. Somehow, I doubted it.

"You honestly thought it was *God* that spoke to you?" I laughed, continuing our earlier conversation. "It was Richard!" How typical. I should have figured that Merodach was pompous enough to actually believe that God would speak directly to him. *What an idiot,* I thought.

Merodach had turned a dangerous shade of red, and his veins bulged across his forehead. "Blasphemy!" he croaked in fury, nearly choking on the word. "How dare you attempt to taint the divine Word? You must never say such things!"

"You're deluded, Merodach. Think of it; God wouldn't need to be meddlesome. He would simply give you a compulsion, right? Demons are the ones that need to trick and disguise themselves." I shouldn't have been surprised by his idiocy. But I was astounded that so many of the Nephilim would actually follow this cretin. "And you are also deluded if you believe that I won't say anything of this. I'll be sure to speak of the *divine* conversation you had with Richard. The others need to know how imbalanced you are."

"I did not speak with a demon!" he raged, shaking the blade at me. "You have now been warned not to spread your insidious lies. Do not mention that cursed demon, Izeil, again!"

"Actually, that's the first thing I plan to do," I informed him, egging him on. "Right after lunch." I probably shouldn't have been so cocky, but knowing that Merodach couldn't kill me made me rather bold.

"Vexatious woman!" he raged, blasting a wall of blue energy at me.

Before I could react, it hit me squarely in the chest, stronger and more penetrating than any physical blow. With my chest burning from the energy, I flew back against a large outcropping of rock, smashing my shoulders and head against the unyielding surface. The sudden impact knocked the wind from my lungs with a forceful cough of air, and lights popped in front of my eyes, obscuring my sight.

My vision cleared only to see Merodach standing over me with the blade, a crazed look in his eyes. "I will silence you," he spat, chopping the blade into my side, "by cutting out your venomous tongue."

My side on fire, I clamped a hand over where he had sliced into me, and tried to roll away. But he wouldn't let me. Merodach stomped his foot directly in front of my roll, and I barreled into him, my hand slipping off the warm wetness at my side. Then before I knew it, he had flung himself on top of me, kneeling sideways on my chest. I was winded a second time, and gaped like a fish while I attempted to draw air into my lungs. But in the brief moment I did so, he had grasped my jaw and worked his fingers into my mouth.

I panicked. I struggled to fling him off me, wriggling and writhing furiously as his large, dirty fingers grasped at my tongue. He brought the blade up to my mouth. My legs free, I tried to kick at him and knee him, but it had no effect. I wrenched my head sideways, but he roughly turned it back. He pressed the point of the blade into the skin just below my eye as he continued to fumble for my tongue.

That worked. I held myself still, feeling the blade's point cutting into my tender skin. If I moved my head too suddenly, I would be certain to lose my eye.

"I cannot see why I should leave you with two of these," he threatened, the blade glinting dully at the base of my vision, "when you only need one to see." He tried to use his fingers to wrench my mouth open wider. My jaw screamed out in pain. "Perhaps after I have finished cutting out your tongue..."

I felt his fingers finally grab hold of it and terror ripped through me. The knife left my eye as Merodach moved to pull my tongue from the safety of my mouth. I couldn't let that happen. Without another thought, I bit down as hard as I could. Blood filled my mouth as I felt my teeth sink deeply into his flesh.

Merodach howled in pain, and I swung my legs up to enclose my shins around his head. As I did so, I opened my mouth to release his fingers and, grasping his head tightly, I slammed my legs back down, bringing Merodach to the ground with them. I heard his head clunk dully off the rocky surface. I released him, and he rolled to his side in a clumsy motion.

Seizing my chance, I scrabbled away from him, finally getting my feet up under me once I had gotten a few paces between us. My right hip throbbed, and I saw that it was slick with blood where Merodach had chopped his blade into me. I pressed down hard, trying to staunch the flow.

I've underestimated him, I told myself as I watched him shake his head and pull himself up off the ground. *He's going to mutilate me.* My heart filled with black dread, and I backed up a few more paces.

Merodach turned and faced me, his eyes narrowed in rage. He shook out his fingers, scattering droplets of blood across the rocky outcropping beside him. "For ye are like unto whited sepulchres, which indeed appear beautiful outward," he quoted, his voice barely a whisper, "but are within full of dead men's bones, and of all uncleanness." He took a step toward me. "Matthew 23:27."

I could hear my heart pounding in my chest. I glanced around for my knives, which I must have dropped when Merodach first attacked. *Where the hell are they?* I thought in panic, not seeing them. I staggered back again, my side aching in pain.

"Woe unto them that call evil good, and good evil; that put darkness for light, and light for darkness; they put bitter for sweet, and sweet for bitter!" His voice was strengthening, and he took another step forward. "Isaiah 5:20."

I tried to hobble further back, but my heel caught on a rock and I stumbled, temporarily throwing myself off balance. I flailed my arms as my body tried to regain equilibrium, and my side exploded in fire.

But the pain I felt didn't originate from the wound alone. Merodach had hit me with another blast of energy—directly on my wounded hip—which propelled me high into the air. I couldn't help the shriek that escaped my lips as his searing strike flung me against the main shaft of a large pine. I hit it on an awkward angle, by body horizontal against its vertical trunk, wrenching my spine with terrible force. Then, gravity taking over, I fell like a dead weight, while sharp stubs from broken branches, protruding from the tree, tore into my back on my way down. My arms felt numb and useless; I couldn't shield my body. My head smacked against a branch. I landed on the ground heavily, where I squirmed like a tangled heap of fresh road kill, too stunned and battered to flee to safety.

"Thou art weighed in the balances," Merodach gloated, standing over me, "and art found wanting." He kicked my injured hip, and I cried out once more. "Daniel 5:27," he added with a smirk. Then, ever arrogant, he crouched down close to my face. "Wormwood was a fool to die for you."

I looked away from him, my anger flaring. I saw that a hunk of branch had imbedded itself in my left arm. Roughly, I yanked it free and without a moment's thought, stabbed it directly into his eye. It penetrated deeply, and I ripped my hand away in disgust.

Merodach roared in pain. Clapping his hands over his punctured eye, he tottered back on his heels.

Forgetting my injuries, I lunged at him. Yet he seemed to expect it. In the brief instant before I could reach him, he had jumped a few paces back, and was standing in a ready pose. I had done nothing but fling myself into the dirt. But I was not through. One of my knives, I saw, was imbedded in the ground beside me. I pulled it out, grasped the blade's tip and flung it at him.

It rotated in the air before sinking into his thigh. He grunted in surprise and reached down to remove the blade. His attention diverted, I charged him again.

Striking and kicking him, my body moved in a flurry of desperation. But he was not through either. He swung his arm up to block one of my strikes, and punched me squarely in the chest. I staggered back, but maintained my footing. I came at him again, this time arching my leg toward him in a reverse kick, throwing all my power behind the swing. It connected with the side of his head, and Merodach went sprawling across the ground, smashing his shoulder against a rock that was perched near the edge of the cliff.

Yet without missing a beat, he turned and blasted me again, his vicious blue arc catching me under the chin and flinging me against a wall of rock. I cracked my head again, and staggered like an old drunk, my vision blurred once more.

"Although I am partial to Genesis 3:19," he growled, spreading his wings. They stretched into an ominous silver-gray backdrop, mimicking the oppressive sky. "Thou shalt return unto the ground; for out of it wast thou taken: for dust thou art, and unto dust shalt thou return."

He's going to kill me, I realized, my stomach turning with renewed dread. I tried to focus on him, and my vision tightened just in time to see the maniacal anger etched into his face. His right eye, the stick still imbedded within it, leaked bloody fluid along the hard lines of his cheek, the collecting drops quivering along the base of his grinding jaw. His glare matched his words; he had lost his reason, and I knew at that moment that he would take my life before giving another thought about losing his command.

I couldn't let him do it. Not him. Not after what he had done to Tiamat. Not after Tiamat gave his life to protect mine. "No," I spat at him, remembering that horrible scene. The images of Tiamat's death burned behind my eyes, and I felt something snap deep inside me. Rage consumed me in an instant. It writhed, lashed and burned through my veins, obliterating any rational thought from my head. My hands balled into tight fists and seemed to pulse with heat. The sensation grew and surged. Unbidden, I vividly remembered what Merodach had done to Tiamat's wings, and I fervently wished the same upon him. Through a haze of red, I saw Merodach's face twisting from a look of anger to one of obvious panic, as stealthy black mists rose from the edges of the cliff and converged upon him.

"Murderer," I whispered, my voice choked with fury. I advanced toward him, watching him double over in pain as I thought of the agony he put Tiamat through. He deserved to feel every bit of the suffering that he caused.

But he received more than simply an experience of the sensation. Through a tunnel of rage I watched as the darkness swirled like smoke around the base of each of his wings. Then, with a shrieking yowl, Merodach convulsed while an electric blue light burst outward from the black mass, tearing his wings cleanly from his back. Blood splattered the ridge as each wing tumbled through the air, spinning toward the raging river far below.

"Filthy whore," he wheezed through his pain. "Remember that I am Death." Merodach raised his hands toward me, likely meaning to blast me to pieces. I jumped to the side—so quickly I surprised myself—and lashed back at him, my hands thrown out in front of me like I was flinging some unseen weapon. Perhaps I was.

The darkness swirled, concentrating with a deadly glow in its center, and, with a shockwave of pale blue, it shot out to skewer Merodach with violent force.

Mirroring Abel's look before he died, Merodach stared at me in wide-eyed shock. He doubled over while he clasped his hands to his stomach. A fountain of crimson gore poured from between his fingers as he staggered backward—right off the edge of the cliff.

Isn't that what Abel had said to me? I wondered numbly, trying to remember. *That he was Death?* Perhaps they all were. I walked closer to the edge of the cliff and watched as Merodach's body crashed into the river far below. My lips curled into a bitter smile as I thought about what I had done. "And I am Retribution," I whispered after him.

The cliff was a good vantage point, and I quietly watched Merodach—now little more than a gray speck—swirl and tumble among the river's hungry waves. After a time, the blue serpent finally consumed him, and I knew he was no more. But even then, I didn't move. I simply stood there, staring blankly at the landscape beneath me.

I supposed that I should have been pleased, but all I felt was shock and emptiness. *Merodach is finally dead,* I told myself, waiting for it to sink in.

"Tiamat—I did it. He's gone," I whispered to the wind. It blew back in response, cool and empty, reminding me—in contrast—of the black smoke that surrounded Merodach's wings, ripping them from his back. *But how did I kill him?* I wondered, playing the scene over in my mind, the dark energy now impaling him. *How?* I didn't feel any more powerful, and was pretty sure I couldn't emulate those strange abilities on demand. If I ran into trouble again, I would have to assume that my newfound skills just might remain dormant. *Was it a way that I moved? Something I said?*

I sighed, resigned to the idea that unless I wished to consult Richard, I couldn't know for certain how to bring about these powers when I needed them—and there was no way in hell I would ever ask him about it. I would have no choice but to try to learn about this on my own.

Yet there would be time for that later. What I needed was to get back to the caves and tend to my injuries, I thought. That had to come first. I saw that my side had stopped bleeding, and the healing had likely already started, but it would be better to be certain. Holding my hand over the wound, I walked to the very edge of the cliff, looking for a decent place to begin my climb back down.

Yet the earth on which I stood had other plans for me. It had been weakened from the spike of energy I had somehow managed to fling at Merodach, and, without warning, the precarious ledge of rock suddenly crumbled beneath my feet.

I tried to leap back toward solid ground, but as the cliff's edge dissolved under me, my feet met with nothing but empty air. Desperate, I flung my arms out toward the remainder of the ledge, scrabbling and grasping onto anything I could. Clumps of dirt exploded under my touch and pebbles cascaded down the side with me.

Then, through a handful of dirt, I felt a stringy root sliding through my fingers. I clutched it as tightly as I could, the friction through my hands ripping the skin from my palms; but I had it. Yet the long growth ripped far too easily out of the crumbly rock on the cliff face, slowing my fall but failing to stop me. It pulled and pulled out of the bluff, my body jerking downward like a marionette. Then, in an instant, it met an obstruction and held, the force of my weight making the thin strands of its roots quiver and snap. I looked around. There didn't appear to be anything else solid that I could hold on to. My feet dangled in the vacant air. My vision blurred as my options ran out; I didn't want to die. The last strands of root snapped.

My stomach lurched as gravity grasped me and hurtled my body downward, while the strong press of wind smoothed the tears from my face. I closed my eyes and waited for the end, hoping that I wouldn't feel the impact.

But it didn't come. A wall of hard flesh smashed against my side, knocking the last of the wind out of my chest. In a flurry of arms, twisting and tumbling, I could feel our bodies crash onto a solid surface, and the impact launched me from my rescuer's grasp. I toppled and skidded across the dirt, landing on my stomach with my face suspended over empty air; the rest of my body safely sprawled out along a sizeable ledge of rock. Based on the distance to the ground below, it appeared as though I was only about half-way up—or down—the entirety of the cliff.

"Thank you, Nathaniel," I whispered fervently, remaining on my stomach. I needed a moment to catch my breath and regroup. "But I thought you had gone. Remember, this isn't your business."

"I disagree, Kali," answered a voice that wasn't Nathaniel's. I knew that voice, and the soft, refined sound of it shot through to my very core.

I inhaled sharply, the gush of my breath cutting through the incredulous silence. As if in slow motion, my fingers pressed into the soft dirt in an effort to raise my body. *It couldn't be him*, I reasoned, preparing myself for disappointment. *It's impossible.* Sitting up, I slowly turned my head to gaze at the speaker behind me, my loose hair falling like a curtain across my vision. I brushed it aside, and my heart stopped.

Leaning over on his hands and knees, an apparition that looked exactly like Tiamat—*but couldn't possibly be him*, I maintained again—raised his chin to look at me. It appeared as though he had hit his head during his rough landing, and a thin trail of blood twisted downward from his dark hairline to curve along the side of his face. Stretching out behind him in vivid, startling white, were a pair of wings that further assailed my sense of reality. Tiamat had not only *died*, but had also lost his wings; further proof that this Nephilim couldn't possibly be him. And the feathers, I noticed, were different—at the very bottom end of each wing, the pristine white suddenly tapered to a jet black, looking like the tips had been dipped into a giant well of viscous ink. The contrast was starkly beautiful.

Could this Nephilim be Tiamat's twin? It didn't seem likely; and that theory hastily fell apart when I saw the way he was looking at me, intensity and anxiety etched plainly in the crease between his brows and reflected in his watchful eyes. This half-angel *knew* me. Despite all my reasoning and any logic at my disposal, there was no doubt that this was Tiamat.

"That's impossible," escaped my lips as a whisper. Like a cautious sparring dance, we both stood in unison, each of us raising our bodies without taking our eyes off the other.

I approached Tiamat as a sleepwalker would, a trance-like deliberateness to my movements, with my gaze fixed steadily upon him. The sound of my heart hammered in my ears as I reached out a hand to touch his face—a face that, the last time I felt it, was cold, slack and lifeless. *My God... was I about to touch an animated corpse?*

He closed his eyes as my hand brushed against his skin, warm and marble-smooth under my fingertips. Tiamat drew in a deep, ragged breath, but held himself still, standing with his eyes closed just as he did the last time I saw him alive—when Daniel violently sawed off his wings. The wings—

I walked a slow circle around him, my bloodied fingers carefully trailing across the smooth whiteness of his feathers. I lightly brushed them down to the inky black tips, the feathers shiny and natural, with a black so vivid the hue took on a bluish iridescence. Tracing the strong lines back to the wing's source, I saw that each one transitioned seamlessly from his bare, unscarred back—like neither wing had ever been severed.

In wonder, I ran my fingers along Tiamat's warm, solid shoulder as I completed the circle, and found myself facing him once more. His eyes remained closed, but his jaw muscles betrayed his tension, and his breathing was deep and rapid. He was obviously struggling with something...

"Oh." I jerked my hand back as my senses returned. *How could I have been so careless?* Tiamat, I remembered, needed to bury his feelings for me, and there I was, tempting him at the first possible opportunity.

"I ... I'm sorry," I stammered, feeling foolish. "I forgot, really. I promise that I'll keep my distance."

His eyes sprung open in apparent surprise and I was blindsided by the full sight of him. It took everything I had to not rush forward and embrace him.

But I wouldn't do that to him. Not again. "Tiamat ... I won't—"

A strange look twisted his face and he suddenly moved, not letting me finish. In a rush of breath, he closed the distance between us and locked his arms around me, silencing my unspoken promise with a fervent kiss. My mind went blank as fire shot through my veins. His mouth and body were impossibly solid and alive, and I pressed myself against him feverishly, incredible waves of energy rippling all through me. It felt as though my body was being filled with starbursts of brilliant light, blasting all other thoughts from my mind. It melted my heart and seemed to burst through my fingers as they stroked his face and clutched at his back.

He broke the kiss and held me to him, the rhythm of his heart pounding against my cheek. "Sorry I cut you off. I don't want you to make promises you cannot keep, Kali," he murmured into my hair, a teasing smile apparent in his voice. "Besides, I would really rather you stayed close to me from now on."

I pulled back to look into his face, confused. "But ... your brothers—they'll know what you're feeling. They'll come here!"

He simply smiled. "The connection has been broken—severed when they cut off my wings." His look sobered then, and as he continued, his voice sounded strained and cautious, "And all ties were completely extinguished when Merodach ended my life."

My breath caught and I stepped back automatically, leaving his arms empty. "You did die. I saw you. I touched your ... your body."

"I crossed over, Kali. My life and wings have been returned. I am no corpse, I can promise you that."

"That's impossible."

"For a human."

"But not for the Nephilim?"

"It is exceedingly rare and incredibly difficult—even for us, but I have a very important reason to be here." His eyes became intense, stopping my breath. He reached out and ran his fingers along my face, tracing the line of my jaw before brushing his thumb lightly across my lips, my skin tingling where his fingers had touched it. "I would cross through the darkest void for you, Kali." He leaned in toward me, and my head spun.

"No, wait. Stop, Tiamat." I took a deep breath and stepped back again, leaving Tiamat looking confused and wounded, the deep crease reappearing between his vibrant blue eyes. I had to pause a moment before my head cleared, but after a beat, I found that I could continue. "How could you simply come back? And how did you get your wings again? Why do they look different?"

"You believe it was *simple*? I am unable to even describe..." he trailed off, at an obvious loss for words. "My wings were returned with my life, though they bear the marks of one who has crossed over. The look of one who has done this is unmistakable, and it feels like that same black has been gouged into my very soul. And I am somewhat changed. I heal at the same rate as a human now, just as you once did." He rubbed his hand across his bloodied forehead and examined it with a wry smile. "That will take some getting used to."

He flicked his eyes back to mine, but when he did, his expression altered. I could see him now focusing on the abrasions on my own face, and he pressed his lips together in response. I felt like squirming away, but held myself still as his eyes began to dart rapidly across my body, surveying for damage. The moment they found my injured side, his face drained to white. He reached toward me in an instant. "Kali—!"

"The wound's already much better," I assured him as he bent to take a closer look, holding my hips firmly. "It stopped bleeding a while ago."

"I see that," he answered without looking up. "Rapid healing is a useful ability to possess, Kali, and one that I'm relieved you have." His hands brisk but gentle, he began examining me all over, tilting my face to the light, running his hands along my arms and pausing at various injuries, then spinning me so he could inspect my back as well. Finally satisfied that I was—I assumed—alright, he faced me once more, and released his breath in a rush of air. He was still pale, the color of his skin contrasting starkly with the vibrant blood from the wound on his head.

I looked at his gash and frowned. It didn't seem fair that I should now heal quickly, while Tiamat, a powerful Nephilim, should not. Not knowing what to say, I pulled out a cloth and pressed it against the cut.

"Ouch." A gentle smile spread across his lips as his eyes watched me carefully.

"Here," I said, motioning for him to hold the cloth on the wound himself. When he did, I took a step back from him again. I felt anxious, knowing I would need to explain the reasons behind my own abilities soon. He deserved to know about my lineage, but I shied away from bringing it up. "Do your wings ... um ... work?" I asked, remembering the hard landing from just moments before.

Tiamat's face became very grave, and the crease returned between his brows. "It will take a while longer for their full strength to return. They were almost unable to carry me up here when I glimpsed you dangling from that cliff top. You were still so far away, and I was ... absolutely terrified ... that my weakened wings would fail to get me to you on time. They almost didn't," he muttered in remembered horror, his pained eyes staring into the vast open air. He turned them back to my face. "Anything else, Kali? Or perhaps I should begin with my own questions now, hmm?" He stepped close again, his expression kind but serious.

I ducked my head, but knew I couldn't avoid the inquiry. To explain how I ended up dangling from a root, I would need to tell him the entire story—from the beginning. I could feel my face flush with prickly heat, and I took a deep breath to begin. "Merodach is dead."

"Oh? So you killed him, then?" He didn't look the least bit surprised.

I stared back at him in disbelief. "Yes." I was dumbfounded by his response. How did he know?

He gently lifted my chin and looked searchingly into my face. "And did you use your knives, or ... other means?"

I glanced down, not able to meet his eyes. "I used ... other means. I killed him like a ... like a demon would," I whispered, ashamed. "Because that's who my biological father was." I pulled my chin away from his hand, and tipped my face toward the ground. My voice was barely audible now. "I don't know *what* that makes me, Tiamat. But I'm probably someone that you shouldn't be around." My heart felt like a leaden weight in my chest. It took everything I had to keep myself from falling apart so I could finish. I cleared my throat. It sounded harsh and unwelcome in the strained silence. "And I did ... *something* to him. It weakened the edge of the cliff, and that's how I fell." I held my breath, waiting for him to shrink back in disgust.

"Ah," he said quietly. "You've remembered your past, then." But instead of recoiling, he leaned forward and kissed my cheek, whispering against my skin, "And do you really believe that I am ignorant of who you are? Remember, Kali, your lineage does not dictate your nature. Richard simply passed down some remarkable abilities; that is all."

I exhaled in a rush, not believing my ears. I pulled back from him so I could see his face. His vivid blue eyes were soft and open. "You already *knew* this about me? How?"

He smiled. "I was aware of you before we ever met, Kali. You see, Richard and I are old adversaries. I had been following his... uh ... *activities* ... with interest, and I watched his relationship develop with your mother." His eyes took on a faraway look as he recalled it, and he shook his head minutely. "And you know, I truly believe that he loved her—as amazing as that sounds. When he learned that she was pregnant, he begged her to terminate it, knowing the birth would kill her. But she would not. The thought of her death consumed him, and like a coward, he left."

"And ... you watched me since I was a child?"

"Actually, no. Your abilities appeared to be dormant, so I failed to pay much attention once I realized that. I didn't even acquaint myself with your name. That is, until we met that day on Lookout Peak. And—I do apologize—but knowing what I did about you, the idea of your father naming you 'Kali' did strike me as something absurdly funny."

I frowned at him.

In response, he gently tucked a strand of hair behind my ear. "Your name only added to your charm," he murmured. "After finally meeting you, I was a lost cause."

"Even though you knew what I truly was?" I couldn't hide the bitter tone to my voice.

"Kali," he said, smiling gently, "you are an absolute angel if you compare your deeds against mine. You always have been, so please do not speak of yourself in that way. Believe me when I tell you that my only concern was that my proximity might awaken your abilities."

It took me a moment to connect the dots. "Oh," I squeaked, remembering exactly when I was first able to make the water palatable. "Proximity, indeed." I grinned at him, but it slowly faded as I remembered the core reason behind my change. "So, I guess Richard knows about me?" I shuddered at the thought.

"To be honest, I am not sure. He never acknowledged your existence when you were a child. I would not be surprised if he had no idea you are his daughter." His eyes took on a playful gleam. "However, if he *was* wise to it, I wonder if this would bother him," he said, soft as a breath, as he leaned in toward me. He kissed me deeply, making my head spin.

When we parted, he looked so pleased with himself that I almost laughed.

His hand lingered under my chin, fingers light on the bone of my jaw. I reached my hand out to touch his face again; amazed that he was standing in front of me, whole and alive. My smile dried up and nearly choked me, thinking about losing him like I did. "I'm sorry for all the pain you've been through; and it's ... so hard knowing that I'm the cause of it—that you died to protect me. You've even lost some of your abilities," I said quietly, my voice catching. "I don't know how you can think that I'm worth it."

His face melted into a blissful grin as he pressed his cheek into my hand and closed his eyes. "It is nothing. I'm just a slow healer now," he murmured, sliding his fingers around to the back of my neck, his light, electric touch causing my nerves to undulate wildly up and down my spine. "And my abilities, I will have you know, are intact." Just as he finished uttering the words, the cliff was instantly struck by a brilliant, honeyed light, reflecting and glowing off the surrounding mass of rock in a warm radiance.

It took me a moment to realize that the nearly blinding glare was from the sun, shining down on us from a sudden clearing in the thick miasma above. I stood enthralled, my hand dropping from his face, and watched in awe as all over the sky, the thick, gray clouds rolled away like a rapid tumble of retreating surf. And as the churning mass departed, it thinned and parted into separate clumps, some of which dissipated into the brilliant blue backdrop as they went. Others, I saw, clustered into large, dark thunderheads that rumbled away to the northeast, seeking to empty themselves as rain onto the parched land below. It was spectacular.

I gazed around me in wonder, the shock of sunlight forcing me to shade my eyes from its beautiful intensity. "Tiamat," I gasped. "The whole sky...! How large of an area—"

"Everywhere." His eyes were soft. He leaned in and pressed his forehead against mine, running his hands up and down my arms as I shivered in response. "It is time for normal weather patterns to return to this place. It is time for things to be as they should; starting with the two of us. We are meant to be together, Kali. You are the catalyst for change and my reason for being. You are more than worth anything that has transpired so far. Do you not realize this?" He straightened and gazed down at me, his expression tender, and slid his hands up to my face. He held it gently, brushing his thumbs lightly across my cheeks. "I love you, Kali Michaels."

I could feel the tears spill over and slide down to where his thumbs traced fiery circles across my skin. Without a word, his mouth turned up in a rueful half-smile as he carefully brushed away the wetness from my cheeks.

"You are my life, Tiamat. So please understand that it's difficult to feel my worth when I know I caused your death..."

"I arranged my own death, Kali. You must not blame yourself."

I didn't answer that one, but let his response hang in the air between us. "One thing's for certain," I continued, an obvious tremble to my voice. "I won't question your feelings for me again."

He watched me quietly, an expectant look on his face that slowly faded as the moments slipped by.

I knew what he was hoping I would say, but after what seemed like an eternity of fighting with my feelings for him, it was difficult to simply state the truth now. Deep inside, I was still afraid of experiencing his rejection. A crease had formed between his brows and the look of anxiety that flickered across his face made my chest tighten. It was time to be honest. "And ... I love you ... so much," I finally choked, the magnitude of feeling nearly overwhelming me. "I always will. Forever."

His immediate smile was broad and warm, but slowly melted—his expression shifting to reflect the hunger that burned in the deep blue of his eyes. "You promise?" He said it in a whisper—harsh and thick like my own voice—and he bent over to run his lips lightly along my neck, his kisses as soft as a feather. Tracing his fingers along my collarbone, he then stroked tingling trails along the back of my neck, down from my hairline, causing shivers to ripple through me. As if sensing my trembling reaction, his breath quickened against my skin, and his hands tightened and gripped.

"With all my heart," I breathed, answering him before I lost control completely. "I promise."

In unison, we closed all remaining distance between us, and the sunlight that shone all around our bodies seemed to shimmer through me as well. Intertwined, we fell down together onto the rocky platform, the feel of Tiamat's body solid against mine, his lips on my mouth and his fingers in my hair. We moved as one; tender, passionate, then ravenous, such that our spoken promise of love whispered like a single, faint breeze against the intense gale of that embrace. The sheer force of it swept us both completely and utterly away.

Chapter 25

The moonlight woke me. Unaccustomed as I was to sleeping in its pale light, the strangeness of it permeated my dreams and slowly brought my awareness to the surface. I opened my eyes in the velvety dark of Nathaniel's cave, to see a splash of silver illuminating my body, cast from the beautiful full moon that appeared to hover just outside the cave's mouth.

I glanced over at Tiamat to see that he slept soundly—with a peacefulness to his face that melted my heart. It was no wonder that the moonlight failed to wake him; Tiamat had trailed me for days, and hardly slept as a result. His wings were not yet strong enough for flights of any distance, so he had been forced to track me on foot—continuing night and day in order to keep up with Nathaniel's wings and my horses. He had rightly feared that Merodach might attempt to end my life after Nathaniel left me on my own, and had pushed on, desperate to reach me before Merodach did.

I stood up and walked out into the silence of the night. The world was bathed in the beautiful washed-out whiteness of the moonlight, the contrast between light and deep shadow as stark as the transition from snow to ink on Tiamat's wings. I sat down with my back against a large rock, and soaked up the quiet serenity of the night around me. The sight of the moon was glorious and my mind wandered as I studied the myriad of shades on its cratered face.

After a time, however, I had the distinct feeling that I was no longer alone. The sensation was neither alarming nor calming; it just *was*.

"Have you come to enjoy the view?" I asked, keeping my eyes momentarily on the moon. "Because I can't think of what other business you might have here, Richard. Or should I call you Izeil?"

It was quiet for a beat, and I wondered if he would respond.

"I will always have business with you two." His usually smooth voice was hushed, almost pensive. It was so unlike him.

I slowly lowered my eyes from the moon and looked over at my visitor. Richard sat stiffly upon a nearby outcropping of rock, gazing back at me with an intensity that was ... surprising. I wondered if he knew about me. If he didn't, I wasn't about to bring it up.

Somewhat flustered, I cleared my throat and slid my eyes back up to the neutrality of the moon. "I see your face and shoulder are nearly healed. How wonderful for you," I said dryly. "I'm sure that you'll be fit to continue your twisted meddling in no time at all."

I heard a huff of displeasure in return. "I explained this to you before. I have a place and a purpose here. I fulfill a need; and I must admit that I am uniquely suited to my position. Yet I did not ask for it."

"But you enjoy it."

"Yes." I heard the slight scrape of pebbles on rock as he shifted, but he stilled shortly after. "The more influence I exert, the stronger my position becomes here. An ineffective demon, you see, loses the right to occupy this realm. So ... it is fortunate that I enjoy what I do, don't you think?"

"You make me sick, Richard. Really. You're nothing but a maggot, feeding off the weak and the rotten." I looked over at him then, hoping to press my point home, and saw that my words had, once again, antagonized him. I didn't really care. "Sorry to disappoint, but I am neither of those things. So go pester someone else, alright?"

"You may be right. But I am also drawn to the delusional. Does the shoe fit, Kali?"

"No. I *know* you to be a meddlesome piece of shit. No delusions there. So please, get lost."

"Silence, now," he growled through his teeth. "Hear this: I have come to claim what is rightfully mine. A Nephilim died because of you, as was part of our bargain. I then fulfilled my end by securing you both places in the first circle. As I told you before, neither of you will ever fall any lower." He paused to ensure that I would comprehend what it was that he had done. Yet when I failed to respond, he glared back at me, as though expecting me to tell him that I fully sympathized with his position. I did no such thing. "What I have arranged for you cannot be undone, even though Wormwood has cheated me by returning!"

"Merodach is dead. I killed him."

"Unsubstantiated. First, show me a body. Then you can enlighten me as to how you managed to do this."

I felt my mouth dry up. "I ... I just killed him. His body disappeared in the river."

Richard considered for a moment. "That sounds a little suspect, don't you think? No details and no evidence. I am afraid that this 'death' you speak of cannot fulfill the bargain, my dear. Unless ... there is something else you wish to say?"

The feel of ice enclosed my heart. I couldn't tell him. "And what is it that you've come here to claim?"

"Tiamat Wormwood," he replied, his look thunderous, daring me to deny him. "He has no right to be on this plane with you, as I am certain you are well aware. His life belongs to me."

I fought to suppress the panic that threatened to overtake my senses. "But he fulfilled his end of the deal as well, Richard. You know he did. Any way you look at it, he died. Whether or not he came back afterward is irrelevant." I glanced back at Tiamat, but saw that he slept on, unaware of this exchange.

"Well now. That's an interesting argument, but the fact remains that he cheated me, Kali, and I'm really not a very good sport. Think about it: who in their right mind *double-crosses a demon?* Tiamat will come with me *now*." With this, Richard got to his feet and started toward the mouth of the cave.

My stomach dropped. "Wait; please stop!" There was something else he wanted, I reasoned, otherwise, Richard would have simply taken him, and he wouldn't have lingered to inform me that he was doing so. "What can I do to pay off his debt to you?"

Richard's fury appeared to evaporate like morning mist. He smiled, slowly. "Ah. You are as sharp as ever," he said in his characteristic smooth voice, turning his gaze out to the stars. Without glancing back at me, he continued, "There is an encampment a few miles south of here. You know this, of course. Everyone is sleeping outside tonight, enjoying the light of the moon. Go there now; walk into their midst, and gently touch one of them. That is all. Then I will relinquish my claim on Wormwood's life. But if you fail, he will be gone by daylight."

Stalling, I stared out at the stars as well, looking desperately for inspiration. "Why would you want them dead? It's like you're asking me to destroy the last of your puppet collection." I shot a glance back at him, but saw that the space beside me was empty.

"Because they will be dead soon anyway, and it tears you up to have to be the one to do it, Kali." Richard's silky-smooth voice was directly behind me, his breath in my hair as he spoke. "Like I told you before, orchestrating these little situations is what I do. I am awfully good at it, am I not?" With a jolt, I felt his hand softly touch my head, yet when I whirled around to face him, he was gone.

Leaping up from the rocky outcrop, I raked my eyes around the surface of the wide ridge, but could not see Richard anywhere.

Intensely agitated, I walked to the mouth of the cave and stood there for a long moment, gazing at Tiamat's peacefully sleeping form. I had not been given much of a choice, and my heart dropped painfully at the thought of either outcome.

I stepped back out into the night, pacing as I watched the play of stark shadows that lay like waiting land mines across the winding, moonlit path. I froze, turned, and paced back again, stopping at the head of the trail, its silvery back twisting like a long snake down to the base of the cliff, tempting me.

Just to my left, back toward the rocky shelf where I sat a few moments before, I could feel Richard's eyes on me again, gloating over my torment and indecision. Refusing to look at him, to acknowledge his seething pleasure, I asked a question that had been niggling at the back of my mind like a boring worm. "What is Achaia like, Richard?" I kept my eyes fixed on the winding path and waited for his response.

He chuckled, slow and deep. "In Achaia, the soul struggles through ceaseless trials, not even knowing that the body is dead. That's funny, isn't it, Kali? Does it sound familiar to you?"

His dirty insinuations were too much. In one terrifying flash, I remembered what it had been like for me since the earth's surface was destroyed; torturously difficult and surreal in the extreme. Panic flared through me like wildfire. "Am I dead? How long have I been dead?" I whirled around to face him, but as I should have expected, there was no one there.

Mind games. He was always trying to mess with me, I reminded myself, fighting to push his alarming ideas out of my head. *I couldn't be dead ... I couldn't be. Otherwise, why would he even bother to take Tiamat if we were already in Achaia? It doesn't make sense!* I knew that I shouldn't listen to him. These tricks were simply what he did. And he was right; he *was* exceedingly good at it. *I must stop playing right into his hand*, I thought angrily.

For now, I simply had to walk into a camp to settle a debt. That's all it was. I owed it to Tiamat to do this for him, after he had sacrificed his life to save mine. *And besides*, I reasoned, *everyone is going to die soon anyway; I'll simply be altering the means of their departure.*

I stood at the foot of the path, a brooding statue, and stayed there for a long time, agonizing over what I had already decided to do. The moonlight illuminated my hands; my fingers twisting in agitation like little creatures caught in a trap. But there was no escape.

I glanced back at Tiamat's sleeping face, and with a deep breath, turned and slipped silently down the pocked ribbon of the waiting path. The moonlight would guide me, and how unfortunate was that? Light, I realized now, was not always a harbinger of good things. It drew the encampment out to sleep in its beguiling glow, and in the end, I knew, it would also bring me.

Acknowledgments

So many people helped me in this journey, selflessly lending their time and support; I believe they should take pride and ownership in every word that is written in this book. I couldn't have done it without you.

I would like to extend a heartfelt thanks...

To my students, who inspired me to write in the first place. I thoroughly enjoyed working with you on your own stories, egging you on as you consistently pushed your creativity to new heights. You amazed me and humbled me. Although you are *definitely* too young to read this book at present, I hope that a few years in the future, you might have a look at the story you inspired me to write. Thank you for believing in me too.

To Nancy Brauer, author of Strange Little Band, who took the time to read Wormwood's manuscript in its early—and rather rough— stages, and give me the critical feedback I needed to hear. *Wormwood*'s ending underwent an incredible transformation, thanks to your direction.

To Nikki Speers-Nevins, who masterfully crafted the Black Wraith Books icon at a moment's notice, and to her sister, Roxanne, who both teamed up (as awesome sisters are wont to do) to help me with *Wormwood*'s promotion over the internet.

To Dave Schultz, who directed hundreds—perhaps thousands—of people to my 'Publish Wormwood' Facebook group. You're a king among men, my friend.

To Serena Aubrey of Serene Promotions, who selflessly gives endless amounts of her time to help Canadian artists and entrepreneurs get their names out there. Your suggestions and support have been invaluable, Serena.

To Anthony Concannon, of the band Dreaming in Waves, for providing many kind words and inspiring me with your beautiful music. I always look forward to your tweets!

To all those wonderful members of my 'Publish Wormwood' Facebook group, who showed support for my book right out of the gate. Your enthusiastic feedback meant (and still means!) the world to me.

To my twitter followers, for diligently retweeting my many lame messages. I'm still mystified as to why you're all following me. The honor is all mine.

To my mother, Madeleine Nevins, who waited (somewhat!) patiently for this book to be published before I let her read it. Your anxiousness to get your hands on the manuscript gave me a wonderful sense of stardom (yes, yes, I'm a terrible daughter. I know).

To a certain editor at Berkley, who asked to see a partial of Wormwood's manuscript after I pitched the premise to her at a conference in New York. You are the first and only editor I ever pitched to (either in person or in writing), and I was heartened by your immediate interest in my book. I realized that others might actually like the story too! After pondering this, I took a leap of faith and decided to publish this baby under my own imprint, Black Wraith Books. Thanks for that.

To my cat, Frog, who purred in my lap for probably two-thirds of this book's creation.

Most importantly, to my husband, Barry, who gave countless hours of support, insight and encouragement. Not only did I receive notes of correction, criticism and praise within the pages of my manuscript, Barry would also spruce them up with the occasional unanticipated diagram. When expecting criticism, it's nice to be served up a laugh instead!

About the Author

D. H. Nevins was educated at Windsor and Brock universities, where she received a Bachelor of Arts degree and a Bachelor of Education degree, respectively. After spending years as a teacher encouraging her students to write, she decided to take her own advice  and began writing *Wormwood*. She lives with her husband and two cats in a rural section of Ontario, where she is at work on the *Wormwood* sequel.